Simon Beckett has worked as a freelance journalist for national newspapers and colour supplements. He is the author of six international bestselling crime thrillers featuring his forensic anthropologist hero, Dr David Hunter: *The Chemistry of Death, Written in Bone, Whispers of the Dead, The Calling of the Grave, The Restless Dead* and *The Scent of Death.* His stand alone novels include *Stone Bruises* and *Where There's Smoke.* He lives in Sheffield.

Acclaim for Simon Beckett's David Hunter thrillers:

'Simon Beckett's masterful storytelling and macabre forensic details make his novels utterly chilling reads'
TESS GERRITSEN

'Beckett is one of the country's best crime writers . . . his books are intelligent, beautifully written and utterly gripping'
SUNDAY EXPRESS

'Beckett's sixth novel featuring the forensic anthropologist David Hunter is arguably his best . . . a superbly strong read'
THE TIMES

'The forensics are chillingly authentic, the writing is both taut and beautifully atmospheric'
ANN CLEEVES

'Bone-chillingly bleak . . . doesn't disappoint'
FINANCIAL TIMES

'Brilliantly original . . . Simon's first crime novel *The Chemistry of Death* absolutely blew me away and he just gets better by the book!'
PETER JAMES

'Strong, pungent writing is Beckett's forte, lethal mind-games that are not for the squeamish'
THE TIMES

'An utterly absorbing, atmospheric mystery that will keep you guessing to the very last page . . . he is a terrific writer'
ANTONIA HODGSON

'Atmospheric . . . a tense, gripping read'
SUNDAY TIMES

'Spine-tinglingly frightening, but also poignant and caring . . . hits the bull's eye'
INDEPENDENT ON SUNDAY

Also by Simon Beckett

Featuring David Hunter
The Chemistry of Death
Written in Bone
Whispers of the Dead
The Calling of the Grave
The Restless Dead

Other novels
Where There's Smoke
Stone Bruises

For more information on Simon Beckett
and his books, see his website at
www.simonbeckett.com

The Scent of Death

SIMON BECKETT

BANTAM BOOKS

TRANSWORLD PUBLISHERS
61–63 Uxbridge Road, London W5 5SA
www.penguin.co.uk

Transworld is part of the Penguin Random House group of companies
whose addresses can be found at global.penguinrandomhouse.com

Penguin
Random House
UK

First published in Great Britain in 2019 by Bantam Press
an imprint of Transworld Publishers
Bantam edition published 2019

A CIP catalogue record for this book
is available from the British Library.

ISBN
9780553824124 (B format)
9780857504340 (A format)

Typeset in 11/13.5 pt Sabon
by Integra Software Services Pvt. Ltd, Pondicherry

Printed and bound in Great Britain by Clays Ltd, Elcograf S.p.A.

Penguin Random House is committed to a sustainable future for
our business, our readers and our planet. This book is made
from Forest Stewardship Council® certified paper.

MIX
Paper from
responsible sources
FSC
www.fsc.org   FSC® C018179

1 3 5 7 9 10 8 6 4 2

To my Dad, Frank Beckett, who always put
things in perspective.
July 1929 – April 2018

Chapter 1

MOST PEOPLE ASSUME they'd know the scent of death. That decay has a distinctive, readily identifiable odour, a foul reek of the grave.

They're wrong.

Decay is a complicated process. For a once-living organism to become skeletonized, reduced to dry bone and minerals, it first has to undergo an intricate biochemical journey. While some of the gases created are offensive to human senses, they're only part of the olfactory menu. Decomposing flesh can produce hundreds of volatile organic compounds, each with its own characteristics. Many of them – particularly those created during the mid-stages of a body's dissolution, those of putrefaction and bloat – possess an undeniable stench. Dimethyl trisulphide, for instance, is reminiscent of rotting cabbage. Butyric acid and trimethylamine have the respective bouquets of vomit and old fish. Another substance, indole, carries the stink of faecal matter.

Yet in lower concentrations indole has a delicate, floral scent that's prized by perfume manufacturers. Hexanal, a gas produced in both the early and later stages of decay, resembles freshly cut grass, while butanol is redolent of fallen leaves.

The aroma of decomposition can encompass all these notes, as complex as a fine wine. And, because death is nothing if not full of surprises, in some circumstances it can announce itself in a different manner entirely.

Sometimes in a way you'd least expect.

'Watch your footing, Dr Hunter,' Whelan warned from ahead of me. 'You step off the boards and you'll be through the ceiling.'

He didn't need to remind me. I ducked under a low beam, careful where I was putting my feet. The cavernous loft was like an oven. The day's heat had been trapped under the slate roof, and the mask I wore made it hard to breathe. The elasticated hood of my protective coveralls cut into my face, and my hands felt slick and hot inside the skin-tight nitrile gloves. I tried again to wipe the sweat from my eyes, succeeding only in smearing it.

The old hospital's loft was huge. It extended off in all directions, disappearing into darkness beyond the glare of the temporary lighting. A walkway of aluminium stepping plates had been laid down, bending and flexing under our combined weight as we clattered over them.

I hoped the joists underneath weren't rotten.

'You know this part of London?' Whelan asked over his shoulder. The detective inspector's accent put his roots far north of where we were now, nearer the Tyne than the Thames. He was a thick-set man in his forties, and when he'd met me earlier the wiry grey hair and beard had been damp and sweat-flattened. Now his face was all but hidden under the mask and white coveralls.

'Not really.'

'No, it's not the sort of area you come to without good cause. Not even then, if you can help it.' He stooped to pass under a sloping roof timber. 'Mind your head.'

I followed his example. Even with the stepping plates, moving around in the loft was hard going. Thick wooden beams criss-crossed overhead, waiting to crack the skull of anyone who didn't crouch low enough, while old pipework snaked across the joists at ankle height, ready to snag a carelessly placed foot. Every now and then, apparently at random, blackened brick chimney stacks rose up to block a direct route, forcing the stepping plates to detour around them.

I brushed away a cobweb that stroked my face. Clogged with dirt, they hung from the rough roof timbers like ragged theatre swags. The dust covered everything in the loft, turning the once-yellow insulation between the joists into a filthy brown mat. Motes of it swirled in the air, glinting in the bright lighting. My eyes already felt gritty, and I could taste it in my mouth despite the mask.

I ducked as a quick movement, more sensed than seen, seemed to flit overhead in the shadows. But when I looked all I could see was darkness. Chalking it up to imagination, I concentrated on watching where I put my feet.

Up ahead, a circle of lights marked our destination. Under their glare a cluster of white-clad figures stood on a wider island of stepping plates set around a chimney stack. A murmur of conversation drifted from them, muffled by their masks. A Scenes of Crime Officer was taking photographs of something that lay at their feet.

Whelan stopped just short of the group. 'Ma'am? The forensic anthropologist's here.'

One of the group turned towards me. What little of her face was visible above the mask was flushed and shiny from sweat. In the baggy white coveralls it would have been hard to say if she was man or woman if I hadn't already known, but this wasn't the first time we'd worked together. As I went over I saw they were standing around an object wrapped in plastic tarpaulin, like a rolled-up carpet. One end of the plastic had been partially undone.

Gazing out from it, toffee-coloured skin drawn taut over cheekbones and hollow eye sockets, was a mummified face.

Distracted, I didn't notice the low roof beam until I banged my head on it, hard enough to jar my teeth.

'Careful,' Whelan said.

I rubbed my head, more embarrassed than hurt. *Good start.* A half-dozen faces regarded me over masks, unimpressed. Only the woman Whelan had addressed seemed amused, eyes crinkled with a smile hidden by her mask.

'Welcome to St Jude's,' DCI Sharon Ward said.

Twelve hours earlier I'd woken from a nightmare. I'd bolted upright in bed, not sure where I was, my hand automatically going to my stomach, feeling for the expected stickiness of blood. But the skin was dry, unmarked except for the trace of a long-healed scar.

'Are you OK?'

Rachel was propped up on an elbow, a hand resting against my chest in concern. Daylight filtered through the heavy curtains, revealing a room that was only now taking on recognizable lines.

I nodded as my breathing slowed. 'Sorry.'

'Another bad dream?'

I flashed to gouts of dark blood and a knife blade glinting in the sun. 'Not too bad. Did I wake you up?'

'Me and everyone else.' She smiled at my expression. 'I'm *joking*. You were just thrashing around, no one would have heard. Was it the same one?'

'I can't remember. What time is it?'

'Just after seven. I was going to get up and make coffee.'

The vestiges of the nightmare still clung to me like a cold sweat as I swung my legs from the bed. 'It's OK, I'll make it.'

Pulling on some clothes, I went out and softly closed the bedroom door behind me. Once I was alone in the hallway my smile faded. I took a deep breath, trying to shake off the after-effects of the dream. It wasn't real, I reminded myself.

Not this time.

The house was quiet, suspended in the early-morning hush that precedes a new day. The heavy *chunk* of a clock punctuated the silence as I padded down to the kitchen. The thick pile of the hall carpet gave way to slate tiles, pleasantly cool under my bare feet. Although the air held some of the previous day's warmth, the stone walls of the old house rebuffed even the heat of the Indian summer we'd been enjoying.

I filled the percolator and set it on the Aga before running myself a glass of water. I drank it at the window, looking out over the orchard to green fields. The sun was already shining from an unlikely blue sky. Sheep grazed in the distance, and a small wood stood off to one side, the leaves on the trees already shading red. They hadn't started to fall yet, but it wouldn't be long.

The scene was like a photograph on a gift-shop calendar, where nothing bad could ever happen.

I'd thought that about other places, too.

Jason had described his and Anja's second home as a cottage. Compared to their main house in London, an enormous villa in Belsize Park, it might have been, but that didn't do it justice. Built of warm Cotswold stone, it was a rambling old place with a thatched roof that could have graced the cover of a homes-and-gardens magazine. It stood on the outskirts of a pretty village whose pub boasted a Michelin star, and where Range Rovers, Mercedes and BMWs crowded the narrow main street every weekend.

When Jason and Anja had invited us over for a long weekend I'd been concerned there might be some awkwardness. They'd been my closest friends, before my wife and daughter had died in a car accident. I'd met Kara at one of their parties, and they'd been godparents to Alice, just as I'd been to their daughter, Mia. I'd been relieved at how well the two of them had hit it off with Rachel, but the occasional drink or dinner was different to spending days in each other's company. Rachel and I had only met earlier that year, during a traumatic murder investigation in the Essex coastal marshes. I'd worried that taking her to stay with friends from my old life would seem strange, that my shared history with Jason and Anja might make her feel excluded.

But everything had been fine. If every now and then I still felt an odd sense of dislocation, a disquieting overlay of my old life over the new, it didn't last. The weekend had been spent walking across Cotswolds fields and woodland, taking our time over pub lunches and long, lazy evenings. By any standards, it had been an idyllic few days.

Except for the nightmare.

The coffee had started to bubble behind me, filling the kitchen with its aroma. I took the percolator off the Aga and was pouring two mugs when I heard the stairs creak as someone came down. From the heavy tread I didn't have to look around to know it was Jason.

'Morning,' he said, looking bleary and rumpled as he shambled into the kitchen. 'You're up early.'

'Thought I'd make some coffee. Hope that was OK.'

'So long as there's a cup for me.'

He sank down on to a stool at the kitchen island, making a half-hearted attempt to adjust the towelling bathrobe around his heavy-set frame before losing interest. A pelt of dark chest hair sprouted from it, creeping up his throat to stop at his shaving line. The stubbled face and thinning hair above it seemed to belong to a different body.

He accepted the coffee I handed him with an appreciative grunt. We'd known each other since we were students at medical school, back in the days before my life had been thrown on to a different track. Instead of medicine, I'd chosen an often-turbulent career as a forensic anthropologist, while Jason had become a successful orthopaedic surgeon who could afford a second home in the Cotswolds. He'd never been a morning person even when he was younger, and the additional years hadn't changed that. Neither had the wine he'd drunk the night before.

He took a drink of coffee and grimaced. 'Don't suppose you've got any tips for a hangover?'

'Don't drink so much.'

7

'That is so funny.' He took a more cautious sip from his mug. 'What time are you and Rachel heading off?'

'Not till this afternoon.'

I'd driven us over from London in my 'new' car, a second-hand but reliable 4x4, and we didn't have to get back until that evening. But the reminder that the weekend was almost over – and the thought of the next day – left a hollow feeling in my chest.

'When's Rachel's flight tomorrow?' Jason asked, as though reading my mind.

'Late morning.'

He studied me. 'You OK?'

'Sure.'

'It's only for a few months. It'll be fine.'

'I know.'

He considered me for a moment, then decided not to pursue it. With a wince, he went to a wall cupboard and took out a box of paracetamol. His meaty fingers deftly popped two tablets from the foil strip.

'Jesus, my bloody head,' he said, opening a bottle of mineral water from the fridge. He washed down the tablets and gave me a sour glance. 'Don't start.'

'I didn't say a word.'

'You don't have to.' He waved a hand at me. 'Go on, get it off your chest.'

'What's the point? I can't tell you anything you don't already know.'

Even when we were students Jason had always been a man of large appetites. Now, though, he'd reached an age when excess had started to take its toll. Always heavily built, he'd put on weight, and his features were developing a puffiness that matched his unhealthy colour. But we'd only recently picked up the friendship

8

again after a gap of several years, and I hadn't felt able to broach the subject as I would once have done. I was glad he'd brought it up himself.

'There's a lot of pressure at work.' He shrugged, staring out through the window. 'Budget cuts, waiting times. It's a mess. Sometimes I think you did the right thing, getting out when you did.'

I made a point of looking around the beautifully equipped kitchen. 'You didn't do too badly.'

'You know what I mean. Anyway, bottom line is I might have been pushing things a bit, but it isn't like I've got a cocaine habit or anything.'

'I'm sure your patients are thankful for that.'

'At least mine aren't dead.'

The comeback seemed to restore his humour. Rubbing his stomach, he headed for the fridge.

'Fancy a bacon sandwich?'

Rachel and I left after lunch. Jason cooked a Sunday roast, a sizzling rib of beef that he tended lovingly, and Anja had made a meringue for dessert. She insisted we take some back with us, along with thick slices of roast meat.

'It'll save you having to shop,' she insisted when I tried to decline. 'I know what you're like, David. As soon as Rachel's left you'll either forget or make do with whatever's in your fridge. You can't just live on omelettes, you know.'

'I don't live on omelettes,' I said, sounding unconvincing even to myself.

Anja smiled serenely. 'Then you won't mind taking something extra, will you?'

Rachel and I were quiet on the drive back to London. It was a glorious evening, the Cotswolds fields green and golden, the trees beginning to take on russet hues as autumn approached. But the spectre of her departure the next day shared the car with us, tainting any enjoyment.

'It's only for three months,' Rachel said abruptly, as though continuing an unspoken dialogue. 'And Greece isn't far.'

'I know.'

It was far enough, but I knew what she meant. That summer she'd let pass a chance to return to her career as a marine biologist in Australia. She'd stayed to be with me, so I was hardly going to complain about a temporary research post in an Aegean marine reserve.

'It's only a four-hour flight. You could still come out and stay.'

'Rachel, it's all right. Really.' We'd already agreed it would be better if she settled into her new job without distractions. 'It's your work, you have to go. It'll pass before you know it.'

'I know. I just hate this part.'

So did I. I suspected that was why Jason and Anja – probably more Anja – had asked us over for the weekend, to take our minds off Rachel's departure.

There was no avoiding it now, though. She went through the limited choice of music I kept in the car. 'How about this? Jimmy Smith's *The Cat*?'

'Perhaps something else.'

Rachel gave up on my music collection and turned on the radio instead. The background murmur of a programme on alpaca farming replaced the silence for the rest of the trip. The fields gave way to suburban sprawl and then the built-up concrete and brick of the city. I resisted the automatic instinct to head for my old flat in

East London. I hadn't lived there for most of the summer, but it still seemed strange to be going somewhere else.

The road I turned on to was tree-lined and quiet. Driving past the white Georgian houses set in wooded gardens, I headed for the jarringly modern apartments that rose above them. Built in the 1970s, Ballard Court was all angles and concrete, a ten-storey complex whose smoked-glass windows reflected a muted version of the evening sky. I'd been told it was an important example of brutalist architecture, and I could believe it. There was certainly something brutal about it.

I stopped at the gates and entered the passcode into the keypad. As we waited for the gates to open I stared unenthusiastically up at the tiered balconies until I realized Rachel was looking at me.

'What?'

'Nothing,' she said, but her mouth was curved in a half-smile.

Once through the gates, I waited again for the electric door to the underground car park to open and pulled into my allotted space. I'd already received a terse letter from the management committee after inadvertently parking in the wrong spot, warning me that such infringements wouldn't be tolerated.

Ballard Court had a lot of rules.

We took the lift up to the fifth floor. There was a reception desk and concierge on duty in the main entrance, but as only residents had passes for the car park the lifts bypassed that and went straight to the apartments. Its doors slid open to reveal a wide landing around which were set well-spaced, numbered teak doors. It reminded me of a hotel, an impression fostered by the faint scent of peppermint that always seemed to gather there.

Our footsteps rang on the marble floor as we crossed to the apartment. I pushed open the heavy door to let Rachel in first, leaving it to slowly swing shut behind us with a soft *click*. A carpeted hallway led to the vast kitchen, where an arched opening gave on to an open-plan dining room and lounge. The same sound-deadening carpet as in the hall ran through there as well, perfectly complementing the kitchen's terracotta tiles. Abstract paintings hung on the walls, and the mocha-coloured leather sofa was deep enough to drown in. It was, by any standards, a beautiful apartment, and a far cry from the modest ground-floor flat where I'd been living before.

I hated it.

It had been Jason who'd set it up. Another consultant at his hospital was moving to Canada for six months and didn't want to leave his home standing empty. He preferred not to let it out through an agent and since I was – grudgingly – looking to move out of my old place, Jason suggested we'd be doing each other a favour. The rent was ridiculously low, and although he denied it I suspected Jason might have something to do with that as well. Even then I'd been reluctant, until Rachel weighed in. It wasn't safe to stay in my old flat, she'd argued, green eyes angry. I'd been attacked and almost died there once: was I really going to ignore police advice and risk my life out of some sort of stubborn pride?

She had a point.

A few years before, a woman called Grace Strachan had stabbed and left me for dead on my own doorstep.

A violent psychotic who blamed me for the death of her brother, Grace had disappeared afterwards and not been seen since. It had taken a long time for the scars to heal – especially the psychological ones – but I'd gradually let myself believe the danger had passed. It was hard to imagine how someone so unstable could avoid capture for so long, not without help. I'd begun to think she must be dead, or at the very least out of the country. Somewhere she could no longer pose a threat.

Then, while I'd been working on a murder investigation in Essex earlier this year, the police had found her fingerprint after an attempted break-in at my flat. There was no way of knowing how long the print had been there, and it was possible it had simply been missed after her knife attack. But it was also possible that Grace had returned to finish what she'd started.

Even then I'd been reluctant to leave. I didn't have any particular attachment to the flat itself – Grace's attempt on my life and a failed past relationship were the two defining memories from my time there – but if I moved out I wanted it to be on my own terms. This felt too much like running away.

In the end, what persuaded me wasn't any advice from the police, or even a belated sense of self-preservation. It was that Rachel often stayed at the flat as well.

It wasn't just my life I was risking.

So I'd moved into Ballard Court, an address where I wasn't listed, and whose security systems, electric gates and underground car parking met with the approval of Rachel and the police. If Grace Strachan *was* back, if she'd somehow got wind of my survival, she'd have a hard time even finding out where I was, let alone getting within arm's reach.

Since that initial fingerprint, though, there had been no further sign of her. To begin with the police had kept surveillance on my empty flat: empty because I wasn't about to sell it or let it out if there was a chance it was being targeted. But as the weeks went by the patrols had been scaled down. By now I'd become convinced the whole thing was a false alarm, and made up my mind to move back once my tenancy in the secure but soulless Ballard Court had ended. I'd yet to break the news to Rachel, reasoning that there'd be time for that later. I wasn't going to spoil our last night together.

As it turned out, someone else did.

My phone rang as we were preparing dinner, both of us determinedly trying to act as though she weren't leaving the next morning. The evening sun gilded the windows, casting long shadows and reminding us that the summer was over. I glanced at Rachel. I wasn't expecting any calls, and couldn't think of anyone who might be phoning on a Sunday evening. She raised an eyebrow but said nothing as I picked it up. The name on the display was *Sharon Ward*.

I turned back to Rachel. 'It's work. I don't have to answer it.'

Her smile crinkled the corners of her eyes, but as she turned away there was a look in them I couldn't read.

'Yes, you do,' she said.

Chapter 2

MOST PEOPLE WOULD regard my profession as odd. Macabre, even. I spend as much time with the dead as with the living, exploring the transforming effect of decay and dissolution in order to identify human remains and to understand what might have brought them to that state.

It's an often-dark calling but a necessary one, and when I saw Ward's name on my phone I knew straight away what it meant. She'd been a DI when I'd first met her, after a body part had been left, quite literally, on my doorstep. But she'd recently been promoted to DCI, heading up one of the Met's Murder Investigation Teams. If she was ringing on a Sunday evening, then it wasn't a social call.

It was a sign of how blasé I'd become that I'd felt barely a flicker of concern. A few months ago it had been Ward who'd warned me that the fingerprint found at my flat belonged to Grace Strachan. Since then we'd been in occasional touch as she'd kept me up to date with developments to locate the woman who'd tried to kill me. Or lack of them, as it turned out. So much so, I never even considered that she might be phoning up now about anything other than work.

She wasn't. A body had been found in the loft of an abandoned hospital in Blakenheath, in North London. The old infirmary had lain unused for years, the haunt mainly of substance abusers and the homeless. The unidentified remains looked to have been dead for some time, and their poor condition meant a forensic anthropologist was needed. Seeing as it was in my neck of the woods, could I pop over to take a look?

I said I could.

It wasn't how I'd wanted to spend my last evening with Rachel for three months. But she'd told me it was better for me to work than have both of us moping around the apartment with last-night blues. Go on, she'd said, don't keep them waiting.

The dusk had been turning to dark as I drove to St Jude's. I didn't know Blakenheath, but its streets were the usual multicultural mix. Takeaways and shops displaying West Indian, Asian and European signage jostled for space alongside dingy units that were shuttered and closed. The number of these increased the further out I went, until the streetlights lit only deserted streets. Then I came to an expanse of high wall that ran parallel to the road. It was topped with old iron railings, through which unpruned tree branches poked, as though trying to escape. I thought it might be a park until I came to an entrance. Curving above two tall stone gateposts was a rusted wrought-iron arch, on which *St Jude's Royal Infirmary* was spelled out in large, ornate letters.

On the wall next to it, a more poignant message was written on a forlorn and ragged banner: *Save St Jude's.*

A young police officer stood sentry next to one of the stone posts. I gave my name and waited until she'd checked my clearance. 'Just follow the drive,' she told me.

As I pulled through the archway my headlights illuminated a sign bearing a hospital map, grown so faded it was barely there. My initial impression of a park wasn't so far off. Mature trees hid the boundary wall, and I guessed the site used to be filled with green spaces and hospital buildings. Now it was a wasteland. Whatever buildings once stood here had been demolished, leaving untidy mounds of brick and concrete on either side.

It was like driving through a bombed-out town, unlit and deserted. The beams from my headlights were the only relief from the darkness. The trees and high wall screened out light from the surrounding streets, making the grounds feel more isolated than they really were. Rounding a shadowy mound of rubble, I saw police cars and vans parked on the forecourt outside the surviving hospital building. It was Victorian, three storeys high with wide steps descending from a Grecian-style central portico. Boarded-up windows stared blankly from blackened stone walls, but despite its dilapidated state it still possessed a severe grandeur. There were elaborately carved cornices, while the portico was supported by fluted stone pillars. Above it all, the angular silhouette of a clock tower rose from the pitched roof, outlined against the night sky like a stern finger.

I gave my name again and was shown to a police trailer to change into coveralls and protective gear. Whelan met me on the steps leading up to the main hospital entrance, introducing himself as Ward's deputy SIO. Covered with graffiti, the big double doors had been pushed right back. Inside it was cold and clammy. The air smelled strongly of damp, mould and urine. Lights had been set up in what had once been the foyer, revealing stained, sagging plaster and a debris-strewn floor. Off to one side was a glass-panelled cubicle with a sign above it proclaiming *Medical outpatients*.

But the beer cans and empty bottles that were scattered around, and the charred remains of campfires, showed that the hospital still had some occupants. My footsteps echoed hollowly as I made my way up the stairs that wound around a lift shaft, long disused. More lights had been set up on each landing, where dust-covered signs pointed off to *X-ray*, *Endoscopy*, *ECG* and other long-forgotten departments.

'Typical hospital,' Whelan said, out of breath when we reached the top of the stairs. Even though it was only three storeys, the high ceilings made it a long haul. 'If you weren't ill when you arrived, the climb's enough to kill you.'

He set off down a long corridor, along which yet more lights had been lined. We passed abandoned wards, where small glass panels set in heavy doors gave a view into blackness. Plaster crunched underfoot, and in places the rotten ceiling had collapsed to expose bare wooden slats. There weren't so many empty cans and bottles up here, but then it was a long way to climb without a good reason.

The lights ended at an extendable aluminium ladder, incongruously new and shiny in the squalid setting. It ran up into a rectangular access panel in the ceiling, from where the walkway of stepping plates had been laid down in the loft to where Ward and the rest of her team were waiting.

Along with the body.

I studied it again now, rubbing my head where I'd banged it on the roof timber.

'We're just about to make a start,' Ward told me. 'Do you know Professor Conrad?'

I did, but only by name. The forensic pathologist had already been an established figure in his field when I was first starting out in mine and had a fearsome reputation for his short temper. He'd be well into his sixties by now and didn't appear to have mellowed with age. Bushy grey eyebrows were knitted in a frown as he regarded me from above his mask.

'I'm glad you could finally join us.'

He had a dry, reedy voice that made it hard to tell if that was a rebuke or not. Once again, out of the corner of my eye I thought I saw movement in the loft's shadows, but this time I ignored it. I'd embarrassed myself enough for one day.

Ward raised an eyebrow at me. 'Well, since we're all here, we'd best crack on. Come on, budge up.'

She gave a SOCO standing next to her an unceremonious nudge. There was a general shuffling as space was made for me. The stepping plates had been arranged around the plastic-wrapped body, providing a platform to work from. But the low roof timbers and chimney stack made it a tight squeeze, and it was hotter than ever under the surrounding lights.

'The hospital's been closed for years, so the only people using it have been rough sleepers and drug addicts,' Ward said, as I moved closer for a better look. 'There was a fair bit of dealing going on from here until the demolition work started on the site a few months back. We could be looking at this being either a fatal overdose or a falling-out someone tried to cover up.'

Neither were rare events. I considered the desiccated features half hidden in the plastic. 'Who found it, one of the demolition crew?'

She shook her head. 'They're supposed to have checked the loft, but I doubt they came this far in. No, it was someone from the bat-conservation society. Came up here to do a survey and found more than he bargained for.'

'Bats?'

'A colony of long-eared ones, apparently.' Her voice held a note of wry amusement. 'They're a protected species, so we've got to be careful not to disturb them.'

I glanced into the shadows above me. So I hadn't been imagining the movement earlier.

'The developers are planning to level the whole site and build a big office complex,' Ward went on. 'There's been a lot of local opposition, so the bat thing was just the latest in a series of delays. The protesters are delighted because it's meant a last-minute stay of execution for St Jude's. Until the bats are rehoused, or whatever it is they do with them, the whole development's ground to a halt.'

'Fascinating as that may be, I cancelled a dinner engagement for this,' Conrad said in clipped tones. 'I'd appreciate not spending all night up here.'

Indifferent to the angry look Ward gave him, the pathologist stiffly lowered himself down next to the body. I went to the other side and knelt beside it as well. Surrounded by a halo of wispy hair, the face inside the plastic was wizened as parchment. The eye sockets were empty, and only stubs remained of the nose and ears. Beneath the loft's pervasive smell of dust and old timber, another odour emanated from within the tarpaulin, sweet and dusty.

'Clearly been dead for some time,' Conrad said, as though passing comment on the weather. 'Completely mummified, by the look of it.'

Not quite, I thought, but kept the thought to myself for now.

'Is that natural?' Ward sounded doubtful. The pathologist either didn't hear or chose not to answer.

'It can be,' I answered for him. Mummification could happen naturally for a number of reasons, from the acidity of peat bogs to extreme cold. But this was down to something else. I looked around the dark loft, seeing how the cobwebs nearby were stirring slightly in some faint air current. 'These are pretty much ideal conditions for mummification. You can feel how hot it is up here, and it'll be dry even in winter. And a big old loft like this has plenty of ventilation, so there's enough airflow to draw out the moisture.'

While I was talking, Conrad was calmly opening more of the tarpaulin, revealing the shoulders and chest. The body lay on its back, slightly twisted and huddled inside the folds of plastic like a dead bird in a nest. The tarpaulin still covered the stomach and lower body, but it was already clear this wasn't a large individual. From its size it looked to be either a juvenile or a small adult. The body wore only a ragged yellow T-shirt, stained by fluids produced as it decomposed. The short sleeves displayed arms and hands that had been reduced to sinew and bone. As with the face, the parchment-like skin had dried out to resemble cured leather.

'The hands look arranged,' Ward said, studying how the claw-like hands appeared to have been folded

21

across the bony chest, as though the body were resting in a coffin rather than wrapped inside a plastic sheet. 'Someone took time to do that. That suggests remorse or at least respect. Could be whoever did it knew her.'

Her? I looked at Ward in surprise. There was nothing to suggest the body was female, and given its condition we might not know for days. Not unless we found some form of ID.

'It's a little premature to start using the feminine pronoun until we've established the gender, don't you think?' Conrad said, giving her a withering glance.

Ward's blush was visible even with half her face hidden behind the hood and mask. It could have been a slip of the tongue, but not one an SIO should have made.

She tried to hurry past her blunder. 'Can you give me a rough idea of the time since death?'

The pathologist answered without looking up. 'No, I can't. Perhaps you didn't hear when I said it was mummified.'

Now Ward looked angry as well as flustered. But Conrad had a point. Once the body reached this level of desiccation, any further physical changes would be so slow as to be virtually imperceptible. There were cases of natural mummification where human remains had been preserved for hundreds of years, or even longer.

'Hard to imagine anyone hiding a body up here while St Jude's was still a working hospital,' Whelan said, filling the awkward silence. 'Must have been after it shut.'

'When was that?' I asked.

'Ten, eleven years ago now. Caused quite an upset.'

'OK, that's an upper limit, but it doesn't help much,' Ward said. 'What's the fastest the body could have

22

mummified like this? Could it have happened in less than ten years?'

'If the conditions were right,' I told her. 'The loft will have been pretty hot over summer, which would speed things up. But, looking at it, I'd say it's probably been up here for at least two summers. There's hardly any smell, even in this heat, which makes me think the mummification finished some time ago.'

'Great. So we're looking at a time since death of anywhere between fifteen or sixteen months and ten years. That really narrows it down.'

There wasn't much I could say to that, so I didn't try. Conrad was pulling back more of the tarpaulin. The stiff plastic was dirty, coated with what looked like cement or plaster dust and smears of blue paint. I was more interested in what wasn't there, but then the pathologist peeled back the sheet covering the lower half of the body, and any other details were momentarily forgotten.

The legs were partly drawn up, bent together and angled off to one side. They looked to be mainly bone beneath the short denim skirt, which showed similar staining as the cropped T-shirt. That had ridden up even more, bunching just below the chest to expose the stomach. Or what was left of it. Most of the abdominopelvic cavity, from below the ribs to the top of the pubic bone, was gaping and open. Within it, what remained of the internal organs were so atrophied and degraded as to be unrecognizable.

But that wasn't what made everyone fall silent. Lying inside the cavity were what looked like tiny pale twigs. I felt something twist inside me at the sight, and Ward's indrawn breath told me she'd recognized them as well.

'Rats have got to it,' one of the SOCOs commented, craning to get a better view. 'Looks like one died inside.'

'Don't be bloody stupid. And show some respect.' Whelan's tone was withering.

'What? I was only—'

'It's a foetus.' Ward spoke quietly. 'She was pregnant.'

She seemed moved, as though the development had undermined her usual professional detachment. Whelan gave the offending officer a glare that promised there'd be more said later, then turned to Ward. 'Looks like you were right about it being a woman, ma'am.'

It did, though Ward could hardly have known. 'How old's the foetus?'

'Looking at the size and development, probably six or seven months,' I told her.

Conrad had ignored the exchange. He turned away from the abdominal cavity as though what it held was incidental, focusing his attention elsewhere.

'The pregnancy's helpful,' he murmured, more to himself than anyone else. 'If she was of child-bearing age that narrows things down somewhat. Fully clothed, underwear still in place, so no obvious signs of sexual assault. Although that's not conclusive, of course.'

'She's not wearing much, though. No coat, just a T-shirt and a skirt,' added Ward. 'No tights, which suggests she could have died during the summer months.'

Whelan made a seesawing motion with his head. 'Unless she was killed somewhere with heating and then brought here. My wife won't wear a sweater indoors even in winter. Just cranks the central heating up and lets me worry about the bills.'

24

Ward didn't seem to be listening. 'What about the, uh, the stomach? Could rats have caused that or is it some kind of wound?'

'Ask me after the post-mortem,' Conrad said. But then he sniffed, considering. 'Rats would be more likely to go for an open wound, so it's possible she was stabbed. But let's not jump to any more conclusions, shall we? For one thing, there aren't any visible bloodstains on the clothes, which suggests, if there was an injury, it didn't bleed significantly.'

He was right. It would be easy to assume that we were looking at some sort of horrific wound, but I knew the tricks nature could play. At the moment there was only one thing I was certain about.

'She was moved.'

Everyone looked at me. I hadn't intended to announce it so bluntly, but the tiny skeleton, still in its mother's womb, had affected me more than I'd thought.

'Her body was somewhere else before this,' I went on. 'It was brought here after it mummified.'

Conrad gave a grudging sniff. 'Yes, you're right.'

'Are you sure?' Ward asked.

I nodded. 'The foetal bones aren't in any sort of ana-tomical position. They've been jumbled up, more than I'd expect, even allowing for scavengers. That suggests they were disturbed by fairly violent movement when there was no fluid left in the womb to cushion them.'

'The body was rolled up in plastic,' Whelan said. 'Maybe it happened then?'

'Possibly. The body wouldn't have mummified if it had been in the tarpaulin all the time. Moisture would have built up inside, so it would've decomposed normally. If that had happened the plastic would be smeared with fluids, the same as the clothing.'

'So it mummified first and then was wrapped in the tarp?' Ward asked.

'It must have. Then there's those.' I indicated a few dark, rice-like specks trapped in the folds of clothing. 'There should be a lot more blowfly casings than this. If her body had been here all the time they'd be scattered all around it.'

Ward frowned. 'Would there even be flies in here? It's pitch black. How could they see?'

'They wouldn't have to, they'd have been guided by the smell.' It was a common assumption that blowflies weren't active in darkness, but it took more than a lack of light to deter the persistent insects. 'These are probably bluebottle casings. If it's too dark for them to fly they'll walk to a dead body instead.'

'There's an image,' Whelan said with a grimace.

Ward gave him an irritated glance. 'Why are there flies if the body was mummified? Wouldn't that put them off?'

'Not if it decomposed first,' I told her. 'You can see from the staining on the clothes there was some initial decomposition before the body started to dry out and mummify. That would be more than enough.'

Blowflies could smell decomposing remains from up to a mile away, zeroing in on the scent to lay eggs in the eyes, nose and any other openings they could find. And while the lack of blood on the woman's clothing suggested she didn't have a major wound, even a small one would have attracted the flies' attention. It would have taken longer to reach her in the loft, but they'd have begun laying eggs long before any rats came along. Once they'd hatched, the ravenous larvae would have fed on the dead tissue, enlarging the original wound and continuing the cycle of feeding and reproducing until the body had mummified. And then they'd abandoned it.

Ward was still frowning. 'So you're saying she was killed somewhere else and then brought here?'

'Not necessarily.' I glanced at Conrad to see if he wanted to answer. But the pathologist had gone back to poring over the remains. 'Wherever her body was at first it had to be somewhere with pretty much identical conditions to this. Dry, a good airflow and hot enough for mummification to kick in quickly. That's asking a lot.'

'You think her body was up here all the time, just moved from another part of the loft?' Ward asked.

'Based on what I can see, I think it's possible, yes.'

'That doesn't make any sense.' Whelan sounded irritated. 'What's the point? If someone was worried her body might be found, why didn't they take it somewhere else? And why wait until it was mummified before moving it anyway?'

'I don't know,' I admitted. 'But I still think you should search the rest of the loft for blowfly casings.'

'OK, we'll check.' Ward was watching the pathologist. He was paying no attention to our conversation, leaning forward to examine the body's folded hands. 'Have you found something, Professor Conrad?'

'There's considerable trauma to the finger ends. Some of it could be from rodents, but I don't think it all is.'

'Can I take a look?' I asked.

He edged aside so I could get closer. Given the body's condition, it was hard to gauge what damage was post mortem and what wasn't. Some of the desiccated fingers had been gnawed by small teeth, and the fingernails had begun to come loose during the initial decomposition. But the finger ends themselves appeared torn, while the nails themselves were broken and splintered, with one missing completely.

'I don't think we can blame rats. It looks like at least some of it could have been done while she was still alive,' I said.

'You mean she was tortured?'

'You insist on asking questions we can't possibly answer,' Conrad said waspishly. His knees cracked as he pushed himself to his feet. 'I've seen enough. Once the hands are bagged you can move the body to the mortuary. I think it's safe to say—'

He broke off as a shadow darted overhead with a fast, flickering sound, like the pages of a book being riffled. The bat was gone in a second, but it startled the pathologist. He stumbled backwards, arms flailing as his foot went off the edge of the stepping plate. There was a dry *crunch* as it broke through the thin ceiling, layers of filthy insulation coming to life in a billow of dust as his leg plunged into them. Whelan managed to grab his wrist as he toppled backwards, and for a second I thought he had him.

Then, with a crash of breaking timber and plaster, Conrad and the whole section of loft beneath him disappeared.

Chapter 3

'BACK! EVERYONE GET BACK!' Ward yelled, coughing.
The air was smoky with dust and sparkling glass fibres. Everyone around me was coughing, the paper face-masks inadequate against the miasma that now filled the air. My eyes felt full of grit as I looked down into the gaping hole that had opened up. One of the spot-lights had toppled over when the plate fell and lay canted beside it, its beam shining into the darkness below.

'That means you, too,' Ward said from beside me. Moving past, she edged closer across the stepping plates towards the hole. Torn lengths of insulation hung down into it, snagged on the ends of splintered joists that jutted out like javelins.

'Professor Conrad! Are you all right?' she called.

There was no answer. This was a Victorian building, and the ceilings were high enough for the fall to break bones even without roof timbers and metal plates cascading down as well.

'Don't bloody stand there, get downstairs and see how he is!' Ward snapped at the officers nearest the loft entrance.

'The joists must be rotten,' Whelan said as the officers hurried off. 'Ma'am, you should . . .'

She nodded, reluctantly turning away from the hole. 'OK, everybody out! Nice and steady, single file and don't get too close together. Come on, move!'

Coughing, we made our way in an uneven line across the stepping plates. They bounced under the scuff and thump of feet, and I was relieved to reach the stepladder. After the dusty heat of the loft, climbing down into the cooler air below was like descending into cold water. Ward and Whelan were last out. She clambered quickly down the ladder, followed by her DI.

'Get paramedics up here, *now*!' she demanded, pushing through the crowd of overalls gathered around the stepladder. She looked around for the officers that she'd sent to help the pathologist. 'Where the hell are Greggs and Patel?'

There was a commotion from further down the long hospital corridor. A young female officer with a torch emerged from the doorway to a ward, looking harassed.

'Here, ma'am.'

Brushing aside a proffered bottle of water, Ward went over. 'How is he?'

The young woman shook her head, blinking nervously. 'Uh, I don't know . . .'

'You don't *know*? Oh, for . . . Come on, get out of the way!'

She unceremoniously barged past the young officer to go into the ward. 'He's not in there, ma'am.'

'Then where the hell is he?'

'We, uh, we can't find him.'

'What do you mean, you can't find him? He can't have bloody vanished!'

30

Ward turned as a torch beam appeared further along the unlit corridor. It bobbed towards us as the other police officer she'd sent down from the loft hurried to join us.

'There are more corridors branching off from this,' he said, breathlessly. 'We looked in the ward we thought was underneath where he fell, and I've just been to the next one along, but he's not in either of them.'

'Well, he can't have wandered off, not after a fall like that!'

'No. I mean, he might have, but . . .' The police officer hesitated, as though reluctant to go on. 'I can't see any hole in the ceiling.'

'Then you're looking in the wrong bloody place, aren't you? Here, give me that.' Ward snatched the torch from his hand and turned to Whelan. 'Jack, I want this floor searched. Every room. And where are the bloody paramedics?'

'On their way, ma'am.'

I moved forward as well, as Whelan began firing off commands, but he gave a quick shake of his head. 'Not you, Dr Hunter. All due respect, but we've lost one forensic expert already. Until we know none of the other floors are going to collapse you're staying put.'

I could see there was no use arguing. Frustrated, I remained by the foot of the stepladder as the others hurried off, torch beams zig-zagging in the blackness. One by one they cut out as they disappeared into adjoining corridors and rooms. As the shouts and footsteps receded, I looked up at the loft entrance. Whelan had told me to stay put, but I couldn't stand around doing nothing.

I climbed up the stepladder until my head and shoulders were in the loft. A haze of dust still filled the air, hanging like smoke in the floodlights. From below, calls echoed along the corridor from the searching police officers. By the sound of it they still hadn't located the pathologist, but I could see now that finding where he'd fallen might not be so straightforward. It was thirty or forty yards from where I stood on the ladder to where Conrad had gone through the ceiling, and the layout of the floor below was completely different to the loft's open expanse. Evidently, it wasn't proving easy to negotiate the warren of NHS wards, corridors, offices and waiting rooms, or to determine which one of them the pathologist had fallen into.

Even so, they should have found him by now. I shifted uncomfortably on the stepladder as the searchers continued to call to each other. *Come on, what's taking so long?* Several minutes had already passed since the loft had collapsed. If Conrad had an open wound, he could be bleeding out while everyone ran around trying to find him.

'Professor Conrad!' I called.

The shout died away. I started to head back down the stepladder, intent on joining the search despite Whelan's warning, when I thought I heard a noise. I stopped, my head cocked to listen. It didn't come again. It hadn't sounded like the searchers, though.

It had sounded like a moan.

'Professor Conrad! Can you hear me?'

Nothing. I stared at the pool of brightness made by the floodlights. Earlier that year I'd been forced to watch helplessly while a man died. I still woke thinking about it, and the idea of history repeating itself was unbearable.

To hell with it.

I climbed the rest of the way into the loft. I tested the stepping plates before trusting them with my weight, but although the joists underneath them creaked and flexed they seemed solid enough. The ceiling below had only given way when Conrad landed directly on them. Providing I didn't do the same, I should be OK.

I hoped.

The loft had been eerie enough when there were other people up there. It was even more so now I was on my own. The glow from the lights strung out along the stepping plates only made the shadows beyond them seem even darker. I kept a wary eye out for bats as I walked across the flexing boards, not wanting to be taken by surprise like the pathologist, but there was no sign of the timid creatures. I guessed the noise and commotion had scared them away.

The tarpaulin-wrapped body lay where we'd left it. It hadn't been disturbed by the collapse, which was something. I edged around the woman's remains, feeling vaguely disrespectful at leaving her alone up here. But it was the living who demanded attention now.

Carefully crossing the stepping plates, I approached the ragged hole. I didn't trust the nearest plates, so I hooked an arm over a roof beam to anchor myself before craning to see down into the room below. Dust swirled slowly upwards, caught in the glare from the toppled floodlight, but it was too dark to see what lay at the bottom.

'Professor Conrad!'

Nothing. Taking out my phone from inside my overalls, I switched on its torch. The shadows grudgingly retreated to reveal a chaotic pile of broken timbers, plaster and insulation. Leaning out further, I tried to see more. The torch beam passed over something blue. I shone it back, searching for it again. It was hard to make out, but then I realized what I was looking at.

A plastic overshoe, protruding from underneath a sheet of insulation.

'What the hell are you doing?'

I almost dropped my phone. Keeping a firm hold on the roof timber, I looked round as Whelan clomped across the stepping plates.

'You were told to stay put. Out. Now!'

'I can see Conrad.'

He hesitated. 'Let me have a look.'

I moved aside. 'Have you found which room he's in yet?'

'Not yet. The layout down there's all messed up. We've got to go along another corridor and then double back, and it's all divided up with panelling and partition walls. Makes it hard to get your bearings.'

It shouldn't be that hard, I thought, but the DI's bristling attitude made it clear he didn't need me to tell him that. Grabbing on to the same roof beam I'd been holding, he leaned out over the hole and shone his torch into the room below.

'Can you hear me down there, Professor?' he called.

There was no reply. 'Can you see him?' I asked.

'I can see something,' he grunted, squinting into the hole. 'Looks like his foot. Maybe we could—'

Footsteps on the stepping plates alerted us to Ward's approach. 'Jesus, Jack, what the hell are you doing?'

We turned to see Ward angrily coming towards us. For the first time I noticed she seemed to be moving awkwardly, bulky in the baggy overalls.

'Sorry, ma'am, I was just—'

'It's my fault,' I told her. 'I thought I heard a moan.'

'What, all the way from here?' She gave me a sceptical glare. I was beginning to wonder myself if I'd imagined it. But I'd heard something.

'We can see him,' Whelan said, saving me any more explanation.

'Bloody hell.' Ward glanced down at the woman's remains as she caught her breath. 'Is he conscious? Please tell me he's still breathing.'

'Can't say. He's buried under half the ceiling, but he's not moving.'

'Let me see.'

'Come on, ma'am, it's not safe,' Whelan warned. 'You shouldn't be up here.'

I don't know which surprised me most, the fact he'd say something like that to his SIO or that Ward didn't take his head off for it.

'Tell me something I don't know,' she said, holding on to the roof beams for balance as she made her way over. She stopped by the huddled remains in the centre of the stepping plates, still breathing heavily in the mask. 'A fire crew's on the way with rescue equipment, as well as an ambulance and paramedics, but we still can't bloody find him! Jesus Christ, this is ridiculous!'

'I could go down—' I began.

'No!' Ward and Whelan snapped in unison. She shook her head. 'The fire crew'll be here soon. They'll have proper rescue equipment.'

'He could be dead by then.'

'You think I don't know that?'

Whelan cleared his throat. 'Hate to say it, but Dr Hunter's got a point, ma'am. We don't know Conrad's condition, and the fire crew have still got to get here and lug all their gear upstairs. I could at least go down and take a shufti, see how things are.'

Ward stared down at the floor, hands bunched on her hips.

'Do it.'

Instructions were shouted at the officers on the floor below and a telescopic ladder was quickly hustled up into the loft. Ward wouldn't allow more than a handful of officers up there to minimize the risk of another collapse. She'd been reluctant to let me stay, until I'd pointed out that my medical background might be useful until the paramedics arrived.

In all of this, the reason why we were all there in the first place was almost forgotten. The body of the dead woman and her unborn child lay off to one side, far enough away from the hole not to be disturbed by the frenzied activity. At my request, a new plastic sheet was brought into the loft, and as Whelan and another officer set about extending the lightweight ladder into the hole I spread it over the near-mummified body. The plastic crinkled as I carefully drew it over the desiccated face, its leathery skin pulled drum-tight over the bones. The sheet would prevent any further contamination from the dust and glass fibre that had been stirred up, though I admitted to myself that wasn't the sole reason I'd wanted to cover her. She'd lain here, alone and undiscovered, for God knew how long.

It didn't feel right to ignore her now.

To my frustration, Ward made me stay well back while Whelan lowered the ladder, careful to avoid the debris that buried the pathologist. Floodlights had been repositioned to throw light into the space below, but the angle restricted

36

our view. They cast enough light to see the mound of timbers and insulation covering Conrad, but beyond that the room disappeared into impenetrable shadow.

Rather than trust the ladder against the hole's crumbling edge, Whelan leaned it against one of the roof timbers overhead and secured its top with a length of nylon rope. He gave it a shake, then swung himself out on to the rungs.

'Watch yourself, Jack,' Ward told him.

'Just like cleaning windows,' he quipped, climbing down.

The aluminium ladder bounced and creaked rhythmically as he descended. In a few seconds it stopped as he reached the bottom. From where I stood he was out of sight, but his voice carried clearly enough.

'OK, I'm down. Let me get some of this stuff off him . . .'

There was a grunt, then the sound of scrabbling. A plume of dust rose up from the hole as the sergeant shifted the debris from on top of the pathologist.

'That's better.' He sounded out of breath. 'He's pretty banged up. Still got a pulse but he's in a bad way. One leg looks broken, and . . . OK, there's a lot of blood.'

'Where from?' I called. 'Is it arterial?'

'I don't know, I can't see where it's coming from. Looks to be from his leg but it's pinned and I don't want to risk moving him. Ma'am, if we don't get this sorted quick we're going to lose him.'

I turned to Ward. 'Let me see if I can—'

Impatiently, she raised a hand to silence me. 'We need to get in there, Jack. Can you see a door or a way out?'

'Hang on.' There was a pause. 'Looks like a small ward. Still some beds and other junk down here, but I can't see a door.'

'There's got to be one *somewhere*.'

'No, it looks like one wall's been bricked up and – *fuck*!'

There was a sudden clatter.

'Jack? *Jack!* Are you all right?'

Seconds passed before Whelan replied. 'Yeah, I just . . . I dropped my torch.'

Ward sagged with relief. 'Bloody *hell*, Jack, what are you playing at?'

'Sorry, ma'am. It's the beds . . .' His voice was strained. 'There's people in them.'

Chapter 4

WARD DIDN'T WANT to let me go down to Whelan. 'I'm not risking anyone else, not until I know what we're facing.'

'We know what Conrad's facing. He's going to bleed to death unless we stop it.'

'The paramedics and fire crew will be here in five minutes—'

'He might not have that long. Come on, I can at least try and slow the bleeding until they get here!'

'Jack's trained in first aid—'

'And I'm a trained doctor! If you're worried I might contaminate a potential crime scene—'

'That isn't it, and you know it!'

'Then let me get down there!'

Ward put her head back. 'Jesus *Christ*! All right, but for God's sake be careful!'

I didn't wait for her to change her mind. Swinging myself out over the ladder, I began clambering down. It creaked and bucked under me but I took no notice. Whelan reached out to steady it as I reached the bottom.

'Careful where you step.'

It was like being at the bottom of a well. Shafts of brightness from the floodlights came through the hole in the ceiling but illuminated only a small area around us. Everything else was in blackness. Whelan was crouching by a mound of broken plaster and timbers, focusing his torch on Conrad. The DI had cleared off most of the debris – at least it wasn't heavy – and the pathologist lay twisted on his side in a nest of torn insulation. Caked in plaster and dirt, his face looked pallid and drawn, blood on it glistening darkly. He was unconscious, and I didn't like the sound of his breathing.

But it was the wound to his leg that was most urgent. Clogged with plaster and glass fibres, blood had formed a pool around his lower body. It was coming from the leg Conrad was lying on, and to get to it would mean moving him. I could see now why Whelan had been reluctant. After a fall like that the pathologist could easily have a spinal injury, and from the rasping breaths I thought a rib might have punctured a lung. He needed more help than I could give him, but at least I could try to see he stayed alive until it got here.

'Hold him still if he moves,' I told Whelan, and slid my hands under the pathologist's trapped leg. Trying not to disturb his position, I gently probed around where the bleeding seemed to be coming from. I was hoping I wouldn't feel a shard of broken bone sticking through the muscle of his leg. If that was the cause of the bleeding there might be little I could do, especially if the bone had nicked one of the arteries. In that case Conrad might well be dead before the paramedics even got here.

But there wasn't the sharp edge of splintered bone I'd been dreading. Instead, through the thin membrane of my gloves, I felt a rip in his coveralls and trousers on his thigh and the warm slickness of blood underneath. Conrad must have caught his leg on a nail or broken joist as he fell through the ceiling. Bad, but hopefully not an artery.

'Get ready,' I told Whelan. 'I'm going to apply pressure.'

My gloves were far from sterile, but they hadn't come into contact with the victim's body in the loft. And infection was the lesser risk facing the pathologist just then. Relying purely on touch, I bunched up the fabric of his trousers over the wound and pressed hard.

He gave a low groan and tried to move.

'Keep him still,' I said.

In response Whelan clamped the injured man more tightly, using his weight to keep him pinned.

'What's happening?' Ward's voice floated down from the hole in the ceiling. 'Is he all right?'

'How far away are the paramedics?' I called back.

'They've just come through the gates. Two, three minutes.'

It couldn't be soon enough. Still pressing on the wound, I shifted to a better position and concentrated on maintaining the pressure. Only then did I take the time to look around.

It was too dark to see much. Whelan had said it was a small ward of some kind, but beyond our island of light the rest of the room was in shadow. As my eyes adjusted, the blockwork of an unplastered wall took shape ahead of me in the gloom. Further away, blurred by the fog of dust, was the angular framework of a hospital bed. Lying on it, little more than a patch of grey in the blackness, was a still figure. I thought I could make out another bed beyond it, although that could have been the shadows playing tricks.

But whatever else this place contained, it would have to wait. Closing my mind to the growing cramp in my forearms, I kept up the pressure on Conrad's wound and willed the paramedics to hurry up.

There was a faint lightening of dawn in the sky as I pulled up outside Ballard Court. I waited for the automatic gates to open, the hum of their motor a bass accompaniment to the morning birdsong. Driving through, I parked in the subterranean car park and switched off the engine. The lift doors chimed open, revealing my neighbour from across the hall. His eyes passed disapprovingly over my rumpled state before he gave a cursory nod as he walked straight past me.

'And good morning to you, too,' I said to the empty lift.

My footsteps clipped out a tattoo on the marble floor as I walked down the hallway to the apartment. I let myself in as quietly as I could, but the smell of bacon told me I was wasting my time. Rachel was at the hob, slicing mushrooms next to a sizzling frying pan. She was already dressed, looking lovely and a lot fresher than I did.

'Hi,' she said, taking the pan off the heat. She came over and put her arms around me, tilting her face up for a kiss. 'Good timing.'

I breathed in the scent of her hair, still slightly damp from the shower. 'There was no need for you to get up yet.'

'Yes, there was. I wanted to cook breakfast. I knew you wouldn't bother if I didn't. Have you even eaten anything since yesterday's lunch?'

I thought back to the over-stewed tea a PC had brought for me earlier.

'I had something.'

Rachel arched a sceptical eyebrow at me before turning back to the hob. 'You've time for a shower.'

I smiled at the unsubtle hint: after hours sweating inside my coveralls I needed one.

But my smile faded as I went into the bedroom and saw the packed suitcase standing by the door. Rachel's flight wasn't until late morning, but she'd have to allow for traffic and delays in getting to the airport. I felt a hollowness under my ribs at the thought.

It wasn't how I'd wanted our last night to be.

The paramedics hadn't taken long to arrive, but it had seemed an endless few minutes. I was grateful to hand over to one of them, a young woman who quickly took over applying pressure to Conrad's wound while her colleague ripped open packets of dressings. I stood back to give them room, holding my bloodied hands away from me. No longer crouched over the pathologist, I was better able to take in my surroundings. The extra light from the paramedics' torches revealed three beds in the shadows. The furthest one was empty, but the other two had motionless figures lying on them. I didn't attempt to go over, knowing better than to contaminate the scene any more than it had been already. But any hopes I'd had that this might have been some sort of hoax, a pair of shop mannequins left in beds by pranksters when the hospital closed, soon disappeared. There was an odour in the air I'd been too busy to notice before. Faint and masked by the smell of dust and plaster from the collapsed ceiling, it was the foully sweet scent of decay. From what I could make out, both bodies were fully clothed, and I could distinguish dark bands across their chests and legs. At first I couldn't think what they could be, but then I realized.

They'd been strapped to the beds.

There was a nudge on my arm. 'Let's give them some room,' Whelan said. 'Here.'

He held out a pair of clean nitrile gloves. Having peeled the soiled ones off, I put them on as the paramedics worked on Conrad, and then went back to the ladder. I paused at the bottom, taking one last look across the shadowed chamber. No doors or any way in or out, as Whelan had said. Only the blank face of the unplastered wall, indistinct in the darkness.

I was ushered out of the loft and back downstairs. I passed the fire crews on the stairs, standing aside to let them past with their equipment. It was a relief to step outside into the cool night. I was sweaty and itching from the loft insulation, glad to be able to take off the filthy and bloodstained protective gear. A sickle moon hung low in the sky, ringed by a milky penumbra, as I accepted a cup of tea from a friendly PC. I stood on the steps outside the doorway to drink it, and hadn't finished when the paramedics emerged from inside. They were carrying Conrad on a rigid stretcher. The pathologist looked in a bad way. His face was bloodied and he was still unconscious, secured by straps and with a cervical collar immobilizing his head and neck.

As soon as he was on board, the ambulance set off in a blare of sirens and blue lights.

Ward appeared not long afterwards. She spoke to several other people, gesticulating angrily at one point, before heading over to where I stood. She'd pulled off her mask and hood and gave a heartfelt sigh as she leaned against one of the stone pillars that flanked the steps.

'Jesus, what a night.' She began peeling off her gloves. 'Thanks for what you did in there for Conrad.'

'How is he?'

She blew a strand of sweat-damp hair from her eyes. 'Too soon to say. The paramedics were able to stabilize him while the fire crew set up the lifting gear. His pupils are responsive, which is a good sign, but until they get him X-rayed and scanned they won't know how serious it is.'

'They brought him out through the loft?'

'It was quicker than knocking through the wall.' She bent and began tugging off her overshoes. 'Took us a while to find the bloody thing, even knowing what we were looking for. It's been built across a sort of ante-room at the end of a ward and painted on the outside to match the rest of it. If you didn't know it was there you wouldn't give it a second glance. Someone went to an awful lot of trouble so it wouldn't be found.'

There was an obvious question waiting to be asked. 'Do you think it's connected with the woman in the loft?'

'Honestly? I haven't a clue.' She threw a wadded-up overshoe at a plastic bin. 'Hell of a coincidence if not, but until we can take a better look at what's in that bricked-up room I'm not jumping to any conclusions.'

I nodded up at a boxy camera fixed high up in the hospital wall, its lens pointing at the pillared entrance. 'What about the CCTV?'

Whoever bricked up the ward had to go in and out, but Ward shook her head. 'They're dummy cameras. Apparently, the developers decided it wasn't worth the expense of real ones. Not that they'd be much help anyway. Recordings are usually erased after a few weeks, and we're looking a lot further back than that.'

'So there was no security here at all?'

'There were security guards to start with, but that was more to keep the protesters out than anything. The office development's caused a lot of ill feeling locally. Social activists think the land should be used for housing, and conservation groups want to have St Jude's listed and a protection order slapped on the entire site. The grounds back on to woodland where there's a ruined Norman church or something. There's been a campaign to have it declared an area of special scientific interest, like Lesnes Abbey Woods in Bexley. Except that's got an abbey and fossils going for it, so they're probably on a hiding to nothing.'

Ward unzipped her coveralls and began wrestling her way out of them. I noticed she seemed to have put on a little weight but didn't think anything of it.

'Once the developers realized it was going to be a long haul, they cut back on security,' she went on, tugging an arm free. 'Usual story. Made do with fences and "keep out" signs and left the place to fall down by itself until they got the green light to demolish it.'

'Until the bats.'

She gave a wry smile. 'Until the bats.'

I looked up at the boarded-up building. 'You think this could have anything to do with the protests?'

'It's somewhere to start. First off, though, we'll need to make sure the building's safe before we send anyone else inside. I'm not risking any more injuries, and we've already contaminated enough crime scenes for one day. Whatever's in that room we found, I don't want any more ceilings dropping on it.' She yanked at one of the coverall sleeves that had become stuck. 'God, I'd forgotten how much I hate these bloody things.'

With a grunt, she finally shucked free. My first reaction was that she'd put on more weight than I'd thought, but then I realized. She cocked an eyebrow at me.

'What's up? Wondering if I've eaten all the pies?'

I smiled. 'How far along are you?'

'Just over six months, but it seems like a bloody age. And, before you say anything, yes, I do know what I'm doing. It's not as if I'm on foot patrol, so I can work as long as I feel fit. I'm not missing my shot at SIO to sit at home knitting bootees.'

I understood now why Whelan had been so concerned about her being in the loft. And why Ward had been so affected by the sight of the dead woman and her unborn child. The victim's pregnancy had been at a similar stage to her own.

'Boy or girl?' I asked, feeling the familiar stab of loss as I thought back to my own wife's pregnancy.

'Don't know, don't care. My husband's hoping for a boy, but I told him if he wants to know the sex he should have got pregnant himself.'

I knew she was married but I'd never met her husband. Although Ward and I had worked together several times, we'd never socialized, and on the occasions we'd met our private lives hadn't really been on the agenda.

Still, her news was a bright note in an otherwise grim evening. I waited by my car, while Ward went into a briefing with senior members of her team and fire-safety officers. Shortly afterwards they were joined in the mobile command post by three more people, a short-haired man in his forties whose authoritative demeanour suggested he could be Ward's superior, and a younger man and woman who trailed behind like his entourage. None of them looked happy. Not only had the pathologist been seriously injured, but now we were looking at multiple homicides that might or might not be connected.

What had seemed like a routine investigation had become a different beast altogether.

After twenty minutes, a PC came over with the message that I might as well go home. All further work had been suspended until the loft was safely shored up and given the all-clear by health and safety: I'd be contacted when I was needed again.

And so I'd driven back to Ballard Court. There was no question of trying to sleep before Rachel left, so after a shower and breakfast we sat at the table over coffee, trying to pretend it was just another morning. That grew harder as the time approached for her to leave. She didn't want me to drive her to the airport, as that would only prolong the goodbye, and I felt my heart sink when her phone chimed to announce the taxi's arrival. I held her close, breathing in the clean scent of her hair to memorize it.

'See you in three months,' she said, giving me a final kiss.

When the door had closed behind her, I turned back to the empty apartment. The gleaming kitchen seemed even more clinical than usual, the abstract paintings on the walls of the lounge and hall more alienating than ever. I was used to being there on my own, yet Rachel's absence shouted out everywhere I looked.

Tired, but knowing sleep was out of the question, I loaded the breakfast plates into the dishwasher and made myself another coffee. The apartment had an elaborate barista-style machine that ground beans, frothed milk and carried out any number of other esoteric tasks. Rachel loved it, but to me it seemed a lot of fuss for a cup of coffee. Taking a jar of instant from a cupboard, I poured myself a mug in half the time and sat down with it at the granite kitchen island.

Now Rachel was gone I felt at a loss. I'd probably head in to the university department later, but that still left me with a few hours to fill. Restless, I went online to see if the grisly discoveries at St Jude's had made it on to any of the news sites. The story was buried away in the regional sections, short on details except that human remains had been discovered at the derelict hospital. There was no mention of either the sealed chamber or Conrad's accident. The site was too public for the police to keep a lid on what had happened for very long, but Ward was evidently hoping to delay the media frenzy as long as possible.

Good luck with that, I thought.

Having read what little coverage there was about the investigation, I ran a quick search on the hospital itself. There was no shortage of information about St Jude's, from petitions and blogs rallying support against the hospital's demolition to amateur websites detailing its history. It had started life in the nineteenth century as a charitable infirmary run by nuns. By the 1950s the hospital had begun to expand, the stern Victorian building presiding over the new departments and facilities built in its grounds. There were numerous photographs chronicling the stages of its life, from sepia prints that showed raw, new-looking stonework and sapling-dotted grounds to more recent snaps taken when the building was a boarded-up wreck. One image that looked to have been taken in the 1970s showed St Jude's in its bustling prime. Where now only rusted posts survived, a large sign detailing the hospital's departments stood next to the main doors. Walking past it were two nurses caught mid-stride, laughing as they smoked cigarettes. Behind them a man and child – boy or girl; it was impossible to tell – were frozen in time as they passed through the big doors.

There was something melancholy about seeing all those images of past lives. It wasn't something I wanted to dwell on right then, and the background reading into St Jude's hadn't provided any great insights. Still, looking at my watch, I saw I'd killed almost an hour. Long enough for me to head into work.

Shutting my laptop, I put it in my bag and collected my jacket from the hat stand in the hallway. Then, with a sense of relief, I went out and closed the door on the opulent apartment.

For the past few years I'd held an associate position in the forensic anthropology department of one of London's larger universities. It was an association based on mutual convenience. My teaching duties were minimal, but it provided me with an income and facilities and allowed me the freedom for police consultancy work. Earlier that year my tenure had looked shaky when I'd been unofficially blacklisted by police forces after an investigation had ended badly. But since the Essex case my star was on the rise again, and I'd recently been offered another two-year contract, on better terms than before.

Yet I'd been putting off signing it. Although my position at the university seemed secure enough for now, I'd no illusions what would happen if my star waned again. And after the uncertainty and upheaval of earlier that year, I wasn't even sure I wanted to wait for that to happen. Rachel's arrival in my life had been a huge change, one that had given me a fresh perspective.

Perhaps it was time for another.

I parked my car a few streets away from the university and walked back to the building that housed the forensic anthropology department. Ever since Grace Strachan's fingerprint had been found on the doorway of my old flat, Ward had advised me to vary my routes into work. Just in case, she'd said. It had seemed a pointless exercise then, and felt even more so now. But I'd promised Rachel, so each day I parked in a different spot and used one of the side doors into the building instead of the main entrance.

The new academic year had started, and the university's chaotic bustle was a welcome distraction after the empty apartment. Brenda, the department's office manager, looked up from behind her desk when I walked in.

'Morning, David. How was your weekend?'

'Good, thanks.'

'I wasn't expecting to see you back so soon. Don't forget there's a faculty meeting this afternoon.'

Damn. 'I can't wait.'

'I can see that. Oh, and that freelance journalist's emailed again. Francis Scott-Hayes.'

I sighed. Scott-Hayes had been pestering me for an interview for weeks, emailing both me and the department in the hope of a response. Or rather, the response he wanted. I'd politely declined his first request, less politely refused the second and ignored his subsequent emails. I wasn't even sure how he'd heard of me. Usually,

51

my involvement in police investigations was strictly behind the scenes, which was how I liked it. Unfortunately, my name had appeared in news reports when two cases I'd worked on made national headlines, one the previous year in Dartmoor, and more recently the Essex inquiry where I'd met Rachel. It was a safe bet that the journalist had seen one of them and decided I'd make a good story.

The fact I disagreed didn't seem to bother him.

'Just ignore him,' I told Brenda. 'He'll get the message eventually.'

'You sure? He writes for all the nationals. Might be nice to get your picture in a magazine.'

'Did I hear someone say "magazine"?' A voice came from behind me.

My heart sank as I turned to find Professor Harris, the Head of Department. Polished briefcase gripped firmly in hand, he was regarding me with a smile that was affable and entirely insincere. He'd been markedly less friendly when my police consultancy work had dried up, but now that the situation had changed, so had his tune.

'It's just some journalist who won't take no for an answer,' I told him, as Brenda mouthed *sorry* and busied herself on her computer.

He nodded, still smiling. 'Then perhaps you should consider it. You know what they say about publicity, and a nice interview would do wonders for your profile.'

And the department's. 'Perhaps later,' I said.

His eyes lit up. 'Ah, yes, I heard a body had been found in an abandoned hospital. Somewhere in North

London, wasn't it? Are you, ah, working on the case? Quite convenient, really, having it so nearby.'

Not for the victims, I thought. 'I can't really say anything . . .'

'No, no, of course. Well, ah . . . good luck with it. And the interview.'

Brenda gave me a wry smile as he bustled off. 'The answer's still no,' I told her.

Going into the cubbyhole that passed as my office, I began sifting through my emails. They were the usual mixture of departmental trivia, newsletter subscriptions and a couple of queries from post-grad students about their research projects. The latest interview request from the freelance journalist was also waiting in my inbox. My first instinct was to delete it, but after the conversation with Brenda I felt obliged to see what he had to say. It was pretty much the same pitch he'd made before. I had to admit he wrote for some prestigious newspapers and magazines and supposed I should be flattered he'd take an interest in me. Perhaps Harris had a point: it *would* raise my profile, and God knows that had taken enough of a beating recently.

But whatever drove me to do what I did, it wasn't to see my picture in a magazine. I pressed delete and the email disappeared.

Chapter 5

IT WAS THE next day before Ward called to let me know they'd been given the go-ahead to recover the mummified remains from the loft. My first reaction was relief. I'd heard from Rachel the night before, tired after her journey but excited at the prospect of starting work. By now she'd be on a marine research vessel, perhaps already heading out for some of the more inaccessible Aegean islands. They'd be spending an extended period out at sea and, while the boat had a satellite phone, it was only for emergencies. She'd only be able to get in touch when they were in range of phone or wi-fi reception, so it could be several days before we'd be able to speak again.

Although we'd known that before she left, when the call had ended I felt her absence more keenly than ever. So when Ward told me they were ready to resume work, I'd cleared the rest of my schedule and driven out there to attend the SIO's briefing. The media had finally realized that whatever was going on at the abandoned hospital was a bigger story than the accidental death of a vagrant or drug addict. Broadcast vans bristling with aerials lined the road, and a cluster of cameras and journalists had congregated outside the main gates. My arrival caused a stir of interest that just as quickly faded as the PCs on the gate let my car through the cordon.

St Jude's didn't have quite the same intimidating presence in sunlight as it had at night. The looming shapes and shadows that had lined the sides of the driveway were revealed as piles of rubble and the empty shells of part-demolished buildings, overgrown with weeds. Without the concealing mask of darkness, the hospital was displayed in all its decaying glory. Once upon a time it would have had the grandeur of a stately home. Two long wings stretched out either side of the faux-Grecian portico that housed the main entrance, its supporting pillars giving it the look of a mausoleum. Wide steps led up to tall double doors inside it, their symmetry marred by the addition of a concrete wheelchair ramp. It was still an impressive structure, but the years of abandonment had taken their toll. Weeds grew through gaps in the stonework, and the pollution-blackened walls were streaked with bird droppings and graffiti. The ranks of high windows that once stared out across landscaped grounds were now boarded up and sightless, while the old signs for long-vanished medical departments added to the sad air of dereliction.

The briefing was held in a police trailer outside the old hospital. It was Ward's first as SIO, and she was clearly nervous. At one point she dropped her notes, offering a muttered 'shit' as she bent to collect them. She left immediately afterwards, so there was no opportunity to speak to her. But after I'd changed into forensic coveralls and made my way through the ranks of police and support vehicles, I saw Whelan at the foot of the hospital steps. A uniformed PC stood nearby, her expression closed as she stared at the third member of the group. He was a big, heavily built man in a yellow high-visibility jacket, and I slowed when I realized they were arguing.

Or rather the big man was. He looked to be in his late forties or early fifties, raw-boned and thick-set, with a barrel stomach that thrust out in front of him like a statement of intent. His yellow jacket was battered and ingrained with dirt, while steel toecaps showed through the worn tan leather of his safety boots. His face had the broken-veined, coarse-pored look of a heavy drinker, and right now it was flushed crimson as his angry voice reached me.

'. . . bad enough with bats! Fucking *bats*, for Christ's sake! And now this! I'm trying to run a business here, do you know how much this is costing me?'

He was a full head taller than Whelan and was using it to full advantage, towering over the deputy SIO, his stubbled jaw thrust out belligerently. Whelan was having none of it, though. His own face was set and impassive as he stared back at the bigger man without giving an inch.

'Like I say, we're sorry for any inconvenience, but—'

'Incon*venience*? Jesus wept!'

'—this is a crime scene now. We can't allow any more work here until we've finished our investigations.'

'And how long will that take?'

'Unfortunately, we can't tell you that at the moment. But the sooner we finish, the sooner you can get your men back to work, so it's in your interests to cooperate.'

'Well, that's bloody great! What am I supposed to do in the meantime? Pay my men for sitting on their arses all day?'

'We're not unsympathetic, Mr Jessop, but it's out of our hands. Now, if you wouldn't mind going with the PC and waiting in the trailer until—'

'Yeah, more fucking waiting! Like I've not had to do enough of that already!'

Turning his back on Whelan, he stomped off, followed by the stony-faced PC. I moved aside as he swept towards me, grubby yellow jacket flapping as he marched past. Something fell from it and clattered to the floor as he went. I looked down and saw a pair of spectacles lying there, one lens fallen out and lying on the gritty tarmac.

'You dropped these,' I called, picking them up.

He looked round, glaring at me as though unable to process the words. Then, leaving the PC to wait, he came back.

'Thanks,' he muttered, snatching the glasses from me.

'There's this as well,' I said, holding out the lens.

A stale smell of sweat, cigarettes and unmetabolized alcohol came off him as he stood blinking, looking down at the broken glasses in his hands. For a bizarre second I thought he was going to cry. Then he turned on his heel and strode off, leaving the unimpressed PC to follow after him.

I went over to Whelan. 'He didn't seem happy.'

'Noticed that, did you? That's Keith Jessop, the demolitions contractor hired to level this place. What with the planning protests and bats, he's been waiting months already, so he's not a happy bunny at the moment.' He gave a cheery smile. 'The good news is we might be seeing more of him. He knows as much about the structural side of St Jude's as anyone, so we've asked him to help locate any more hidden rooms there might be. As you saw, he's only too happy to assist.'

'You think there might be more?' It was a stupid question: I'd been so busy thinking about the pregnant woman and the other two victims that it hadn't occurred to me there could be others.

Whelan considered the dark face of St Jude's, blackened walls looming above us with their blind windows. 'We've found three bodies already without even trying. The size of this place, God knows what else is in there.'

He motioned with his head for me to follow him.

'Come on. Before you start on the recovery there's something else you need to see.'

The ward was in the paediatric wing. It was on the top floor, some way further along the corridor from the loft hatch I'd used before. I'd forgotten how cold it was inside the hospital, and the odour of damp and mould was heavy in the breezeless air. A daisy chain of floodlights had been rigged up along the corridor here as well, spaced out to show the way but creating pools of shadows in the corners. The floor was littered with rubble and broken plaster that crunched underfoot, the larger pieces big enough to turn an ankle. Posters warning against tobacco, alcohol and drugs hung from the walls, while others forbade the use of mobile phones. We passed a large area of curtained cubicles, where a sign declared *X-ray: Do not enter when light is on* next to a cobwebbed red bulb.

The ward was a little way past that. Its double doors had been propped open and more floodlights set up inside. They cast a harsh, ethereal light on the dingy walls, where faded murals of cartoon characters capered to an empty room. The smell of mould was even more overpowering in here. Dangling sockets for oxygen cylinders protruded from the walls, and an assortment of broken junk was scattered about: a rusted bed frame lacking a mattress, a bedside cabinet missing both cupboard door and drawer, even a pair of old car batteries. A worn teddy bear slumped tiredly against the skirting board, next to a broken abacus whose colourful beads had spilled off the wires.

'I know. Gets you, doesn't it?' Whelan said, seeing me looking round.

'Can't you take some of the boards off the windows?' I said, sobered by the atmosphere in the dank ward. Some of the windows still had ragged curtains hanging over them, but all were boarded up so that not a chink of daylight penetrated the darkness.

'We could, but then we'd be letting any nosy bastard with a drone or telephoto lens get a good look inside as well. At least this way we know what we're doing isn't going to be on the front pages tomorrow.'

He continued to the far end of the ward, where bigger floodlights illuminated a group of anonymous figures in blue coveralls. They were working in front of what at first appeared to be an ordinary wall. Four yards long and three high, it was made of breezeblocks painted a close match to the pale green of the other walls. It was easy to see how the police officers searching for Conrad had overlooked it. Completely featureless, there was nothing about it to attract a second glance.

Not unless you knew what lay behind it.

It was only when you looked more closely that the false notes began to sound. Whereas the interlocking rectangles of the individual blocks were clearly visible on this area of wall, the rest of the walls had been finished in plaster. And instead of the blocks being keyed into the walls on either side, they'd been crudely butted up to them, as though there'd been an opening here that had been filled in.

'How's it coming along?' Whelan asked, stopping by an assortment of heavy-duty electric power tools, lump hammers and chisels assembled nearby. His voice echoed in the empty room.

One of the figures working on the wall paused to answer. 'Not far off now. We've been in the other side and rigged up a plastic sheet to keep down the dust and stop any fragments flying into the room. It's about as good as we're going to get.'

'It better be. We can do without any more mishaps.'

Whelan didn't make it a threat, but it didn't sound like a joke either. As the hammering started up again, I noticed an empty paint tin and plastic decorator's tray in the corner. Both were smeared with the same colour emulsion as the breezeblock wall. Next to them was a large paint roller, its sponge caked with green paint and set rock hard.

'Are they what I think they are?' I asked.

'Yep,' Whelan said. 'Somebody went to all this trouble to camouflage the wall, then left their tools behind. We lifted some nice sets of fingerprints off them, too. Even left a thumbprint in the mortar, which was considerate. Big bugger, if the size is anything to go by.'

'Seems a bit of an oversight, doesn't it?'

He shrugged. 'It happens. People try to be clever and then cock up something obvious. Anyway, let's leave them to it. We're back out here.'

We went into the corridor again. The floodlights continued past the ward and around a corner, ending at a doorway. Beyond it was a flight of wooden stairs, rising out of sight. We stood aside to let a SOCO come out, her coveralls blackened and grubby, then went through.

'This leads to the clock tower,' Whelan told me, as we climbed up the narrow stairway. There was a peppery smell of dust, and the wood creaked drily under our weight. 'Nothing much up there any more. All the clock mechanism was taken for scrap, but we're not going that far. This is us.'

We'd reached a small landing. A floodlight shone on a low doorway in the wall, no more than five feet high. The plaster on the walls around it had crumbled to expose the wooden laths underneath. The small door was open, smudges of talc-like fingerprint powder dusting the doorframe and edges. There was a sturdy catch on the outside to hold the door shut, a simple metal bar that swung down to sit in a bracket fixed to the frame.

'There's about a dozen hatches and access doors like this scattered around,' Whelan said. 'Apart from the one we used last time, this one's closest to where we found the body. Mind your head.'

He ducked through the low doorway. I did likewise, straightening once I was inside. We were in a different part of the loft to where the pregnant woman's remains had been found. The brick wall of the clock tower rose up at our backs, while in front of us the supporting timbers of the roof disappeared into darkness like the ribcage of a dead whale. The air in here was different to the rest of the building, closer and seeming to have more weight. It would be easy to give in to claustrophobia, I thought, turning to where Whelan was waiting.

A platform of stepping plates had been set up just inside the loft doorway, forming a temporary floor on the joists. A space had been left clear in the middle, exposing a patch of filthy loft insulation. In the white glare of floodlights, two SOCOs were poring over it on their hands and knees.

'We found this a few hours ago,' Whelan told me. 'What do you make of it?'

I crouched down beside the uncovered area of insulation. It was very close to the doorway, and the uneven, dirt-matted surface was covered with hundreds of tiny dark specks, like grains of black rice. They were arranged in an approximate ring, more or less oval in shape. Its centre was almost clear, but then the flecks grew in density before thinning out at the edges.

I picked one up, turning it carefully in my gloved fingers. The papery husk was split in half and hollow, the creature it contained long gone. Most of the others were the same, although I could see a small number of whole pupae where the insect inside had failed to hatch. We were old acquaintances, *Calliphoridae* and I. The maddening buzzing of the adult flies provided an accompaniment to many of the crime scenes I attended. Although I'd no love for them, I respected the role they played. Not only in breaking down decaying organic matter, including human flesh, but in determining how long ago an individual had died. Blowflies were nature's stopwatch, their lifecycle – from eggs to larvae to adult insect – an invaluable aid in estimating time since death.

The clock here had stopped a long time ago – too long to be any use now. Even so, that didn't mean these empty shells had nothing to tell us.

'I'd get a forensic entomologist to confirm it, but they're mainly blue- and greenbottles,' I said, examining the empty casing. 'I can't see any larvae among them, but there wouldn't be after all this time.'

Any larvae would have either pupated and hatched, or died and disintegrated once the food source was no longer available. But although the body that once lay here was gone, there were clear signs of its presence. The glass-fibre insulation was stained and matted where decompositional fluids had leached on to it, and the random pattern of the discarded fly casings had been disrupted. In places the husks were crushed and flattened.

'Looks like you were right,' Whelan said. 'The body lay here until it mummified, then it was moved further into the loft.'

'Did you get anything from the tarpaulin she was wrapped in?' I asked.

'Maybe.' He sounded deliberately non-committal. 'There are what look like dog hairs on it, and we found a human hair caught in one of the eyelets. Different colour to the victim's so it isn't one of hers. We'll check the DNA from it against the database, see if we can find a match, but that's going to take time. The tarp itself is the sort of thing you could find in any DIY outlet or builder's yard. The powder on it was a mix of cement and plaster dust like we thought, and the blue paint's fairly generic, so we can't pin it down to any particular brand. I'd say whoever moved the body was in a hurry and grabbed whatever they had to hand rather than buy a new one. Although that doesn't explain why they waited so long in the first place.'

'They?'

He gestured around us. 'This is a good twenty or thirty yards from where we found her. Unless someone took the time to put boards down the body would have to be carried. Easier with it wrapped in the tarp, but I can't see one person managing on their own. Not the weight so much, just balancing all that way on the joists without putting a foot through the ceiling.'

It was a good point. And if the woman's body had been dragged it would have left a trail of disturbed insulation in its wake, as well as causing substantial post-mortem damage to the fragile remains. I'd seen no indication of that.

I looked again at where the body had been. As well as discolouration from the decomposition, there was a lighter patch of staining on the insulation, as though some paler fluid had dried there. 'What's that?'

One of the SOCOs shook her head. 'Not sure. It's not dark enough for blood. We found splashes of what could be the same stuff on the wooden steps outside, so it might not even be from the body. Could be something that somebody just spilled. We've sent samples for analysis, but whatever it is it's too old and dry to tell us much.'

'We did find something else, though,' Whelan said. He pointed at the inside of the doorframe. 'See here?'

There were splintered gouges in the unpainted timber, lighter than the surrounding wood.

Scratches.

'Explains the damage we saw on the woman's hands,' Whelan said. 'We dug one of her fingernails out of the woodwork. The door was fastened from the outside and it's pretty solid. Too heavy for her to prise open or break down, but she gave it a good go.'

God, I thought, imagining it. We'd thought the woman had been killed somewhere else and then her body had been carried up to the loft. We were wrong.

Someone had locked her in here and left her to die.

'What I can't understand is why she didn't get out through one of the other exits,' the second SOCO said.

He was an older man, with worried eyes above his mask. 'It's not like this was the only one.'

'How would *you* feel, crawling around up here if you were pregnant? You made hard enough work of it with your beer gut,' his colleague countered. 'And how would she know where they were? It'd be pitch black, and we haven't found a phone or cigarette lighter she could have used for light. One slip and she'd have been through the ceiling.'

'I was only saying,' he muttered, sounding hurt.

I was still trying to make sense of what had gone on here. 'Why would anyone lock her inside and then just leave her?'

Whelan gave a shrug. 'I suppose there's a chance it could have been unintentional, some sort of prank gone wrong. People do all sorts of things when they're drunk or high, and we know a lot of addicts use this place. But I can't see a pregnant woman hiding in a loft for a laugh, high or not. I'd say someone either forced her in here or else she was being chased and tried to hide. Either way, someone fastened her inside and then left her. Leastways until months afterwards, or however long it was. Could be when they heard the hospital was going to be knocked down they decided to shift the body to where it was less likely to be found.'

It was as good a theory as any. But the idea of the pregnant woman being chased reminded me of something the SOCO had mentioned earlier.

'The pale stains on the insulation,' I said, looking at the matted glass fibre. 'You said there were splashes of something similar on the steps outside. Could it be amniotic fluid?'

The female SOCO sat back on her heels, considering. 'Yeah, I suppose it could. But I think the stains will be too old to say one way or the other.'

'You're thinking her waters broke?' Whelan asked me.

'It's possible. But if they did, from what I saw of the foetus it would have been premature.'

'So she could have died from that.'

I nodded, sobered by the thought. Without medical attention, if the membranes around the amniotic sac ruptured early it could be life-threatening in far better conditions than this. Trapped in a loft without even food or water, the woman and her child would have had no chance of survival. Only a slow death in the dark.

No one spoke, then Whelan turned back to the doorway.

'Come on,' he said heavily.

As we tramped down the wooden stairs I stopped by the dried splashes the female SOCO had spoken about. They were only faint, more like watermarks than blood. There were several of them, some little more than drops that led in an uneven trail up the stairs to the loft.

They might still be something entirely innocent, I reminded myself, some liquid spilled by a workman or some trespasser. It was easy to read too much into things, especially in an emotive case like this.

But as I followed Whelan back into the empty hospital corridor, the image of a young woman fleeing along it from some faceless pursuer – or pursuers – was hard to shake. She'd sought sanctuary in the loft, then found herself trapped there. I thought again about the scratches on the wooden doorframe, each gouge one of fear and desperation. Exhausted, her waters prematurely broken, she'd fought for her life and her child's in the only way left open to her.

And when that had failed, she'd lain down in the filthy loft and died.

Chapter 6

IN THE END, the recovery of the woman's remains went without a hitch. The dust had settled, literally, when I climbed through the ceiling hatch and crossed the stepping plates to where the desiccated body waited. Everything in the loft was as we'd left it, except now the hole that Conrad had fallen through had been covered over with plastic sheeting and cordoned off with blue-and white police tape.

I'd been told the forensic pathologist was out of danger, although a bad concussion, broken hip, ribs and shoulder meant he wouldn't be carrying out post-mortems any time soon. There had been talk about waiting for a replacement before resuming the recovery, but Ward hadn't wanted to wait any longer. Even though the structural engineers had decided there was no imminent risk of any more of the loft collapsing, no one wanted to put it to the test. The priority now was to get the body out of the loft as quickly as possible. Anything else could wait until it was in the mortuary.

Ordinarily, recovering the woman's body would have been relatively simple. Even fragile mummified remains wouldn't cause too many problems, though care would have to be taken when it came to lowering them through the narrow hatch. The complication here was that the victim wasn't only mummified, she'd been pregnant. And without the womb's cushioning fluid to protect it, any attempt to move her body with the foetus still inside would cause the tiny bones to shift around, like seeds in a dry gourd. We couldn't afford to damage them more than they had been already, which left me with no option.

Before we recovered the mother's remains from the loft, I'd first have to remove her baby.

It wasn't something I'd been looking forward to. There seemed something deeply wrong – sacrilegious, almost – in separating the two of them in that way. I waited while a SOCO carefully fastened plastic bags around the woman's claw-like hands with their shredded finger ends and broken nails. Then, as another SOCO videoed the operation, I closed my mind to the macabre nature of what I was about to do and set to work.

I hadn't done anything quite like this before. In effect, I was looking at two individual sets of remains, because the conditions for them both would have been markedly different. Whereas the mother's body had been exposed to air, flies and scavengers virtually straight away, inside her uterus the foetus would have been more protected. That also applied to the process of mummification. The mother's body would have desiccated from the outside, with internal organs gradually shrinking as they dried out at a slower rate. Ordinarily, the child she carried would have been similarly protected. Cocooned in the womb's amniotic fluid, the foetal remains might not have mummified at all.

There was nothing ordinary about this, though. The entire abdominopelvic cavity was open and hollowed out, exposing the tiny bones nestled inside. Had that been caused by a wound, there would have been extensive bloodstains on her denim skirt and T-shirt. Since there weren't any, it meant this was down to something else. Rats were one possibility. They were known to inhabit lofts, and the woman's body would undoubtedly have been visited by them before it mummified.

But, contrary to popular belief, rodents aren't major scavengers of human remains. Foxes, dogs and even domestic cats are all more voracious, although nothing of that size was to blame for this. Even if one had managed to gain access to the loft, larger scavengers generally devour a body in a recognizable sequence, starting with the soft tissues of the head and neck and ending by the disarticulation of the cranium and long bones. Sometimes that can allow a rough time-since-death to be estimated, based on how long each of these various stages are known to take.

Nothing I saw suggested that had happened here. The gnawing and teeth marks were mainly limited to the more vulnerable extremities. As well as damage from the woman's futile attempt to escape from the loft, the finger ends had been badly chewed, which would rule out any hope of making an identification from fingerprints. The ears, nose and eyes had been similarly targeted, resulting in a grisly death's mask of a face. That suggested nothing larger than a rat had been at work. Although the edges of the open cavity had been gnawed – and the much, much smaller foetal bones had received even more attention – that was more likely to have come later. The remains of empty pupae casings inside the cavity told me that *Calliphoridae* larvae had been busy, and I was inclined to think they were the main culprits rather than rats.

Yet flies would have laid eggs on the abdomen only if there was some kind of open wound. It didn't have to be big: even a minor cut or graze would have provided all the invitation the questing insects required. But there was no sign of anything to indicate a pre-existing injury, such as a dressing or plaster either on the body or in the folds of the tarpaulin enclosing it. And nothing had been found at the other site where the body had been originally.

That was a mystery that could wait till the mortuary, though. Angling one of the floodlights closer, I turned my attention to the cluster of pathetically small bones.

As I worked, loud hammering from the floor below announced that the false wall was being dismantled. I didn't let it distract me. Handling the delicate foetal skeleton was fine work. Not all of it was present, since some of it had been carried off by whatever scavengers had discovered it in the loft. The remaining bones had become disconnected from each other and lay in an untidy scatter, probably disturbed when the mother's mummified body had been moved, as well as by the attentions of scavengers. One by one, I began to carefully lift them out and place them into small storage bags, wherever possible separating the left and right bones. The minuscule size meant it was an agonizingly slow business, baking hot under the glare of the floodlights.

Intent on extracting a miniature vertebra with a pair of tweezers, I didn't look up as the tramp of feet approached on the stepping boards.

'How much longer do you think you'll be?' Whelan asked after a moment.

'As long as it takes.'

It came out more sharply than I'd intended. I'd tried to detach myself from what I was doing: evidently, I hadn't succeeded. I waited until I'd slipped the tiny vertebra into a bag and then straightened.

'I'm about halfway there,' I told him. 'I can't go any faster without damaging the bones. And I don't want to miss any.'

'Fair enough. Just checking.'

I tilted my head towards the hammering coming from below. 'How's that coming along?'

'Getting there. We decided against power tools, so we're using old-fashioned hammers and chisels. Not as fast but they don't kick up as much dust. We should be through by this afternoon, then once the ceiling's shored up we can get the SOCOs in there.'

'Where's Ward?' I asked. I hadn't seen her since she'd disappeared after the briefing that morning.

'Tied up in a meeting, but she'll be along later. She'd like a word with you when she gets here.'

I nodded, but I wasn't really listening. As Whelan left, I was already leaning over the remains again, intent on teasing out a rib the size of a fish bone.

It never occurred to me to wonder what Ward might want.

The rooks perched on top of the ruins like monks on the skyline. They might have been carved from stone themselves. Every now and then one or other of them would cock its head or ruffle its feathers, then it would subside and the birds would go back to their silent waiting.

Choked with ivy, the roofless church stood in a clearing surrounded by autumnal trees. Only one gable wall remained standing, an arched window in its centre framing blue sky. The rest had tumbled to crenellated mounds of stone centuries ago, their edges softened by moss and bracken. Lying in its centre was a lightning-struck oak. Although not as ancient as the church itself, it was still old, its gnarled trunk blackened and split a few feet above the ground where the lightning had hit. The mortally wounded tree had thrown up a thicket of new growth around its charred bole, and a few sparse leaves still clung to its branches as though in denial of its own death.

It was hard to believe I was only a stone's throw from the hospital, still part of London's urban sprawl. A squirrel paused to scold me as it skittered up a tree trunk, then shot up into the rustling branches. From where I was sitting I watched it go, then closed my eyes and turned my face up to the sun again.

I'd needed to clear my head after I'd finished in the loft. Once the foetal bones had been removed and taken away, recovering the woman's remains had been straightforward. Even so, I was glad when it was over. The floodlit loft was close and airless, and I was running with sweat inside the coveralls long before I'd finished. It wasn't just the physical discomfort: I'd grown accustomed enough to that by now. Nor was it purely the sad nature of what I was doing. It was the old hospital itself. St Jude's seemed to exert a malign pressure, one that grew the longer you were inside. I thought it might lift once I'd climbed down from the stifling loft. But the long, echoing corridors were just as bad. Stinking of mould and urine, they seemed to go on for ever, lit by receding lines of floodlights that served to darken the blackness around them. Open doors offered glimpses into shadowed rooms, empty except for an upended chair or broken trolley. If ever this had been a place of healing, the peeling walls held no memory of it. Only desperation would bring anyone here now.

It was a relief to step outside into daylight. Even the diesel-tainted air tasted sweet in comparison. The respite was only temporary, though. The post-mortem on the woman and her unborn child wasn't scheduled until the next morning, and in the interim there were still the other victims in the sealed room. As soon as the wall was down I'd be going back inside St Jude's.

Taking off my coveralls, I'd collected a sandwich and a bottle of water and gone around to the back of the hospital to see what was there. Behind St Jude's was a scene of ordered devastation. The cracked tarmac was marked with the faded white lines of car-parking spaces, and head-high mounds of rubble showed where the out-buildings had once been. Protruding from one of these, a weed-covered hummock of broken bricks and concrete, was a battered sign that read *Morgue deliveries around rear.*

Fifty yards beyond it was a dark green line of trees. Remembering what Ward had said about the woods behind St Jude's, I'd set off towards them. I'd almost been turned back by a police-dog handler patrolling the outer cordon that had been set up, but after a brief explanation he'd let me pass.

The wood wasn't very big: in this part of the city it couldn't be. A line of rusted railings, pointed like spears and canted at odd angles, formed a boundary between its trees and the hospital grounds. They were half hidden behind undergrowth, and I wasn't sure at first if I'd be able to find a way through. But a section of the spearlike railings had collapsed, leaving a yard-wide gap. A thin ribbon of worn path showed I wasn't the first person to discover it so, pushing through the scratching branches, I stepped into the wood.

It was a different world. This wasn't some recent planting, the fast growth of inner-city landscaping. The trees here were ancient: broad, twisted oaks and beech. They closed around me as I walked in, and after a few paces St Jude's and the rest of London might not have existed.

I didn't plan to go very far, but when I saw a brighter dapple of sunlight through the branches up ahead I headed towards it. Ward had mentioned there were the ruins of a Norman church in the woods, but I'd forgotten until I entered the clearing and saw the crumbling stone walls. The church must have been quite a landmark when the land surrounding it had been fields or forest. Now only a solitary gable remained standing, overgrown with ivy that clambered over its stones as though slowly drawing it into the ground.

Stepping over a worn stone block draped with moss, I picked my way into what would have been the church nave. Open to the sky, it was almost filled by the lightning-struck oak. Skirting round the massive trunk, I sat down on a grass-covered mound of fallen masonry and ate the tasteless sandwich. If I strained I could just make out the distant sound of traffic, a muted rushing that could almost be the sea. Then a breeze stirred the branches and even that was lost. With my eyes closed and the sun on my face, I felt St Jude's finally begin to loosen its hold.

I must have drifted off. Suddenly, I came awake, with a prickling awareness that I was no longer alone.

A woman was standing on the edge of the clearing.

I hadn't heard her approach. Stoutly built, she looked in her seventies, though it was hard to tell. Her brown coat looked too heavy for the weather, and the scuffed training shoes were an ill match for the thick tights she wore with them. An empty bin bag hung from one hand, rustling slightly in the breeze. Her grey hair had a russet tinge that gave it the look of a rusty wire pan-scrub, while the face below it was jowly and had an unhealthy pallor. She was breathing hard, with an asthmatic wheeze I could hear even from where I was.

If she was surprised to find me there she didn't show it. 'Who are you?'

I climbed to my feet. 'Sorry, I didn't mean to startle you.'

'I didn't say you had.' The eyes that regarded me from above the doughy cheeks were small and suspicious. She jerked her chin at the trees behind me. 'One of that lot, are you?'

'What lot?'

'Police. Here for them murders that's been on the news.' She looked me up and down. 'You don't look like police.'

'I'm not.'

'Then what're you doing here?'

'Just leaving,' I said, resigned.

It was time I went back anyway. I picked up the water bottle and the remains of the sandwich, but she hadn't finished.

'If you're not police, what are you? You don't look like a druggie, neither. And you're wasting your time if you are. Nobody's selling.'

'That's OK, I'm not buying.' But she'd snared my interest. 'How do you know nobody's selling?'

Ward had told me drugs were dealt from the abandoned hospital, and there was a good chance at least one of the victims could be either a user or a dealer. If this woman had seen anything she might make a potential witness.

She gave a scornful huff. 'What, with police crawling all over the place? It's like an ants' nest.'

'But before they came. Was there a lot of dealing round here?'

'Open your eyes. Streets aren't fit for decent people no more.' A look of indignation came over her face. 'Why're you asking?'

'I was just—'

'You think *I'm* one of them scum?'

'No, I—'

'Filthy bastards! They deserve stringing up, the lot of 'em! Ruining decent lives, but nobody cares about that, do they?'

I tried a change of tack. 'I'd no idea this place existed. Do you live nearby?'

'Near enough.' She looked around her, tutting when she saw a couple of empty drinks bottles in the grass. Opening the bin liner, she bent and picked them up, flinging them into it in disgust. 'Look at this. Dirty sods, leaving all their rubbish.'

'Is that why you come here?' I asked, realizing now why she'd brought the empty bag.

'No law against it, is there? Who else is going to do it?' Her jaw worked ruminatively as she considered me, the eyes unmistakably hostile now. 'For someone who says they're not police you ask enough bleeding questions.'

I held up my hands in surrender. 'I didn't mean to pry.'

She glared, shifting her grip on the empty bin bag as she weighed me up.

'Piss off.'

With that, she turned around and walked off through the woods. Well, that's told me, I thought, watching the dumpy figure trudge through the trees. Then, making sure I'd not left any litter behind, I went back to St Jude's.

Chapter 7

THERE WAS STILL no sign of Ward by the time I'd walked back to St Jude's. I changed into fresh coveralls, gloves and overshoes and pulled on my hood and my mask. Then I went back into the hospital's dark interior.

It was like stepping into a pit. Even climbing the stairs somehow felt like being underground, far beneath fresh air and daylight. At the top, I paused when I saw the windowless corridor stretching ahead of me. It seemed to go on for ever. Floodlights were dotted along its length, disappearing into the distance like a night-time landing strip. Giving an involuntary shiver, I set off down it.

The sound of hammering told me the wall still hadn't been dismantled. As I drew nearer to the ward, a floodlight in the corridor illuminated a haze of cement dust in the air. It was even thicker inside. Two burly police officers were pounding away at the wall with lump hammers and chisels. Their shadows jerked under the glare of the floodlights as they hacked out the mortar around each breezeblock, removing them one at a time to make a crenellated hole. The sheet of protective plastic draped on the other side as a dust barrier shimmered with each blow like a dirty shower curtain.

A number of white-suited officers and SOCOs had gathered in the ward, almost indistinguishable from each other in their coveralls, hoods and masks. I managed to pick out Whelan among them, but he turned away when he saw me. Evidently, he wasn't in a mood to talk. He wasn't the only one. A palpable tension, as thick as the dust, hung in the air as we waited.

There was a disturbance in the corridor outside. 'Excuse me, coming through, let the dog see the rabbit, thank you . . .'

I recognized the voice even before I saw its owner. It was low but strong, with a throatiness that suggested a bad cigarette habit. Falsely, because the person it came from was a devout anti-smoker. The police officers and SOCOs standing in the ward's doorway hastily stepped aside as a small woman bustled through. She seemed tiny compared to the officers who hurriedly moved out of her way, yet she neither slowed nor gave them a glance as she breezed through, taking it for granted that they'd clear a path. She stopped beside me, setting down a leather Gladstone-style bag that looked almost as big as her. Her dark face crinkled in a smile behind her mask.

'Hello, David. Been a while.'

It had. Riya Parckh had been one of the first forensic pathologists I'd worked with. She'd been a senior figure in her field even then, much older than me and already at the top of her profession when I'd been starting out. That was a long time ago now, longer than I cared to remember.

A lot had changed since then.

Including Parekh herself. Even under the concealing mask and hood, it was apparent how she'd aged. Never a tall woman, she seemed to have physically shrunk, developing the beginnings of a stoop around her shoulders. The jet eyebrows were now grey, and her eyes surrounded by wrinkles, with dark shadows etched underneath them.

I returned her smile, genuinely pleased to see her. 'Hello, Riya. I didn't know you were working on this.'

'I wouldn't have been if Conrad hadn't bolloxed things up.' She gave a sniff. 'Typical.'

Some things, at least, hadn't changed. 'How are you?'

'Oh, you know. Older. Creakier. The same.' The eyes scrutinized me. 'You're looking well.'

'So are you.'

'Liar.' But she looked pleased as she turned away to consider the partly demolished breezeblock wall. 'Puts me in mind of Edgar Allan Poe. *The Fall of the House of Usher*. Are you familiar with the story?'

'Not really, but I'm guessing someone gets walled up.'

'Entombed, actually, but close enough. Although it isn't in a hospital, so let's hope the similarities stop there.'

'Similarities?'

'Poe's victim was still alive.'

I thought about the restraints I'd seen strapping the bodies to the beds when I'd been in the chamber helping Whelan with Conrad. But there was no point speculating: we'd know soon enough. We watched as another breezeblock was lifted out and carried to the growing pile. A big enough section of wall had now been removed to allow access. Flushed and out of breath, one of the

80

SOCOs heaved the block on to the pile with the others and turned to Whelan.

'That should do it.'

Whelan came to speak to Parekh while the worst of the dust and the debris was sucked up with a heavy-duty vacuum. Again, he didn't seem inclined to acknowledge me, but I was too distracted by the crenellated black hole to wonder why.

'No SIO?' Parekh asked him. 'Where's DCI Ward?'

I'd wondered about that myself. It must be an important meeting to keep her away from this.

'She's on her way,' Whelan told her. 'She'd still like a word with you when she gets here, Dr Hunter. You might want to wait for her outside.'

I didn't like the sound of that. For the first time I began to wonder what Ward might want to talk about, but Parekh spoke before I could quiz the DI.

'Nonsense, we're about to go in. If DCI Ward can't be here on time then she should invest in a better watch.'

Whelan seemed to be about to speak before thinking better of it. He turned to face the hole, not meeting my eye as a SOCO drew aside the plastic sheet like a translucent curtain. Beyond it was blackness. The section of wall where the breezeblocks had been removed now looked like the mouth of a cave.

'Who has a torch?' Parekh asked, holding out her hand.

'I think we should wait until the ceiling's been shored up and we've got some lighting in there,' Whelan said. Blue-suited figures were already lifting steel props from a stack and carrying over portable floodlights. 'We're going to rig up a tent over the beds, as well. We want to keep any more plaster dust from coming down on the bodies.'

'Then I can take a look while you're doing it.'

She left no room for argument. Whelan still didn't acknowledge me as torches were supplied.

'Don't go far in. And keep away from where the ceiling's collapsed,' he warned Parekh as she switched on her torch.

'You can stay out here if you're worried,' she told him.

I heard a muttered 'Shit' under his breath as he followed the pathologist through the hole. Turning on my own torch, I went after them.

My breathing sounded too loud in my mask as I stepped through the opening. The smell of decomposition was still noticeable, but fainter than before. This was the odour of old death, not recent. I'd only had a glimpse of the chamber before, too busy with Conrad to study it closely, even if there had been enough light. The torch beams showed a chamber perhaps thirty feet long by twenty wide. The walls were bare and peeling, the ceiling high for a room that size. At one side was a mound of rubble, broken timber and torn insulation from where the ceiling had fallen in.

Then Parekh's torch picked out the beds. The three of them were lined up in a row, their tubular metal frames the heavy and institutional design of outdated NHS stock.

Two of them were occupied.

Our torch beams converged on the nearest. Clothed in a stained sweatshirt and jeans, the motionless figure lay face up on a bare, fouled mattress. Its large stature suggested the body was male, although I knew that didn't necessarily follow. It was secured to the bed by two broad rubber straps, of a type used to restrain unconscious patients during surgery. One was fastened across the torso and forearms, the other below the knees. The hair had mostly slipped off the skull and so had the skin, which had the colour and texture of waxed leather. The head was tilted back, teeth bared as if in a cry or snarl.

A wadded-up cloth had been crammed in the mouth. It had come loose as the lips and cheeks had shrunk and now lay between the teeth like a dirty bridle.

The second body was considerably smaller but also strapped down and gagged. Like the first, its skin had sloughed off the bones like too-big clothes. But this individual had a lot more hair. Coarse and dark, it lay pooled on the mattress around the skull.

Parekh started forward, but Whelan deferentially held out an arm to stop her. 'Sorry, ma'am, we need to get the ceiling shored up before we do anything else.'

'I'm not proposing to swing from it, I just want to take a closer look,' the pathologist retorted.

'And you'll be able to. Just as soon as we've got things set up.'

Parekh clicked her tongue in annoyance but this time didn't argue. She'd put on a pair of tortoiseshell glasses and the torchlight glinted off them as we played the beams over the bodies.

Unlike the pregnant woman's remains, these hadn't mummified. The concealed chamber was much colder than the loft, lacking both the baking heat and airflow of the roof above. Although the sloughed skin had begun to dry out, the decomposition of these two bodies had been able to continue uninterrupted, progressing through bloat and putrefaction to their current state. The only similarity with the woman's body from the loft was that, like the mummification those remains had undergone, this process had also ended some time ago.

There was also another, major difference. I'd been shining my torch over the bodies and the floor below their beds, checking for empty pupae casings. There weren't any. Nor did the bodies show any ravages of blowfly infestation. A single fly in here would have been enough: its eggs would have hatched into larvae, fed and pupated, then repeated the cycle again and again, until all the available soft tissue had been consumed.

If that hadn't happened, it meant the room had been well sealed.

I turned my torch back on to the nearest body. Both hands had contracted into semi-claws, the yellowed fingernails calloused like talons. The sweatshirt cuffs had ridden up, exposing forearms reduced to bone and tendon beneath the baggy skin. The skin itself had darkened to a rich caramel colour, although that was a normal feature of decomposition and had no bearing on its original pigmentation.

'Don't think we're going to have much luck getting an ID from fingerprints,' Whelan said, shining his own torch over the hands of both victims. The sloughed skin was draped from them like badly fitting gloves, stiffened from where it had dried in the air.

He was wrong, but there'd be time for that later. I was more interested in how the rubber straps had cut into the victims' arms. The skin had contracted away from the wound like a pushed-back sleeve. Both victims were wearing jeans, and where the straps passed over the legs the denim was frayed and stained with dried blood.

'So what are we looking at here?' Whelan asked, his voice hushed. It was a natural reaction in that place. 'Some sort of torture scenario?'

Parekh made a *hmming* noise in her throat as she shone her torch beam on to the restrained arms of first one body, then the other. 'Possibly. But I can't see any trauma except for the lesions from the straps.'

'Poor sods must have done it trying to get free,' Whelan said.

'They might have, but these aren't just surface abrasions,' I pointed out. 'It's hard to tell with the skin slippage, but it looks like the edges of the straps have cut into the underlying muscle. That would have been excruciating. To inflict that sort of damage on themselves they'd have to have been frenzied. It's like a snared animal trying to gnaw off its own leg.'

He shook his head. 'Can you blame them?'

'Perhaps not, but there's no sign of torture. Not physical, anyway,' Parekh said, peering at the nearest victim's body. 'No pulled teeth or fingernails, and no obvious cause of death. I can't rule out something like strangulation at this stage. But the fact the only visible trauma looks to have been self-inflicted makes me suspect they might have been alive and conscious when they were walled in.'

'Christ.' Whelan sounded shaken. 'How long for?'

Parekh gave an elaborate shrug. 'That depends. If they died of thirst or starvation it could have been several days or longer. Impossible to say right now, but it wouldn't have been quick.'

'Could they have suffocated?'

'If the room was airtight, then yes, I suppose so.'

'I don't think it was,' I said. I'd wondered the same thing, because there weren't any flies in here. And flies would have found their way in through the smallest crack. But if the chamber had been airtight the atmosphere in it would have been much fouler than it was, since the gases produced during decomposition would have been trapped in there as well.

I ran my torch beam over the walls and ceiling. 'Over here.'

Set low in one corner was the grille of what looked like an air or heating vent. Going over, I angled the torch into it. A fine mesh screen was fixed to the inside, and I could see a dark mass banked up in the duct behind it. In the torch beam it glinted with pinpoints of iridescence.

'It's full of dead flies,' I said, climbing to my feet. 'It kept them out but there'd have been enough air getting in here for two people to breathe.'

'So they didn't suffocate,' Whelan said. 'I'm not sure if that's good or not.'

Neither was I. Suffocation would have been relatively quick, causing gradual hypoxia as the oxygen in the chamber was replaced by carbon dioxide. Starvation and thirst would have taken longer. Strapped down and helpless, when the last breezeblock had been eased into place the two victims would have been left in utter darkness, without hope of rescue or escape.

No wonder they'd torn their own skin trying to break free.

Parekh and I left the chamber to the SOCOs and technicians while floodlights and ceiling props were set up. She stood in the ward's doorway, frowning as she stared back inside.

'Seems an awful lot of trouble to hide two bodies. Especially when the building was going to be pulled down anyway.'

'Perhaps whoever built it didn't think that far ahead. Or they might have assumed the remains wouldn't survive the demolition.' I said. They probably wouldn't have. Even the bones would have been pulverized, and the chances of anything being spotted among tons of debris were remote.

'True,' Parekh conceded. 'But why bother building the wall in the first place? A place as big as this, there's no shortage of hiding places. It'd have been much easier to bury them somewhere in the grounds. Or conceal them in the loft like the other victim.'

I'd been thinking the same thing. The woods behind the hospital would have made a convenient burial ground.

'Perhaps whoever killed them didn't want to risk being picked up by CCTV,' I suggested. The cameras were dummies but they wouldn't have known that. 'And it's still possible these two victims aren't connected to the woman's body in the loft.'

Parekh gave me an admonishing smile. 'Now you're playing devil's advocate. They were all interred. Two people walled up, quite possibly while they were still alive, and I understand the woman had been locked in the loft. And then there was that empty third bed. That looked to me as though it was meant for somebody.'

I thought about the splashes on the wooden stairs leading up to the loft, the possibility that the pregnant woman had fled in there to hide from some pursuer. But that was still just speculation at this stage.

'Dr Hunter.'

I looked round. Whelan had been talking to a police officer who'd arrived a few moments ago. He glanced in my direction as they spoke, then came over.

'DCI Ward's waiting for you downstairs.'

'She wants to talk now?' I looked back through the hole in the breezeblock wall. Light now came from inside, and SOCOs were busy videoing and taking photographs while the ceiling props were put in place. It wouldn't be much longer before we could go back inside.

'If you wouldn't mind.'

Whelan's face gave nothing away, but I was starting to have a bad feeling about this.

'Don't be long,' Parekh instructed as I left. 'I don't like being kept waiting.'

The floodlit corridor seemed a longer walk than usual as I made my way downstairs. After the perpetual night inside the hospital, the bright sunlight outside came as a surprise. Blinking, I looked around for Ward. She was standing by one of the trailers, talking to the Crime Scene Manager. As I headed over I noticed several dark grey vans parked at the bottom of the steps. They were sleek and new, with a discreet logo on their sides showing a stylized DNA molecule's double helix with the name *BioGen*. Underneath, in smaller lettering, it read *Biological and Forensic Services*.

'Dr Hunter?'

A smartly dressed man in a navy suit and tie was coming towards me. He looked familiar, and then I remembered seeing him at St Jude's with his entourage on the night Conrad had fallen through the loft. He wasn't so grim-faced now, fit-looking and in his late forties, with the easy walk and confidence of a natural athlete. The fair hair was impeccably cut and his face was so closely shaved it looked chiselled. A strong smell of cologne came off him. Not excessive, just pungent.

'We've not met, but I've heard a lot about you. I'm Commander Ainsley,' he said, extending his hand.

He had a firm grip that stopped barely the right side of a challenge. As we shook I wondered what had brought such rarefied company all the way out to St Jude's. In the Metropolitan Police's unique structure, Commander came between Chief Superintendent and Deputy Assistant Commissioner. That put him several ranks above Ward's DCI. The investigation was evidently attracting the Met's big guns.

'I wanted to thank you personally for helping Professor Conrad,' he said with a brisk, professional smile. His teeth were straight and white, and he had disconcertingly blue eyes. 'It was a bad situation that could easily have been a lot worse. Well done.'

I nodded, a little bemused. I wasn't used to being thanked by high-ranking police officers. 'How is he?'

'As well as can be expected.' The blandness of the answer made me wonder if he knew. From the corner of my eye I saw Ward look across and hurriedly detach herself from her conversation with the CSM. 'I'm surprised to find you still here rather than at the mortuary. When's the post-mortem scheduled for the loft victim?'

'Not till tomorrow morning.' I was about to add that I still had two more victims to help recover, but some instinct stopped me.

'Well, I'm glad of the opportunity to say hello. I hope you understand why we decided to bring in a private forensic service provider, by the way,' he said glancing over at the vans. 'BioGen have an excellent reputation, and first-class people, by all accounts.'

I was still wondering how to respond when Ward reached us. She was out of breath from hurrying and I saw her cheeks colour as she overheard her superior.

'Ah, Sharon. I was just saying how much we've appreciated Dr Hunter's contribution.' Ainsley turned to me. I realized that it wasn't just the colour of his eyes that was disconcerting. Until he blinked, his eyelids left the whole of his iris visible, like bright blue marbles. It gave his stare a doll-like, slightly manic quality. 'Perhaps you should consider a move into the private sector yourself. I'm sure there'd be plenty of openings for someone of your experience.'

'I'll bear that in mind,' I said, looking at Ward.

'Good man. I'm sure Sharon can arrange an introduction to BioGen's CEO?'

He raised his eyebrows, making it a question. Ward kept her face studiedly neutral. 'Yes, sir.'

'Excellent. Well, good to meet you, Dr Hunter. I'll look forward to reading your report. I'm going to be taking a personal interest in this inquiry. Back seat, of course,' he added with a brief nod at Ward.

He shook my hand again before he left. I watched him go, striding confidently across the car park towards the grey vans.

'I was going to tell you,' Ward said quickly, as soon as he was out of earshot.

'You're bringing in a private forensic company?' It was only now starting to sink in. No wonder Whelan had wanted me out of the way.

'Only for the victims we found walled up. You aren't being fired, we still want you to work on the original inquiry. But until we know whether or not there's a connection between the woman in the loft and these new victims, it makes sense to treat them separately.'

I looked at the vans with the BioGen logo. 'What if they aren't separate?'

'Then we'll cross that bridge when we come to it.' She sighed. 'Look, for the record, it wasn't my idea. The decision was made above my pay grade, but I don't disagree with it. The investigation's literally tripled in size and we're faced with an entire hospital as a potential crime scene. And after Conrad's accident there's a lot of nervousness. Using a company that can handle all the lab work as well as providing technical and forensic support means there's one less thing to worry about.'

I was beginning to understand what a Met Commander like Ainsley was doing at St Jude's. Although Ward's first outing as Senior Investigating Officer had started out as a routine inquiry, it was now something very different. Her superiors were understandably nervous, but having a high-ranking police officer looking over her shoulder was hardly going to help her confidence. Or ease the pressure.

'I haven't heard of BioGen,' I said. I still wasn't happy, but I knew the argument was already lost.

'They'd heard of you. Said all sorts of nice things, but they still weren't happy about keeping you on.' She gave a wry smile. 'I didn't see why they should have it all their own way, though.'

'Thanks,' I said, meaning it. It would have been easier for her to have gone with a private company, especially if there'd been pressure from above. Suddenly, Commander Ainsley's enthusiasm for me to join the private sector didn't seem quite so coincidental.

Ward shrugged it off. 'They're an unknown quantity, and I've worked with you before. Just don't balls it up.'

She didn't sound like she was entirely joking. 'Who's their forensic anthropologist?'

'Daniel Mears. Comes very highly rated. A real perfectionist, by all accounts. Do you know him?'

I shook my head: the name meant nothing to me. 'Where's he based?'

'Not sure, but you can ask him yourself.' She nodded towards the BioGen vans. 'This is him now.'

A young technician and an older man were walking towards the hospital steps. Their coveralls were the same grey as the vans and bore the BioGen logo on the chest. Their hoods were down at the moment, revealing that the older of the pair was about fifty, tall with aquiline features and a shaved head. I was surprised I'd never heard of him before. Forensics had exploded in the last few years, with newly qualified graduates in all its disciplines flooding the market. But this was an older individual, and if he'd been around for any length of time I'd have expected to have come across him.

'Hello, Dr Mears,' Ward said. 'This is David Hunter. He's been working on the other half of this investigation.'

I was on the verge of offering my hand, but the newcomer didn't stop. 'See you up there,' he said to the young technician, and carried on walking.

The younger man had halted in front of us. Realizing my mistake, I tried to recover from my gaffe. And my surprise. *God, how old is he?* Mears must have been in his mid- or late-twenties at least, but he didn't look it. Fresh-faced, he had flaming red hair and a complexion to match, milky skin dotted with freckles that made him seem even younger. He was carrying an aluminium flight case similar to mine. It wasn't a standard piece of kit, but I knew one or two other people in my line of work who had them. The lightweight aluminium was tough and waterproof, protecting my camera, laptop and various other pieces of equipment I carried around with me. But whereas my case was battered and scuffed from years of use, the one Mears had was as pristine as everything else about him. In his fresh grey overalls, he put me in mind of nothing so much as a schoolboy decked out for the first day of term.

Ward had said he came highly recommended, though. He must be, or he wouldn't be here.

'Dr Hunter,' he said stiffly. His voice was unexpectedly deep, as though to compensate for his youthful appearance. The pale cheeks had darkened in a flush that told me my slip hadn't gone unnoticed. 'I read one of your papers on decomposition a couple of years back. Interesting.'

I wasn't sure how to take that, but let it go. 'Always good to meet another forensic anthropologist.'

'Actually, I'm a forensic taphonomist.'

'Oh. Right.'

Ward had got his job title wrong, but it was an understandable mistake. In a basic sense, taphonomy was the study of the processes a biological organism undergoes after death, up to its eventual fossilization. In a forensic context that meant looking at any and all post-mortem changes to a human body, from decomposition to trauma. It encompassed a broad range of forensic disciplines, but there was nothing particularly new about it. In a lot of respects, it was only what I already did myself.

Yet I wouldn't have called myself a forensic taphonomist and, while I was aware of a few people who did, it was more common in the US than the UK. Still, earlier in my career I'd experienced bias myself from more established experts who didn't like the idea of change. I'd no intention of becoming one of them.

'So is your background anthropological or archaeological?' I asked.

'Both. I take a broad-spectrum approach, including palaeontology and entomology,' he said, snapping a skin-tight glove into place by way of emphasis. They were the same steel grey as his coveralls: BioGen obviously took their corporate image very seriously. 'The old single-disciplinary approach had its time, but it's outdated now. Forensics has moved on. You need to be able to bring a wide range of skills to the table.'

'I thought I did,' I said lightly.

He smiled to himself. 'Really.'

Now there was no mistaking the implied put-down. Ward was frowning as she looked at us.

'Well, I'll leave the two of you to it.'

She headed towards the police trailer. Mears and I regarded each other. I was struck again by how young he looked. *Give him a chance.* He might just be nervous and overcompensating.

'Have you been inside yet?' I asked, nodding at the blackened walls of St Jude's.

Mears's blush had faded, but the faintly supercilious air remained. 'Not yet.'

'It's pretty grim. They've just finished opening the walled-up chamber in the paediatric ward. I'll be interested to hear what you make of it.'

'You've been in there?'

'Only just inside the false wall.'

That wasn't strictly true. I'd gone down into the chamber to help Conrad, but I didn't think there was any point mentioning that. Something told me Mears would be territorial, and we'd started off badly enough as it was.

'Really?' Colour was flooding back to his cheeks. 'I know we're supposed to extend professional courtesy to each other, so I won't make a formal complaint this time. But I'd appreciate it in future if you'd stay out of my crime scene.'

I was too surprised to speak. The only reason I'd been there in the first place was because no one told me I'd been replaced.

'Technically, I think it's DCI Ward's crime scene,' I said, trying not to lose my temper. 'But don't worry, I've no reason to go in again. It's all yours.'

'Good. In that case we won't have any problem.'

He brushed past me. The back of his neck was red as his hair as he carried his shiny flight case up the steps.

Then the Gothic entrance of the hospital swallowed him into its dark maw.

Chapter 8

I WAS STILL fuming as I went back to my car. Mears might look young, but he wasn't lacking in ego. Or nerve. I'd come across more than a few prima donnas in my work, but the forensic taphonomist came close to the top of the list. I wasn't impressed with Ainsley either, patronizingly offering me career advice after instigating my removal from the investigation. Or this part of it, anyway. And while I didn't blame Ward for what had happened, she should have told me sooner. Not let me wander into a crime scene believing I was going to be working on it.

Feeling aggrieved and hard done by, I wrenched on the zip of my coveralls as I made my way through the parked police vehicles. It was only when I was nearly at my car that I realized I'd gone past the bins left out for discarded coveralls.

Wonderful. But the slip was enough to puncture my sulk. As I turned around and walked back the air began to leak out of my indignation. There were bigger things at stake here than pride, I reminded myself, looking up at the austere walls of St Jude's. At this time of day the sun was behind the old hospital, casting its shadow across the car park. When I stepped into it there was a noticeable drop in temperature, as though the hospital's dank atmosphere extended even out here. I didn't want to imagine what it must have been like for the two victims I'd seen, strapped to the beds inside a sealed room. The memory of that scene swept away the last of my self-pity. It was hard to say how long their bodies had been there, left to die and decay in the cold darkness. But in those conditions – dry with a cool, constant temperature, insulated from even the summer heat – it would have been months. Perhaps even years, because once the decomposition was in its final stages a sort of stasis would be reached, the remaining physical changes slowing down and down until they were almost imperceptible.

I paused by the bins, for the first time really taking in the hospital's size. It was huge. With its blackened walls and boarded-over windows, it looked like a giant, derelict mausoleum. A tomb. Seeing it from the outside, I gave an involuntary shiver.

What else is in there?

Turning away, I retraced my steps back to my car. I would have liked a chance to examine the two interred victims, to find out what their remains could tell me. Even so, as St Jude's receded in my rear-view mirror, I wasn't sorry to see it go.

I'd forgotten about the media pack outside the hospital gates. As I approached I could see it had grown since that morning. A sizeable crowd was now gathered outside the gates, along with the press. Demonstrators carrying placards spilled off the pavements on to the road in front of the entrance. They were a mix of ages and ethnicities, and more police officers had been brought in to keep them out of the hospital grounds. Portable metal railings had been set up between the stone gateposts, forcing me to slow as I reached them. I wound down my window.

'What's going on?' I asked the young PC who came over.

'Bit of a protest,' she said, sounding unimpressed. 'They're not causing any bother, just showing off for the cameras. Hang on, we'll let you out.'

I waited while the railings were swung back. The placards bore messages ranging from straightforward pleas to *Save St Jude's* to more political slogans. A home-made banner proclaiming *People need homes, not offices* was fixed to poles carried by protesters, and underneath it a man stood on a bench as he spoke to the crowd. I wound down my window further to hear what he was saying.

'. . . should be ashamed! Ashamed that innocent people are scared to walk their own streets. Ashamed of the deprivation families in this borough are forced to endure. And ashamed that individuals could be left to die like animals in what used to be a hospital! That's right – a *hospital*!'

He was in his thirties, strikingly handsome in a black jacket and white shirt that set off his dark skin. Pausing for emphasis, he looked around the crowd.

'Are the politicians, and the corporate investors who pull their strings, are they *blind* to the tragic irony of that? Or don't they care? What happened to *community*? Shops are forced to close, houses boarded up. And now this!' He extended an arm, finger pointing towards the hospital. 'We tried to save St Jude's from closure and were ignored. We tried to have new homes built, instead of offices that will stand empty for years. And were ignored. Well, how much longer are we going to *let* ourselves be ignored? *How many more of us have to die?*'

An angry cheer went up, placards were waved and arms thrust in the air. I began to edge my car forward as the police barrier was opened. The fringes of the crowd moved aside to let me through, but I had to stop again as a young woman pushed in front of my car. She crammed a leaflet behind one of the windscreen wipers, and as a PC began to steer her away she thrust one through my open window.

'Public meeting tomorrow night! Please come,' she said as she was led off.

The leaflet had landed on my lap. It was cheaply printed, with a black-and-white photograph of St Jude's in all its dilapidated glory. Below it was the caption *Don't let this be a symbol for our lives!* together with details of the meeting's location and time.

Putting the leaflet on to the passenger seat, I closed my window. As the glass slid up, I glanced back at the speaker. His attention must have been drawn by the disturbance, because at that moment he looked directly at me. For a second I thought there was something like recognition in his eyes, then the moment had gone. Leaving him exhorting the crowd, I put the car into gear and drove through the gateway.

Pulling out, I saw a lone figure standing at a bus stop on the opposite side of the road, well away from the demonstrators and press. The only reason I noticed him was because of the rapt way he was staring at the hospital. Ward should sell tickets, I thought uncharitably, as I drove away.

*

It was far too early to even consider going back to the apartment, so with my afternoon unexpectedly empty I went into the university. Buying a sandwich and a coffee at the cafeteria, I took them up to my cramped office and switched on my computer. I hadn't checked my emails while I'd been at St Jude's, so went through them now. There was nothing of note, only another request for an interview from Francis Scott-Hayes, the freelance journalist. The man just couldn't take no for an answer, I thought, irritably deleting it.

That done, I opened the crime-scene photographs from the loft. As a rule, I prefer to take my own, but as there hadn't been the opportunity to do that at St Jude's Ward had given me access to the SOCOs'. Although they were high resolution and competent, they didn't convey anything of the atmosphere inside the old hospital. Still, the images were stark and shocking. Bleached out from the flash, the desiccated remains looked utterly out of place in the loft. The pregnant woman and her unborn child lay in the dirty insulation like skeletal Russian dolls. Looking at them again now, it was depressingly obvious how hard it would be to produce an accurate estimate of time since death.

I spent a while considering the gaping abdominal cavity and its pathetic jumble of tiny bones, then systematically did the same for the rest of the woman's body. Although I'd be able to examine her remains at the mortuary the next day, it didn't hurt to remind myself of how her body had looked when it was found in the loft. I paused when I came to the right shoulder. There was something wrong with it, I decided, zooming in on the image. The angle seemed unnatural and, while that could just be how the body was lying, it might also suggest something else.

I also spent time studying the wrists and lower legs, at least as much of them as was visible in the photographs. Like Parekh, I hadn't missed the fact that only two of the three beds in the walled-in chamber had been occupied. So it was possible that the third might have been meant for the pregnant woman.

But if she'd somehow escaped, she'd managed it without suffering any injuries from the straps. Unlike the other two victims, there were no signs of any abrasions or cuts to her bare forearms or lower legs. The skin had mummified and shrunk, but the photographs showed that it was still intact. I found myself wishing I'd taken photographs of the two victims interred in the chamber, then I remembered that wasn't my case any more. I needed to focus solely on the woman and baby and forget the rest.

It was late by the time I switched off my computer. I sat back, rubbing my eyes and feeling my lower back protest from the length of time I'd been at my desk. There'd been no need for me to stay as long as I had, except that I was in no hurry to go back to the empty apartment. One by one everyone else in the department had gone home, Brenda pointedly reminding me that the office cleaners would be in at seven the next morning. I'd smiled and assured her I'd be going home soon.

That had been some time ago, though, and now I was the only person there. Dusk had settled outside, I realized, seeing my reflection looking back at me from the window. Turning off the lights, I closed the door on my office and took the lift to the ground floor.

I didn't even think about using a different exit until I was going out of the main doors. I offered a silent apology to Rachel and Ward, but I was tired and couldn't be bothered to use one of the side entrances. If Grace Strachan was waiting outside, then too bad, I thought, pushing through the doors.

It was a cool evening. The Indian summer seemed long gone and there was no denying the autumn chill in the air. I'd parked a few hundred yards away, and the streetlights threw multiple shadows as I walked across the concourse. Except for me, it was empty, deserted by the staff and students that filled it during the daytime. As my footsteps rang on the concrete I was thinking about Rachel, wondering whereabouts she was now. I was halfway across before I registered the sense of unease that had begun to settle over me. I stopped, looking around. There was no one in sight.

The hairs on the back of my neck began to prickle.

Under the skin, we're all just animals. The same survival mechanisms that protected our primitive ancestors are still present, atrophied and below our awareness most of the time, but there all the same. I could feel my pulse speed up, the shakiness in my muscles as adrenaline was dumped into my system. *What the hell's this . . .?*

And then I smelled it.

It was only faint, the merest hint of a spiced, musky perfume, but it ran through me like an electric shock. I heard the scrape of a shoe behind me and spun round.

''Night, Dr Hunter.'

Two of the department's post-grad students smiled as they went past, giving me a curious look. I hadn't been the last to leave after all, I realized, raising my hand in a weak acknowledgement. Their footsteps receded as they disappeared across the concourse.

My heart was still thumping, though more slowly now. I looked around again, but I was alone. The air held only exhaust fumes and the burnt-leaves smell of autumn, without any trace of perfume.

If there ever had been.

That was the power of suggestion for you, I thought, setting off across the concourse again. I'd been thinking of Grace Strachan as I'd left the building and my imagination had done the rest. Grace had been one of the most beautiful women I'd ever met. Raven-haired and with a dazzling smile that blinded almost everyone to her fractured, psychotic nature, her physical presence had been overwhelming. Her distinctive perfume had been the last thing I'd been aware of when she'd stabbed and left me for dead. It had branded itself into my memory, and for a long time afterwards I would have panic attacks, believing I could smell it and that Grace was nearby. The clinical term was phantosmia, or olfactory hallucination, but I thought I'd put that behind me.

Until now.

Annoyed with myself, I walked to the back of my car, throwing my bag into the boot with more force than was necessary. I switched on the car radio as I drove off, catching the tail end of a news report about St Jude's. The demonstration outside the gates had brought a fresh element to the story, allowing the old grievances against the hospital development to be aired again. But when the report had finished the rest of the news failed to hold my interest. Although I tried to forget about it, the incident outside the university had rattled me. I drove automatically, without paying attention to where I was going, and it was only when a road sign registered that I realized I was heading for my old flat.

Oh, great. I was well over halfway there now, on a ring road that didn't allow me to turn around. The next exit would take me close to where I used to live anyway, so I decided to carry on. It wasn't as if I had anything to hurry back to Ballard Court for.

It seemed preordained that, on a street lined both sides with parked cars, there'd be a vacant space right outside the Victorian villa. I pulled into it. Despite Ward's warnings, this wasn't the first time I'd visited my old flat. I'd driven by two or three times, but this was the first time I'd stopped. Objectively, I knew Ward – and Rachel too, for that matter – was right. If Grace Strachan were still alive and intended to try to kill me again, this was where she'd come. It would have been stupid to stay there.

Yet moving out still seemed like running away.

The freshly painted front door, where Grace's fingerprint had been found after the attempted break-in, had lost some of its shine since the last time I'd been here, but otherwise the house looked as it always had. The ground-floor flat was still empty, its 'To Let' sign standing on a post by the path. Rachel had suggested I sell it, but I'd baulked for the same reasons I hadn't rented it out. For one thing, I wasn't quite ready to give it up. Not yet.

For another, if there was even a slight chance that Grace Strachan was back, then I couldn't let anyone else live there.

But I didn't believe that any more. My panic at the university seemed embarrassing now, a momentary lapse. I put it down to lack of sleep and an overactive imagination: the oppressive atmosphere at St Jude's must have got to me more than I'd realized. Still, coming here had resolved one thing, I thought as I pulled away. With Rachel in Greece there was no longer any reason to stay at Ballard Court. Once the investigation was over I'd look at moving back into my old flat.

I'd had enough of hiding.

Chapter 9

THE WEATHER BROKE during the night. Rain pitched down from a gunmetal sky as I drove to the mortuary next morning, bouncing off the pavements and dashing the autumn leaves from the trees. I found a parking place nearby and ran through the downpour, pausing under the covered entrance to shake off my wet coat.

The mortuary was relatively new, a custom-built building that served most of this part of North London. I'd worked there in the past, though not for some time. Parekh was there already, and greeted me with her customary dryness.

'You were a long time coming back yesterday afternoon,' she commented, a mischievous twinkle in her eye.

I hadn't seen her since the day before: when I'd come away from the sealed chamber at St Jude's I thought I'd be returning soon.

'There was a change of plan.'

'So I gather.'

I hadn't wanted to broach it myself, but I couldn't pretend I wasn't curious. 'How did the recovery go?'

'Slowly. There was a delay while more of the ceiling was shored up, so only one body was recovered. The other should be removed later today.'

'And what about BioGen?'

'Our new private service provider?' She gave a shrug. 'They have very nice grey outfits. Other than that, I had little to do with most of them. Although I found your replacement something of a surprise.'

Tell me about it. 'Why's that?'

'I've never worked with anyone calling themselves a forensic taphonomist before. I have to say, if he hadn't told me I would have thought he was just another forensic anthropologist. Grey overalls aside, obviously.'

I tried not to smile. 'Apparently, he comes highly recommended.'

'I'm sure he does. He seems capable enough. Young but very methodical. And certainly not lacking in self-confidence.'

That was one way of putting it. But then he wouldn't have regarded a forensic pathologist like Parekh as a rival. Not if he'd any sense.

She smiled at me, her face cross-hatching with fine wrinkles. 'Stings, doesn't it?'

'What does?'

'Finding the next generation snapping at your heels.'

I started to protest, then gave it up. She'd known me too long. 'Was I that arrogant when you first met me?'

'Not arrogant, no. Confident, yes. And ambitious. But you've seen a lot more of life since then. I daresay Daniel Mears will improve once he's had his own rough edges knocked off. And I've no doubt he will.'

I thought that was likely, too, but I didn't really care. I'd already decided that the less I had to do with Mears, the better we'd both like it.

The SIO's post-mortem briefing was scheduled for ten o'clock. Whelan and the other team members who were attending began to arrive fifteen minutes before the start, but Ward herself was late. She was the last there, shucking out of her wet coat as she bustled into the briefing room.

'Sorry, sorry,' she sighed, dumping her shoulder bag on the table before taking her seat.

She looked frazzled and tired, her swollen stomach more obvious in the charcoal jacket and grey dress-skirt than when she'd been wearing coveralls. The briefing itself was routine, essentially just making sure the pathologist and SIO were on the same wavelength before the post-mortem started. The police were still no closer to establishing the dead woman's identity. She hadn't been carrying a driver's licence or any other form of ID, and her clothing and shoes were cheap, mass-produced brands that told us nothing. No useable fingerprints had survived on the torn and rat-gnawed skin of her hands, and while the victim's pregnancy might help when it came to sifting through the missing-persons database, we would need a better idea of how old she was to refine the search criteria. Her pregnancy narrowed it down a little, but not enough. Child-bearing age could mean anything from a juvenile to someone in her forties.

That meant the main hope for identification now lay with dental records and whatever Parekh or myself could turn up. While Ward, Whelan and other members of the Murder Investigation Team filed into the

108

observation booth, the two of us changed into scrubs and went into the examination room.

Mortuaries are the same the world over. Some may be more modern and better equipped than others, but the basic design doesn't vary. And the chilled air and smell of disinfectant that overlies the other, more biological odours remains constant.

The door shut behind us, enveloping us in a cool quiet. The woman's body lay on an examination table. Her knees were drawn up and bent off to one side, while arms the colour and texture of pemmican were folded in the traditional funeral pose across her lower chest. The decay was even more obvious against the table's stainless-steel surface. Her clothing had been removed, sent off to the lab along with tissue samples for analysis and testing, and the remains had been rinsed down. Most of the loosened hair had washed away to be collected separately, leaving a few lank strands lying forlornly on the scalp. Waiting nearby were the surviving bones of the foetus.

'What a sad job we do sometimes,' Parekh murmured, looking down at the two sets of remains. Mother's and child's. Then, with a shake of her head, she set to work.

The post-mortem itself was her domain, so apart from assisting I stayed in the background. It didn't take very long. With the remains in such poor condition there wasn't much a forensic pathologist could do. There was no obvious trauma, such as a fractured skull or broken hyoid, which would have pointed to a probable cause of death. Like me, Parekh thought it was possible that the young woman's waters had broken, which in those conditions could eventually have proved fatal, especially if

109

she'd sustained some other injury as well. But with her body so badly degraded, that was only speculation.

The mummification also ruled out any chance of establishing how long ago the woman had died. I saw nothing to make me change my original estimate, that her body had been in the loft for at least one full summer and probably longer. Like so much else about this, however, that was little more than an educated guess.

Even so, one or two things did emerge.

'I don't think her hands and arms were arranged like that,' Parekh said, studying the remains over her mask.

'I don't think so either,' I agreed. 'Not at the same time as the body was moved, anyway.'

It was possible that someone had arranged them soon after she'd died, either just before or just after rigor mortis when the body was still pliant. Except that didn't fit with the theory that the young woman had been shut in the loft and left to die.

One thing I could say with certainty was that her arms hadn't been posed when her remains had been wrapped in the plastic sheet and moved. Her body would have already mummified by then, the dried-out skin and soft tissues locked in the posture in which she'd died. As brittle as they were, any attempt to reposition them would have caused obvious damage.

There was none I could see, which meant the apparently deliberate arrangement of her arms had another explanation.

'She was hugging herself,' Parekh said. 'The way her knees are drawn up and twisted to one side, it's almost a foetal position.'

I'd reached the same conclusion. Exhausted after God alone knew how long in the dark loft, the young woman

110

had curled up, covered her pregnant stomach with her arms and waited to die. And as her body had dried out the whipcord tendons had contracted, drawing her arms higher up her chest.

The pose wasn't one of respect. Just a happenstance of nature.

The only discernible trauma was to the right shoulder. I'd noticed in the crime-scene photographs that its position didn't look normal, and when I examined the post-mortem X-rays I saw why. It had been dislocated.

'Perimortem, do you think?' Parekh mused, looking at the ghostly black-and-white image. 'It could have been caused by a fall or during a struggle. Perhaps as she tried to escape, assuming that's what happened.'

I nodded. Although we were into the realms of speculation now, I knew from painful experience how agonizing a dislocated shoulder was. It wasn't something that anyone would endure without treatment, at least not willingly. But there was nothing to suggest the woman had been restrained, such as the abrasions we'd found on the other two victims. And a post-mortem injury when the body was moved would have damaged the mummified tissues around the joint, possibly even caused the limb to completely detach.

That made a perimortem injury – at or close to the time of death – most likely. It also added weight to the theory that she'd gone into the loft to hide. A pregnant woman with a dislocated shoulder wouldn't have been able to run very far, or very fast. If she'd been trying to escape from someone, the loft might have been her only option.

As well as her last.

Parekh moved aside to let me take a look at the dead woman's teeth. A forensic dentist would be able to give a more exhaustive analysis, but I could provide an initial assessment. Carefully shining a pencil light in, I peered into the gaping mouth. The tongue and lips had gone and only shrivelled scraps of gums remained.

'Two of her wisdom teeth have erupted, but the upper two haven't fully broken through,' I said. 'So she's late teens at least, but probably not much older than her mid-twenties.'

Wisdom teeth usually emerge between the ages of seventeen and twenty-five, so while the woman – the *young* woman, I could now say – had been old enough for the process to start, the fact it was still ongoing put an upper limit on her age range. That was supported by the relative lack of wear shown by her teeth, which suggested a younger person. But their condition was revealing for another reason as well.

'She doesn't have many fillings, but there's a lot of discolouration and a few visible patches of caries,' I told Ward, when we were back in the briefing room after the post-mortem. 'She hasn't visited a dentist recently.'

'Consistent with drug use?' she asked.

'I'd say so, yes.'

Whelan had been listening while he was on the phone. He put it away now as he joined the conversation. 'If she was buying or selling drugs that'd explain what she was doing at St Jude's. We know some dealing went on there, and dental hygiene isn't high on an addict's list of priorities.'

'Perhaps not, but her teeth used to be well looked after,' I said. 'I think the decay and staining are relatively recent. None of her fillings looks particularly new, so if she's only in her twenties they were probably done when she was a child or in her early teens. And two of

112

her back molars have white fillings rather than silver amalgam. The NHS only pays for those on front teeth.'

'So she had private dental work when she was younger. That doesn't sound like someone from a deprived background.' Ward nodded to herself. 'OK, that tells us a bit more about her. Early to mid-twenties, six to seven months pregnant with a likely history of substance abuse. If she went to St Jude's she was potentially still using, but she could be from a family who could afford to pay for white fillings.'

'Nice girl gone bad,' Whelan said. 'Very bad, if she was looking for drugs when she was pregnant.'

I saw Ward give him an annoyed glance, folding her arms across her stomach in an unconsciously protective gesture. It wasn't hard to guess her thoughts: the dead woman's pregnancy had been at a similar stage to hers. I'd been able to confirm my original estimate from measurements of the foetal skeleton. The foetus was between twenty-five and thirty weeks old, meaning its mother had been in either the later stages of her second trimester, or possibly the start of her third.

But, despite my best efforts, that was all I could say. X-rays had revealed hairline fractures on the tiny radius on the right forearm and ulna on the left, but in all likelihood the damage was post-mortem, caused either when the mother was moved or by scavengers. I'd take a closer look once the minuscule skeleton had been cleaned, but I didn't expect to learn very much. Sex characteristics only developed after puberty, so there would be no way of even knowing if the unborn child was a boy or girl.

It was a sad job sometimes, as Parekh had said.

*

After Ward and Whelan had gone, and Parekh had returned to St Jude's to supervise the recovery of the remaining body, I was left on my own for the next grisly stage. X-rays can only reveal so much. I needed to examine the unknown young woman's bones in greater detail, a task more related to butchery than to science. First, as much of the remaining soft tissue as possible would have to be removed using shears and scalpels. Then the skeleton itself would have to be systematically disarticulated, by cutting through the connective cartilage and tendons at the joints. Skull from spine, arms from torso, legs from pelvis: all had to be carefully separated one from the other. Then, once the body had been reduced to its component parts, any residual soft tissue had to be removed by macerating the bones in warm water and detergent.

It was a laborious process, but at least this time the task would be a little easier. The condition of the remains meant there wasn't much soft tissue left to remove.

Especially on the second, tiny skeleton.

I'd turned down the mortuary assistant's offer of help. I was accustomed to doing this alone, and by then the melancholy nature of what I had to do was starting to weigh on me. I was better left to my own thoughts, and my own company.

It was several hours before I'd done. I left the adult bones to simmer gently overnight: by morning they'd be clean enough to rinse and then reassemble for examination. The more delicate foetal skeleton I put to soak in plain water at room temperature. It would take longer, but there was precious little tissue left on its bones, and I didn't want to risk damaging them.

Once I'd cleared everything away, there was nothing more I could do. I checked my watch and felt a heaviness when I saw how early it was. I'd no plans, and the prospect of an empty evening alone at the apartment held little appeal.

It wasn't raining when I left the mortuary, but it started again as I walked back to my car. Fat, heavy drops began to spatter on the pavement, and within seconds it was coming down in earnest. I ran the rest of the way, ducking into my car as the heavens opened. Rain drummed on the roof as I brushed water from my face, obscuring everything outside the smeared glass of the windows. It was too heavy for the wipers to cope with, so I sat back to wait it out.

I was in no rush.

I switched on the radio while I waited. I caught the end of the six o'clock news, the segments that weren't quite important enough to make the opening headlines. The rain drowned it out at first, but when I heard St Jude's mentioned I turned up the volume. A local historian was being interviewed, trying hard not to sound too excited.

'Of course, tragic as the, er, *current* events are, this is far from the first misfortune to strike St Jude's,' he said. 'Several of the nuns who worked in what was then an isolation wing died during a typhoid outbreak in 1870, the very same year an unknown number of patients were also killed in a fire. Then in 1918 almost a quarter of the hospital staff, ah, *succumbed* to the Spanish flu outbreak. And during the Second World War a bomb fell on the east wing. Luckily, it didn't explode, but it brought down a section of roof that killed a nurse. The story goes that she's the Grey Lady.'

'Grey Lady?' the interviewer prompted on cue.

'The hospital ghost.' The historian couldn't keep the smile from his voice. 'Reportedly seen by patients and staff throughout the years, although actual eyewitness accounts are hard to find. Supposedly a harbinger of death, if you believe the legend.'

Oh, for God's sake. I shook my head, irritated.

'So it's fair to say the hospital is cursed?' the interviewer asked.

'Well, I wouldn't necessarily go *that* far. But it's certainly had its share of bad luck. Which is ironic given that St Jude is the patron saint of lost causes, one of the original apostles who—'

I turned off the radio. It was a filler piece, making up for the fact that the police had released so few details about the deaths at the old hospital. But that sort of sensationalism wouldn't help the investigation.

Still, it had reminded me of something. Reaching for the glove compartment, I took out the leaflet for the public meeting the protester had given me the day before. Below the old photograph of St Jude's were details of when and where it was going to be held. I looked at my watch. I could just about make it.

It wasn't as if I'd anything else to do.

The rain had eased by the time I reached St Jude's, but the downpour had cleared the streets. There was no sign of the media scrum that had congregated outside the gates the day before. The entrance was now guarded by a single police officer, his yellow waterproofs shockingly bright in the gloom, while only a few diehard journalists remained. Most were dressed for the weather or huddled under golfing umbrellas, although one bedraggled woman who'd been caught out stood dripping and forlorn under a tree.

I drove on past the derelict hospital. The public meeting was being held in a church hall not far away. It didn't start for another twenty minutes and I'd thought I'd be able to find it easily enough. But as I turned down yet another street of demolished houses and boarded-up shops, I was regretting not using the satnav. Taking what I hoped was the right turning, I found myself back on the main road that ran behind the abandoned hospital's grounds. A solitary figure plodded along the deserted street. It was a woman, laden with carrier bags as she trudged through the downpour. She wore a heavy coat but no hood and walked with a slightly awkward gait, favouring her left side. Something about her seemed familiar but I'd gone past before I realized it was the woman I'd encountered at the ruined church the day before.

Remembering her final 'Piss off', I almost carried on, but then the decision was made for me. As I glanced back in the mirror I saw the bus behind me splash through a puddle at the pavement's edge. The old woman was almost obscured by the sheet of dirty water it threw up, tottering sideways as it soaked her.

Cantankerous or not, I couldn't leave her like that. I pulled over, earning an irate flash of the bus's lights. It was possible its driver didn't know what he'd done, but I couldn't drive away now. The woman was standing where she'd been splashed, mouthing something at the disappearing bus. Then, hoisting her dripping bags, she set off walking again with slump-shouldered resignation.

I wound down the window as she drew level with my car. 'Do you want a lift?'

She looked round. Her grey hair was plastered to her head, and water dripped from her eyebrows and the tip of her nose as she scrutinized me.

'Who are you?'

'I saw you in the woods yesterday.' She didn't say anything, just regarded me with sullen hostility. I tried again. 'By the ruined church, at the back of St—'

'I remember, I'm not stupid.'

She still didn't move. Rain was blowing in the open car window, drenching me as well. 'Where do you live?'

'Why?'

'If it's not far I can give you a lift.' I hoped it was nearby: the meeting was due to start soon.

She scowled. 'I don't need charity.'

A gust of wind blew more rain into the car. I wiped it from my face. 'Look, it's a filthy night. I can drive you home if you like, but if you'd rather walk that's fine.'

She gave the car a doubtful look before she grudgingly answered, 'All right.'

I reached into the back and opened the car door. She dumped her wet carrier bags on to the seat, then climbed in after them with a grunt.

'So where am I going to?' I asked.

The face in the rear-view mirror stared back at me suspiciously. There was another pause.

'Cromwell Street. Take the next left.'

I checked the clock on the dashboard as I pulled out: I was cutting it fine if I was going to make the start of the meeting. The car smelled of wet wool and old fabric, and a sour odour that said my passenger didn't bathe very often.

'I'm David,' I said, taking the turning.

'Good for you. You want the next right. No, *that* one, are you blind? You've missed it now!'

The road was already disappearing behind us. 'It's OK, I'll turn around.'

She sniffed. 'Don't bother, you can take the next one instead. They all go to the same place.'

Now she tells me. I tried again. 'It's bad weather to be out in.'

'Not like I've any choice when I need shopping, is it?'

'Aren't there any shops nearby?'

'You think I'd be out in this if there were?'

I gave up trying to make conversation. We drove in silence for a while.

'Lola,' she said abruptly.

'Sorry?'

'That's my name. Lola.'

The hostility in her voice had been replaced with tiredness. I glanced in the mirror and saw her staring listlessly out of the window, the pouchy face loose and sullen.

She didn't look like a Lola.

Her street was a few hundred yards from the woods where I'd first seen her. Rows of pebble-dashed terraces ran on both sides of the road. A few had lights on but most looked empty, while some had been demolished altogether.

'Here.'

I pulled up outside the house she'd indicated. The pebble-dashing was unpainted and starting to spall and the window frames were badly in need of paint. Only the front door looked new, a sturdy slab of panelled wood, glossy with varnish.

Capricious as ever, the rain had all but stopped as I got out of the car. She'd already opened the door and was struggling to climb out herself.

'Here, let me,' I said, reaching for her carrier bags.

'I've got them,' she said brusquely.

I stood back while she heaved herself out. Awkwardly clutching her shopping, she rummaged in her handbag as she went to the front door. But instead of unlocking it she stopped, keys held ready as she fixed me with a stare.

'If you're expecting me to pay you, you can think again.'

'Don't worry, I was just seeing if you can manage,' I told her.

'Well, I can.'

It looked like I'd already outstayed my welcome. 'OK, then. Take care.'

She didn't respond. Turning back to my car, I checked my watch, swearing to myself when I saw the time. I briefly considered asking Lola – her name still didn't seem to fit – for directions to the church hall, but immediately decided it wouldn't be worth the aggravation. I'd find the place myself.

From behind me I could hear the snick of a lock as she opened her front door. Suddenly, there was an exclamation, followed by an explosive smash of breaking glass. I looked back to see that one of her carrier bags had burst, spilling jars, tin cans and packages on to the ground. The top had come off a container of milk, and bacon, sausages and broken eggs lay in a spreading white pool on the wet pavement.

I put my foot out to stop a tin of baked beans from rolling into the gutter, then started picking up the other groceries that had come to rest nearby. Still standing in front of the doorway, Lola stared down at the ruined food spread around her feet, as though unwilling to believe what she saw.

'Shall I bring these in?' I asked, going over with the tins and packages I'd retrieved.

Her expression clouded. 'I told you, I don't want any help.'

She turned to thrust her remaining carrier bags inside, then began grabbing the items I was holding. The front door behind her stood ajar, and from inside the house came a low moan. I saw Lola's mouth tighten, but it wasn't until the moan was repeated, more loudly this time, that she responded.

'Give me a chance, I heard you the first time!' she snapped over her shoulder.

The noise had come from a person, not a pet, I was certain of that. I looked through the open doorway, trying to see inside. The house was in darkness, but now I saw that a bulky parcel had spilled from one of the carrier bags she'd put down. It was a pack of adult incontinence pads.

'Is everything OK?' I asked.

She gave me a look as though the question were too ridiculous to answer. 'What do you care?'

I sighed, giving up any hope of making it on time to the meeting. 'Look, why don't I clean this up while you put your shopping away?'

I don't know if she was tempted or just surprised. She stared at me as though unable to decide what she was seeing. Then she snatched the last tin from my hand.

'Leave us alone.'

The front door slammed in my face.

Chapter 10

I MISSED THE first ten minutes of the meeting. Although the church hall wasn't far from where the old woman lived, there were no road signs and by then I was already running late. In the end I had to resort to my satnav, which took me back to streets I'd already been on at least once, before leading me to one that had been frustratingly close all along. The rain was still holding off as I locked my car and hurried across the road. Only a few drops pattered down, but the smoke-coloured clouds overhead promised the break was only temporary.

The church was a severe Edwardian building, with a mismatched 1970s extension protruding from one side. A fug of humidity and wet clothing greeted me as soon as I stepped through the doorway. Posters for social clubs and events decorated the walls, and a torn trampoline was folded and propped up against one wall. I'd expected the weather would put a lot of people off, but the hall was full. All the seats were already taken, and people were standing in the aisles and at the back. Someone on a stage at the front was already speaking as I went in, the amplified voice constantly on the verge of feedback.

Half a dozen people sat behind microphones at a long trestle table. The speaker was in the middle, a tired-looking woman with cropped hair and an assortment of necklaces and bangles dangling over a brightly coloured top. Standing at one end of the table but set slightly apart from it was an empty chair. It looked out of place on the stage by itself, as though it had been put there deliberately. Sitting at the table next to it was the man who'd been speaking at the demonstration outside St Jude's. Once again he wore a plain black jacket, jeans and crisp white shirt, and while there was nothing flamboyant about him he was by far the most imposing figure on the stage. Even silent he managed to command attention. The woman who was speaking kept glancing his way, as though checking for approval. A discernible flush made its way up her throat when he nodded in agreement, the lights in the hall gleaming off his shaven head.

I saw space against a wall and made my way over. Although I tried not to make a noise, my entrance hadn't gone unnoticed. As I eased into the gap I realized I was being watched. Turning to the stage, I found the man who'd been at St Jude's was staring at me. I'd thought I must have imagined the recognition in his eyes the day before, but there was no mistaking it now. He gave me a short, barely perceptible nod before switching his attention back to the woman speaker.

Do I know him? Baffled, I racked my brain to recall. If we'd met before I didn't remember it, yet he seemed to know me. I was still puzzling over it when a low voice murmured next to me.

'Wasn't expecting to find you here, Dr Hunter.'

The Geordie accent identified Whelan before I even looked round. The deputy SIO squeezed in beside me, giving a quick smile to a woman who shuffled aside to make room.

'You must be a glutton for punishment,' he whispered. If he'd seen the nod I'd got from the man on stage, he didn't mention it. 'What brings you here?'

'Just curious,' I said, keeping my own voice down as well. I could hardly admit I'd nothing better to do.

'Does DCI Ward know?'

'I didn't know myself until about an hour ago.' If I'd had a chance I might have cleared it with Ward, but I couldn't see there was any real need when it was a public meeting. 'What are you doing here?'

'Oh, just keeping a quiet eye on things.'

'Is Ward expecting trouble?' She'd told me that local feelings over St Jude's were running high even before the bodies had been found. But there weren't any uniformed police in the hall, and I couldn't see any other of Ward's officers.

Whelan shook his head. 'No, nothing like that. Doesn't hurt to keep tabs on these things, though. You never know who's going to turn up.'

Or not, I thought, looking again at the unoccupied chair at one end of the trestle table. I nodded towards the people on stage.

'Who are these?'

'Community leaders and small-fry activists, mainly. The woman talking now's a councillor. The one next to her runs a food bank.' He shrugged. 'Well-meaning, most of 'em.'

'What about the man sitting by the empty chair?'

A hard smile touched the policeman's lips. 'The jury's still out on that one. That's Adam Oduya. Local activist, but in a different league to the rest of them up there. Used to be a human-rights lawyer but he's set himself up as a self-styled campaigner for "social justice". He orchestrated most of the protests and rallies to save St Jude's, and he's the one who got the bat-protection league or whatever involved. Without him the place would've already been flattened.'

There was no clue there why this Oduya might think he knew me. 'He won't be popular with the developers, then.'

'I doubt they're losing any sleep over it. They're some big international conglomerate so it's just figures on a balance sheet to them. It's the poor sods who live here that get the shitty end of the stick.'

'You sound like you're on the protesters' side.'

'I'm sympathetic, I don't deny it. You might not think it to hear me talk but I grew up only a few streets from here.' He nodded at my surprise. 'I lived in Blakenheath until my folks moved to Newcastle when I was eight. Married a Londoner, that's how come I'm back, but this is the first time I've been here since. Shocking what's happened to the place. It was never a rich neighbourhood but not like this. Drugs everywhere, everything knocked down or boarded up, and a twelve-mile trip to the nearest hospital since St Jude's closed. It's enough to make you weep.'

He'd begun speaking more loudly, earning an irate look from the woman who'd made room for him. He gave her an apologetic nod and leaned closer, dropping his voice again.

'The whole area's crying out for redevelopment, but instead of affordable housing the developers want to throw up another shiny office block. And they're trying to get their hands on the woods behind St Jude's as well. It's ancient woodland, but they say if they're allowed to develop it they'll be able to build houses. Oduya says they're blowing smoke up everyone's arse, and he's probably right.'

'So what's your problem with him?'

Whelan hitched a shoulder. 'I can't disagree with a lot of what he says, I just don't buy this "social messiah" act he puts across. He's too much of a self-promoter for my liking. He's got a popular blog, a massive Twitter following, and he knows how to play the media. Photogenic bugger, I'll give him that, but I'm not convinced he doesn't have his own agenda. St Jude's hasn't exactly done his profile any harm.'

I looked at the handsome man sitting on the stage. He wore a thoughtful frown as he listened to the woman drone on. 'What sort of agenda?'

'Who knows? Whatever ambitions made him jack in a law career. Politics, maybe. The man's a natural politician, and he could pick his own ticket around here. Ah, here we go. The main event's starting.'

The speaker was finally winding down, turning to Oduya as she introduced him. As she sat back in her chair, he applauded enthusiastically, prompting a more muted response from the audience. Then, instead of staying seated like the last speaker, he lifted his microphone from its stand on the table and rose to his feet.

'Thank you, Tanja. And thank you all for coming here tonight. If not for the rain, we might have had a full house.'

He gave an easy smile, deliberately looking around the crowded hall to underline the joke. Amplified, his orator's voice was even more impressive, and a ripple of laughter came from the audience. It quietened as he grew serious again.

'Some people say there's no such thing as community any more, that the ties binding our society have broken down. That nobody *cares*.' He nodded, pausing for effect. 'Well, standing here tonight that's not what I see. What I see are people who *do* care. People who're concerned for their families and neighbours, people who want to make better lives for their children. People who are *sick* and *tired* of not being heard!'

His voice climbed to echo off the hard walls of the church hall, earning a spontaneous round of applause. But I noticed how he also moved the microphone slightly away from his mouth, so there wouldn't be feedback. Whelan was right: Oduya knew exactly what he was doing.

For the next ten minutes he spoke eloquently and with controlled passion. I already knew some of the background to St Jude's, but then so did everyone there. It made no difference. Oduya commanded everyone's attention, and I doubt there was an eye in the hall that wasn't fixed on him.

Coming out from behind the table, he made a show of stepping around the empty chair as he came to stand at the front of the stage and stared out. A hush fell on the audience. He let the silence build.

'I know I'm not saying anything you haven't heard from me before.' He was speaking more quietly now but still held everyone gripped. 'The closure of our hospital, the theft – and it *is* theft – of our rights and land to satisfy corporate greed, that's all old news. We've been there and done that. But this isn't just about land, or buildings, or greed any more. This is about *lives*. People have died. Yet what do we have from the police? Silence.'

'Uh-oh,' Whelan muttered, straightening.

Oduya swept an arm towards the empty chair on the stage. 'This was an opportunity for the police to speak directly to the people of this community, but instead they chose to say nothing. So where are they? Why aren't they here?'

Whelan's voice was tight with anger. 'This is a stitch-up. We weren't bloody invited.'

But Oduya's words went down well with everyone else. A threatening rumble went up from the audience as he stood beside the vacant chair. A prop, I saw now.

'All we know is that three individuals have died, their bodies left to rot in what was once a *hospital*. We don't know who they are, we haven't been told anything about them. But one thing is for sure. They didn't deserve to die like rats, as neglected and forgotten as St Jude's itself. And neither does anyone else!'

There was furious applause, whoops and angry shouts of assent. Oduya was prowling around the stage now, his voice rising.

'How can it have come to this? Are lives – *our* lives, yours and your children's – are they really worth so little? Because make no mistake, it is our children's lives that are at stake here! I have it on good authority that one of the poor souls who died in there was *pregnant* . . .'

Beside me, Whelan stiffened. 'Oh, shit.'

'The police don't want you to know that, because they're ashamed. And they should be ashamed!' Oduya was impassioned now. 'What's happened at St Jude's isn't just a tragedy, it's a symptom. A symptom of the infection that's affecting our society. Are we really going to sit quietly and do nothing while it spreads even more?'

People were on their feet now, applauding wildly and shouting their outrage. Whelan was already on his way out, pushing his way through to the exit. And in the calm centre of it all Oduya stood at the front of the stage silently now.

Head held high as he soaked it in.

I stayed until the end, but after Oduya the other speakers were an anticlimax. They did little more than add their voices to his, trying unsuccessfully to tap into the same wellspring of feeling. The man himself remained in his seat, apparently content to sit back and politely listen to the rest. But people were already starting to leave before the last speaker had finished.

When the meeting finally wound down I joined the shuffling queue for the doors. There was no sign of Whelan, but he'd be busy briefing Ward on what had happened. There would be some furious discussions going on after Oduya's bombshell. He'd blindsided the police completely, revealing sensitive details no one outside the inquiry team should have known, clear proof there was a leak from within the investigation. Now Ward was facing a PR nightmare and had some hard questions to answer.

The rain was still holding off when I left the church hall, although there was a faint mizzle in the air that promised the lull wouldn't last. A few people were still trailing out, but I was one of the last. Feeling the chill through my jacket, I set off back to where I'd left my car. I hadn't gone far when there was a shout.

'Dr Hunter!'

I turned to see someone hurrying over. As he drew closer I saw with surprise that it was Adam Oduya. He was smiling broadly.

'I thought it was you when I saw you yesterday. How are you doing?'

My face must have shown my incomprehension. His smile became rueful.

'It's been a long time. We met, oh, must be eight or nine years ago now. The Gale Fairley case? I was on Kevin Barclay's defence team.'

It took me a moment to place what he was talking about. Gale Fairley was a runaway seventeen-year-old whose decomposed body had been found in woodland. Kevin Barclay, an unemployed thirty-year-old with learning difficulties, had been charged with her murder after police found items belonging to her in his bedsit. I'd been brought in as an expert witness for the defence and had managed to establish that the teenager had been dead for between four and six weeks when her body was found. Since Barclay had been in hospital after a car accident during that time, he couldn't have killed her.

It hadn't gone down well with the police or the CPS. The prosecuting counsel did her best to undermine my findings during the cross-examination, but they couldn't argue with the facts. Barclay was cleared, and a short time later his housemate was charged and later found guilty of murdering Gale Fairley.

But although I could recall the case, I couldn't remember Adam Oduya.

'I had hair back then,' he said with a grin, passing a hand across his smooth skull. 'You probably didn't notice me much anyway. I was only a junior barrister so

I was in the background most of the time. Most of your dealings were with James Barraclough.'

Barraclough I did remember, an officious Queen's Counsel with an overblown sense of his own importance. And now I was beginning to place Oduya.

'Quite a change from criminal counsel,' I said, glancing at the church hall. 'Interesting speech you gave in there.'

'It needed saying. And I'll keep on saying it until people start to listen.'

'It looked to me like they already were.'

'It'll take more than a few hundred people in a church hall to change things.' For a second he sounded dispirited. 'Look, I've got to tie up one or two things inside, but how about grabbing a beer afterwards?'

The warning bells that had been sounding began to clamour more loudly. 'Thanks, but I can't.'

'Some other time, then? We could meet up for a coffee if you'd rather.'

'I don't think so.'

He smiled, giving me a quizzical look. 'Don't want to collaborate with the enemy, is that it?'

He'd seen me at St Jude's, so he already knew I was part of the inquiry team. 'Let's just say I don't want a conflict of interest.'

He raised his outspread hands, signifying surrender.

'I'm not looking to put you in a difficult position, I give you my word. Believe it or not, we're on the same side. You want to help victims and give them justice. So do I.'

'By giving away leaked details from a murder inquiry?'

'If you're talking about one of the victims being pregnant, then yes. I notice you aren't denying it.'

Careful. 'It's not down to me to confirm or deny anything. Where'd you hear about it, anyway?'

The leak could have come from anyone connected with the investigation. As well as dozens of police officers, it could have been someone at the mortuary or even one of the fire officers or paramedics who'd been at the scene.

Oduya smiled, shaking his head. 'You know I can't tell you that. But it's from a reliable source.'

'And you think using it to score cheap points is the best way to help?'

'Is that what you think I was doing?' He seemed genuinely taken aback. 'Each of those victims has a family or friends somewhere. Don't you think they've a right to know what happened to them?'

'Of course, but not like that.' I didn't need a lecture from him, not after what I'd been doing at the mortuary that afternoon. 'It's not your decision to make.'

'Oh, come on, Dr Hunter! You're seriously suggesting we should blindly trust the authorities? You're not that naïve.'

Stung, I was about to argue before I stopped myself. This was what Oduya wanted. He was a former barrister, trained in adversarial argument. I wasn't going to let him provoke me into giving anything away.

Perhaps realizing this, he changed tack. 'Look, I promise I'm not after information, that's not why I came after you. I mainly wanted to say hello. We've worked together once, and I'd like to think we can again. Perhaps not now, but sometime.'

'OK.'

His smile was regretful. 'I can see you don't trust me. That's fair enough. All I ask is that you keep an open mind.'

'I always try to.'

'Then I can't ask any more.' He held out a card: after a moment I took it. 'Good to see you again, Dr Hunter. Despite what some of your associates in the police may say, I'm really not the enemy. I hope you'll remember that.'

I put the card in my wallet as I watched him walk away.

Chapter 11

I SET OFF early next morning. I wasn't due at the mortuary until later, by which time the remaining soft tissue should have fallen off the bones I'd left macerating overnight. They'd probably be ready now, but an extra hour or two's soaking wouldn't hurt.

There was somewhere I wanted to go first.

I'd woken in a good mood. Rachel had called the night before. I hadn't been expecting to speak to her again for another couple of days, but the boat had made an unscheduled stop at an island with good mobile coverage. She sounded upbeat and excited, telling me how they'd tracked a pod of dolphins, even rescued one from an abandoned fishing net. Her talk of blue sea and skies was a far cry from the autumnal grey of London, and even further from the pall of St Jude's. The call had been a welcome bonus after the mire of the investigation.

But my good mood lasted only until I switched on the radio. Although I hadn't noticed any media at the public meeting, either journalists must have been in the audience or Oduya had contacted the press himself afterwards. Either way, he'd been busy.

'The police have declined to comment on your claim that one of the bodies found at St Jude's was pregnant,' the interviewer was saying. 'How did you come by the information? Was it leaked to you from someone inside the inquiry?'

'Obviously, I'm not going to reveal my sources, so let's just say I'm not the only person uneasy about the way the investigation is being handled,' Oduya's now-familiar voice replied. 'But I was told by a very reliable source. And it was confirmed for me last night by someone I trust who's in a position to know.'

What? Burning my mouth on my coffee, I hurriedly set it down to listen.

'So why do you think the police are withholding these details?' the interviewer asked.

'That's a very good question. I can't answer it, which is why I'm appealing to the police now. Please, for the sake of this unknown woman and baby's family, just tell the public the truth. We have a right to know, so why all the secrecy? What are they afraid of?'

Oh, come on! I poured my coffee down the sink in disgust, no longer interested in breakfast. Releasing sensitive details when we'd still no idea who the young mother was was bad enough. It risked swamping the switchboards with frantic relatives, hoax calls and false alarms. Even so, after talking to him I'd begun to believe Oduya was acting with the best intentions in making it public.

But that final 'What are they afraid of?' was a cynical attempt to ramp up the story. It was the sort of attention-grabbing soundbite that people would latch on to, implying cover-ups and conspiracies where none existed. Whelan had told me that Oduya knew how to play the media. Now I saw what he meant.

And I had a pretty good idea who the 'trusted' some-one might be. Anonymously or not, and despite all his protestations, Oduya was prepared to use me to bolster his cause. Although I'd done my best to sidestep his question about one of the victims being pregnant, I hadn't flat out denied it. I couldn't, not when it was true.

That was all he'd needed.

I tried calling Ward but her phone went straight to voicemail. That was hardly surprising. She was in a difficult position and would be busy working on a damage-limitation strategy. Details of the young victim's pregnancy were out there now; there was nothing she could do about that. But if she responded to Oduya straight away it would look as though he'd forced her into it. And if she didn't, it would feed his claims that the police were deliberately keeping the public in the dark.

I tried to put the radio interview from my mind as I took the lift down to the garage. The morning traffic was the usual ordeal of gridlocked roads and frayed tempers, and my day was shaping up badly enough already. It wouldn't be improved by getting into a scrape with another car.

The row of terraces looked abandoned when I pulled up outside. A cat stared at me impassively from the out-side windowsill of a boarded-up house, while at the bottom of the road a tired-looking woman was pushing twin toddlers in a double buggy. Other than that, the street was empty.

There was an ancient doorbell next to the new front door. When I pressed it there was only a grating of broken plastic and silence from inside. I knocked on the door instead, the glossy wood solid against my knuckles.

At my feet, a faint stain on the pavement marked where the eggs and milk had been dropped, but all other evidence had been cleared away.

I wasn't sure what sort of reception I'd get. Lola had made it clear she wanted to be left alone, so I doubted she'd be pleased to see me. Ordinarily, I'd have accepted that, but it wasn't so much her I was worried about. There had been that moan from inside the house when she'd let herself in, and then there were the incontinence pads she'd had in her shopping. I didn't need to have been a GP to realize what that meant. An old woman managing on her own was one thing, but if she was caring for a sick husband or relative I couldn't walk away without making sure everything was OK. Earlier that year I'd encountered another vulnerable individual during the Essex investigation who'd needed help. On that occasion I'd done nothing, and came to bitterly regret it.

I didn't want to make the same mistake again.

I waited a few more seconds then knocked again. The sound died away without a response. I began to think I'd had a wasted journey, but when I stepped back from the doorway I saw the blinds twitch at the window.

'Hello?' I called.

Nothing. But at least I knew someone was home. I lifted up the carrier bag I was holding so it could be seen.

'I've brought you some shopping.'

Nothing happened, but just when I thought I'd had a wasted trip, there was the click of the door being unlocked.

It swung open a few inches before being brought up by a chain. Lola's pouchy face regarded me through the gap.

'What d'you want?'

'I gave you a lift home last night and—'

'I know who you are, I asked what you want?'

I raised the carrier again. 'I brought you some groceries. To replace the ones you dropped.'

She looked down at the carrier bag, suspicion warring with temptation. 'I'm not paying for stuff I didn't ask for.'

'I don't want any money.'

'And I don't want any charity, neither!'

I tried another approach. 'It's the least I can do. I feel bad for not helping with your shopping. You'd be doing me a favour.'

She scowled, then the door closed in my face. *Well, I tried.* Then there was the rattle of a chain and the door opened again. Lola favoured me with a last suspicious look before grudgingly stepping aside to let me in.

There was no hallway. The front door opened directly into a small room. It was dim inside, the venetian blind on the window blocking out most of the natural light. The smell hit me right away, a thick odour of human waste and unwashed bedding that took me back to my time as a medical doctor. A clock was ticking, counting off each second with a slow, metronomic *tock*, and as my eyes adjusted I saw I was in a sitting room that at some point had been converted into a kitchen. Now it doubled as a sickroom. A man lay in a bed in its centre, covered by dirty sheets and blankets. It was hard to put an age to him, but he was obviously much younger than the woman, with greasy brown hair and an unkempt beard covering his sunken cheeks. His mouth was open, and for a bad moment I thought he was dead. Then I saw his eyes were still alive and aware, watching me keenly from the loose face.

'Here, give me that.' Lola almost snatched the carrier away. Then, as though as an afterthought, she glanced towards the bed. 'That's my son, in case you're wondering.'

I'd guessed as much. A cabinet at the end of the bed was cluttered with framed photographs taken when he was much younger. They ranged from him as a small boy, plump and round-faced, to snapshots of a hulking teenager. Overweight and clearly self-conscious, he wore the same shy smile in all of them.

But he wouldn't be doing much smiling now, shy or otherwise. Illness had burned away any excess flesh, leaving an emaciated ruin in its wake. Apart from the dark hair, the man in the bed was unrecognizable now as the teenager in the photographs. I smiled at the gaunt wreck of a face.

'Hello, I'm David.'

'You're wasting your time, he can't answer you,' Lola snapped, unceremoniously dumping the carrier bag down on the kitchen worktop. Next to it was a sink overflowing with dirty dishes. 'He had a stroke.'

'That's OK, I was just introducing myself.'

I wasn't going to assume her son couldn't understand what was going on just because he was physically incapacitated. Certainly, the eyes that were watching me now seemed alert enough. They'd never left me since I'd stepped inside.

This was the other reason I was there. As well as replacing the spoilt groceries, I'd wanted to find out who I'd heard moaning the evening before. As his mother began unpacking the carrier bag, I took in the rest of the room. Packets of incontinence pads were piled in a corner by a folded-up wheelchair. Other medical aids and products were scattered around the room, and a sideboard was all but covered by junk mail and unopened post. I read the name on the top envelope: *Mrs L. Lennox.*

'It can't be easy,' I said, taking care to include the man in the conversation as well. 'Do you have any help or do you manage by yourself?'

'Who else is going to do it?' She pulled out a packet from the bag. 'I don't need sausages, I washed the others off.'

'What about social services?'

She was still delving into the carrier and didn't look round. 'What about them?'

'Can't they arrange for carers to come in?'

'I keep telling you, I don't want any help. Not from the likes of them.' She examined a box with disdain. 'What'd you bring apple pies for? I don't like them.'

'Sorry.' I tried again. 'How do you manage things like changing the bed and bathing on your own?'

'I know what I'm doing. I used to be a nurse.'

'At St Jude's?' I asked, before I could stop myself.

'You wouldn't catch me working at that dump. It's bad enough living near it.' She turned to glower at me. 'You ask a lot of questions, don't you?'

'I was just making conversation.'

It was time to change the subject. I indicated another framed photograph, this one hung on the wall. It showed a well-fleshed young woman in a tight-fitting red dress, hair elaborately taken up and lacquered. The photograph was faded, but the styles and oversaturated colours had the look of the 1970s. The woman in it

141

was attractive, staring at the camera with a knowing smile as she struck a model's pose. I'd have guessed who it was anyway, but the eyes gave it away. They hadn't changed.

'Is that you?' I asked.

Her expression softened when she saw what I was looking at. 'In my heyday. Had men after me like flies back then. Not like now.'

A grimace of either regret or distaste crossed her face. Then it had gone, replaced by annoyance as a low groan came from the bed. I looked at the man lying in it. He was staring at us intently, a line of spittle trickling down his chin. Agitated, he began shifting around weakly, knocking a plastic feeder cup on to the floor.

'We'll have none of that,' his mother snapped, going to retrieve it. 'Shut up, I'll get to you in a minute.'

'Is he all right?'

'He needs changing. I'll sort him out when you've gone.'

Turning away from him, she went to her handbag. Taking out her purse, she began counting out money.

'Really, I don't want paying—'

'I've said, I don't want charity.'

Her voice was like iron. I didn't waste any more breath, knowing there was no use arguing. I looked uneasily at her son. He'd quietened a little, as though even that exertion had tired him, but was still watching us. On the mantelpiece above an unlit gas fire, the old clock continued its monotonous duty. Poor devil, I thought. Having to lie there listening to it count off each second must be slow torture. More spittle ran down his chin as his mouth worked, laboriously opening and closing, like that of a fish.

'Here.' Lola thrust the money into my hand. 'I'm not paying for the sausages or the apple pies, though. I didn't want them.'

She'd still kept them, I noticed. But I'd clearly out-stayed my welcome, if I'd ever had one. I turned to go, then paused.

'I forgot to ask your son's name,' I said, addressing the man in the bed as much as his mother.

She stared at me, looking as though the question was difficult.

'Gary. His name's Gary.'

I felt her son's eyes on me as I opened the door and went out. 'Bye—' I started to say, turning, but it had already closed behind me.

After the fug of illness in the cramped room it was a relief to be back outside. But I was still bothered by what I'd seen. Lola's son was a chronically ill man in need of twenty-four-hour domiciliary care, at the very least. His mother might have been a nurse once, but I'd seen no sign that she had the facilities to look after him properly. And there was her age, as well. She had to be in her seventies, and while she seemed robust enough apart from the stiffness, dealing with bedpans, bedsores and bed-baths was exhausting work even for someone much younger.

The question was, what should I do about it?

'Miserable old cow, isn't she?'

A woman was standing in the doorway of a house several doors down. She looked to be in her forties, although the heavy make-up made it hard to tell. Her hair was an unnatural jet black, while her face and neck had the orange tint of tanning cream. It gave her a jaundiced look as she leaned against the doorframe. She waved a cigarette towards the door that had just shut in my face.

'Whatever you're after, I wouldn't bother. Won't give you the time of day, that one.'

I gave a non-committal smile as I started over to my car, not wanting to be drawn into a conversation. The woman didn't take the hint.

'You social services?'

'No.' But I slowed. 'Why?'

She took a drag of her cigarette, eyeing me through the smoke. 'It's about time somebody did something. It's not right, her keeping her son at home like he is. He should be in somewhere, the state he's in. You can smell the stink out here.'

I glanced at Lola's house. The blinds appeared shut but I still moved further down the street so I was out of earshot and view. 'How long has he been like that?'

She gave a shrug. 'No idea. I've lived here nearly a year and he was like it when I moved in. Only time I've seen him was not long after, when she'd got him out in a wheelchair. Poor bastard. They should shoot me if I end up like that.'

It was said without any real feeling.

'Does anyone come to help them? Another son or daughter?'

'Not that I've seen. Can't blame them, though, can you? Sour-faced old bitch. I asked what was wrong with him once and she told me to mind my own business. Gave me a right mouthful. I didn't ask again, I can tell you that.' She looked me up and down, tapping the cigarette thoughtfully in her fingers. 'So if you're not social services, who are you? A doctor or something?'

'Something like that.' It wasn't a lie, and it saved long-winded explanations.

'Thought so. Got that look about you.' She sounded pleased with herself. 'Son taken a turn, has he? I'm not surprised, with someone like her looking after him. Rather him than me, after what she did.'

It was said in such an arch way it was an obvious invitation. I didn't want to ask, but curiosity won.

'What did she do?'

The woman smirked. 'She tell you she used to be a nurse?'

'Yes, she did.'

'Did she tell you she got the sack as well?'

The neighbour was watching me, gauging my reaction. 'Sacked for what?'

'She was lucky she wasn't thrown in prison, from what I've heard.' She took another drag on her cigarette, enjoying herself. 'They reckon she killed a kid.'

Chapter 12

I DROVE PAST St Jude's after I left Lola's. It wasn't far, and I wanted to see what impact Oduya's leak had made. The previous evening there had been hardly any journalists outside, and it wouldn't have been the rain that kept them away. With no further developments to sustain it, media interest had begun to die down.

But Oduya had changed all that. The gates outside St Jude's were once again surrounded by press vans and journalists. Not as many as when the victims' bodies had first been found, but enough to show interest in the story had taken a definite upswing. Some of them had spilled on to the road, forcing me to slow as I drove by. It was as well I did. Coming from the opposite direction, a young man in a hooded sweatshirt was walking on the pavement towards them. He'd turned his head to stare, obviously more interested in the TV cameras than where he was going, and in one of those half-intuited moments I knew what was going to happen.

I'd already started to brake when he stepped off the kerb. Even so, it was a close thing. He was right in front of me, and if I hadn't already slowed I would have hit him. As it was, I was rocked against the seatbelt, my flight case thudding over in the boot as the car came to a sudden halt. The youth stood frozen in the road, his hooded face washed with shock as he stared at the car that had suddenly appeared. Then his expression changed.

'Watch where you're fucking going, prick!'

He seemed about to launch a kick at my car before remembering the police across the road. Giving them a furtive glance, he put his head down and hurried off.

The near-miss had shaken me as well. My heart was bumping as I moved into gear and pulled away. The commotion had drawn the attention of the nearest journalists. Conscious of their stares, I didn't look back as I drove down the road.

I didn't want to give them any more headlines.

As St Jude's disappeared in the rear-view mirror, I thought over what had happened back at Lola's. Her neighbour had clearly enjoyed spreading the rumour that she'd been sacked after a child in her care had died, but it was quickly apparent that she didn't know any more than that. If there was even anything to know: I'd once been a victim of malicious gossip myself and knew how easily it can stick, regardless of whether it was true or not.

Yet Lola had told me she used to be a nurse. And just because I didn't like the way some people revelled in spreading slander, it didn't mean there couldn't be a kernel of truth in it sometimes.

It was an unlooked-for complication, especially after seeing the squalid conditions Lola and her son were existing in. It was clear she was struggling to look after him on her own and, while I didn't want to interfere, her wish for independence had to be balanced against his welfare. I might not be a doctor any more, but now I'd seen how Lola and her son were living I couldn't pretend I hadn't.

The question was, what to do about it?

It was a relief to step inside the cool, clinical quiet of the mortuary. Here at least I had some control over what was going on. I signed in and changed into scrubs, switching my phone to silent before putting it into an inside pocket. If I was carrying out particularly demanding work I would often leave my phone in the locker. But today's task should be relatively routine, and I didn't want to be out of touch.

I knew Ward would be trying to get hold of me.

I checked on the delicate foetal bones first. Even though there had been precious little soft tissue remaining, it would take several days of soaking in plain water for the last of it to dissolve and fall away. But examining them was only a formality. There was nothing to indicate that the mother had been stabbed or suffered some other physical trauma that could have left its mark on the tiny bones. Inside the womb, her unborn infant would have been protected from whatever final moments its mother had endured.

At least until she'd died.

Changing the water the bones were soaking in each day was as much as I could do to speed the process along. I did that now, then turned my attention to the mother. The overnight maceration, simmering gently in a weak detergent solution, had effectively removed tissue and grease from her disarticulated bones. Pulling on a pair of elbow-length rubber gloves, I set about the next stage.

As a piece of biological engineering, bone puts man-made constructions to shame. The smooth exterior is made from layers called lamellar bone, within which is a honeycomb structure known as trabecular bone. This serves to strengthen without adding weight. In longer bones, such as those of the arms and legs, the hollow centre – or medullary cavity – is filled with bone marrow, the fatty tissue responsible for producing blood cells. It's a masterpiece of structural design which, when viewed under a microscope, reveals an even more intricate world.

I'd carry out a full examination later when I reassembled the woman's bones in their correct anatomical positions. That didn't mean I couldn't make an initial assessment now. Lifting the dripping skull from the pan where it had been macerating, I rinsed it off in clean water. It gave little clue of the person it had once been. Bone might form the underlying framework, but it's the skin and muscles that give our faces animation and character. Without them the skull is only a calcium relic.

Though still a useful one.

The skull's angular shape suggested white ancestry, as did the narrow, high-bridged nose and relatively small jaw. Although that was far from conclusive, it might help Ward when it came to searching for a possible match on the missing-persons database. I'd already seen the general condition of the young woman's teeth during the post-mortem, enough to give me an idea of her age and lifestyle. More interesting now was the slight but distinct overbite, the upper front teeth overlapping the lower. It would have been noticeable in life, which was another feature that might help with identification.

Setting the skull in the fume cupboard to dry, I began taking the rest of the cleaned bones from the soup-like detergent bath and rinsing them off. I was keen to take

149

a closer look at the ball-like head of the right humerus, the long bone of the upper arm, and the corresponding socket on the scapula, or shoulder blade, to see if the dislocation had caused any damage not shown on the X-rays.

It hadn't. Both were in good condition. If the dislocation was the result of manhandling when the mummified body was moved, then it hadn't caused damage to either the desiccated soft tissue or the joint itself. Although it wasn't necessarily conclusive, it was another indication that the injury had occurred while the young woman was still alive.

Though not for long.

As I continued rinsing and putting the cleaned bones to dry, I found more evidence to support my earlier estimate of the victim's age. The pubic symphysis – a part of the pubic bone that over time changes from ridged to flat – suggested an individual still in her twenties. So did the femurs. In childhood, the end of the thigh bone is capped by a thick pad of cartilage. Over adolescence this ossifies, transforming into bone and gradually fusing with the femur's shaft. The process is known as epiphyseal union, and at first a line marks the junction of the two surfaces. Soon even this fades until, by the mid-twenties, it disappears altogether.

Faint lines were still visible here, but only just. And the sternal rib ends were smooth rather than displaying the more granular appearance that develops in later life. Taken together, it was another confirmation that the victim was no older than her mid-twenties at most. Probably younger, given that not all her wisdom teeth were fully erupted.

I was placing the last of the ribs in the fume cupboard when my phone started to vibrate. *Damn*. Pulling off my gloves, I left the examination room. The phone stopped before I could take it from my scrubs' inside pocket. Even though I'd had a good idea who it would be, I felt a sinking feeling when I saw the name in the display.

Ward.

I found a secluded corner of the corridor and called her back. She picked up straight away.

'I just missed a call—' I began.

'Hang on.' The connection became muffled. I heard her speaking with someone else in the background, then she came back on. 'What did you tell Adam Oduya last night?'

I'd not gone into details in the voicemail message I'd left earlier, only that I'd spoken to the activist after the public meeting. I hadn't expected Ward to be pleased, but her tone was brusque and accusing.

'I didn't tell him anything. He came up to me outside as I left and introduced himself. It turns out I was a defence consultant on a case he worked on as a junior barrister.'

'And you're only just letting me know now?'

'I didn't know myself until he reminded me. It was years ago, I didn't even recognize him.'

'So did you tell him anything about the investigation?'

'Of course I didn't.'

'Well, Oduya's going on national TV and radio claiming *someone* confirmed the leaked information. Someone he knows and trusts, so are you asking me to believe he might have another old associate apart from you?'

151

'I'm not asking you to believe anything,' I shot back. 'I'm just saying I didn't tell him anything. He asked me to confirm it and I refused.'

'But you didn't deny it either.'

Here we go. I took a breath. 'No.'

There was a pause. I could almost hear Ward trying to keep hold of her temper. 'Tell me exactly what happened.'

I went through it all, missing nothing out. She said nothing until I'd finished.

'OK.' She gave a long exhalation. 'I don't suppose I can blame you for not denying the pregnancy angle, but it's given Oduya more ammunition. The press are all over it, so I'm going to be making a statement at St Jude's this lunchtime. I'd rather have waited until we knew more but I don't have any choice now. So if he tries to speak to you again, for Christ's sake do us both a favour and keep walking.'

I didn't need to be told. Tension had started to stiffen the muscles in my neck. I kneaded them to try and ease it. 'Have you found out where the leak came from?'

'Not yet. It could be someone on the inquiry, but after Conrad's accident there were too many people swarming round St Jude's who might have overheard something. Could be any one of them.'

She sounded more weary than angry, but with the investigation lurching from one crisis to another that was understandable. I couldn't imagine that Commander Ainsley would be giving her an easy time over it.

'There's another reason I called,' she went on, in a calmer tone of voice. 'How long before you've finished at the mortuary?'

I thought about what there was left to do. 'I'll have to come back to examine the foetus, but apart from that I should be done by the end of today.'

'Good, because I want you out at St Jude's tomorrow,' Ward went on. 'We need to make sure there aren't any more surprises hidden away in there, so I've got a cadaver dog coming out to help with the search. I'd like you there as well.'

I'd expected that a cadaver dog would be brought in at some point. With a sense of smell hundreds of times more developed than ours, the animals were trained to sniff out decomposition too faint for the human nose to detect. They could pick up on traces of decay even through several feet of concrete, so a false wall shouldn't pose much of a problem.

But as useful as they were, cadaver dogs weren't able to distinguish between human and animal remains. That didn't matter so much when an entire body was discovered, but partial remains and scattered bones weren't always so easily identified. Which was why a forensic anthropologist was needed.

Still, I was surprised Ward was asking me. 'What about Mears?'

'He's got his hands full already. Parekh's scheduled to do the first of the post-mortems on the interred victims this morning, so he's going to be busy with them for the next few days. And I'm not having anybody else brought in, not when I've already got the two of you.'

I thought I'd seen the last of the old hospital. I hadn't been sorry to leave the place, but now I felt excitement stir at the thought of going back.

'What time do you want me there?' I asked.

*

I'd been intending to tell Ward what I'd heard from Lola's neighbour, but at the last minute I decided against it. She'd got enough to contend with as it was, and I didn't want to waste her time on what was probably just malicious gossip. For a former nurse rumoured to be implicated in a child's death to be living near St Jude's might raise eyebrows, but the more I thought about it, the less confident I felt that it was worth mentioning. Even if what the neighbour said was true, it was hard to see how it could have any bearing on the case. An old woman and her bedridden son were hardly credible suspects. They were a matter for social services, not the police.

Putting away my phone, I headed back to the examination room. Depending how long the reassembly of the young mother's bones took, I thought I might drive over to St Jude's at lunchtime to hear Ward's statement. It was her first as SIO, and I was interested to witness how she handled it. Thinking about that, I almost walked into the changing-room door as it swung open. Someone came out wearing full scrubs, including a surgical cap. But I didn't need to see the red hair to recognize the youthful face of Daniel Mears.

He hesitated, flushing when he saw me. Then his chin came up and he let the door swing shut behind him.

'Morning,' I said.

That was met with a stiff nod. 'Have you seen Dr Parekh?' he asked, looking past me, as though expecting her to materialize.

'Not so far. She's doing the post-mortems this morning, isn't she?'

'That's right.' He paused. 'Should be interesting.'

It was a transparent attempt to make me ask why. I was tempted not to bite, but then I'd have spent the rest of the day wondering. 'Why, what have you found?'

I'd only seen the interred victims briefly. Mears would have had a chance to study the bodies much more closely before they were removed and brought to the mortuary.

But I immediately regretted asking. He made a poor attempt not to look smug. 'Oh, this and that. You probably saw for yourself that they'd been tortured?'

Tortured? Except for the deep chafing of the restraining straps, the torch beams I'd played over the victims hadn't shown any obvious signs of physical trauma. Being walled up alive would qualify as torture by any criteria, but I knew that wasn't what Mears meant.

'I didn't get a good look,' I said, aware it sounded like an excuse.

'Well, it *was* easy to miss,' he said, with false magnanimity. 'The skin slippage and discolouration made it hard to see, but there was localized scorching to parts of the epidermis.'

'They were burned?'

'Isn't that what I said?'

His look of confusion was badly feigned. I hadn't seen the two victims close up, and the condition of their bodies would have camouflaged any burns to some extent. That didn't make hearing about it now rankle any less.

'The injuries were relatively small and too contained to have been caused by a naked flame,' Mears continued, enjoying himself. 'Some sort of heated implement, probably, rather than a blowtorch. Of course, I'll have a better idea once I can examine them properly.'

'Whereabouts were they burned?' I asked.

'All over. I found scorching on the head, limbs, torso. It looks random from what I've seen.' He couldn't keep the condescending smile from his face. 'If it's any consolation, I had to point them out to Parekh, as well.'

'That's because these old eyes don't see so well in the dark,' Parekh's voice came from behind us. 'Although in my defence I was concentrating on the injuries from the straps at the time.'

I hadn't noticed the pathologist approaching. Evidently neither had Mears. His face flushed scarlet as the diminutive figure stopped.

'Dr Parekh, I, uh, I was just . . .'

'Yes, I heard. Hello, David.' She gave me a smile, but there was a dangerous glint in her eye. 'How are you getting on with the loft victim? Almost done, I imagine.'

'Getting there.'

'You never were one to waste time. Well, I'll look forward to reading your report. I'm sure it'll be as thorough as ever.' She turned to Mears, whose flush had deepened. 'If you're ready, Dr Mears, I'd like to make a start on the first post-mortem. I'll try not to miss anything but feel free to point it out if I do.'

Without waiting, she headed off down the corridor. Small as she was, she set a surprisingly fast pace, forcing Mears to hurry after her.

I was smiling as I turned away. But it died as I thought about what the taphonomist had said. The two victims who'd been walled in had faced a horrendous death however you looked at it. If they'd been tortured – burned – as well, it took their ordeal to another level of cruelty.

It was an horrific thought. Pushing aside the selfish regret that I couldn't take a look at their remains myself, I went back into the examination room where the bones of the young mother were waiting.

Chapter 13

I ALMOST MISSED Ward's lunchtime press statement. The young woman's cleaned bones didn't yield any surprises as I rinsed them off and put them to dry, but I couldn't let go of what Mears had said. When the last of them were in the fume cupboard, I pulled up the photographs taken at the crime scene and during the post-mortem. Even though I knew I would have seen any burns already, I checked the photographs again for any evidence of charring on the young woman's body I might have missed. Pale skin darkens during decomposition, while dark skin lightens, making it impossible to use skin colour as an indicator of ancestry. Even allowing for that and the drying effect of mummification, severe burns such as Mears had described finding on the interred victims would still be visible. I couldn't rule out the possibility that she'd been burned on parts of her body destroyed by maggot activity – a suppurating burn on her abdomen would have been a target for flies to lay their eggs and wouldn't have left bloodstains on the clothing, which might explain the gaping abdominopelvic cavity.

But I'd found no physical evidence to support that. Except for the close proximity of their bodies, there was nothing to suggest the deaths of the victims walled up in the hidden chamber and that of the pregnant woman in the loft were connected. I didn't like coincidences, but it was beginning to look as though that's all this was. Perhaps Commander Ainsley had been right to want Ward to treat the two crime scenes separately, I grudgingly admitted. Hidden away from prying eyes and all but forgotten, the derelict old hospital could hide all manner of secrets.

After poring over the photographs I finally accepted that I hadn't overlooked anything. There had been no visible burns on the pregnant woman's remains.

Leaving her bones drying in the fume cupboard, when I checked my watch I saw it would soon be time for Ward to give her statement. Hurriedly changing from my scrubs, I left the mortuary and drove to St Jude's. Summer already seemed a long time ago; the year had swiftly embraced autumn. The light was subtly different now, the shadows longer and harder edged, while an underlying chill in the air bit like a harbinger of winter.

When I reached the hospital a small crowd was gathered around the hospital's main gate. Cameras, TV vans and boom microphones clogged the road outside, and one lane had been cordoned off with metal barriers. I parked a couple of streets away and hurried back. I found a spot by the barrier on the edge of the scrum, where I'd have a good view from the sidelines. A microphone faced the waiting media just inside the gates, but no one stood at it as yet. Looking round, I saw Ainsley standing by himself at the back of the press. No one paid any attention to the commander, but in plainclothes there was nothing to identify him as a police officer.

I wondered if it was significant that he was standing on this side of the microphone rather than behind it with Ward.

There was no one else there I recognized. Including Oduya. The activist was nowhere to be seen, which was surprising. I'd thought he'd have jumped at the chance to present his case again in front of TV cameras. As I was wondering about that, a dark car drove down the hospital's access road and pulled up inside the gates. Ward climbed out, together with Whelan and a smart young woman I took to be a police press officer.

The hubbub of conversation fell quiet as Ward stepped up to the microphone. Her face was deadpan, but the way she cleared her throat before she spoke betrayed her nerves. She'd made an effort to look the part, tethering the wayward hair into some sort of style and wearing a belted black mackintosh that concealed her pregnancy. I wondered if that was deliberate. It would be another unwelcome distraction if the press found out the SIO was pregnant as well as one of the victims.

I felt someone's eyes on me and turned to find Ainsley looking over. He didn't acknowledge me at first, and I wondered if he'd forgotten who I was. The disconcerting china-blue eyes stared for a moment, then he gave a short nod, turning away as Ward began to speak.

'On Sunday evening . . .' She flinched as a drone of feedback swelled from the PA speakers, drowning her out. The press officer whispered something and Ward moved a little further away from the microphone before continuing. 'On Sunday evening, following information received from a member of the public, police officers discovered the body of a young woman in the derelict main building of St Jude's Hospital. A subsequent search revealed the bodies of two more victims also inside. Pending formal identification, I am unable to release any of the victims' details. However, I can confirm that all three deaths are being treated as suspicious.'

It was a typically bland holding statement, avoiding anything contentious and skirting around how little we knew so far. I noticed Ward had avoided mentioning the gender of the other two victims: that would have to be confirmed later.

She paused, more confident now as she looked out at the press.

'There has been a claim made regarding the condition of one of the victims at the time of her death. At this present time, I can neither confirm nor deny such rumours, since to do so would risk compromising the ongoing inquiry. This is a highly complex and far-ranging investigation, so I would therefore ask . . .'

She trailed off as a commotion rippled through the crowd. Heads were turning towards a group of people making their way towards the front, journalists shuffling aside to let them through. Craning for a view, I saw it was a middle-aged man and woman, faces etched with strain. To one side and slightly behind was a much younger man, either in his late teens or early twenties, who walked with downcast eyes.

Leading them was Adam Oduya.

The activist's expression was solemn as he forged a path through the journalists. His aura of confidence was a marked contrast to the unease of the three people accompanying him. They followed close behind, huddled together and darting nervous glances to either side.

161

Ward made an attempt to recover. '. . . I would therefore ask for patience while we continue our inquiries . . .'

But no one was listening. All eyes were on Oduya and the people with him as he stopped in front of Ward. He paid no attention to the microphones and cameras that were now being turned towards him.

'This is Sandra and Tomas Gorski,' he announced, loudly enough to be clearly heard by everyone there. He gestured to the young man with them, who ducked his head even further. 'This is their son, Luke. And this is their twenty-one-year-old daughter, Christine.'

Holding up a large, glossy photograph, he turned it so everyone could see the young woman's face. The press officer with Ward hurriedly stepped up to the microphone.

'I'm sorry, this isn't a public meeting. If you have any information—'

'This family have a right to be heard!' Oduya didn't shout, yet his voice still dominated. I saw that uniformed officers were making their way through the crowd towards him. 'Christine went missing from Blakenheath fifteen months ago. No one has seen or heard from her in all that time. Yet despite repeated appeals to the police, *nothing* has been done to find her!'

'If you have any information please speak to one of our officers—'

'Sandra and Tomas contacted me this morning in desperation!' he continued relentlessly. 'They'd nowhere else to turn, because their daughter—'

There was jostling as the first police officers hurried to reach him. Oduya brandished the girl's photograph above him like a sword.

'—because their daughter, Christine Gorski, was *six months pregnant*!'

Pandemonium broke out as a police officer tried to take hold of him. Journalists were yelling questions, but Ward put a hand on the press officer's shoulder before she could say anything more. She spoke quickly to Whelan, who gave a nod and spoke into his phone. The police officers who had reached Oduya stopped, backing away slightly but still watchful.

'All right, quiet, please,' Ward said into the microphone. 'Excuse me, can we have *QUIET*!'

Feedback from that last word whistled over the crowd of media. Silence fell, broken only by the whirr of camera shutters. Ward began to speak but Oduya was there first.

'DCI Ward, out of consideration for the Gorski family, will you confirm if it's true that one of the victims found at St Jude's was pregnant—'

'Out of consideration for *all* the victims and their families, I'm not going to release any information that could compromise an ongoing police inquiry. They deserve better than that,' Ward responded. Twin patches of colour in her cheeks betrayed her anger. 'However, I sympathize with Mr and Mrs Gorski and their family over their missing daughter. I understand how distressing—'

'Our daughter's been gone over a *year*!' Sandra Gorski's anguished cry cut across Ward. Next to her, her husband stared dead ahead, his face clenched. 'We don't want your sympathy, we want you to *do* something!'

Ward looked as though she'd been slapped, but then rallied. 'And we will, I promise you. But a public forum isn't the place to have that discussion. If you go with one of my officers now, then I give you my word I'll hear what you have to say. After that, if you still want to air your grievances publicly that'll be your decision. Thank you, that's all.'

She'd turned and left the microphone before anyone had a chance to realize that she'd finished. As the press futilely shouted questions, I saw Whelan push his way towards Oduya and the Gorski family. There was a quick conversation, then he led them back through the police cordon towards the unmarked car Ward had arrived in.

The shouted questions continued, but the crowd of journalists was already starting to break up. They'd come hoping for news. Well, they'd certainly got it.

As I turned to leave myself I had a sudden feeling of being watched. I glanced back to where Ainsley had been standing, thinking it might be him. The police commander was nowhere to be seen, though, and the melee of journalists, photographers and TV cameras made it impossible to pick anyone out.

But the feeling persisted all the way back to my car.

The young mother's bones had dried by the time I got back to the mortuary. Reassembling them was straightforward enough, and a more thorough examination produced nothing I didn't already know. There were no healed fractures or other significant skeletal features that might help with identification, and the only new detail I'd been able to come up with was an estimate of her height. Gauging stature wasn't as straightforward as simply measuring the remains from head to foot, as when someone is alive. Loss of soft

164

tissue and deformation of the spine if the body was in a contorted position can either of them skew the results and potentially complicate any identification. While it's possible to gain a rough estimate of height based solely on the lengths of some long bones from the limbs, since there was a full skeleton it was more accurate to use individual body segments, such as the skull, vertebrae and femurs. Using calipers to take measurements, I calculated that in life the woman would have been approximately one hundred and sixty-three centimetres tall. Around five foot five, give or take half an inch.

As I worked I did my best not to dwell on what had happened at St Jude's, but it was never far from my mind. I was acutely aware that the mummified remains – now reduced to smooth, pale bone – had once been a young woman with parents and friends. A life. It might have ended in a dirty loft, yet there was more to a person than the manner of their death. And while I didn't need reminding how important it was to remain detached, knowing who this individual might be brought a subtle change of perspective. I could tell myself that it wasn't confirmed, that it might have been a different young woman's grieving family at the hospital that afternoon. But even the possibility of a name had a personalizing effect, removing a layer of distance between me and the victim.

Now when I handled the slender bones they seemed to have more weight.

I'd almost finished when my phone vibrated in my scrubs pocket. I'd been half expecting a call and felt no surprise when I saw it was Ward again. She didn't waste any time.

'Are you still at the mortuary?'

'Just finishing up.'

'Stay there. I'm sending a set of dental records I want you to check against the loft victim. How soon can you let me know if they match?'

'It depends if you want a detailed examination or just a basic comparison.' The latter was no problem: any forensic anthropologist had enough knowledge to compare ante-mortem dental records with the teeth of a dead individual. But anything more complicated was better done by a specialist.

'Basic is fine. We'll get a forensic dentist to do a formal identification later, and we'll be running a DNA test as well. They'll both take time, though, and I need something to go on now. Can you do that?'

I could. 'Are the dental records Christine Gorski's?'

'Heard about that, did you?' Ward didn't sound surprised, but by then it would have been all over the news and social media.

'I was at St Jude's earlier when Oduya turned up with her family.'

'Then you'll understand why I don't want to wait days to find out if the body's hers or not.' Her exasperation was clear from her voice. 'The annoying thing is Christine Gorski's name was already on our radar even before Adam bloody Oduya pulled that stunt this afternoon. She's not the only pregnant woman who's gone missing but her description matches what we know about the body from the loft. Right sort of age, six months pregnant and been missing for fifteen, which fits your estimated time since death. We don't know what clothes she was wearing on the day she disappeared, but it was during summer so a T-shirt and short

166

skirt's not out of the question. Her family seems decent enough. Father's Polish, as you probably guessed, works for a sports retail company. The mother's a secretary, brother's a final-year arts student. Not exactly well off but they could afford white fillings for Christine when she was fifteen.'

I thought about the condition of the dead woman's teeth. 'Did she use drugs?'

'She'd been in and out of rehab for heroin addiction since she was seventeen. The family lost touch with her for nearly two years, until she turned up out of the blue one day and announced she was pregnant. She was broke and said she wanted their help to get cleaned up for the baby's sake.'

'What about the father?'

'Her parents don't know, and it doesn't sound as though Christine did either. My guess is she probably wound up working on the streets, because she was in no state to hold down a regular job. Her parents didn't ask too many questions, they were just glad to have her back. They insist the change of heart was genuine, although they still didn't trust her enough to give her any money. It was all set up for her to go into rehab again, but she disappeared the day before it started. That was when they reported her missing, and they haven't seen or heard from her since.'

Sad as it was, I could understand why Christine Gorski's disappearance hadn't been prioritized by the police. Her disappearance would have been seen in the context of her addiction, just another drug addict deciding to avoid rehab, rather than anything more sinister. That must have made it all the more agonizing for her family. The months of being in limbo, of not knowing what had become of their daughter, must have been sheer torture for them.

If I'd been in their shoes, I would have gone to Oduya as well.

I told Ward I'd be in touch and went back into the examination room. The circumstantial evidence that the reassembled skeleton on the table was the physical remains of Christine Gorski was stacking up, but I couldn't let myself be swayed by that. Nor did I want to look at the dental records that Ward was sending through. Not yet.

There are several stages involved in establishing a positive dental identification. To start with I made sure all the teeth were present – which they were, with the exception of a missing back molar – and recorded the location and nature of crowns and amalgam fillings. That done, I checked for any untreated conditions, noting a cracked tooth next to the missing molar as well as several small patches of caries.

I entered all these details on to a dental chart. It perhaps wasn't as exhaustive as a forensic dentist's would be, because I didn't have the same breadth of experience. But I was confident it would be enough for Ward's purposes.

Once I'd finished my inventory, I compared the chart I'd drawn up with the dental records Ward had emailed as a password-protected file. She'd included a photograph of Christine Gorski with them. It looked to have been cropped and enlarged from a group photo, taken when she was in her late teens. The brown hair was tied up in a semi-formal style, exposing a roundish face that was both attractive and ordinary. She'd been caught looking off to one side as though not entirely engaged in what was going on, and although she was smiling it looked artificial, a self-conscious pose summoned up for a camera rather than anything spontaneous. I studied it for signs of an overbite, but it was hard to tell.

Occasionally, a single unique feature can be enough for a positive ID. I'd once had a case where I'd been able to make an informal identification from a distinctively crooked front tooth. That had been an unusual situation, though. Ideally, there should be an absolute match between the dental records taken when a person was alive and the post-mortem dental exam. That wasn't the case here. Neither the caries, missing molar, nor cracked tooth were present in Christine Gorski's records.

But she hadn't visited a dentist for five years before she'd disappeared, which was more than enough time to account for the changes. And the cracked molar that sat next to the empty socket hinted that the missing tooth could have been dislodged by force. Knocked out rather than extracted.

More compelling than these inconsistencies were the similarities between the two. According to her records, Christine Gorski had an identical overbite to the one I'd noted on these remains, and the dental work of the woman from the loft matched hers to the last detail. Even down to the white fillings in two back molars. I went through it all again just to be sure, but there wasn't any doubt.

We'd found Christine Gorski.

Chapter 14

ONE OF THE holy grails of forensic scientists has been to devise an artificial way of detecting the gases produced as a body decomposes. That would not only help locate buried or hidden human remains but also serve as a means of determining how long an individual has been dead. So far, though, science hasn't come up with anything that can compete with nature.

The Labrador could barely contain its excitement. It was only young, its sleek coat pitch black except for a splotch of white on its head. Fairly quivering, it shifted from paw to paw, casting hopeful glances up at its female handler as it gave a tremulous whine.

'Shush,' she told it, tousling its ears. 'Be still, Star.'

'Glad someone's keen,' Whelan commented, looking at his watch.

There were six of us standing at the bottom of the steps outside St Jude's. Seven, including the cadaver dog. Ward had said she might be out later, but at the moment she was busy dealing with the fallout from my identification of Christine Gorski. Not that there was any need for the SIO to be there. In addition to the handler, Whelan and myself, there was the police search adviser, a rotund man in his fifties called Jackson, and two SOCOs I recognized from the loft. One of them toted a video camera on a strap around her neck, the other carried a case of equipment. All of us wore white coveralls and the usual protective paraphernalia, although for the moment our hoods and masks were down. They weren't necessary until we went inside, so we were making the most of the fresh air while we could. By now, though, it wasn't only the Labrador that was impatient. We'd been standing in the grey drizzle at the bottom of the steps for the past ten minutes.

Waiting.

Whelan's radio came to life. He answered it bad-temperedly. 'Go on.' I didn't catch the reply, but the deputy SIO gave an exasperated huff. 'About bloody time.'

He ended the call.

'He's here,' he announced.

We watched in silence as another white-clad figure approached from the police trailers. The newcomer walked slowly behind a young PC, his coveralls strained tight around his heavy gut. A battered but clean holdall was slung over one shoulder, while in his other hand he carried an equally well-used case for a heavy-duty drill.

'Glad you could join us, Mr Jessop.' Whelan spoke tonelessly, not openly sarcastic but not welcoming either. The demolitions contractor looked at him sullenly, his eyes jaundiced and bloodshot.

'I'm here now, aren't I?'

The coveralls were the smartest thing about him. Above them his thinning hair was unkempt and two or three days' growth of grey whiskers shrouded his jowls. When I'd called Ward the night before to tell her I'd identified Christine Gorski, she'd confirmed that Jessop would be helping out on the cadaver dog search.

'He knows the building as well as anyone,' she'd said. 'He's got copies of the original blueprints as well as equipment to check behind any false walls.'

I said nothing. Jessop hadn't seemed exactly enthusiastic about the investigation when I'd seen him with Whelan, and he'd failed to show up that morning for the SIO's briefing. The signs weren't good, but it was up to Ward who she used as a civilian consultant. And it made sense to have someone along who had structural knowledge of the derelict hospital. Jessop had been hired to knock the place down: he could bring a useful perspective to the search. Even so, I had my doubts as I followed the big man up the steps to the entrance. Then I stepped through the doorway into St Jude's.

The few days I'd been away had dulled the physical memory of how dismal it was. Inside the hospital's vast interior it was permanent night. Even the police floodlights only accentuated the shadows in the recesses and corners of its echoing corridors, and no amount of light could take away the stink of mould and urine. When Ward had asked me to go back there I'd been pleased: now, as we left daylight outside and the scale of the task sank in, I felt my enthusiasm wane. It would take days to work our way through every ward, anteroom and corridor.

In St Jude's claustrophobic darkness, that would seem a long time.

The hospital had been divided up into zones so it could be systematically searched, starting at the top, where the two interred bodies had been found, and working down floor by floor to the basement. The police were carrying out a fingertip search of the entire building, and the plan was for the cadaver dog team to follow along behind to ensure there were no more decomposing remains concealed behind false walls, or anywhere else.

Normally, the forensic pathologist would accompany the search, to certify death if a body was discovered and oversee its removal. But this was an unusual situation, where it was uncertain there was even anything to find. I'd be able to determine if any remains were human, and whatever the Labrador located would likely be concealed and inaccessible anyway. There'd be ample time for Parekh to come out when – and if – she was needed.

The dog's claws clicked like knitting needles as we made our way up the stairs. Our heavier footsteps set up a reverberating echo that bounced off the stairwell's hard walls. I was behind Jessop and could see that the big contractor was making heavy work of the climb with the drill case and holdall. He hauled himself up by the handrail, and by the time we reached the top his breath was wheezing in his mask.

'You OK?' I asked when he stopped.

The yellow eyes turned to look at me, the barrel chest rising and falling. Even through his mask I got a waft of his breath, sour with old alcohol.

'I'd be better if I wasn't in this shit heap.'

'Do you want a hand with one of the bags?'

He stared at me, his affront obvious even under the mask.

'No.'

Hoisting the holdall further on to his shoulder, he set off along the corridor. Lit by floodlights, it seemed to go on for ever, a black tunnel disappearing into the distance. The search was starting at the far end, but part way along Jessop stopped again. I thought he might still be having difficulty after the stairs until I saw where he was looking. Off to one side, a cordon of police tape sealed off the access to the loft where we'd found Christine Gorski's body.

He gave me a quick glance, realizing I was watching him. 'That where they found her?'

'I expect so.'

Jessop stared at the darkness beyond the police tape, breathing nasally in his mask. 'Said on the news she was twenty-one. Same age as my daughter.'

Without waiting for me to comment, he turned and clomped off down the corridor.

Even though I knew there were other police search teams in the building, as our small group began the slow trek through St Jude's dark expanse it felt as though we were completely alone, stranded from any other living thing. I was no stranger to hospitals, knew how maze-like they could seem at the best of times. But the ones I'd worked in had been full of life and noise, not empty and silent like this. It would have been easy to become disorientated.

At least the dog was happy. With the exception of the Labrador's handler, the rest of us hung back so as not to distract the animal as it worked. Not that there was much chance of that: Star was wholly engrossed in exploring the wonderful new world of scents the old hospital offered. Consulting rooms, wards, examination cubicles, even storage cupboards: all had to be checked by the cadaver dog.

I hadn't given much thought to the practical aspects of the search. Like most old NHS hospitals, St Jude's had been renovated and modernized over the years. The outside might look the same, but the interior bore little resemblance to the original building. The layout of rooms, wards and corridors had all changed over the years. Walls had been taken down in places and erected in others. Some of these were obviously old and had been there for decades. Others were less so.

The Labrador made its first find within the hour, its ears cocked intently as it explored the recesses of a dusty closet. A quick check by a SOCO produced the leathery corpse of a bat, crumpled under broken shelves like a discarded glove. The dog's handler rewarded it with a well-chewed tennis ball.

'Must be nice to be easily satisfied,' Whelan remarked, as the dog thrashed its tail happily.

Not long after that I saw why Ward had wanted Jessop along. We were in a former waiting room, a row of broken plastic chairs still fixed to the wall below a sign that read *Please take a seat and wait to be called*. A torn poster showing an electron microscope image of an influenza virus was stuck next to an empty hand-wash dispenser.

The Labrador had been snuffling along a dusty skirting board when it suddenly came alert. It tracked back and forwards along one length, then looked towards its handler and barked.

Fussing it, the woman turned to Whelan. 'Looks like he's got something.'

Jessop had said virtually nothing all this time, his moody presence adding to the oppressive atmosphere. Now, beckoned forward by Whelan, he banged the wall above where the dog had reacted with his fist. It produced a hollow thump.

'Plasterboard,' he grunted.

Opening the plastic case, he took out a battery-operated drill and bored a small hole low down the wall. From his shoulder bag, he took out an inspection endoscope, a fibre-optic probe connected to a small hand-held screen. Inserting the probe through the hole he'd drilled, he rotated it this way and that. Light shone on his face as he studied the image on the screen. Then he stopped, minutely adjusting the controls to improve the picture.

'What is it?' Whelan asked.

Instead of answering, Jessop set down the endoscope. Reaching again into his bag, he pulled out a crowbar. Before anyone could do anything, he smashed it against the wall, knocking a hole in the flimsy plasterboard. Whelan leapt forward as the contractor thrust his arm inside.

'Jesus, what the hell . . .!'

But Jessop was already withdrawing his arm from the hole. He had something dark and furry in his hand. He held it up by its thin tail.

'Just a rat. Probably got through the skirting.'

Whelan said nothing as he went over to the hole in the wall. He peered through it, shining his torch to see inside. I got the impression it was as much to give himself a chance to calm down as to make sure there was nothing else in there. His eyes were cold as he turned to Jessop.

'Pull a stunt like that again and I'll charge you with interfering with evidence. You see anything in future, you let me decide what to do about it. Clear?'

'Christ, it was only a bloody rat—'

'Are we clear?'

The contractor looked away. 'All right, calm down,' he muttered.

He tossed the dead rat into a corner. The dog leapt after it excitedly, earning a rebuke from its trainer. It slunk back, looking hurt. Whelan took a deep breath.

'OK, let's call it lunchtime.'

The weather had eased to a light mizzle outside, a fine spray that hung in the air and clung to hair and clothing. I considered walking over to the church ruins in the woods behind the hospital, but with the ground wet and muddy I decided on a sandwich and mug of tea in my car instead.

I was staring blankly out of the window, chewing mechanically and wondering what Rachel was doing, when there was a rap on the passenger window. It was Ward.

'Got a minute?'

I reached across and pushed open the door for her to get in. I hadn't seen her since her press statement had been hijacked by Oduya, and I was struck now by how tired she looked. There were shadows under her eyes and lines on her face I couldn't recall seeing before. She eased herself into the car seat with a sigh, awkward because of her stomach.

'Nice to take the weight off my feet. I'm not staying long, just wanted to see how you were getting on.'

I gave a shrug. 'So far, so good, I suppose. We haven't found anything else yet.'

'Please God. I'd like one day when we're not making new headlines. How are you getting on with our resident demolition expert?'

'Jessop? I can't say we've spoken that much.'

'Very diplomatically put. I hear he's not the most enthusiastic member of the team.'

'Let's say I think he'd rather be knocking the place down than working in it.'

'Can't really blame him. All these delays must be costing him a fortune. If he wasn't such an awkward sod I'd feel sorry for him.' She shifted in her seat, trying to find a more comfortable position. 'Have you spoken to your friend Mears recently?' She gave 'your friend' an ironic emphasis.

'I saw him at the mortuary yesterday. He said he'd found burns on both victims.'

'Oh, it's a bit more than that now. He thinks they could be brands.'

'Brands? As in cattle brands?' That was news to me.

'Or something similar. They're only small and they were difficult to spot, given the state the bodies were in. But he says a naked flame would have left a lot more charring to the skin. He thinks someone used something like a soldering iron on the victims. Something hot enough to scorch the bone but only cause localized burns.'

'Hang on, the burns penetrated to the *bone*?'

Ward nodded. 'Doesn't bear thinking about, does it? He hasn't examined the larger victim yet, so for the moment we're still assuming it's probably male. But he's confirmed the other victim was a woman in her late thirties or early forties. And he's found marks on her skeleton that correspond to the scorching on her skin.'

Christ. I was still trying to think of anything that could burn so deep without causing much more visible damage to the epidermis. Small or not, I hadn't noticed any burns when I'd seen the remains in the concealed chamber. I could tell myself that it had been dark and I'd only had the chance to take a brief look, and even then only from a couple of yards away.

But still.

'It gets better,' Ward went on grimly. 'The post-mortem X-rays showed fractures on the arms and legs of both victims. Only hairline, but it looks like someone gave them a real working over. Mears is speculating it might be gang or drug related.'

'Is he an expert on that as well?'

She smiled. 'No, but it's a reasonable theory. We know drugs were being dealt from St Jude's, and this has all the hallmarks of either a punishment or a revenge killing. Both victims strapped down and tortured and then bricked up while they were still alive. You can't tell me that doesn't sound like someone had a grudge.'

'Would a gang go to all that trouble?' Torture I could believe, but I couldn't imagine gang members taking the time and trouble to wall up their victims, even if they'd had the skills.

Ward rubbed her eyes with the heels of her hands. 'I said it was a theory, I didn't say it was perfect. But it doesn't make much sense to me either. If somebody wanted to make an example of them they'd have left the bodies somewhere obvious. And if they didn't, why take the risk of them being found when the building was pulled down?'

I'd had a similar conversation with Parekh. I didn't have an answer then either. 'Have you had any luck with the fingerprints from the paint tins?'

'No, we drew a blank on those, and the one left in the mortar. They're from the same person and probably male from their size, but nothing's come up on the data-base. So we could be looking at someone without a criminal record, which isn't much help.' She sounded flat, but then brightened. 'One bit of good news is that Mears managed to lift the victims' fingerprints.'

'You've identified them?'

'Not yet, but with the skin sloughed off I wasn't holding out much hope of getting any prints off the bodies at all. Mears might look like an undergraduate, but he knows his stuff. Get this – he soaked the skin from the hands in water to soften it and then used it like gloves.' She shook her head, impressed. 'Never heard of that one before.'

I had. It only worked in certain circumstances but I'd used the same technique myself on several occasions. Still, I had to concede it took skill when the body was as old and decomposed as this.

'Pity you couldn't do the same for Christine Gorski,' Ward went on, stifling a yawn. 'Might have saved us some embarrassment if we'd identified her sooner.'

'Her finger ends had been chewed by rats. She didn't have any viable fingerprints left,' I said, smarting at the comparison.

'I know, I'm not criticizing.' She paused. 'And there were definitely no burns on her? Nothing to suggest she might have been tortured as well?'

'I'd have told you if I'd found anything.'

'You're certain?'

I bit back the retort I'd been about to make and just gave her a look. Ward knew me well enough not to ask, and must have realized it herself. She nodded, acknowledging as much.

'OK, I was just making sure.' She glanced at her watch. 'I've got to go, but the reason I came over was to warn you there'll be visitors later. Christine Gorski's family want to see where their daughter was found.'

'Is that a good idea?' I asked, surprised.

'It's happening, whether it's a good idea or not,' Ward retorted, then sighed. 'Look, we were caught out by them turning up like that. It didn't exactly paint us in a good light, and now the body's been identified as their daughter we don't want to seem unsympathetic. They'll just be brought here to see what we're doing to find the people responsible for her death. We won't be taking them inside the hospital building, so there's no reason you should even see them. I'm just giving you prior warning so you know what to expect.'

She sounded as though she was trying to convince herself, and I could see why. Letting Christine Gorski's family visit St Jude's was a bad idea. They might not be under any illusions about the sordid nature of their daughter's death, but seeing the squalor of where she'd died for themselves wouldn't help them understand. Or bring them any comfort.

The whole thing smacked of a PR exercise. I knew Ward well enough to know she was unhappy herself, and guessed Ainsley was probably behind it. After the public debacle of her press statement, the commander would be keen to have something that would play well on TV.

It was only after Ward had left the car that I realized I'd missed the chance to tell her about Lola.

Chapter 15

THE AFTERNOON'S SEARCH started in the same way as
the morning's. After lunch, the team assembled
once more on the hospital's steps. The rain had started
again, not heavily, although the dark clouds promised
that could soon change. We sheltered underneath the
faux-Grecian portico, its fluted columns streaked with
bird droppings and graffiti. Not for the first time, it
struck me how much the entrance to St Jude's resembled
that of a mausoleum. Standing under the shadowed
gloom of the portico's roof, with the heavy doors opening into the dark interior, was like being on the threshold
of a tomb.

It wasn't the best association for a hospital.

Once again, we found ourselves waiting for Jessop.
The contractor had taken himself off when we'd broken
for lunch and had failed to come back. In a reprise of
that morning, Whelan looked at his watch with barely
suppressed irritation.

'Bugger this. We'll start without him.'

But he'd no sooner said it than the contractor
appeared, strolling with an almost insulting lack of
urgency from the direction of the portable toilets. He

was still fastening his overalls, frowning as he struggled to zip them over his gut.

'We've been waiting for you,' Whelan said, tight-lipped.

Jessop wriggled his thick fingers into a tight glove. 'I was taking a dump.'

'We were supposed to be starting ten minutes ago.'

'Yeah, well, I'm here now, aren't I?'

Whelan studied him expressionlessly, then spoke to the rest of us. 'You all go on up. Mr Jessop and I will be there in a minute.'

It took them slightly longer than that. We'd trooped back up to the top floor and were standing around at the top of the stairs. No one spoke, and only the Labrador was oblivious to the uncomfortable atmosphere. Footsteps echoing up the stairwell announced Whelan and Jessop's arrival, the big man lagging behind the DI like a reprimanded schoolboy.

'Right, let's get to it,' Whelan said, setting off down the floodlit corridor.

Pausing at the top for breath, Jessop stared after him sullenly but said nothing.

I can count on the fingers of one hand how often time has dragged while I've been working on an investigation. More often than not the opposite holds true, and I'll emerge from some task to realize the day's gone by without my noticing. Inside St Jude's, though, time seemed to congeal. There was nothing to do except slowly follow the dog along one endless corridor after another, searching empty rooms that all seemed to merge. I'd glance at my watch, convinced that an hour or more had passed, only to find that the hands had hardly moved at all.

But at least Jessop was behaving himself. Whatever Whelan had said to him seemed to have worked, although as the afternoon wore on his truculence began to reassert itself. There were several more false alarms that came to nothing, each one prompting mutterings and impatient sighs from the contractor. When the last one produced the fur and bones of another dead rat, his restraint finally broke.

'I thought these things were supposed to be trained?' he burst out, as the Labrador's handler rewarded it with the tennis ball again. 'My own dog'd do a better job than this! Can't it tell the difference between a dead body and a bloody rodent?'

'No, can you?' its handler shot back. She straightened, staring at Jessop as though daring him to criticize her dog again. The contractor appealed to Whelan instead.

'This is bollocks! How much longer are we going to spend farting around like this?'

The police officer spoke without looking at him. 'As long as it takes.'

'Oh, come *on*, we're just wasting time. There's nothing here!'

'Then the sooner we confirm that, the sooner you can bring your bulldozers back and start breaking things.'

'You think it's funny?' Jessop's bloodshot eyes seemed to bulge over his mask. 'While you all stand around with your thumbs up your arse, this is costing me money!'

Whelan regarded him. 'No, I don't think it's funny, Mr Jessop. I'm sorry if it inconveniences you but this is a murder inquiry. That takes precedence over your profit margin.'

'*Profit . . .?*' Jessop gave a bitter laugh, shaking his head. 'Jesus. You've no idea, have you?'

Whelan was saved from responding by his radio. Giving Jessop a baleful stare, he moved off to answer it.

Silence fell. The SOCOs exchanged glances with each other, and one of them looked at me and rolled his eyes. Indifferent to it all, the big contractor stood with his head bowed and shoulders slumped. He was shaking his head, grumbling to himself under his breath.

'You know what? Fuck it.'

Abruptly, he yanked down his hood and took off his mask. His face was flushed and sweating, thinning hair plastered to his head. His cheeks bore red lines where the mask straps had dug in.

'Whoa, you can't do that,' one of the SOCOs told him.

'No? Watch me. I've wasted enough time on this fucking place.'

He started back down the corridor towards the main stairs. Whelan's voice stopped him.

'Mr Jessop!'

The contractor slowed, then turned. His face was sullen and angry as the DI came over.

'That was the PolSA. Looks like one of the other search teams has found asbestos in the basement. You wouldn't know anything about that, would you?'

A change came over Jessop's features. He blinked, his mouth working as though silently trying out words. 'What? No, I didn't . . . I haven't . . .'

He trailed off. Whelan stared at him, then turned to the rest of us.

'OK, let's take a break.'

*

185

I sat in my car with the door open. A polystyrene cup of stewed tea steamed on the dashboard, slowly cooling. It was almost an hour since we'd come out of the hospital, and I was yet to hear when – or if – we were going back in again. A fine mist of rain speckled the windscreen as I took a drink of tea. Taking my time.

Something told me it could be a long wait.

Jessop had looked haggard as we emerged from the hospital into daylight, his face ashen beneath the whiskers. All his bluster had deserted him, as much an admission of guilt as any confession. His firm was supposed to have carried out a survey at St Jude's before any demolition work started. That should have included checking for any asbestos in the antiquated hospital, which, if found, would have to be safely removed. That was time-consuming and expensive and could only be carried out by a licensed company. At best, Jessop was guilty of negligence for missing it. At worst, he knew it was there and deliberately said nothing, which could mean criminal charges.

No wonder he'd been so desperate to knock the place down.

It left the police search of St Jude's in limbo, at least until the risk had been assessed. And possibly even longer, if the operation was suspended until the place had been made safe. Either way, it meant more delays until a decision was reached.

I climbed out of the car and stretched, debating if it was even worth staying any longer. I couldn't see anyone being allowed back inside for the rest of the day, and there were more interesting ways of passing an afternoon than sitting in a car park. I'd decided to try and find Whelan when I saw someone come out from one of the police trailers.

It was Jessop.

If anything, he looked even worse than before, as though he'd aged ten years in the space of an hour. I didn't want to talk to him, but I needn't have worried about him seeing me. He wasn't in any state to notice anyone just then. His walk was slightly stumbling, as though he'd lost coordination, and his face had a dazed expression. Watching him, I wondered if he was in shock. The question was answered a moment later. As he passed a line of police cars his legs suddenly buckled. He tried to support himself against one but only slid down it, sitting with a thump on to the wet tarmac.

I ran over. He made no attempt to get up, just stayed where he was with one arm draped along the car.

'Are you OK?' I asked. He stared at me without answering, blinking owlishly. It could be more than shock, I thought, looking around for help. 'All right, stay here. I'll go and get—'

'No!' Colour was coming back to his face now, a red flush starting in his cheeks. 'I don't want anything to do with those bastards.'

He started trying to haul himself up, leaning against the car for support. I hesitated, then put my arm underneath his to help him.

'Get off me,' he said dully.

But there was no feeling behind the words, and he didn't try to shrug me off. He was every bit as heavy as he looked, too heavy for me to lift on my own. He was already recovering, though. His grip on my shoulder was strong as he pushed himself upright, and after a brief wobble his balance was good. Probably just shock, then, I thought, as he let go of me and straightened on his own.

'Where are you parked?' I asked.

'I can manage,' he muttered, before adding, 'Over there.'

His car was an old Mercedes that in better condition might have been a collector's item. As it was, like its owner it looked like it was barely hanging on. Jessop could walk under his own steam now, but I stayed with him while he searched for his car keys and then unlocked it.

'You shouldn't drive yet,' I told him, hoping he wouldn't try. I didn't relish trying to get the keys off him.

'I'm all right.'

He made no attempt to get into his car, though. I was wondering if I should leave or stay with him when his shoulders started heaving.

'They've got rid of me,' he said, tears rolling down his grey-stubbled cheeks. 'Bastards have thrown me out. Said they're going to look at charging me.'

He'd been threatening to walk out anyway and done nothing but complain since we'd been there. And even if he hadn't known about the asbestos, his negligence had still put his own employees, as well as other people, at risk. But even though Jessop might have brought this on himself, he cut a pathetic figure now. As much as he might deserve it, I couldn't leave him in this state.

'Here, sit down.'

Opening the car door, the first thing I saw was a plastic container of orange juice in the passenger footwell. Lying next to it was a half-empty bottle of vodka. I'd already had Jessop down as a drinker. He'd smelled of alcohol that morning, and I'd noticed it still clung to him as I'd helped him to the car. I'd assumed it was in his system from the night before, never thinking he'd be stupid enough to drink in the middle of a police operation. Whatever pity I'd had for the contractor dried up. This wasn't just about making sure Jessop was all right any more. My wife and daughter had been killed by a drunk driver. I wasn't about to let one behind the wheel now.

The contractor sank heavily on to the car seat, facing outwards with his feet planted on the ground. He sat limply, his big hands dangling between his knees and a lost expression on his face.

'That's it. I'm fucked.' He'd stopped crying, at least. 'It's all gone. Everything. All of it, up in smoke.'

There was a beaten air about him. Then his expression hardened as he looked up at St Jude's.

'This fucking place. I wish I'd never set eyes on it. All that time and money, buying new plant, taking on more men. Jesus. I should've blown the fucker up weeks ago.'

I was looking round, half hoping to catch sight of Whelan or someone else who could intervene. There were a few white-clad figures at the far end of the car park, but none of them was looking this way.

'Why don't I call a taxi . . .?' I said, already knowing how that would go down.

He squinted up at me. 'What the fuck are you talking about? I don't want a taxi, I've got a car.'

His belligerence was back. I knew there was little chance of convincing him, and before I could try one of the trailer doors across the car park opened. With relief I saw Ward emerge with a group of uniformed senior officers. I recognized Ainsley, but it was only when I saw the civilians with them that I realized what was going on.

Oh, Christ.

I'd forgotten about Christine Gorski's family visiting St Jude's that afternoon. Her mother and father were leaning together for support as they walked, faces shell-shocked and etched with grief. They were smartly dressed, as though for church or a formal event. Their son was separate from them and off to one side. He wore jeans and walked with his head down and his hands thrust into his pockets, a noticeable distance between him and his parents.

The fourth civilian was Adam Oduya.

Even in his casual clothes, the activist still stood out more than the senior police officers around him in their crisp dark uniforms. The visit was clearly at an end. I was too far away to hear, but there were handshakes and earnest nods from the police officials. Then the group was breaking up, most of the police splintering off back to their cars. Ward and Ainsley stayed with Oduya and Christine Gorski's family, accompanying them as they walked away from the trailer.

Towards where I stood with Jessop.

They hadn't noticed us yet, and the contractor was facing away from them. Even so, it was only a matter of time. I looked around desperately, searching for some way to avoid what was about to happen. Their voices grew clearer as they approached, with Oduya's distinctive baritone carrying above the rest. Jessop's head came up as he heard it. He rose to his feet, his thick eyebrows knitting together as he saw the group.

'What's that bastard doing here?'

Until then I'd only been worried about the grieving family encountering the contractor. It hadn't occurred to me that Jessop would know Oduya. But the activist had been leading the campaign to save St Jude's, had been responsible for its stay of execution over the bats. And, after producing Christine Gorski's family in front of the press, his face had been all over the TV and news sites for the past twenty-four hours.

Jessop would definitely recognize the man responsible for the delays.

I put a restraining hand on his shoulder. 'You should get back in the car . . .'

'That fucker,' he breathed, glaring at Oduya.

I tried to block his path as he started towards them, but he pushed past me. His earlier weakness had been forgotten, replaced by adrenaline and anger. Knowing we were making exactly the sort of scene I'd wanted to avoid, I made one last attempt to stop him.

'Don't, that's her family . . .' I began, but he wasn't listening. Jessop was a big man, accustomed to using his bulk, and he shrugged me off as he strode out from behind his car.

'You!'

He stabbed a finger at Oduya. The group were already looking over, drawn by the disturbance. I saw Ward's eyes widen, while a look of cold fury compressed Ainsley's features. The others stared at us, confused. Including Oduya. Jessop might have good reason to know him, but the recognition was one-sided: the activist had probably never set eyes on the demolition contractor before.

'This is your fault!' Jessop spat, still closing the distance between them. 'Are you fucking happy now? Eh?'

Oduya looked bewildered. 'I'm sorry, do I know you . . .?'

'All right, that's enough.'

Ainsley came towards Jessop, athletic and impressive in his police uniform and peaked cap. The contractor ignored him.

'Do you know what you've fucking *done*?' he snarled at Oduya. 'All the grief you've caused? Who gives a fuck about a few bats or some junkie whore who—'

'I said that's *enough*!' Ainsley stepped in front of him, taking hold of his arm. 'DCI Ward, I want this man—'

I don't think Jessop intended to hit him, but the big contractor was past caring. He jerked free from Ainsley's grip, his arm flying up and striking the uniformed commander in the face. Ainsley's head snapped back, his cap falling off as he stumbled backwards. I could hear footsteps as police belatedly raced towards us. I ran to restrain Jessop, seeing Ward doing the same as Christine Gorski's family watched in shock.

But Oduya was closest of all of us. There was a look of concentration on his face as he stepped out to meet Jessop. As the bigger man lunged, the activist sidestepped and gripped his outstretched arm. Letting the bigger man's momentum carry him past, he swept the arm up and behind Jessop's back, locking it rigid. With an oath, the contractor stumbled, dropping to one knee with his arm extended painfully backwards.

'You need to calm down,' Oduya told him.

'Bastard! Get off!' Jessop gasped, trying to wrench free. In response Oduya twisted his arm higher.

'Don't make me hurt you.'

Ainsley had recovered from the glancing blow, but the police commander had lost his cap and his nose was bleeding. His face was tight with anger as he went to them. 'All right, we've got him.'

Other officers were rushing over as well. Oduya stepped back as Jessop was swamped by uniforms. He gave me a nod, not even breathing heavily.

'Hello, Dr Hunter.'

I returned the nod, still shaken. Whelan ran up, out of breath, as the bedraggled contractor was hauled to his feet. 'What the hell . . .?'

'Later,' Ward told him. She gave me a furious look before turning away. 'Mr and Mrs Gorski, I am so sorry . . .'

She was interrupted by a splashing noise. Standing in the background, forgotten by everyone, Christine Gorski's teenage brother bent double as he vomited noisily on to the broken tarmac. His face was chalk white as he slowly straightened. For a second he seemed on the point of saying something.

Then his legs folded from under him and he collapsed.

Chapter 16

THE LIGHTS CAME on automatically when I let myself into the apartment, lamps and uplighters steadily brightening to a warm glow. I supposed the mood lighting was designed to ease away the stresses and strains of the day, a touch of luxury to welcome you home. I just found it annoying and wished there was a switch I could flick on.

Dumping my aluminium flight case in the hallway by the front door, I took off my coat and went into the kitchen. Right then I didn't want to think very far past food and a drink.

Definitely a drink.

I opened the fridge door to see what there was to eat. After staring at the sparse shelves without any inspiration, I offered up a silent apology to Anja, took out eggs and cheese and set about making myself an omelette.

I might not have mastered the apartment's NASA-standard coffee machine but I'd learned how to operate the sound system. Setting it to play randomly, I poured myself a beer and took my plate over to the dining-room table, trying not to think about the empty seat opposite me. The mournful tones of jazz piano swelled from the speakers as I sat down. It wouldn't have been my first choice but it filled the silence. Good enough.

Taking a drink of beer, I tried to unwind.

It had been pandemonium after Christine Gorski's brother had collapsed.

There had been calls for medics and an ambulance, but I could see he was already starting to revive. It looked like he'd only fainted, probably just reaction or shock.

There was a lot of it going round.

Jessop had been quickly hustled away, the big contractor beginning to look more than a little shell-shocked again himself. Once she was satisfied that Luke Gorski was OK and being attended to, Ward had come over to me. Grabbing hold of my arm, she'd led me away.

'What the *fuck* was all that about?' she'd hissed.

I'd told her as much as I knew. She'd listened in silence, the skin around her nose white. When I'd finished she exhaled angrily.

'Couldn't you, I don't know, have kept him *away* or something?'

'I tried. You saw what happened.'

She'd screwed her eyes shut and massaged the bridge of her nose. 'Jesus, what a fuck-up.'

'So where does this leave the search?'

Ward had looked back towards St Jude's and shaken her head. 'I don't know yet. I need to talk to Whelan and the PolSA, find out what the situation is with the asbestos. We'll have to take it from there.'

'And Jessop?'

'God knows. By rights we could charge him with assaulting a police officer, but that's down to Ainsley. Jesus, Oduya's going to have a field day with this.'

'Will I?'

The mellow voice had come from behind us. Great timing, I'd thought, turning round to face the activist. Neither Ward nor I had noticed him coming over.

Ward had made an attempt to rally. 'Mr Oduya, on behalf of the inquiry, I can only apologize . . .'

He'd waved her off. 'Forget it. I know a bully when I see one. Whatever disagreements we might have over St Jude's, I'm not going to hold you responsible for the actions of a man like that. I'm only sorry Tomas and Sandra had to hear what he said. And Luke, too, of course.'

'Keith Jessop will be dealt with, and if you decided to press charges yourself then you'll obviously have our full support.'

'Thanks, but I'm not going to waste time on the Jessops of this world. Life's too short.' His eyes had crinkled in a wry smile. 'Besides, I'll be dining out on this for years. Getting assaulted while surrounded by police officers? I couldn't make that up.'

Ward had done her best to smile, but she wasn't in a joking mood. 'That's very gracious of you, Mr Oduya . . .'

'Adam. You can call me Adam.'

But that was going too far. She'd nodded, sidestepping the invitation. 'You'll have to excuse me, but I've got to see how Luke Gorski is.'

'Of course. I'll be there myself in a second.'

Ward clearly hadn't liked the idea of leaving him with me, but there wasn't much she could do about it. Giving me a warning look, she'd headed back towards where a paramedic was helping the teenager to his feet.

'Heartbreaking, isn't it?' Oduya had said, looking over. 'It was bad enough for them without this.'

'They shouldn't have come.'

I didn't try to keep the accusation from my voice. Oduya nodded heavily.

'I agree. I tried to talk them out of it. Tomas didn't want to, and you can see what it's done to Luke. But Sandra insisted, and I'm not going to argue with a mother whose daughter's been murdered.' It had been his turn to look at me. 'Anyway, thanks for what you did back there. I saw you trying to stop Jessop.'

'Not very effectively. That was quite a move you pulled.'

He gave a shrug. 'In my line of work it pays to know how to defend yourself.'

We'd watched as Luke Gorski was led, weakly protesting, to a waiting ambulance. 'Has he taken it hard?' I'd asked.

'Very. I think even his parents are surprised at how it's affected him. He and his sister don't seem to have been particularly close.'

Death could do that. Sometimes you only realized how much someone meant when it was too late.

'This isn't the right time, but there is something else I'd like to talk to you about,' Oduya had gone on. 'If I give you my word it's nothing to do with this case, would it be OK to call you to discuss it?'

I'd just been starting to let my guard down: now it snapped back up. 'So you could quote me as a known and trusted source again, you mean?'

He hadn't flinched. 'I did what I had to, I'm not going to apologize for that. And whether you meant to or not, your reaction did confirm the pregnancy. I'd do the same thing again if it meant a missing young woman's family could know what happened to her.'

He'd had a point. Although Christine Gorski would have been identified before much longer anyway, Oduya's intervention had ended her parents' uncertainty sooner. Even so, although I couldn't blame his motives, I still didn't like being used. 'Like you said, this isn't the time.'

'No, of course.' He'd given me a regretful smile. 'Perhaps later, then.'

It would be much later, if I had anything to do with it. Oduya's motives might be laudable, and it was hard to argue with results. But for him the end would always justify the means.

That made him a hard man to trust.

By the time I'd made a statement about the Jessop incident it had been late afternoon. There was no question of going back inside St Jude's. The entire search operation had been suspended because of the asbestos and wouldn't be resumed until the building was declared safe. I might not relish spending time inside the old hospital, but I didn't welcome yet another delay. First the loft, now the basement.

St Jude's sprang traps from every angle.

It had been too early to go back to Ballard Court, so with nothing better to do I'd called into the university. I hadn't checked my emails since that morning, and when I did I found another one waiting from Francis Scott-Hayes. The freelance journalist was becoming a nuisance, I'd thought, deleting it. Other than that, it was all routine stuff. Anything was better than spending an evening alone at Ballard Court, though, and it had only been when my stomach started growling that I'd reluctantly called it a day.

The reason for my restlessness wasn't only work. The truth was I missed Rachel. We'd both known she'd be out of touch for days and possibly longer, but her absence was starting to gnaw at me. I'd grown used to her being a part of my life. For the last couple of months we'd virtually lived together, rarely been apart for more than a couple of days at most. Knowing she was there had made the soulless apartment more bearable. For the first time in years I'd begun to think in terms of *we* rather than *I*.

Now I was having to get used to being on my own again.

Stop feeling sorry for yourself. She has a job to do. And so do you. Finishing the omelette and beer, I saw it was almost time for the late news. I washed and put away my few dishes, then took one of the ridiculously heavy crystal tumblers from a cupboard and poured myself a bourbon. I'd taken to drinking the occasional glass of Blanton's in memory of an old friend and had brought a bottle with me to the apartment. There was an extensive – and expensive – drinks cabinet, and the owner had said I could help myself. But that wouldn't have felt right. I was only there because Ward felt my own flat wasn't safe and, while I was grateful to Jason for arranging it, I didn't want to make myself too comfortable. Not when I didn't plan on staying.

Settling into one of the deep leather armchairs, I turned on the TV. St Jude's was again featured on the news, but it had slipped down the headlines. There was footage of the Gorskis being driven through the hospital gateway, their faces pallid ovals behind the smoked glass of the car, but it wasn't the lead story. No mention was made of the incident with Jessop, but that had taken place inside the hospital grounds, well away from media scrutiny. To his credit, Oduya evidently hadn't told the press, although I thought that was more from consideration for Christine Gorski's family than for the police.

Ward would still be relieved.

When the segment on St Jude's had finished, I remembered my bourbon. I reached for the glass and almost knocked it over as my phone rang. Hoping it might be Rachel, even though I wasn't expecting to hear from her again so soon, I quickly picked up. The number wasn't one I recognized, though.

'Is that Dr Hunter?'

The voice sounded familiar, but I couldn't place it. Disappointment made me irritable. 'Who's this?'

'It's, er, it's Daniel Mears.'

Mears? I couldn't think why the forensic taphonomist would be calling, let alone so late. 'What can I do for you?'

I heard him breathing. 'It doesn't matter. Forget it.'

'No, wait,' I said, before he could ring off. Now I really *was* curious. 'What's wrong?'

'Nothing's *wrong*.' The arrogance was back. And just as quickly gone again. 'Not as such, it's just . . . Could you come out to the mortuary?'

'You mean now?'

'Yes, I mean—' He stopped himself. 'If you wouldn't mind.'

Any thoughts of bourbon or an early night were forgotten. I sat up. 'Why, what's happened?'

There was silence. Finally, Mears found his voice.

'I need your help.'

Chapter 17

MORTUARIES ARE STRANGE places even during day-time. At night they take on a character all their own. Not because there's anything profoundly different then. There are few windows: for obvious reasons, most rely on artificial lighting. And, like hospitals, mortuaries are a twenty-four-hour business.

Yet, for all that, I've always felt that something still changes. Never noisy or bustling even at their busiest, at night mortuaries slow even more. The quiet that descends has a different quality, pensive and more hushed. Weighted, almost. The awareness of the silent dead who inhabit the building, their bodies laid out on metal tables or stored in cold, dark cabinets, seems heightened. Perhaps it's a primitive response to the fall of night coupled with the proximity of death which, on some instinctive level, we still baulk at. Or an effect of our body clock running down as we approach the small hours, a psychological and physiological protest at the disruption to its natural, diurnal rhythm.

Or perhaps it's just me.

My shoes squeaked on the floor as I walked down the corridor. A night-shift mortuary assistant told me where to find Mears, though not without a sniff of disdain when I'd explained who I was there to see.

'Rather you than me.'

Mears certainly knew how to make friends, I thought. *So why are you here?* I didn't owe the forensic taphonomist any favours, and I'd had a long enough day already. But I'd worked on cases before where egos had got in the way, and I knew how damaging it could be. Even if Mears and I didn't like each other, the investigation shouldn't suffer because of it.

Besides, I was keen to take another look at the interred victims' remains.

I found him in the small examination room the mortuary assistant had directed me to. The first surprise was that he was in full scrubs and wellington boots rather than a lab coat like the one I was wearing. Mears hadn't wanted to say over the phone why he needed help, but he should be well past the earlier stages of the examination process by now, when scrubs would be necessary.

He was leaning over a reassembled skeleton laid out on an examination table, carefully adjusting the position of one of the bones. He straightened when I entered, and I was shocked by the sight of him. His already pale face looked bone white, making the freckles and red hair more noticeable than ever. Unshaven and with dark rings under his eyes, he looked like he hadn't slept in days.

'Ah, you're here!' He sounded so relieved he was almost effusive. 'You made good time.'

At that time of night there hadn't been much traffic. I went over to the skeleton he'd been poring over. I knew from its relatively small size which one it was.

'This is the female victim?' I said, taking a pair of gloves from a dispenser.

'Yes, I, er, I was just finishing off.'

I couldn't see how there could be much left to finish. He'd carried out the same procedure as I had for Christine Gorski, disarticulating the bones and cleaning them of soft tissue before reassembling them for examination. It was a fundamental part of our work, a process that with practice soon became second nature. I was so familiar with it by now I could almost do it blindfolded.

Although, I had to admit, I'd struggle to improve on the job Mears had done here. The unknown woman's bones were pristine and laid out immaculately. Each one had been positioned exactly the same distance from its neighbour, virtually to the millimetre, as far as I could tell. It was an impressive piece of reassembly that could have graced the pages of any textbook, bestowing a symmetry no living skeleton would possess.

'Nice work,' I commented, pulling on the gloves.

Privately, I thought that degree of precision was unnecessary, but it would have been churlish to say so. And right then I was more interested in the dark marks I'd seen on the bones. The smallest was roughly the diameter of a thumbnail, while the largest – this one on the pubic bone – was the size of a small hen's egg. All were a yellowish brown in colour, like splashes of weak coffee on blotting paper.

I could also see hairline cracks on the left ulna and radius, the long bones of the lower arm, as well as on several of the ribs. Ward had mentioned fractures, but these weren't the sort of injuries I'd expect from torture or a beating. There were no radiating fracture lines from a single point of impact, or complete fractures where the broken ends had separated from each other. These looked more like they'd been caused by bending or shearing forces. And the bones of the skull appeared intact. If the victim had been beaten, her assailants had avoided her face.

Turning my attention back to the patches of discolouration, I picked up a right metacarpal, one of the slender bones of the hand. A dirty yellow blemish marred its creamy surface.

'So these are the burns? How many are there?'

'Thirteen. On the arms, legs, feet. Skull.' Mears was starting to regain his poise, either the compliment or the shop talk restoring his equilibrium. *Good.* 'All places where the bone was thinly covered by skin. I also found additional burning on the sloughed epidermis where there was no underlying bone, like the abdomen and leg muscles. Seems like they were inflicted at random.'

'And they're definitely burn marks?' They certainly looked like it, but the only way to be sure would be to take sections of the discoloured patches to examine under a microscope. I could see excisions in some of the bones where Mears had done just that.

'There's cracking at the microscale and the periosteum's been damaged,' he said, an edge creeping back into his voice. 'Given the discolouration as well, there's nothing else they could be.'

'Do you still think a soldering iron could have caused them?' I asked doubtfully.

'Or something like it, yes, without a doubt.' His confidence was growing now he could expound on familiar territory. 'I wondered about the end of a cigarette, because of the general size. But that wouldn't be hot enough. It would have to have been held in place for longer for the heat to penetrate to the bone, so it would have burned right through the skin. There was localized scorching to the epidermal and dermal layers over the bone, but that's all.'

That didn't make sense. I'd have expected heat so intense as to discolour the bone to cause far more damage to the overlying tissues, regardless of what was used. 'How localized?'

'Approximately the same size as the bone burns.' Mears was obviously feeling more like himself, enough for his smile to verge on condescending. 'That's why I think something that can focus intense heat into a small area, like a soldering iron, was probably used.'

That still didn't sit right with me, but this was Mears's case, not mine. And he sounded certain enough. I set the metacarpal back where I'd found it. 'Is it the same on the other victim?'

Mears reached out to adjust the bone I'd just put back, minutely altering its position until it was perfectly aligned with its neighbours. He didn't answer at first, and when I looked up I saw the blood had rushed to his cheeks.

'I, er, I'm not sure. I think so.'

'Can't you tell?' I asked, surprised.

'Yes, of course. I mean . . . not yet.' He cleared his throat. 'That's sort of why I called you.'

'OK, I can certainly give you a second opinion,' I said, still bemused.

I couldn't see why he was so flustered if that was all he wanted. There was nothing wrong with asking for another viewpoint if something wasn't clear cut. I'd done it myself on more than one occasion, particularly early in my career when I was still finding my feet.

But Mears shifted uncomfortably. Again, he fractionally altered the position of the phalange. 'Er, that isn't . . . I mean, it's not . . .'

He made a needless adjustment to a floating rib, then started to do the same to one at the other side. I put my hand on it to stop him.

'Why don't you show me what's going on?'

He nodded, still colouring crimson. 'Yes. Yes, all right.'

I followed him into the corridor, peeling off my gloves and dropping them in the bin on my way out. He went along the corridor and opened the door to one of the bigger examination suites. It was in darkness. Lights flickered on overhead, buzzing to life as he clicked a switch. I blinked at the sudden brightness, then saw what was waiting in there.

It was like something from a butcher's shop.

There were three stainless-steel examination tables in the room. Lying on the one at the far end was the second victim's body. It had been denuded of bulk soft tissue and a start had been made on disarticulating the connective tissues of its joints. The left foot had been separated at the ankle, and the lower leg had been neatly severed at the knee. The results bore a superficial resemblance to a butcher's block, but it was all beautiful, painstaking work.

But although cuts had also been made to the pelvic joint, these had been less carefully executed. This was a much bigger individual than the other victim, and the main joints correspondingly harder to sever. The creamy white ball and socket of the hip were exposed but still connected, the tough tendons and cartilage hacked at and torn as though someone had wrenched at them in a tantrum. A fine-bladed scalpel lay discarded on the table nearby, along with several larger knives. All were soiled and greasy from use, and I saw now that attempts had been made to cut through other joints before being abandoned.

I'd halted, taken aback when I saw the remains. Now I understood why Mears had called me. He should have been much further along than this. I'd expected the reassembly of the other victim to be almost finished. At the very least the bones should have been macerating by now.

I looked at Mears, at a loss. He attempted to draw himself up.

'I, er . . . I seem to have fallen behind schedule.'

That was an understatement. But I was less shocked by how long it was taking him as by *why*. He'd done a flawless job of cleaning and reassembling the woman's remains, so it was hard to see why this should be any different. Although the victim's larger size might make the physical aspects more difficult, that didn't explain the mess Mears had got himself into.

'What happened?' I asked.

'Nothing *happened*. It's, uh, it's just it's taking longer than I expected.'

'So why didn't you ask one of the assistants for help?'

Mears looked wretched as he struggled for an answer. 'I – I thought I could manage.'

I was beginning to understand what was going on now. I thought again about the female victim's skeleton, perfectly laid out in the other examination room.

Too perfectly.

'How long did you spend on the woman's remains?' I asked.

It was like watching a balloon deflate. He shrugged, trying to affect nonchalance. 'I don't know. You know how it is, you can't rush these things.'

No, you couldn't. But there was a world of difference between taking long enough to do something properly and wasting time. Parekh had commented on how methodical he was, and the reassembly of the woman's skeleton showed he was clearly a perfectionist. But that wasn't always a good thing. He'd let himself become too wrapped up in the minutiae of the first reassembly, obsessing over unnecessary details at the expense of the larger picture. Then, when he ran out of time, he'd panicked and made things worse.

'Does Ward know?' I asked, although I could already guess.

'No!' He looked horrified. 'No, I . . . I didn't want to bother her with it.'

Of course he didn't. And he wouldn't have been in any rush to tell his employers, either. Mears wouldn't have wanted to admit there was a problem, probably not even to himself. So he'd dug himself deeper and deeper into a hole of his own making, until he'd grown desperate enough to call me.

What puzzled me was that he'd allow himself to make such a basic mistake in the first place. It was the sort of mistake a rank novice would make, not an experienced . . .

I realized then. Mears was watching me, looking flustered and scared. And younger than ever.

'This is your first time on a murder investigation, isn't it?' I said.

'What? No, of course not!' But he avoided my eyes, and the flush on his face deepened even more.

'How many have you worked on?'

'Enough.' He shrugged. 'Three.'

'On your own?'

'That's beside the point.'

No, it wasn't. The pressure of a murder inquiry could be overwhelming. Not everyone was able to cope. And there was a huge difference between assisting someone and working a major investigation on your own. I could remember the first time it happened to me, the sweat-inducing fear that I would embarrass myself. No amount of training or study could prepare you for that.

This showed Mears's behaviour in a new light. Beneath the arrogance and bluster was a core of self-doubt. He'd been overcompensating to hide his inexperience.

'I was supposed to be accompanying Peter Madeley,' Mears blurted. 'There was some sort of falling-out, though, and he quit. There wasn't time for them to find anyone else, so I . . . I said I could do it.'

I'd heard of Madeley. He had a reputation as a solid forensic anthropologist, although I hadn't realized he'd joined the private sector. But this was beginning to make more sense. Talented or not, Mears hadn't been the first choice. He'd been a last-minute substitute to keep BioGen from losing their forensic services contract. No wonder I hadn't heard of him.

No one had.

I rubbed my eyes, thinking it through. Ward needed to be told if one of her forensic consultants wasn't up to the job. It might not be wholly Mears's fault, but someone untried and untested couldn't be entrusted with this sort of responsibility. There was too much at stake to take the risk. And it wasn't as though I owed him anything.

Yet he'd shown with the fingerprints – perhaps the burns, too – that he was competent enough. Perhaps even more than that. It was possible this was just a case of first-night nerves. If I went to Ward now he wouldn't only be thrown off the inquiry, it could permanently blight his career. I wasn't sure I wanted that on my conscience either.

Mears was watching me worriedly, chewing his lip. 'I'm not going to cover for you,' I told him. 'Ward has to know about this.'

'I'm sure she'd be too busy to—'

'She's the SIO. If you don't tell her I will.'

He looked away, but only as far as the butchered remains. His shoulders slumped. 'OK.'

'And if anything like this happens again, you need to tell someone. Don't try and bluff your way through.'

'It won't—'

'I mean it.'

His mouth clamped in a tight line, then he nodded. 'Fine. But it won't.'

I hope not. I looked at the wall clock and saw it was after midnight. I sighed.

'I'll go and change into scrubs.'

The larger victim's remains looked worse than they actually were. Mears's meltdown hadn't resulted in anything catastrophic. None of his hasty attempts to disarticulate the joints had resulted in cuts to the bone and there was no post-mortem trauma to the skeleton. The damage was purely to the connective and soft tissue, which would be discarded anyway. It was just shoddy workmanship born of panic and, while that was bad enough, no real harm had been done.

He was subdued and quiet as we set about removing the last of the bulk soft tissue from the man's body. Even though the underlying skeleton was far from fully cleaned, I could already see some of the bones bore the same yellowy-brown burns as were on the female victim. I would have liked the opportunity to study them more closely, but the priority now was to get them soaking so Mears could carry out a proper examination.

He worked painfully slowly, not so much from perfectionism now as nerves. For all his strutting, his self-confidence was a brittle thing. If he was going to recover from this, let alone be any use to the investigation, that had to change.

'Looks like a big individual,' I said. 'Have you any idea of stature?'

'I've estimated the height at a hundred and seventy-eight centimetres,' he said sullenly.

So, about five eleven. A little over average height for a male, but no giant. 'Any thoughts on gender?'

Determining if a badly decayed body was male or female wasn't always straightforward. If the genitals had decomposed beyond recognition then the only way to attribute gender was by examining the bones themselves. Even then it wasn't always easy, so it was unfair to put Mears on the spot.

But enough soft tissue had been stripped from these remains to reveal some skeletal characteristics, and I wasn't asking for a definitive verdict. He sighed, as though this was all rather tiresome.

'Well, obviously, I can't say for certain at this stage. But the brow ridges are pronounced and the mastoid is large and clearly projects. Taken with the overall stature and heaviness of the bones, I don't think there's much doubt he's male.'

I noticed that '*he's* male', suggesting that Mears had already made up his mind. That could be dangerous, though it was hard to disagree. The eyebrow ridges and bony protuberance of the mastoid process below the ear were usually reliable sex indicators. Although it doesn't always follow, sometimes things are exactly as they seem. We already knew that the smaller victim who'd been tortured and interred behind the false wall was a woman. It was reasonably safe to say that the person who'd died with her was a man.

Mears was beginning to work more fluidly, I noticed, wielding the scalpel and saws with more assurance. An abrasive manner and confidence seemed to go hand in hand for him, but that was OK. I'd rather him be obnoxious and functional than an affable liability.

I began to cut through the connective tissue around the left hip. 'What about age?'

He gave a listless shrug. 'Thirty-five to fifty, judging by wear to the teeth.'

'What sort of condition are they in?'

'Why don't you see for yourself?' he said truculently.

I didn't look up from what I was doing. 'Because I don't want to waste time checking something that's already been done. I'm assuming you *have* done it?'

'Of course I have! There's staining that suggests he was a smoker who liked coffee, and enough fillings to say he didn't look after his teeth but at least went to a dentist. Now, if you don't mind, I'm trying to concentrate here.'

I smiled under my mask.

Mears's confidence grew after that. He handled the physical aspects of the work with all the delicacy of a surgeon, and I could see why he'd come with such a glowing recommendation. Soon it was as though the panic attack had never happened. It wasn't long before his innate sense of superiority reasserted itself.

'You macerate at a higher temperature than I like,' he sniffed, as we placed disconnected bones to soak in vats of warm detergent solution.

'That's fine when there's time. You don't always have that luxury during an investigation.'

'Mm,' he said blandly. 'Each to their own, I suppose.'

Telling myself not to let him get to me, I flicked on the switch for the fume hood, letting the drone of the airflow drown him out.

But, ego restored, Mears had one last salvo to fire. We were in the changing room. The last of the victim's bones had been left to soak overnight, ready to be rinsed and examined by lunchtime the following day. Make that later today, I amended, seeing the time. I'd changed back into my own clothes, dropping the scrubs into the laundry basket before I left. Neither of us had said anything since we'd left the examination suite, and I'd wondered if Mears would want any help with the reassembly. It should be straightforward enough now but, given the chance, I'd like to examine the burn marks on the victims' bones more closely.

Mears showed no sign of offering, though. The silence stretched on between us. The forensic taphonomist didn't so much as look my way as he packed his things away in his flight case, as though ignoring me might wipe out his loss of face. It was only when I was putting on my coat to leave that he finally spoke.

'Well, thanks for the assist, Hunter.' He had his back to me and addressed me without looking round. 'I'll be sure to tell DCI Ward you helped out. Let me know if I can return the favour.'

I stared at him. *Thanks for the assist?* Mears still didn't look around, apparently preoccupied with fastening his shoes. I waited a moment, but that was obviously all he had to say. Unbelievable, I thought, letting the door swing shut behind me as I walked out.

It was after two in the morning and the streets were empty. I was fuming as I drove away. I should have let Mears sort out his own mess, I told myself, angrily crunching the gears. I didn't want gratitude but I hadn't expected him to revert to form so soon either. He was already rewriting what had happened, revising events into a more palatable version. By the time he told Ward – and I'd make damn sure now that he did – it'd probably sound like he'd done me a favour.

Still seething, I turned on to the cul-de-sac that housed Ballard Court and saw flashing blue lights outside. A fire engine was parked by the apartment block, its bulk out of place in the peaceful setting. The building itself seemed normal: there were no flames, and lights still shone in many of the windows. A few people were gathered in the grounds, some of them in nightclothes and dressing gowns, but they were already filing back inside.

No one tried to stop me as I went through the gates, which I took to be a good sign. I couldn't see anyone I knew in the straggle of residents filing back through the doors, so I pulled over by the barrier to the underground car park and got out of my car. The cool night air was fouled by a stink of burning plastic. I went over to where fire officers were gathered by the big tender. Two of them were rolling up a hose with a distinct lack of urgency, while the rest stood around chatting.

'What's going on?' I asked one of them, a woman whose curly hair crept out from beneath her helmet.

She gave me a wary look. 'Do you live here?'

'On the fifth floor.'

'You sure?'

'I can show you my keys, if you like. I've been working.'

'No rest for the wicked, eh?' But she relaxed. 'Sorry, nothing personal but we've already had to escort one of your neighbours away for being too nosy. She wasn't best pleased, but fires always bring out the weirdos.'

Thanks. 'What happened?'

She gestured towards the apartments. 'Some idiot tried to set fire to the bins. Not much damage, but the smoke carried up the chutes. Didn't trigger the sprinklers but it set off the alarm.'

There were discreetly hidden refuse chutes on every floor in Ballard Court, where residents could drop their bags of rubbish into the bins below. They would have acted like chimneys, funnelling smoke up to the residential levels.

'Who did it?'

'Kids, more than likely. Bloody stupid, whoever it was. At least a place like this has proper safeguards, but these days you'd think people would have more sense.'

You would, but they rarely did. Still, Ballard Court was lucky. As well as security that included electrically operated doors and a twenty-four-hour concierge, it had a state-of-the-art fire-safety system as well. The same couldn't be said for every block of flats.

'Can I go in?' I asked.

'No reason why not. The fire's out but we'll be here a while yet. And seeing as you're already up, there is one thing you could do.'

'What's that?'

She grinned. 'You couldn't stick the kettle on, could you?'

Chapter 18

THE WOMAN WAS a shadow surrounded by sunlight. Motes of dust floated in the air around her, barely moving flecks of light. I could only see her silhouette in the doorway, but I knew who she was. The knowledge froze my heart. Slowly, her face gained form and feature as she came nearer. Long, raven hair. Dark eyebrows above dead eyes and skin white as bone. Her beauty was terrifying. I wanted to scream, to run.

I couldn't move.

The full mouth was parted in a smile as she leaned towards me. I could smell her scent, a subtle, spiced musk. Her breath feathered against my skin as she put her lips to my ear.

'Hello, David.'

She was closer now, staring at me with a gaze so empty it burned. Knowing what was about to happen, I watched helplessly as she took out the knife. Its blade caught the sunlight.

'You let me go,' Grace said, and slid the knife into my stomach . . .

I jerked awake with a cry. A ghost-odour of musk and spice seemed to linger, but it was gone even as I searched for it. Gasping for breath, my heart thudded as I stared into the shadows in the bedroom. Outside the window it was still dark, but enough light came from the street below for me to see that the room was empty. I sagged, the tension draining from me.

Christ. What the hell brought that on? The glowing numerals of the bedside clock showed it was after five. Knowing I'd slept all I was going to, I threw back the duvet and stood up. Night-sweat cooled on my skin as I padded over to the window and looked down. The fire engine had gone, but there was still a faint odour of smoke in the air.

That was probably what had triggered the nightmare.

It was the first time in several days I'd had the dream, and I'd begun to think I'd left it behind. I passed my hand over my face, shaky with adrenaline. Dawn wasn't far off. Even as I stood there, a bird began singing from one of the trees outside. Within moments it had been joined by others, nature's chorus announcing a new day.

My feet sank into the thick-pile carpet as I went into the en suite bathroom and turned on the shower. I stayed under the steaming jet until the last vestiges of the dream had been sluiced away, then made sure by running the water cold for a few seconds.

Feeling more awake, I switched on the radio as I made breakfast. Scrambled eggs and toast, with coffee. I considered making an effort with the elaborate coffee machine but soon lost interest: instant was fine.

The memory of what had happened with Mears the night before continued to rankle, but less than it had. When it came down to it, I'd done it more for the investigation – and Ward – than him. Even so, once was enough. If he fouled up again he was on his own.

218

Rain beat against the window as I ate at the granite kitchen island. I still had the grainy, out-of-sorts feeling that comes from too little sleep, but I felt better when I'd eaten. And my mood improved more when there was no mention of St Jude's on the morning news. The story had obviously dropped from the cycle, which was no bad thing.

A muddy day was dawning outside as I washed my breakfast dishes. It was still early so I made myself another coffee while I considered what to do. It was too soon to hear when the search operation would resume, but it was unlikely to be that morning. Perhaps not even the following week, either. It all depended on how widespread the asbestos was and how quickly it could be made safe so we could go back into the hospital. Not long, I hoped: Jessop wasn't the only one who'd be frustrated by any more delays.

I could go into the department later, but since I had an unexpectedly free morning I might as well use it. The situation with Lola and her son had been preying on my mind ever since my last visit. They clearly needed help from somewhere, but I still hadn't settled on how to go about it. Lola wouldn't welcome any interference from me or anyone else, and I was reluctant to simply report them to social services. But she was clearly struggling to cope with her ill son on her own, and at her age that wasn't going to get any better.

Then there was the neighbour's story. The more I'd thought about it, the less credible it seemed, but it was something else that had been nagging at me. Another visit might help me decide if it was worth mentioning to Ward or not.

Assuming Lola would let me in.

*

The street of boarded-up terraces was even more dismal in the overcast morning. It wasn't raining but the air felt damp and the heavy clouds turned day into a grey twilight. I parked on the road outside Lola's house. There was light leaking through the slats of the window blind, so at least I knew she was home. It was possible she'd left it on for her son while she went out, but she hadn't bothered on the rainy evening when I'd given her a lift home. I had the feeling she'd view that as a waste of electricity.

As I climbed out of the car I glanced over at the neighbour's house. No lights or signs of life there, which was a pity. I'd have liked the chance to talk to her again.

I went to Lola's and knocked on the glossy front door, keeping my eyes on the window blind. Sure enough, after a few seconds the slats shifted as someone peered out. I held up the brown paper bag I was carrying, hoping curiosity would counter any inclination to leave me standing outside.

The slats closed, but nothing else happened. I looked up and down the semi-derelict street, telling myself this had always been a fool's errand. I raised my hand to knock again when I heard the latch being turned. The front door opened a few inches and then Lola's unfriendly face appeared over the chain.

'What do you want?'

'I brought you this.' I showed her the brown paper bag again.

She peered at it through the door, scowling. 'What is it?'

I opened the bag, not so much to let her see as smell what was inside. 'It's a roast chicken.'

I'd stopped off at an up-market delicatessen near Ballard Court. The prices were geared more to the neighbourhood's well-heeled residents than a relocated forensic anthropologist, but I'd shopped there a few times with Rachel. As well as artisan cheeses and cured meats, there was a glass-encased rotisserie on which slow-basted chickens turned, fresh each morning. The smell filled the street, and it had occurred to me that virtually all of Lola's shopping had been processed or canned. Certainly nothing like the still-warm chicken she could smell now.

I saw her nostrils twitch as the savoury odour of roast meat reached them. I wasn't proud of trying to manipulate an old woman, but I told myself it was for a good cause. Of course, she might just take it and shut the door in my face. In which case I'd at least know she and her son had some decent food.

She looked at the paper bag again. Then the door closed and I heard the ratchet of the chain being undone. It opened again, wider this time, and Lola reached out to take the carrier.

'Can I come in?' I asked, keeping hold of it.

She glared at me, but her eyes kept going to the bag. 'What for?'

I risked a smile. 'A cup of tea would be nice.'

I waited for the door to slam. It didn't. The small eyes scrutinized me, then Lola turned back inside, leaving it open. I followed before she could change her mind.

The fug of human waste and unwashed flesh enveloped me. Music was coming from an ancient CD player on the sideboard, some sort of faux-classical piano that competed with the slow ticking of the clock to set my teeth on edge. The house was as grimly chaotic as I remembered, a single overhead bulb giving off a sickly light that somehow made the stiflingly hot room seem cold.

The man in the single bed was watching me, his face slack but his eyes alert. There were flecks of food caught in his beard, while the plastic infants' cup, with a lid and non-spill spout, lay empty on the rumpled sheets. At the foot of the bed, the framed photographs of the boy he used to be stood facing him on the cabinet like a premature shrine.

'Hello, Gary,' I said. 'I've brought a few more groceries.'

The bag was plucked from my hand. Lola took it to the worktop by the overflowing sink and delved inside. Next to her, an electric kettle hissed as it heated up.

'There are a few other things in there as well,' I said, as she pulled out the chicken.

'I can see that,' she snapped, pausing to inhale the greasy foil wrapper before setting it aside. I had to hide a smile as she continued to forage in the brown paper bag, as engrossed as a child at Christmas. Poached salmon, a wedge of farmhouse Cheddar and a pork pie all joined the chicken on the worktop. It wasn't the sort of food a dietician would approve of, or that I'd have advised when I worked as a GP. But Lola and her son looked like they could do with a treat. Sometimes the soul needed feeding as well as the body.

I watched as Lola unwrapped the warm chicken and tore off a piece of skin with her fingers. She gave a little grunt of pleasure when she put it in her mouth, actually closing her eyes for a second as she chewed. I looked back at her son, wondering if he'd be able to enjoy it as well. He might not be able to eat solids, and I couldn't see anything like a food processor where his meals could be liquidized. Perhaps that was something else that needed looking at.

The kettle began to bubble on the worktop, mercifully drowning out the tinny piano music. Lola crammed another piece of meat into her mouth before wrapping up the chicken again. Sucking the grease from her fingers, she wiped them on her cardigan before turning to regard me.

'What're you after?'

You're welcome. 'I'm not after anything.'

'I'm not stupid. You didn't bring all this for no reason. If I was younger, I'd think you were trying to get in my knickers.'

'Well, I'm not.'

I kept a straight face, wondering what her son was making of the conversation. Lola made a wheezing noise, as though she was clearing her chest. I realized she was laughing.

'Don't worry, I'm not blind either.' The laughter died, as though switched off. 'I told you before, I don't want charity.'

'It isn't charity. I just thought you and your son might enjoy it.'

For some reason that was the wrong thing to say. Her face hardened. Behind her, the kettle switched itself off with a *clunk*. Lola stared at me a moment longer, then turned back to the kettle.

'You might as well sit down now you're here. Milk and sugar?'

'Just milk,' I said, taken by surprise.

The trilling piano music fought with the clock as I went to the small kitchen table. I was conscious of Gary's eyes on me as I pulled out a chair and sat down.

'You going back there again today?' Lola asked, pouring boiling water into mugs.

My mind went blank. 'Where?'

'St Jude's, where do you think?' She gave me a crafty look. 'I told you, I'm not stupid. I can tell you're not local, and there's no other reason you'd be hanging around this place.'

I'd ducked her questions before, when I'd seen her at the ruined church. But there didn't seem much point in being evasive any more.

'No, I'm not going there today.'

'You're not police, though.'

There was a calculation in the way she said it, as though she wanted it confirming. 'No.'

'So what are you? One of them forensic types? CSIs, or whatever?'

'Something like that.'

She nodded, satisfied. 'Thought so. You've got that look about you.'

I didn't know what sort of look she meant, but didn't ask. 'How about you?'

'What do you mean?'

The suspicion was back. 'You were collecting litter in the woods. Is that something you do regularly?'

'Not when the weather's like this. My sciatica's bad enough without falling in there.' She mashed the teabags against the sides of the mugs with a spoon. 'I like it in there, though. It's a change of scenery. You could be miles away.'

I knew what she meant. Surrounded by the mature woodland, the ancient church ruins seemed a long way from these run-down streets.

'So how long were you a nurse for?' I asked, hoping to steer the conversation to one of the reasons I'd gone there.

'Long enough.'

'Where did you work? You said it wasn't St Jude's.'

She glared at me. 'Why are you so interested?'

'I'm just making conversation.'

Lola favoured me with a dark look before spooning three heaped sugars into one of the mugs. 'I worked all over. You married?'

The abrupt change of subject caught me off guard. 'No.'

'You should be, man your age. Something wrong with you?'

I didn't want to get into my personal life, but I'd just been quizzing Lola about hers. 'I'm a widower.'

It's a sentence that can elicit all types of response, from embarrassment to sympathy. Lola's was none of them.

'How'd she die?'

Her tone was as disinterested as when she'd asked if I took milk in my tea. But at least I could answer without having to worry about it being awkward.

'It was a car accident,' I said, feeling the usual sense of unreality about it even now. 'What about you? Are you married?'

'I was. Still am, I suppose.' She gave a contemptuous shrug. 'My husband slung his hook years ago. Good riddance. Worked in the merchant navy so he was hardly here anyway, and when he was he was filthy drunk. Rotten bastard. He was a sod to my Gary sober, and when he'd had a drink he was even worse. We were better off without him.'

It was the most I'd heard her say. There was a stiffness about her actions as she took a container of milk from the fridge, as though she was self-conscious after her outburst.

'You got any kids?' she asked, pouring the milk.

'We had a daughter. She was in the car with my wife.'

Lola turned to look at me, the milk container poised in her hand. Then she set it down and began stirring the tea.

'You know what it's like, then. You put all your life and soul into them. Do your best, try to protect them. Then something happens, and that's it. All gone.'

She threw the teabags into the sink with a wet *slap*. I glanced over at her son, uneasy at having this conversation in front of him. His mouth worked feebly as he watched us. Right then I couldn't have said if I felt worse for him or for his mother.

'Don't mind him, I'm not saying anything he doesn't know,' Lola said. She turned to him. 'He knows what's what. Don't you?'

Her son stared at her.

'When did the stroke happen?' I asked, including her son in the question as Lola brought over the teas.

'It must have been . . . no, hang on.' She frowned, setting down the mugs on the table. The rim of mine was chipped and stained brown with old tannin and a film of grease glinted on the tea's surface. 'Must be eighteen months ago now. Came right out of the blue. No warning. One minute he was fine, the next . . .'

She went to the cabinet and picked up the largest of the framed photographs. It showed her and her son on a windswept seafront, hair streaming sideways with their coats buttoned up to the neck.

'This is my favourite. He was fifteen when that was taken. Southend,' she said, holding it out to show me. 'You can see what a big lad he was. Strong as an ox, my Gary. Always liked physical work. He could turn his hand to anything. Did all this kitchen himself. Plumbing, joinery, you name it.'

I studied the photograph to conceal the effect of her words. Her son stood with his eyes downcast, a large, overweight teenager with crooked teeth. His shy smile verged on apologetic. Next to him, his mother stared at the camera with a pride that was almost defiant.

'Is that what he used to do for a living?' I asked, with a glance at the man lying in the bed. His sunken eyes were on me, his mouth a wet gash in the beard. The gulf between the hulking teenager and the wreck he'd become was shocking.

'He didn't get paid for it, if that's what you mean. Not with all them bloody foreigners taking all the work.' She set the photograph back in its place. 'He could have, if he'd pushed more. But he never would. Too soft, that was his problem. I used to tell him he should stand up for himself, not let people . . . Well. That's by the by.'

It had the sound of an old complaint, but by then I'd noticed something else. I'd been looking at the rest of the photographs, paying them more attention this time. In one of them her son looked to be in his late teens. He stood by the same fireplace in the room where we now were, wearing a royal-blue top over black trousers. It was a variation of a uniform I'd seen daily before I'd switched careers from medicine to forensics.

I nodded towards it. 'Did Gary use to be a hospital porter?'

'He had a lot of jobs,' Lola snapped. 'What's it got to do with you anyway?'

'Nothing, I was—'

'It's time you went.' She stood up, her face hard. 'I need to get him cleaned up.'

I got to my feet as she went to the door, knowing I'd gone too far. She opened it and stood back, holding it for me to go. I paused in the doorway, reluctant to leave on such a sour note.

'Thanks for the tea. I can get you some more shopping if—'

'I don't want nothing.'

She was already closing the door, forcing me to step out on to the pavement. Her son gave a low moan.

'And don't you start . . .' I heard her say before the door shut in my face with finality.

I looked around. The skinny cat was watching me indifferently from the same windowsill as before, but otherwise the street was empty. My mind was in a turmoil as I went back to my car. I had the sense of having done something irrevocable, though good or bad I'd no idea. I drove until I was a few streets away and then pulled over. I'd gone to Lola's concerned for the welfare of an old woman and her incapacitated son, and hoping to disprove the rumour that she'd been responsible for a patient death. Instead I'd learned that Gary Lennox had been a hospital porter with a knack for DIY.

I wondered if his skills extended to building a false wall.

I told myself not to get carried away. For all I knew, he might not even have worked at St Jude's and all this could be just a coincidence. His mother had said he'd had his stroke a year and a half ago. That would rule him out of Christine Gorski's murder, since she'd only been missing for fifteen months when we'd found her body.

But we couldn't say for sure when the two interred victims had died. And there was no longer any question of not wanting to waste Ward's time: she needed to know about this.

I took my phone out to call her and jumped when it rang. It was Whelan.

'We're back in,' he said.

Chapter 19

ANY ILLUSIONS I might have had that Ward would be pleased to hear about Gary Lennox were soon dispelled. After I'd briefly explained to Whelan, the deputy SIO had sworn under his breath.

'She's going to want to talk to you,' he'd said.

It wasn't far from where Lola lived to the hospital, but the road layout meant I had to take a meandering route. Whelan hadn't said much, only that the cadaver dog search was being resumed. That was sooner than I'd expected, so either the asbestos scare was a false alarm or it wasn't as bad as they'd thought. The press pack outside St Jude's had thinned, reduced to a token presence now the investigation had slipped out of the headlines. Traffic was sparse, but as I drove up to the main gates a lone bus was coming the other way. A solitary passenger waited at the bus stop but made no attempt to flag it down as it went by. It was only as I saw his hooded top as I turned into the hospital driveway that I registered who it was.

It was the same man who'd stepped out in front of my car, too engrossed with what was happening at St Jude's to look where he was walking.

I'd seen him at the bus stop before, I realized. Not that there was anything wrong with that, except that he'd just let the bus go past. *You're getting paranoid.* After what had happened at Lola's I was probably a little twitchy. I slowed to a stop and wound down my window as one of the police officers at the gates came over. It was the same round-faced young woman who'd been on duty the other times I'd been there.

'Back again?' she said cheerfully. 'OK, go on through.'

I smiled but didn't drive on. 'Do you know how many buses run along here?'

She gave a nonplussed smile. 'Just one, I think. Every hour. Why?'

Let it go. I tapped my fingers on the steering wheel, looking in the rear-view mirror. The bus stop and its sole occupant were out of sight.

'It's probably nothing, but I've seen the man across the road here before. Late teens or early twenties. He's just let the bus go past.'

'Probably nothing better to do. Not much else happening round here if you're out of work.'

I nodded, wishing I'd not said anything. But now she was looking across the road, taking a few steps backwards to get a better view.

'Can't see from here.' She turned to the other policeman on gate duty. He looked old for a uniformed PC, unfit and nearing retirement age. 'Hey, Carl, mind holding the fort for a couple of minutes? I'm going to check out somebody across the road.'

'Want me to go?'

She grinned. 'I don't think you can walk that far.'

I got out of the car, moving so I could see across the street. The young officer started across the road but the hooded man at the bus stop had started walking away as soon as he saw her approaching. She watched him go, then turned around and came back.

'Doesn't want to say hello.' She shrugged. 'Could be a junkie waiting for us to clear out. We'll keep an eye out in case he comes back.'

'Fat chance,' the older officer said. 'He'll make himself scarce now you've scared him off.'

'Good job he didn't see you then, he'd have run a mile.'

The banter had an ease to it, the familiarity of people used to spending long hours in each other's company. At least I'd broken the monotony for them, I thought, driving away from the gates.

Ward was in the trailer where the briefings had taken place. Whelan was with her, along with Jackson, the search adviser, and several other officers I didn't recognize.

'Come in, we're done,' she told me, waving me inside when I hesitated in the doorway.

Jackson nodded to me as he went out, while Whelan gave me a look I couldn't decipher. Ward was sitting behind a table, plastic stacking chairs scattered in an uneven row around it. They weren't designed for comfort at the best of times, and her pregnancy didn't help. She looked cramped and awkward, but I didn't think that was the reason for her bad mood.

'Sit down.' She sounded tired and irritable, her face puffy and ringed under the eyes. A disposable cup of what smelled like mint tea stood on the table in front of her, the teabag's string still dangling down its side. She waited until I'd taken a seat. 'Jack tells me you've been busy.'

I told her about Lola and her son, beginning with the accidental encounter in the woods behind St Jude's and ending with what had happened that morning. Ward stared into her tea as I spoke. Only when I'd finished did she look across at me.

'So why is this the first I've heard about it?'

'It didn't seem important until now.'

'Since when has it been your job to decide what is and isn't important?'

'It was uncorroborated gossip. I only found out about Gary Lennox an hour or so ago, and I would have told you straight away if Whelan hadn't called first.'

'You shouldn't have been at their house anyway. What the hell did you think you were doing?'

I'd never seen her so angry, but I wasn't happy about this either. 'Visiting an old woman and her son who're struggling to cope,' I shot back. 'If I'd known about any of it sooner I'd have done things differently, but I didn't. Would you rather I'd just ignored them?'

'Right now, yes! And this had better not be a backdoor way of getting social services to help them out.' She held up a hand to stop me as I started to object. 'All right, that's not fair. But you shouldn't be talking to potential witnesses, let alone possible *suspects*, behind my back. Oduya was bad enough, but after this I'm starting to wish I'd let Mears . . .'

She didn't finish, but she didn't have to. 'Let Mears what?' I demanded. 'Examine Christine Gorski as well?'

Good luck with that, I thought, furious. After the mess he'd got into with just two victims, God knew what he'd have done faced with the responsibility of all three.

But I couldn't say that without making the situation worse. And Ward seemed to be regretting her loss of temper as well. She made a visible effort to rein herself back.

'OK, let's both calm it down. I know you didn't do it deliberately. And I appreciate you offering to help Mears like you did.'

I thought I'd misheard. 'Sorry, say that again?'

'Don't get me wrong, I know it was well meant. But Mears is a big boy, he doesn't need any help. You should stick to your own responsibilities in future.'

Jesus. 'What exactly did he say?'

'Just that you'd stopped by the mortuary and offered to lend a hand. He wasn't complaining, as such. He was very polite about it.'

I bet he was. I tried to keep a lid on my temper. 'You seriously think I'd just "stop by" the mortuary at eleven o'clock at night?'

Ward studied me for a moment. 'OK, probably not. But whatever's going on between you two, either sort it out or keep it between yourselves. We've enough problems as it is without the pair of you getting into a pissing contest.'

I didn't trust myself to respond to that. *Bloody Mears.* 'So do you still want me on the cadaver dog search?'

'If I didn't, you wouldn't be here. I just want you to stop all these extracurricular activities you seem to find.'

'I don't go looking for them.'

'Maybe not, but they seem to find you anyway.' She sighed. 'Look, we're under a lot of scrutiny. *I'm* under a lot of scrutiny. Ainsley's still furious about yesterday, what with Jessop kicking off and then Luke Gorski nearly passing out.'

I was glad to get back on to less contentious ground. 'How is he?'

'If you mean the brother, it was just a faint. He was visiting the place his sister was murdered, he's entitled to be a bit overwrought. The point I'm making is that we've had enough cock-ups already, some self-inflicted, some not. I don't want any more, OK?'

I had the impression there was something about Luke Gorski that Ward wasn't saying. I knew when to take a hint, though: I was on thin enough ice already.

'So what happened with the asbestos?'

Ward massaged the back of her neck as she answered. 'There's an old service tunnel in the basement that used to link the hospital to the morgue. That's been knocked down, but the tunnel's still there, and now it turns out there's asbestos in the ceiling. It should have been removed before any demolition work started, but as far as we can tell it's only in the tunnel. We can cordon it off for now, so providing everyone wears masks and protective gear down there it shouldn't be a problem.'

I'd seen the remains of St Jude's morgue around the back of the main building, now just a mound of bricks and concrete overgrown with weeds. The tunnel would have been to transfer patients' bodies to it from the hospital, well away from public view.

'Did Jessop know about it?'

Ward's smile was hard. 'He says not, but I don't believe that for a second. We've found out he lost his licence for asbestos removal six months ago. Some foul-up over red tape because he didn't fill in the right forms, or something, which doesn't surprise me. But it meant another company would have been brought in to remove it, which would probably have lost him the contract. At the very least it would have caused delays and he couldn't afford that. He'd pared his costs down to the bone to win the tender, even re-mortgaged his house to buy new equipment. It'd have ruined him.'

'There were delays anyway,' I said.

'That's his problem,' Ward said unsympathetically. 'I'm more bothered about how it affects the investigation. And it makes me wonder what else he might have done.'

'Like what?'

But she shook her head. 'Never mind. I need to get on.'

She heaved herself to her feet, grimacing and rubbing her lower back.

'How are you?' I asked, standing up as well.

'This, you mean?' Ward rested her hand on her stomach. 'Peachy. My back aches, my bladder's got a mind of its own and I've got this pain-in-the-arse forensic consultant who won't do as he's told. Other than that, everything's great.'

'Business as usual, then.'

'Pretty much.' Her smile died. The tension between us had thawed a little but it hadn't gone completely. 'Seriously, we can't afford any more cock-ups. *I* can't afford any more. Let's keep our focus, shall we?'

I didn't think I'd ever lost it, but I wasn't about to argue. 'Can I at least ask what's going to happen with Lola and her son?' I chanced as we left the trailer.

'We'll look into it.' Ward's tone seemed to end the conversation, but then she paused. 'This Lennox and her son, do they have a dog?'

'I didn't see one.' I was about to ask why, then I realized. There were dog hairs on the tarpaulin that Christine Gorski's body had been wrapped in.

'OK, I just wondered,' Ward said.

Her expression was thoughtful as she walked away.

*

Back inside St Jude's again, it was as if I'd never left. Shut off from the outside world, the old hospital seemed to exist in a bubble all its own. Its interior hadn't seen fresh air or sunlight for years, and the dankness seemed to have soaked into its stones. Not even the Labrador was immune to the oppressive atmosphere. The animal had taken to whining more often, looking to its owner for reassurance before venturing into yet another dark corner. Even the well-chewed tennis ball it was rewarded with seemed to have lost its appeal.

But at least we were making better time. By late afternoon we'd finished searching the rest of the top floor and were well on with the middle. There'd been fewer false alarms down here, perhaps because this floor was less accessible to any birds and rodents from the loft. Armed with power tools and an endo-scope, another SOCO had replaced Jessop in case any suspect walls were found. So far, they hadn't been.

We'd got as far as the hospital chapel when Whelan received a call.

'They've found something in the basement,' he said, coming back over 'No need for the dog, I'll just pop down to take a look with Dr Hunter.'

'Don't they want the dog to check it out as well?' I asked, my voice echoing as we went down the stairwell.

'Not this time. It's hard to get at but they can see it.'

'See what?'

'They think it's an arm.'

Hospital basements are a world unto themselves. They're its beating heart, home to the unseen boilers and pumps that keep the building alive. Even though St

Jude's had been a corpse of a building for years, this netherworld remained intact. Like the fossilized organs of some long-dead beast, the mechanisms that had kept it warm and breathing still remained.

It was the first time I'd been down there, and the difference could be felt immediately. The smell of damp and mould became stronger as we descended the stairs. If I'd thought the upper floors were bad, this was even worse. Upstairs had been the hospital's public face, where over the years cosmetic attempts had been made to disguise the building's antiquated roots. Down here, away from the gaze of any patients, there was no need for such efforts. It was in its basement that St Jude's showed its true age.

There were no long, sweeping corridors. Instead, the stairs ended at the junction of a warren of narrow brick passageways where ducting and pipework clung to walls like angular intestines. Cold and damp as the upper floors were, at least they had some ventilation. Surrounded by earth on all sides, unheated and shuttered for years, the basement had become an aquatic environment. Water dripped from the ceiling and pooled on the floors, beading and trickling like clammy tears down the walls.

'Lovely, isn't it?' Whelan said.

We followed the spaced-out floodlights that ran off down one of the passageways, splashing through the puddles that reflected their glow. Every now and then we'd have to duck under some low pipe or duct. Once upon a time this place would have fairly hummed with boilers, pumps and fans, the background rhythm of the hospital's pulse. Now it was silent except for us.

After a few minutes we came to a service-lift shaft, where folding metal doors were pulled back to reveal a refuse-strewn interior. A little further along was the rectangular opening of a passageway, dank and unlit. It had been cordoned off with a diagonal cross of yellow tape, from which hung a sign warning *Danger! No Entry!*

'Is that where you found the asbestos?' I asked. Ward had told me it was in a service tunnel that linked the hospital to the morgue.

'Don't worry, it's at the far end. Some of the ceiling came down when the morgue was demolished. The passageway's all blocked off with rubble so you can't get through to the morgue any more. Not that one, anyway.'

I didn't know what he meant, but then he went to a set of double doors near the passageway entrance. A sign was fixed above them that looked as old as the hospital itself. It bore a single word, so faded it could only just be made out.

Morgue.

'There were two morgues?' I said, looking back at the cordoned-off opening.

He nodded. 'This is the original. The passageway leads to a bigger one they built in the 1960s. It can't have been worth stripping out the old fittings all the way down here, so they just left it. Out of sight, out of mind.'

That could have been St Jude's motto. Whelan pushed open the doors, revealing a scene from a history book. Lit by police floodlights, the ancient morgue resembled a filthy museum exhibit, unchanged in a half-century or more. Three porcelain post-mortem tables stood side by side in the middle, coated with dust and grime. Hanging above each of them were oversized light fittings, conical metal shades from which bristled ancient, twisted wiring.

Rusted taps spouted over dry, cracked sinks, while at one end the heavy doors of a body-storage cabinet hung open like a giant refrigerator to reveal empty shelves.

The entire morgue was a relic from the past. The hospital had simply closed the doors and forgotten all about it, leaving a time capsule of mortality to silently gather dust. Turning away from the husks of dead spiders that lay curled on the crazed ceramic tables, I went to see what the search team had found.

They were in a small office at the far end, ghostly in their white suits. Inside was a metal desk, behind which lay a broken chair. Everyone was gathered around a huge rusted filing cabinet that was canted at an angle against the wall. I recognized one of them as Jackson, the police search adviser.

'It's on the floor behind the cabinet,' he said. 'The thing weighs a ton and it's been fixed to the wall. We wanted you to see it before we tried moving it.'

'Let's have a look.' Whelan knelt down and shone his torch into the narrow gap between the wall and cabinet, peering to see behind it. 'It's an arm, right enough. Dr Hunter, do you want to take a shufti?'

He straightened, stepping away so I could take his place. I'd been looking around the rest of the room, listening for something that should have been there. Chalking up its absence, I went and crouched down by the filing cabinet.

It was difficult to see into the narrow gap. Pipework ran behind the cabinet, and at first I couldn't make out what else was there. Then my torch picked out something pale. Covered in dirt, the hand was lying palm down with the fingers half curved, a slender wrist and forearm extending beneath the cabinet.

'No sign of blood or any discolouration,' I said, pressing my face against the wall in an attempt to see more. 'Doesn't look like much decomposition either.'

'Can't have been there very long, then,' one of the search team said.

'Well, it's got to have been at least a week,' Whelan commented. 'Nobody could have got in after we showed up. It's pretty cold down here, though. Could that have preserved it?'

'Not to that extent.' I put my face to the gap and sniffed. My mask got in the way, but there was no discernible odour.

'Might be embalmed,' another search-team officer offered. 'Maybe it was a specimen or something that got left behind.'

'How the hell do you leave an arm behind?' Whelan asked irritably. 'And that'd mean it had been here for years.'

'I think it has,' I said. I'd wondered about embalming as well, but I couldn't smell any trace of embalming fluid or formaldehyde either.

Getting to my feet, I crossed to the other side of the cabinet, trying for a better view. From there, concealed behind the cabinet like another pipe, I could just make out that the arm ended below the elbow. A neat, straight cut, without any ragged edges or torn skin.

'Have any of you noticed any flies?' I asked.

No one had. A freshly severed arm would have attracted them in droves, even down here. Unlike the room upstairs, there was no false wall to keep them out, yet the old morgue was blessedly free of the droning insects.

Sliding my hand down the gap between the cabinet and wall, I gently touched the top of the arm.

'Should we get Dr Parekh out to take a look?' Whelan said uneasily.

'There's no need.' Reaching further in, I took hold of the arm by the wrist and gave it a hard tug.

'Whoa!' Whelan yelled.

But the arm had already slid free from behind the cabinet in a shower of rust. I examined the blunt end where the forearm ended below the elbow, then rapped it against the filing cabinet. It made a solid *clunk*.

'It's plaster,' I said, holding it up so they could see for themselves. 'I don't even think it's a medical prop. Looks more like an old shop mannequin.'

Whelan took the dummy arm from me, turning it as though not entirely convinced even now.

'Bad case of rigor mortis, sir,' one of the search team commented.

Whelan gave him a baleful look and slapped the arm against the man's chest. 'Funny. Next time you call us all the way down here for nothing I'll jam it up your backside.'

He set off back through the old morgue without waiting for me.

Chapter 20

THE NEXT DAY started promisingly enough. I'd slept well, with no further call-outs from Mears to disturb my night. I'd gone to bed in a better frame of mind anyway, after receiving an unexpected call from Rachel. The research boat had made an unscheduled stop at an island due to bad weather. The mobile coverage was non-existent so she was calling from a public landline.

My mood had instantly brightened at hearing her voice. There was a hollowness to the line and a slight delay.

'How is it over there?' I asked.

'Well, yesterday we were tagging a pod of bottle-nosed dolphins and spent the night anchored off an uninhabited island. Then this afternoon there was a terrific thunderstorm, so we've been in a taverna most of the evening.'

'Sounds awful.'

'It's a nightmare. How about you?'

'Oh, the usual.'

'The usual,' she echoed. 'There's no internet out here, but Dimitri picked up a two-day old *Times* this afternoon. I read they'd found more bodies in that old hospital. That's the case you're working on, isn't it?'

'We're coming to the end of it.' I didn't want to talk about St Jude's. *Dimitri?* 'Do you know how much longer you'll be out for?'

'Another three weeks at least before we're due back at the mainland. But we'll be making stops at a couple of bigger islands, so I won't be out of touch all the time. Honestly, we have to come out here sometime. I can't tell you how *blue* the sea is . . .'

She tried, all the same. I was content to listen, enjoying hearing her. All too soon I heard someone calling her in the background. 'Yeah, coming,' she said to whoever it was. 'Got to go. I'll call you in a day or two. Just be careful, OK?'

'You're the one in the middle of the Aegean. I'm stuck in London.'

'I know, but . . . Let someone else take the risks this time, OK?'

I knew she was thinking back to what had happened earlier that year, when her sister had been murdered and Rachel and her surviving family had almost lost their lives. That sort of trauma didn't just disappear, regardless of how blue the sea was.

'I'm surrounded by police. The only risk is catching cold from standing around all day,' I told her.

There was a pause. I could almost see the pensive 'v' between her eyes. 'OK, but—'

The same voice as before called something in the background. I couldn't make out what, but it was male, deep and richly accented.

'If that's Dimitri, tell him to wait,' I said.

Rachel laughed, the mood of a moment ago apparently lifted. 'No, that's Alain.'

'There's an Alain *and* a Dimitri?'

'What can I say? It's a multinational crew,' she said, still laughing. 'And some of them are waiting to use the phone, so I really have to go. I'll speak to you soon.'

Buoyed up by talking to her, I'd celebrated with a glass of bourbon to make up for the one I'd missed the night before. Warmed by the phone call and the drink, I could have believed that what I'd told Rachel was true, that the St Jude's investigation was coming to an end. The fingertip search hadn't uncovered evidence of any more victims, and there wasn't much more of the basement left to check. While the warren of narrow passages and ducting would take the cadaver dog longer to work through, another couple of days should see us finished as well. When I finally went to bed, I was already letting myself think that there was nothing else to find, that the old hospital had relinquished the last of its secrets.

As though encouraging that view, the sun was back out that morning. It had the thin, hard-edged quality of autumn rather than the summer heat of little more than a week before, but it was a welcome change after the recent grey clouds and rain. I actually felt optimistic as I drove to St Jude's. Pulling up at the cordon by the gates, I saw that the bus stop across the road was empty. It seemed a sign that things were going to run more smoothly from now on, and as I parked outside the hospital even the sight of the bleak walls and boarded-up windows failed to dim my mood.

It didn't last.

Whelan was waiting as I pulled up. 'Don't bother getting changed. The SIO wants to see you.'

What have I done now? 'Why, has something happened?'

'I'll let her tell you herself.'

He still hadn't forgiven me for catching him out with the mannequin's arm. The hospital cast long shadows across the tarmac as I went to the same trailer where I'd had the conversation with Ward the previous day. A briefing had just finished. Officers were filing out, along with people in casual clothes who clearly weren't police. I stopped outside and waited for Ward to emerge. She did, business-like in her flapping mackintosh and shoulder-strapped briefcase. Seeing me, she motioned for me to walk with her.

'Glad you made it in time. You can ride with me.'

'Ride where?' Now I really was confused.

She didn't slow, keeping up a brisk pace towards the parked police vehicles. 'Didn't Jack tell you? We're going to arrest Gary Lennox.'

Ward gave me the details in the car. After our conversation, she'd had her team dig into Lola's son's background.

'You were right about Lennox,' she told me, as we pulled away from the kerb. 'He worked as a porter at St Jude's from when he was eighteen. He was sacked the year before it closed, but he'd know the hospital layout like the back of his hand. Before that he took a City and Guilds in Construction. He struggled with the classroom side of things so he didn't finish, but he scored high marks on the practical aspects. He'd certainly have the skills to build and plaster a breezeblock wall.'

246

I remembered Lola proudly telling me how her son could turn his hand to anything. Perhaps more than she knew. 'Why was he sacked?'

'The details are pretty sketchy, but it was some sort of trouble over drugs disappearing from the hospital pharmacy. Painkillers, tranquillizers, steroids, all the sort of stuff there's a ready market for. No criminal complaint was made, but it caused enough of a stink for him to be fired. Which ties in with the theory that the murders might be drug-related. Maybe he had some sort of scam going selling pilfered drugs from St Jude's and set up shop in his old stomping ground when the hospital closed. It's only circumstantial at his stage, but however you look at it Lennox is starting to tick a lot of boxes.'

He did, but I still felt uncomfortable about this. 'How are you going to question him if he can't talk?'

'We'll have to get him medically assessed and take it from there. If we find enough evidence to charge him, we can see if his fingerprints match the ones from the paint tins and mortar. If they do, then it won't matter whether he can talk or not. We can tie him to two of the murders, and his building background potentially connects him to the tarpaulin Christine Gorski's body was wrapped in. If his DNA matches the hair we found on that, we've got him for her murder as well.' She looked at me quizzically. 'What's wrong? You don't seem very happy about it.'

I didn't know how I felt. Even though I'd been the one to bring Gary Lennox to Ward's attention, I hadn't really believed there was anything to it. While I wanted whoever was responsible for the atrocities at the abandoned hospital to be caught, I was uncomfortable with the idea of bringing yet more trouble into the lives of Lola and her son.

'I wasn't expecting things to happen so fast,' I admitted.

'Neither was I, but I'll take it. And I've not told you the best part yet.' Ward tried not to show it, but I could hear her excitement. 'We got a positive ID on the fingerprints Mears took from the male victim. His name's Darren Crossly. Thirty-six years old, had a conviction for possession of cannabis when he was eighteen, otherwise a clean record. But he used to be a porter at St Jude's as well, right until it shut. He'd have known Gary Lennox.'

Christ. I fell quiet, trying to take it in. When I'd told Ward about Lennox I'd been worried I was wasting her time. I hadn't expected this.

'Well, say something,' Ward said. 'I didn't expect you to punch the air but I thought you'd be a bit more enthusiastic.'

'What about the woman who was walled up with him?' I asked.

'Nothing on her yet. We haven't come up with a match for her fingerprints, so it doesn't look like she had a criminal record. We're still waiting on DNA and dental, but now we've identified Crossly we can start looking into his friends and associates. See if she was someone he knew.'

'When did he go missing?'

Ward hesitated. 'It was reported thirteen months ago.'

I looked at her. 'Lola told me her son had his stroke eighteen months ago. That's five months before Darren Crossly went missing.'

248

'I said that's when it was *reported*,' Ward said, with a touch of irritation. 'Crossly doesn't have any family and he'd been out of work since St Jude's closed, so we can't say exactly how long he's been gone. We only found out when we did because he was claiming benefit and his landlord reported him for falling behind on his rent. But we think he probably disappeared closer to fifteen months ago, which puts it around the same sort of time as Christine Gorski was last seen. And we've only got the word of Lennox's mother for when her son actually had his stroke.'

'You think she's covering for him?'

Ward gave a shrug. 'We've applied for a court order to access his health records, so we'll see then. But in view of everything else, we didn't want to wait. Mothers have been known to lie, and she hasn't got an unblemished record herself. We checked into what the neighbour told you about a patient death. Lola Lennox used to work at the old Royal Infirmary in South London. It's gone now, but twenty-two years ago a fourteen-year-old boy died from an insulin overdose while she was the nurse on duty.'

'It was true?' Even though I'd felt obliged to tell Ward about it, I'd never really believed the neighbour's story.

'Well, the basics are. The hospital's internal investigation ruled it was an accident but Lola was dismissed and never worked as a nurse again. Getting sacked from hospitals seems to run in the family.'

Leaving me with that thought, Ward fell silent as the car turned on to Lola's street. Still absorbing the news, I felt my stomach knot at the thought of what was to come.

'You haven't told me yet what I'm doing here,' I said.

'Apart from you starting the whole thing off, you mean?' She gave a dry smile. 'Don't worry, it's not a punishment. Lennox's mother knows you, so I thought it wouldn't hurt to have a familiar face along.'

'I'm not sure that'll make any difference.'

'Maybe not, but it's better than a house full of strangers. She seems to trust you, anyway.'

Not after this, I thought.

We pulled up outside the house, along with several other cars and an ambulance. Gary Lennox might be a suspect, but he was also a vulnerable adult. Social services were accompanying the police, as well as an ambulance and paramedics to check on Lennox's physical condition and transport him to hospital. I felt a weight of responsibility on my shoulders as I got out of the car. I'd wanted to get help for Lola and her son. I hadn't anticipated this.

Car doors slammed as the police entourage climbed out on to the pavement. Drawn by the commotion, faces were appearing in windows of the houses that weren't boarded up. A few people had emerged into the street to watch, staring with undisguised curiosity at the unexpected entertainment.

Whelan had been in one of the other cars. Now he went to the front door and knocked. I kept my eyes on the blind in the window, watching for a movement that would betray Lola's presence. It stayed still. Whelan waited a few seconds then knocked again, harder this time.

'She's gone out.'

It was the same neighbour who'd spoken to me on a previous visit. She stood watching from her doorway, a bathrobe wrapped around her and another cigarette in hand. It looked as though she'd only just got out of bed, and without the thick make-up her face appeared older and unfinished.

'Do you know where she is?' Whelan asked.

She shrugged a shoulder. 'How should I know?'

'Do you know how long she's been gone?'

'I don't know. Hour, hour and a half.' Taking a drag on her cigarette, she gave me a faintly mocking smile. 'Brought reinforcements, did you?'

Whelan turned back to Ward. 'What do you think, ma'am? Shall we—'

'Sir.'

One of the uniformed PCs was looking further up the street. A forlorn woman was trudging towards us on the pavement. She carried shopping bags in both hands, limping along with her head bowed. Lost in the effort of walking, she hadn't noticed us, but then something must have registered. She looked up, stopping dead at the sight of the police outside her house. For a second or two she didn't move. Her eyes rested briefly on me. Then, mouth set in a determined line, she hoisted her carrier bags and continued towards us with the same unhurried pace as before.

Ward stepped to meet her. 'Lola Lennox? My name's DCI Sharon Ward. We're here about Gary.'

Lola ignored her, walking past Ward and everyone else as though none of us were there.

'Did you hear me, Mrs Lennox? I said we'd like to speak with you about—'

'I heard. You can piss off.'

'Mrs Lennox, we have a warrant for your son's arrest.'

'Shove it up your arse.'

Without putting down her shopping bags – more incontinence pads, I saw – Lola fumbled with her keys to unlock the front door.

Ward tried again, making an effort not to lose patience. 'We don't want to cause you any more distress than we have to, but it's in your own and your son's interest for you to cooperate.'

She might as well have been speaking to a stone. Still holding her bags, Lola continued to struggle with her keys, face reddening with the effort.

Whelan went to help. 'Here, why don't I—'

'*Get your fucking hands off me!*' Lola snarled, turning on him.

'All right, let's all calm down,' Ward said as Whelan backed off, hands raised placatingly. She beckoned me forward. 'I think you know Dr Hunter—'

'Keep that back-stabbing bastard away from me.'

So much for a familiar face. I took a breath. 'I'm sorry, Lola, I didn't want to—'

'Fuck off!'

She'd managed to get her key into the lock but, hampered by the shopping bags, was now struggling to turn it. By now more people had emerged on the street to watch.

'You should be ashamed of yourselves!' a woman called from across the road. 'She's an old woman, leave her alone!'

I could see the indecision on Ward's face as she tried to decide what to do. The last thing she needed was accusations of heavy-handed policing, especially towards the elderly mother of a sick man. But the longer this went on, the more danger there was of losing her authority.

Abruptly, the front door unlocked with a *snick*. Lola tried to squeeze through the gap while still blocking it with her bags.

'You can't come in!' she yelled, trying to force the door shut. 'This is my house, you've no right!'

They had, though. Abandoning the attempt to keep them out, she hurried inside, leaving the door to swing open. I let the police and social workers go in first. Whelan recoiled as he entered and the smell of the sickroom hit him.

'Jesus,' he muttered under his breath.

Lola was standing in front of the bed, as though to keep everyone away from her son. 'I don't want you in here! Go on, get out!'

One of the paramedics approached the bed, smiling reassuringly. 'It's all right, we just want to take a look at your son.'

'Get away from him!'

Lola swung a carrier bag of incontinence pads at the paramedic, but Whelan got in the way and took them from her. As this went on, Gary Lennox's eyes darted from one person to the other, the only outward sign of his agitation. The paramedic smiled down at him.

'All right, Gary. How're you doing? I'm Kalinda, I'm a paramedic. I'd just like to do a few tests—'

'No!' Lola wailed, trying to get past Whelan and a uniformed PC who were doing their best to restrain her. 'No, you can't, I won't let you!'

I tried again. 'Lola, why don't you come with me—'

'Fuck off!' she spat, the small eyes glittering with rage. 'Bloody Judas, this is your fault!'

'Leave it, you're making it worse,' Whelan told me over his shoulder as he stood between us. He was right, so I moved aside to let one of the social workers try. As I did there was a commotion outside. Voices were coming from the street, and I saw a uniformed PC blocking someone from coming through the doorway.

It was Adam Oduya.

'I'm here to see Lola and Gary Lennox.' The activist wasn't shouting, but he didn't need to. 'Let me speak to them.'

'Oh, great,' Ward breathed. 'Jack, get him out of here.'

Leaving Lola to the uniformed PCs, Whelan went to the doorway. 'This is none of your business. You need to move away.'

'Anything to do with this community *is* my business,' Oduya replied. 'Why are you harassing an old woman in her own home?'

'We're not harassing anyone. This is a police operation, we're here with social services and—'

'You don't call this harassment? Forcing your way mob-handed into the home of an elderly woman and her son? They have rights.'

'You've been asked to move on, I won't ask you again—'

'Mrs Lennox?' Oduya called into the house, trying to see past Whelan. 'Lola Lennox! I'm a lawyer, I can help you!'

'Right, get him out of here,' Whelan snapped at a PC.

But the shouting had attracted Lola's attention. 'Who's that?' she demanded, turning towards the doorway as a uniformed officer tried to hustle Oduya away.

'My name's Adam Oduya,' the activist called as he was herded back. 'If the police are here against your wishes I can help you. Just tell them I represent you and you want to speak to me!'

A look of calculation passed across the old woman's face. She turned to Whelan.

'You heard him.'

'Mrs Lennox, there's no need to—'

'I want to see him!'

Whelan gave a look of appeal at Ward. She nodded, disgusted. 'All right, let him through.'

Reluctantly, Whelan and the PC stepped aside. Oduya took a moment to straighten his jacket before coming inside. He didn't seem surprised to find me there.

'Hello, Dr Hunter . . .' he began, but stopped when he saw the man lying in the room's squalor.

'Still think we're violating anyone's rights?' Whelan asked.

The activist quickly recovered his composure. He went towards Lola, extending his hand.

'Thank you for inviting me into your home, Mrs Lennox.'

She ignored the outstretched hand, staring at him with an expression of distaste. I realized she would only have been able to hear him outside, not see him.

'You're one of them.'

'I'm a lawyer, yes,' Oduya said, smoothly reaching up with the hand he'd offered and taking out a business card from his jacket. 'My name is Adam Oduya, and if you'll permit me I'd like to represent you and your son.'

'I'm not paying you.'

'You don't have to. I run a not-for-profit organization. We offer help to members of the community who need legal advice and representation.'

'She doesn't need representing,' Whelan said irritably.

'But her son does. Or are you denying him legal representation because he's incapacitated?'

Ward came forward. 'Mr Oduya, our priority is making sure Gary Lennox is in a good state of health. He would have been offered legal representation as soon as was appropriate, but now you're here that obviously won't be necessary. And, while we're on the subject, why *are* you here? Please don't try to tell me you were just in the neighbourhood.'

He gave her a smile. It was warm but let her see they understood each other. 'As I've told you before, I have my sources. None of them present at the moment, I hasten to add.'

That was for my benefit. Nor was I the only one to realize it: I was aware that Whelan was giving me a hard look.

'What are you standing there for?' Lola demanded to Oduya. 'This is my house. If you're a lawyer, tell them to get out!'

I wondered how long it would be before the activist regretted what he'd taken on. 'I'll do my best, but first I have to—'

'We need to get him to hospital.'

The paramedic's voice cut through everyone else's. While the argument had been going on, she'd been quietly examining Gary Lennox. His eyes were wide and frantic, darting at everyone in the room. His breathing was fluttering and rapid, loud enough to be heard now the room had fallen silent.

'His stats are all over the place,' the paramedic went on. She tore the Velcro blood-pressure cuff off the emaciated arm with a ripping noise. 'His oxygen levels are way down, his BP and pulse are—'

'No!' Lola sounded as though she'd been struck. 'He doesn't need a hospital! I can look after him!'

The paramedic briskly rolled up the cuff. 'Sorry, but he can't stay here. He looks malnourished and dehydrated, and I think there could be liver and kidney problems. He needs proper medical attention.'

'You've no right! I won't let you!'

'Mrs Lennox, I think perhaps you should listen to the paramedic,' Oduya said, his tone reasonable and reassuring. 'I'll come to the hospital with you and—'

'No! Please!' Lola didn't seem aggressive any more, just desperate. And scared. 'Don't take him as well! He's all I've got left!'

She began to wail as an oxygen mask was strapped to her son's face, oblivious to anything either Oduya or the social workers could say. The room was overcrowded and I was getting in the way. Unnoticed, I stepped outside as a stretcher was wheeled across the pavement from the ambulance.

'Tell DCI Ward I've gone back to St Jude's,' I told one of the PCs stationed by the front door. Pushing through the small crowd of onlookers who'd gathered in the street, I started walking in the direction of the hospital.

I could still hear Lola's cries behind me.

Chapter 21

THE CADAVER DOG search had made good progress while I'd been away. There had been no more false alarms, and the middle floor was mainly wards, which were larger and easier for the dog to search than the cubbyholes and crannies of the level above.

I rejoined them after lunch. It took longer to walk back to St Jude's than I'd expected, and I didn't exactly rush. The search team would call if they found anything, and after what had happened at Lola's I needed time to clear my head. I'd driven part of this route before but never walked it and, although I knew there was a short-cut through the woods, finding it was another matter. The streets all looked the same, run-down terraces and boarded-up properties scrawled over with graffiti. I was beginning to think I'd got myself lost when I turned a corner and saw trees at the end of the road, a dark green border among the tired bricks and concrete.

The woods on this side were fenced by ramshackle metal railings. A gap in them revealed a muddy path, covered by fallen leaves and overgrown with hawthorn bushes. Pushing through them, I found myself sur-rounded by gnarled trunks and twisted branches, unable to see the road that lay only a few yards away. I halted for a few moments, enjoying breathing air that smelled of earth and leaf mulch. I couldn't see where the path was leading as it weaved around tree trunks, but I had a good idea. It came as no surprise when I found myself in the clearing with the lightning-struck oak inside the ruins of the ancient church.

I stopped at its edge, realizing I'd followed the same route Lola must have taken when I'd seen her here. A lone rook launched itself from the ivy-choked stones, but otherwise the clearing was deserted. In the days since I'd been there the rain had stripped most of the leaves from the trees. Set against the nearly bare branches, the crumbling gable wall looked even more stark.

I went to the same fallen pillar as before and sat down. The memory of the ugly scene at Lola's ached like a bruise. Ward was right. The circumstantial evidence against Gary Lennox was compelling. He would have known at least one of the two entombed victims, had the building skills to build the false wall and had lost his porter's job at St Jude's under a cloud over missing drugs. Yet none of that would count for anything if he'd been incapacitated by a stroke for the past year and a half. That would rule him out of any involvement not only in Darren Crossly and the unknown woman's murders, but Christine Gorski's death as well. Lennox couldn't have been responsible for any of them if he'd been a bedridden invalid at the time.

Unless his mother had lied.

The dates could be easily checked once the police had a court order to see his hospital and GP records. It might have been better for Ward to have waited until then, but

I could understand why she hadn't. Accessing confidential medical information wasn't always straightforward, and Ward was under mounting pressure for results. Lennox's guilt could be quickly established if his fingerprints matched those from the crime scene. If they did, this would be a huge coup for Ward on her first outing as SIO.

If they didn't, then it would effectively end the police case against Gary Lennox, regardless of how long he'd been ill. And I'd have brought down all this fresh misery on Lola and her son for nothing.

Telling myself I hadn't had a choice didn't make me feel any better. Nor did the fact that Gary Lennox clearly needed proper medical care. That could have been arranged without what amounted to a police raid.

But I'd spent long enough brooding. Climbing to my feet, I brushed myself down and made my way back through the woods. The police officer patrolling the perimeter at the back of the hospital didn't want to let me through, fixing me with an unfriendly stare as he made a call on his radio to confirm it was OK. It had started to cloud over as I walked through the wasteland of demolished outbuildings behind St Jude's. I paused next to the mound of rubble where the morgue used to be. The *new* morgue, I reminded myself, remembering the cobwebbed original in the basement. The mound of broken concrete and bricks reached above my head, but as I paused to look at it fat drops of rain began to spatter down. The respite was over.

Leaving what remained of the morgue behind, I went to get changed.

*

It was late afternoon before Whelan came back to St Jude's. The cadaver dog had worked its way down to the ground floor by then, where the open main doors at least allowed a trickle of fresh air and daylight inside. Even though the Labrador still had the basement to search, there was too much ducting and pipework for any false walls not to be immediately obvious. There was a sense that we were approaching the end now, that St Jude's had exhausted its supply of surprises.

I should have known better.

We were in an X-ray suite from which all the equipment had been removed. Torn notices to switch off mobile phones hung from the walls, while the doors of empty changing cubicles stood open like looted sarcophagi.

'Dr Hunter?'

I looked round to see Whelan in the doorway. Even in his mask I could see he didn't look happy.

'You're needed in the basement,' he said, turning and setting off down the corridor without waiting.

He'd reached the steps leading down to the lower level by the time I'd caught him up. 'Has the search team found something?' I asked.

'They've got a piece of burnt bone in the boiler room, but they can't say if it's human or not.' I was behind him on the steps but he didn't look around. 'We wondered where you'd got to earlier.'

'Didn't you get my message?'

'That's not the point. You should have told us before you left.'

'You were busy and I was just getting in the way,' I said, irked. 'I thought I'd be better doing something useful.'

'Well, next time clear it with us first.'

As far as I was concerned, there wouldn't be a next time. But I guessed I wasn't the only reason for the DI's bad mood. 'How did it go after I'd left?'

His sigh was answer enough. 'Oduya's causing problems. He's advised Lennox's mother not to give consent for her son's fingerprints to be taken. Or hers, either. Says if we want them we'll have to charge them first.'

That would be a blow for Ward. Unless they were given voluntarily, the police were only legally allowed to take a suspect's fingerprints once they'd been charged. Gary Lennox was in no condition to give his consent, so permission would have to come from his mother. If she refused, it prevented the police from comparing her son's fingerprints with those found at St Jude's. The investigation would be at a stalemate.

'What's Oduya hoping to gain by that?' I asked, as we reached the bottom of the steps.

'Nothing, it's just a spoiler tactic.' Whelan set off down one of the passages. Pipes and ducting ran along the walls and ceiling, and small floor lights had been spaced out to show the way. 'He's trying to stop us seeing Lennox's medical records, as well. He says if we've a case we should present it, otherwise we should stop persecuting a sick man.'

'But if Lennox is innocent it's in his own interests to be ruled out.'

'Try telling your friend that.'

He's not my friend. I didn't blame the DI for being angry, though. If Lennox's fingerprints were at the scene, left on the paint cans and in the mortar of the wall itself, then it would effectively confirm his guilt.

Being blocked from establishing that on a point of law would be incredibly frustrating for the police.

But I could also understand why Oduya was doing it. Gary Lennox couldn't speak for himself, so Oduya was going to speak for him. He'd represent the man as best he could, even if it meant delaying the police investigation. For all his self-promotion, I was starting to realize that the activist was genuinely doing what he thought was right, not simply posturing for effect.

It wasn't going to win him any popularity contests.

'Don't you have enough on Lennox to bring charges?' I asked.

Whelan shook his head. 'Arrest, yes. Charge, no. Without the fingerprints it's all circumstantial.'

'Didn't you find anything at the house?' They would have carried out a search for any incriminating evidence at Lola's when they arrested her son.

'Nothing that helps. A pile of old comics and bird-watching magazines, but that was about it. Lennox was a real Billy-no-mates. He didn't even have a computer or a mobile phone.'

The more I heard, the worse I felt. 'How is he?'

'Not good. The hospital have got him on fluids, antibiotics and God knows what while they run tests, but he's in a bad way. Whether he's guilty or not, we did him a favour getting him out of that place. If that's how she cares for her own son, I wouldn't like his mother looking after me, nurse or not.'

'Has she said anything?'

'Swear words, mainly. She's got a foul mouth on her, that one. Turned the air blue when she talked about you.' Whelan found that amusing, at least. 'I don't think you're on her Christmas-card list any more.'

He veered off along another passageway. Its low ceiling dripped with water and the walls were beaded with condensation. The boiler house lay at the end of it, hidden behind heavy metal doors. Inside was a complicated assembly of tanks, pipes and valves that disappeared into shadow. In its prime it must have been like a furnace down here, hissing with fire and steam like the engine room of an old ship. Now the huge machinery was cold and dead. Beneath the smell of corrosion was the taint of old oil, so faint it was barely there. But the further in we went, the more another odour asserted itself. Soot and cold ashes. Something had been burned in here. Not recently, but not so very long ago either.

The search team were waiting by the boiler. Rusted and ringed with protruding rivets, the huge metal cylinder was eight or nine feet in diameter, like a giant tin can laid on its side. In one end was an open circular hatch, set low down by the floor. Floodlights had been positioned around it, backlighting the ghostly white figures so it looked as if they were huddled around a campfire.

'Show me,' Whelan said.

One of the figures, barely identifiable as a woman in the coveralls and mask, stepped forward. 'This was buried in the ash inside the boiler. Pretty sure it's bone, but I can't say if it's human or not.'

She handed Whelan a plastic evidence bag containing something small and dark. Whelan examined it under the light before passing it to me.

'What do you reckon?'

The object resembled a burnt peanut shell. It was tubular in shape, no more than a centimetre or two in length with slightly flared ends. The surface was blackened, with a few charred tags of soft tissue still clinging to it.

'It's an intermediate phalange,' I said. 'A finger bone.'

'So it's human?'

'Unless you get many chimpanzees or brown bears in North London, yes, it's human.'

Whelan gave me a sour look, but I wasn't being flippant. The phalanges of brown bears and some primates were superficially similar to ours, and I'd worked on cases before where animal bones had been mistaken for human. Even so, I wasn't in any real doubt about what we'd found here.

'They burn body parts in hospitals, don't they?' one of the search officers asked. 'Could it be from an amputation?'

'They'd have proper incinerators for that,' Whelan told her, looking up at the metal cylinder. 'This is an old coal boiler. It'd be for heating and hot water, not burning surgical waste.'

'This didn't happen when the boiler was running,' I said. 'Coal burns at a high temperature. It'd have been as hot as a crematorium in there, so any bone would have been calcified. It'd be white, not black like this. That's a sign it burned at a lower temperature.'

Bone follows a predictable path when it's exposed to fire. First it darkens, changing from the dirty cream of its normal colour through brown to black. Then, if the fire is hot enough, the bone turns to grey and then chalk white. Eventually, it will become light as pumice as the natural oils are burned away and only the calcium crystals are left.

265

Whelan looked towards the hatch. 'Anything else in there?'

'Don't know yet,' the officer said. 'We backed off as soon as we found the bone. No obvious body parts, but it's full of ash and cinders. There's no way of saying what else is buried under it.'

Whelan was examining the floor in front of the boiler, where pale smears of grey marked the filthy concrete. 'There's ash spilled here. That from you?'

'No, it was there already.' The woman sounded offended.

'Was the hatch open or closed?'

'Closed.'

Whelan considered it for a moment longer, then bent to peer inside the hatch.

'Can't see much.' His voice boomed inside the boiler. 'Pass me a torch.'

Someone stepped forward and handed him a flashlight. Whelan leaned further inside, upper body disappearing into the round hatch.

'Hard to tell what was burned in here. There's a lot of ash but that could just be from before it was decommissioned.'

Extricating himself awkwardly, he straightened. He was holding a small, blackened cinder on his palm.

'That isn't bone,' I told him.

'No, but it's not coal either. Looks like charcoal. There's a load of it in there. Someone's been burning wood.'

'Can I take a look?'

Whelan handed me the torch and moved aside. A sooty, metallic smell of combustion filtered through my mask when I crouched down and leaned into the boiler's mouth. My head and shoulders cast a shadow that blocked the floodlight, but the torch beam revealed a mess of cold ash and cinders, black islands in a grey sea. Whelan was right: there was a lot of what looked like burnt wood in there, carbonized to charcoal. It was possible that there could be more bone among it, but there was nothing immediately recognizable as human. I started to back out, then stopped as my torch beam passed over the back of the boiler.

'There's something else.'

Barely visible, an object was partially buried in the ash. Only its uppermost tip was showing, flattened and roughly triangular in shape. To a casual glance it could have been another piece of charred wood.

'I think it's a shoulder blade,' I said.

I made way for a SOCO to take photographs, then bent through the hatch again. The curved rim dug against me as I leaned inside, reaching for the buried object. It shed ashes as I pulled it free, its triangular shape emerging from the cinders like a shark fin. Giving it a gentle shake to dislodge the clinging ash, I levered myself back out of the boiler and turned to show Whelan.

'It's a scapula. Human,' I added, before he could ask.

The surface of the shoulder blade was blackened, but like the phalange there was still a weight and heft to it. The fire had been hot enough to burn away most of the soft tissues, but not enough to calcify the bone.

Whelan examined it. 'We can rule out surgical waste anyway. I could see the odd finger finding its way inside, but not something this big. Question is, where's the rest of the body? Unless it was dismembered and they only burned some of it in the boiler.'

That was one possibility. This wouldn't be the first murder where the victim had been cut up and the various parts disposed of in separate locations. But I didn't think so.

I took the blackened scapula back from Whelan. 'Cutting up a shoulder's a different proposition to an arm or a leg, or even a head. It'd mean sawing up the torso, which is a big, messy job, and I can't see any cuts on this. The body can't have all burned away either. A wood fire wouldn't be hot enough, even if an accelerant was used as well.'

'What about the wick effect?' the SOCO who'd taken photographs suggested. 'You know, when the body fat catches fire and burns like a candle till there's next to nothing left. I've heard of that happening.'

So had I: I'd even come across the grisly phenomenon once myself. Under certain conditions, when the body burns, its layer of subcutaneous fat can melt and soak into clothing. The fabric then literally acts like the wick on a candle, causing the body to slowly burn away until little more than ashes are left.

But that was a freakishly rare occurrence, and I doubted it was the explanation here. 'It takes a lot of body fat for that to happen, and even then not everything burns away. Some of the bigger bones and extremities usually survive.'

'They could be hidden under the ash,' the SOCO offered.

'Not an entire body,' I said. 'We should be able to see more than this.'

We could rule out scavenger activity as well. Animals couldn't have got into the boiler if the hatch was closed, and I doubted they'd have tried anyway. Even if a larger scavenger, like a fox, had ventured this far into the basement, the bones would have been too burnt to be of any interest.

Whelan had squatted down to examine the ashes spilled on the floor below the boiler's hatch. 'So you're saying somebody burned a body in here, then came back afterwards and took away what was left.'

'Not all of it,' I said, putting the scapula into an evidence bag.

Chapter 22

WHILE THE CADAVER dog search continued without me, I stayed in the basement to sift through the cold ashes in the boiler. If I was needed they would send for me: in the meantime, I was more use down there, carefully trowelling ashes through a fine-grade sieve with the SOCOs. Most of what we recovered were just fragments of charcoal that hadn't been fully consumed by the fire, but there were other finds as well. Several more phalanges, from feet as well as hands, along with a small number of larger bones, were concealed beneath the ashes. All were crazed and distorted by the heat. Two pieces of broken ribs were recovered, their ends sharply splintered, and what looked like a rounded piece of clinker turned out to be the head of a right tibia, with the rest of the long shin bone buried under the ash. Uncovered nearby, though still further away than it would have been in life, was the rounded triangle of a patella. A kneecap, though from the left leg rather than the right.

As we worked, we began to form a clearer picture of what had happened, if not why. As Whelan had noted, the ashes on the surface were mostly burnt wood, salted with blackened chunks of charcoal. Underneath them was an older layer of ash and cinders, left over from when the boiler had burned coal to heat the hospital. That suggested that the body had been put inside, had wood piled over and around it, and then been set alight. While it wouldn't have burned as hotly as a coal fire, the boiler would have trapped and intensified the heat, enough for the soft and connective tissue to burn off until only the charred skeleton remained.

Then, when the fire had died and the bones were cool enough to handle, someone had come and taken them away.

The SOCOs had discovered an ash-covered rake and shovel nearby, probably used by boiler-room staff when the hospital was still functioning. They'd also been put to more recent use. The burnt remains would have come apart when anyone tried to remove them, the surviving ligaments and tendons too brittle to maintain the skeleton's integrity. Judging by the tracks in the ashes, the tools had been used to clumsily drag the remains closer to the hatch, jumbling up the bones and causing some of them to be buried in the process.

And not just bones. There were other non-organic finds as well. A metal belt buckle, a zip fastener and circular eyelets from either shoes or boots, all charred but enough to show that the body burned in here had been wearing clothes.

Parekh had been to the basement for the start of the recovery but hadn't stayed. There was little for her to do except agree that the bones were human, and when she'd been called out to another, unconnected death across the city she'd left us to it. Ward had come as well, bulky and uncomfortable in the coveralls and her face pale and strained.

271

'Are we looking at one set of remains or multiple?' she asked, looking at the boxes of evidence.

'I can't say for sure yet,' I said. 'I haven't seen any duplications, but—'

'Just tell me if it's one or two.'

Her sharpness betrayed her tension. The excitement she'd shown earlier, on the way to arrest Gary Lennox, had evaporated. Not only had Oduya's intervention stymied her hopes of establishing Lennox's guilt through his fingerprints, now we'd uncovered what appeared to be a fourth victim.

Today hadn't turned out as she'd hoped.

'One. So far,' I added.

If we'd found duplicates of any of the bones – two right tibias, say – it would mean we were looking at commingled remains from two or more people. I'd found nothing to support that yet, though.

'What else can you tell me?'

'The bones we've found are all large and heavy, even allowing for them shrinking in the fire. I'd say from that we could be looking at a male, but that's only a first impression.'

'Height? Age?'

'You know I can't—'

'I'm going to be reporting to Ainsley and standing in front of a pack of reporters later. Just give me something.'

I was about to say that it was too early to be speculating on age and stature when we were still sifting through the ash and cinders, but then I saw the lines of strain around Ward's eyes.

'From what I've seen, it's probably an adult male,' I told her. 'Heavily built and between one eighty-four and one eighty-eight centimetres tall, based on the length of the tibia. I'll be able to give you a better estimate when I've done all the calculations, but he was probably six foot one or two. Probably.'

I stressed the last word, letting her see I wasn't happy saying even that.

'How old an adult?'

'It's hard to say.'

'Give me your best guess.'

'I just have done.' I could understand Ward's impatience, but there was only so much I could tell from a few burnt bones.

'Fine. If you're not up to it I'll ask Mears,' she snapped.

She turned and walked out. I stared after her, my face burning. None of the SOCOs would meet my eyes. I picked up the sieve, then put it down again.

'I'm taking a break,' I said.

I left the boiler room myself, silently fuming. Ward and I didn't mix socially, but we'd always got on. There had never been any friction when we'd worked together in the past, and she'd shown real concern during the scare over Grace Strachan earlier that year. She was obviously feeling the strain, but that didn't make me feel any better after she'd publicly torn a strip off me. Stoking a sense of injustice, I walked along the dimly lit passageway. My footsteps rang off the dank walls, the echo bouncing back in a staccato counterpoint. It was only when I turned a corner and found that the floor lights abruptly ended that I realized I'd taken the wrong turn.

In front of me the passageway disappeared into darkness. Now I'd stopped, the only sound was my breathing as I took in where I was. Up ahead was the black mouth of a larger passageway, and when I saw the cross of tape stretched diagonally across it I realized it was the blocked-off tunnel leading to the demolished morgue. Opposite it, unlit and barely visible in the shadows, was the old morgue entrance.

My breath steamed in the cold underground air, and I was suddenly aware of how alone I was. I told myself that was ridiculous. There were SOCOs in the boiler room I'd just left and the entire site was full of police. Yet, standing in the dark passageway, it felt as though I were the only person in the entire hospital.

Idiot. Now you're just frightening yourself. I must have been this way when I'd first come down with Whelan, and even if the floodlights had been taken away I had a flashlight on my phone. I could probably find my way to the stairs if I carried on.

I didn't, though. Ignoring the urge to look back over my shoulder, I turned around and headed back the way I'd come. Even though I didn't like to admit it, the sound of my feet splashing through the puddles was a welcome relief after the heavy silence. I speeded up, telling myself it was because I didn't want to waste any more time, and turning the corner, I almost walked into Whelan.

'Christ, don't do that!' he said, putting a hand on his chest. 'What're you doing down here?'

'I took the wrong turn.'

My own heart was thumping, but the feeling I'd had by the old morgue was fading already. We set off along the passageway.

'They said in the boiler room you'd gone upstairs, but I didn't pass you on my way down, so I figured you'd wandered off,' Whelan said.

'I was going to get some fresh air.'

He slowed. 'Look, I heard what happened back there. The boss . . . she's under a lot of pressure. Don't take it personally.'

This was another surprise. Whelan wasn't exactly apologizing for Ward, but it came close. 'Is she serious about bringing in Mears?'

'She was just letting off steam. This morning we thought we'd had a break with Lennox. Now that's bogged down over the bloody fingerprints, among other things, and we've found another victim.' The DI's tone changed. 'Trust me, she won't be letting Mears anywhere near this.'

We'd reached the junction in the passageway where I'd gone wrong before. Floodlights ran off towards the boiler room on one side, and towards the stairs on the other. I turned to face Whelan, wondering what he'd meant by that last statement.

But he'd clammed up again. 'Go and get yourself a cup of tea, then come and finish up down here. It's been a long day.'

Leaving me with that, he headed off down the passageway.

It took several more hours to sift through the rest of the ashes in the boiler. By the time were done only pale smears remained on the metal base, like a dusting of chalk. The bones we'd recovered had been taken to the mortuary. Parekh would be carrying out a post-mortem on them the following morning, or at least as much of one as was possible with so little to go on. With luck, I'd have a chance to examine them as well.

Assuming Whelan was right and Ward didn't ask Mears to do it instead.

From what I'd seen, I didn't expect the bones to tell us very much. But we had recovered one item that might. Although there was no skull, we did find a melted dental prosthesis buried among the ashes. It was a partial dental palate, a twisted lump of blackened plastic and metal to which the stubs of broken-off porcelain teeth were still attached. There was no sign of the teeth themselves and, although it was a potentially important find, without the jaw to match it to we couldn't be certain it belonged to the victim. For all we knew it could have found its way into the boiler after being lost or discarded by another owner.

I didn't think so, though. Like the bones, it wasn't damaged enough to have been subjected to the heat of a working coal boiler. The higher temperature would have vaporized the plastic and shattered the porcelain. These appeared to have been snapped off rather than shattered, and while the palate was badly deformed it hadn't been subjected to that sort of heat. That pointed towards it being the victim's, which could be a significant factor when it came to identifying the remains.

It was late by the time we'd finished. Whelan was right: it had been a long day. As I pulled through the electric gates at Ballard Court, I was debating whether to make myself a late supper or settle for a drink and an early night. I'd had a pre-packaged sandwich earlier at St Jude's, a tired affair of limp lettuce and tasteless cheese masquerading as a ploughman's, so bourbon and sleep were winning when I noticed one of my neighbours by his car.

Only the apartments on the first floor and above had underground car parking. The rest had spaces in the grounds. I didn't know the neighbour's name, although

I'd nodded to him once or twice. He was bending over by the driver's side of his car, a much newer and higher-spec version of the 4x4 I drove myself.

'Everything OK?' I asked, slowing and winding down my window.

'Some swine's keyed it.' His voice was tight with anger. 'Both doors, right through to the metal!'

'Kids?' I asked, thinking back to what the fire officer had told me when the bins had been set alight.

'Or someone living here. The whole place has been going downhill ever since we allowed apartments to be sublet. If I could get my hands on whoever . . .'

I said something vaguely sympathetic and left him to it. By the time I'd parked and taken the lift up to my apartment, the question of what I was going to do had resolved itself. Pouring myself a glass of bourbon, I decided I'd had enough news for one day. Instead I turned on the sound system and sank into the leather armchair.

I'd barely sat down when the intercom sounded.

I put my head back and closed my eyes. If this was my neighbour wanting to complain some more . . . With a sigh, I went into the hallway and pressed the intercom button. The night-time concierge's accented voice came out of the speaker grille.

'I have a DCI Ward to see you.'

This really would get the neighbours grumbling, I thought, looking at my watch. It was almost midnight, and I'd no idea why Ward might be calling so late. Telling the concierge to send her up, I opened the front door and waited, watching the lift at the end of the hall corridor apprehensively. I'd put what she'd said earlier about bringing in Mears down to frustration: now I began to wonder.

The lift chimed and then its doors opened. Ward came out, mackintosh draped open and bag slung carelessly over her shoulder. She looked exhausted as she stopped in front of the door.

'Do I get to come in, or aren't we talking?'

I stood back to let her inside. She slipped off her shoes in the hallway.

'God, I'd forgotten how thick this carpet is. It's softer than my bed,' she said, wriggling her toes in the pile.

Ward had visited the apartment when I'd first moved in, to approve the security arrangements when it seemed Grace Strachan might have re-emerged. As we went through into the open-plan kitchen and dining room, I felt embarrassment as I saw her taking in the opulent surroundings.

'Can I get you a drink?' I asked.

'I'd kill for a gin.' She gave a tired smile. 'Joke. Well, not really, but I'll settle for anything decaf. Fruit tea, chamomile. Water's fine if not.'

'I think there's some mint tea.' There had been a packet in a cupboard when I'd moved in, but I didn't think the owner would miss one sachet.

'Perfect.' She sat down at the dining table, lowering herself into a chair with a sigh. 'Sorry to be calling so late. I was on my way home, so . . . Look, I shouldn't have bitten your head off like I did earlier. It was unprofessional and unfair, so I wanted to clear the air.'

I switched on the kettle. 'You didn't have to come here to do that. You could have phoned or waited till tomorrow.'

'I wanted to say it in person. And I'd rather get it out of the way. It's one less thing to keep me awake.' She sounded as tired as she looked.

'Tough night?' I asked.

'Tough day. And to cap it off, I've just come from an interview with Luke Gorski. We've found out why he threw up the other day at St Jude's.'

I paused, a teabag in my hand. 'Please don't tell me he was involved in his sister's death.'

'No, thank God, nothing like that. Not directly, anyway. But he's admitted he gave Christine money for a final fix before she went into rehab. She promised him it was the last time, that she just needed something to see her through until she checked in. The idiot believed her. Still, at least we know now what she was doing at St Jude's.'

We'd thought Christine Gorski had probably gone to buy drugs; now it was confirmed. No wonder her brother had looked so strained. 'How have his parents taken it?'

'About as you'd expect.' She ground the heels of her palms into her eyes. 'You don't have a biscuit or any chocolate, do you? Never mind. Stupid question.'

'I can make you a sandwich.' I realized as I offered that I might struggle to manage even that. I should have bought some groceries for myself when I'd gone shopping for Lola.

'No, I'm fine.' Ward stopped rubbing her eyes and straightened in the chair, a weary attempt to get back to business. 'So, are you OK to examine the bones from the boiler tomorrow?'

'What about the cadaver dog search?' I asked, pouring boiling water on to the teabag.

'Finding out whatever we can about this new victim has to take precedence. If you're needed at St Jude's we'll let you know.'

I couldn't resist a last dig. 'I thought you were going to use Mears?'

Ward grimaced. 'OK, I deserve that, but I was just venting. Apart from anything else, Mears has his own problems.'

Does he now? 'Like what?'

But she shook her head. 'Let's change the subject.'

Her irritation was edging back, but at least this time it wasn't directed at me. I took the mint tea over, then fetched my bourbon from the living room and joined her at the table.

'That's really rubbing it in,' Ward said, looking from my glass to her mug.

'I wouldn't have poured it if I'd known you were coming.' I took a drink and set the glass down. 'How's Gary Lennox?'

'They're still trying to stabilize him. His heart's arrhythmic, he's got liver and kidney damage, fluid on both lungs and dozens of partly healed skin lesions that look like pressure sores. He's suffering from malnutrition and dehydration, and the doctors think he's had at least one massive neurological "event", as they're calling it. Probably more, but they're not sure exactly what. They're going to be doing more scans tomorrow, but there's some confusion over his medical history.'

'What sort of confusion?' Whelan had said Oduya was trying to stop the police from seeing Lennox's health records, but his doctors would still have access to them.

'Apparently there are gaps. We know Lennox was diagnosed with a heart defect when he was nineteen, but his doctors say they can't find any record of anything like a stroke. No hospital admission, no treatment, nothing. As far as anyone can tell us, he hasn't even seen a GP in the past three years.'

'That can't be right.'

'Not in the state he's in, no. They're still checking, but we're starting to think he might not have even *been* hospitalized. Whatever happened to him, it looks like his mother didn't tell anyone about it. Just decided to nurse him herself.' Ward shook her head, perhaps unconsciously resting her hand on her stomach. 'Takes "mother-love" to a new level, doesn't it?'

God, I thought, shocked. If that was true, then Lennox had been in an even worse purgatory than I'd realized. I'd seen earlier how desperate his mother had been not to have him taken away, but I'd never imagined she'd go that far. And it meant there was no way to verify the alibi she'd given her son: we'd still only her word that he'd been incapacitated when Darren Crossly had gone missing.

'Has she said anything?' I asked.

'Nothing printable. She's still refusing to cooperate or give us consent to take their fingerprints. His or hers. It's possible she's just being awkward, but I'm beginning to think there's more to it than that. She obviously couldn't have physically built a wall herself, but maybe she knows more than we thought. If she's kept her son from getting critical medical treatment, then I wouldn't like to say what else she's capable of.'

Neither would I. Yet I found it hard to believe Lola would be selfish enough to risk her son's life like that. 'You still sound convinced Lennox is guilty.'

Ward shrugged. 'The more we find out, the likelier he looks. We've been checking into Darren Crossly's acquaintances, and think we might have a lead on the woman he was walled up with. He had an on-off girlfriend by the name of Maria da Costa who seems to have disappeared as well. She hasn't been reported missing, but she was out of work and tended to flit from place to place, so it could be another case of no one noticing. We know she sometimes stayed with Crossly, and the last confirmed sighting has them both together. So it's possible that they disappeared at the same time. She doesn't have a criminal record, which would explain why we haven't had any luck matching the fingerprints from the woman's body.'

'If she was only Crossly's on-off girlfriend, would Lennox have known her?'

Ward gave a tired smile. 'Sorry, I didn't mention that, did I? Da Costa used to be a cleaner at St Jude's. She worked there for five years, until it closed. If we can confirm she's the woman we found with Crossly, then that means Lennox would have known both victims. Add to that his sacking because of missing pharmacy drugs and Darren Crossly's conviction for possession of cannabis, and there's a definite picture starting to form.'

St Jude's again. Somehow everything seemed to come back to that place. 'You think the three of them were dealing and had a falling-out?'

'I think "falling-out" puts it mildly, but yes. And maybe Christine Gorski went along looking to buy a fix and got in the middle of it. Except . . .'

'Except?' I prompted.

She shook her head, troubled. 'I don't know. Lennox just doesn't fit the profile. I mean, how many drug dealers in their thirties live at home with their mother?'

'With nothing worse than comics and birdwatching magazines, you mean?'

'Jack told you about that, did he?' Ward smiled, but it soon faded. 'OK, it's possible Lennox had another place or a lock-up we don't know about. I could even accept that he somehow managed to stay off our radar all this time. But it doesn't quite gel. Apart from his sacking, nothing we've found paints him as a drug dealer, let alone a violent sadist. Social services already had a file on him from when he was a kid. The social workers described him as physically big but lacking in confidence and with borderline learning difficulties. He was bullied at school, and he was almost taken into care because they thought his father was physically abusing him.'

'Lola said pretty much the same thing. Not about the care, about her husband,' I told her. Lola's phrasing had been more colourful, though. *Rotten bastard. He was a sod to my Gary sober, and when he'd had a drink he was even worse.*

'She wasn't lying about that, anyway,' Ward said. 'Patrick Lennox was a nasty piece of work, by all accounts. He worked on container ships doing the South America routes, so he wasn't at home all that much. But when he was he was a heavy drinker and handy with his fists. Especially against his son. It didn't stop until he left when Gary was sixteen.'

That fitted what Lola had told me as well. 'Where is he now?'

'Abroad, we think. We haven't been able to trace him, but I can't see that he's got anything to do with any of this. Except possibly in a formative sense.'

'As in, victims of abuse becoming abusers themselves?'

Ward shrugged. 'We know it happens. People change, and just because Lennox used to be bullied twenty years ago doesn't mean he couldn't dish out the same treatment himself. Maybe it gave him a chip on his shoulder.'

'Now who's putting it mildly?' I said.

'You know what I mean. Anyway, time I went home.' She drained her mug and pushed herself heavily to her feet. 'Thanks for the tea. For future reference, you might want to check what bags are actually in the box.'

'It wasn't mint?'

She smiled. 'Whatever it was, it was very nice.'

'What's going to happen to Lola?' I asked, as we went into the hallway, where Ward retrieved her shoes.

'Too early to say. She could be facing charges of criminal neglect if it turns out she prevented her son from receiving medical treatment. But a lot depends on what happens with the fingerprints.'

'Do you have enough to charge Gary Lennox without them?'

'No, but there might be a way round it,' she said cryptically. 'Alternatively, I was hoping to appeal to your friend Oduya to persuade Lola it was in their best interests to grant consent. Prove their innocence, that sort of thing. That's not going to happen now, though.'

'He's not my friend,' I sighed, then picked up on what else she'd said. 'Why isn't it?'

'Because he isn't Lola's friend any more either,' Ward told me, as I unlocked the apartment's front door. 'She fired him this afternoon.'

Chapter 23

AFTER ITS BRIEF resurgence, the sun had given up the fight again by the following morning. The rain-dreary roads were lit with headlights long after it should have been light as I drove to the mortuary. I'd set off earlier than I needed to. I was due to meet Parekh later for the post-mortem on the bones recovered from the boiler, but before I did that there was something else I had to attend to.

The tiny bones of Christine Gorski's foetus had been soaking for several days. Each morning I'd called into the mortuary to check on them and change the water for fresh. They hadn't had much soft tissue left clinging to them to begin with: now even that had fallen away. There was nothing to keep me from examining them, but I knew Ward would want a report on the burnt remains from the boiler first. The foetal skeleton would have to wait.

The delicacy of the miniature bones seemed sadly poignant as I carefully removed them from the water. Some were so small that I could only pick them up with tweezers. The hairline fractures the X-rays had revealed in both tiny forearms were almost too small to see with the naked eye. I tried anyway. They would probably have been caused by scavengers or – more likely, given their subtle nature – when its mother's mummified body had been moved further into the loft.

But they were too small to make out, no more than the faintest of lines against the bone-white slivers. Putting the bones back into clean water, I left them to their slow immersion and went out.

The post-mortem briefing for the burnt bones from the boiler didn't take long. With only a left tibia, right patella and assorted phalanges from hands and feet to work on, there'd be precious little for the forensic pathologist to do, a fact Parekh seemed aware of when she breezed into the briefing room with an airy, 'Morning, morning, let's move this along, shall we?'

The briefing itself was a perfunctory affair, and as we filed out Parekh walked alongside me.

'Have you seen your colleague recently?' she asked.

I couldn't think who she meant. 'Who?'

'Well, I'm not talking about the cadaver dog. Our esteemed forensic taphonomist, Daniel Mears.'

The last time I'd seen him was when he'd called asking for my help. I imagined he'd be finishing up by now, although since Ward had threatened to bring him in to examine the burnt bones instead of me, he was obviously still around.

'Not for a few days. Why?'

'Oh, no reason.' The shrewd eyes held mine for a moment. 'While you were here, I thought you might stop by and ask how he's doing.'

She pushed through the door, leaving me to wonder what that meant as I followed. Ward had been similarly cryptic the night before when she'd mentioned that

Mears was having problems. I'd assumed it was something to do with confirming the woman found interred with Crossly was Maria da Costa, perhaps using dental or medical records.

But he shouldn't need my help with that. And even if he did, I'd had my fingers burned after bailing him out once. Parekh wouldn't be aware of that, but I wasn't going to make the same mistake twice. Whatever trouble Mears was having, this time he was on his own.

The post-mortem was as routine as expected. X-rays revealed no healed fractures that could potentially help with identification, and the rest merely confirmed what I'd already seen as I'd removed the bones at the scene. The considerable size of specimens such as the spade-like scapula pointed to a large stature, suggesting this individual was probably – though not definitely – male. Using the tibia's measurements, I'd refined my preliminary estimate of height and calculated it to be around one hundred and eighty-five centimetres. An inch or so over six foot. But that wasn't definitive: although the shin bone was a useful indicator of height, ideally any sort of estimate would be based around the length of other long bones as well.

It was the best I could do, though. And neither Parekh nor I could even hazard a guess at the probable cause of death. Although the two broken rib sections we'd recovered had obviously been caused by some sort of blunt trauma, there was no way of saying if they were a contributing factor or not. The ribs had both broken on the diagonal, in what were known as simple fractures. Common in falls, the bone had been snapped clean in two, creating a jagged, knife-like edge. An injury like that could easily have been fatal if the sharp bone had

287

pierced the heart or severed an artery, or even punctured a lung, although that would have had less immediate consequences.

The problem was, I couldn't say for sure that's what had happened. The injuries could also have happened post mortem, after the victim was dead. The only thing I could say for certain was that the ribs were already fractured when the body was burned. Their broken surfaces were as blackened and charred as the rest, a sure sign they'd been exposed to the fire. If they'd been damaged afterwards – when the brittle remains had been taken from the boiler, say – then the exposed interior would show the pale ivory of unburnt bone.

Still, some interesting facts did emerge. Gently brushed clean of soot, I could see that the head of the right tibia and the inner surface of the patella showed some wear, though not very much. The phalanges told a similar story: this was an adult who'd lived long enough to show early degenerative changes in the joints, but not enough to suggest they'd reached an advanced age.

'Based on that, I'd estimate mid-thirties to forties,' I told Whelan. Ward had left immediately after the post-mortem, summoned to another briefing with Ainsley. Her deputy had the shadow-eyed look of someone who'd had another late night himself.

'How sure are you about the height?'

'I'd feel happier if it was based on more than one bone, but the tibia length is usually fairly reliable. Why, do you think you know who this is?'

'Maybe.' He seemed to debate how much he should say, then shrugged. 'We're still looking into associates of Darren Crossly, particularly anyone who used to work at St Jude's. As well as Maria da Costa, we've turned up someone else whose description more or less matches what you've said about the remains from the boiler. His name's Wayne Booth, worked as a porter with Crossly. Forty-five years old, single, a shade under six foot and heavily built.'

It wasn't far out from my estimates for age and stature, but not as close as I'd like. 'Forty-five's at the upper end of the range, but still possible. I'd have expected someone taller, though. When did he go missing?'

'Eleven months ago.'

That was seven months after Lola had said her son had his stroke, and considerably less than the fifteen months since Darren Crossly, Maria da Costa and Christine Gorski had last been seen alive. But Whelan anticipated my objection.

'We've still only his mother's word for how long Lennox has been ill and, given what we know about her, I'd put as much faith in that as a fart in a thunderstorm. And you said yourself the age and height were only estimates. No offence, but how much can you tell from a shin bone and a kneecap?'

It was a fair point. I liked to think my estimates were reasonably accurate, but I wasn't going to let my pride get in the way if the facts said otherwise.

Still, I wasn't entirely convinced. 'What else do you know about him?'

Whelan grinned. 'That's the good bit. After he was laid off as a porter when the hospital shut down he got a job as a security guard. Guess where?'

'You're joking. At St Jude's?'

'Night-watchman, believe it or not. Didn't last long, because it was only a few months later they decided it didn't need actual guards and made do with the dummy

CCTV cameras instead. But I'd say Booth's the odds-on favourite to be who we found in that boiler.'

'Did he have a dental palate?' I asked, thinking about the crisped piece of wire and plastic with the attached porcelain teeth we'd uncovered from the ashes.

Whelan gave a frustrated shake of his head. 'The description we have of him doesn't say. We're checking to see if he went to any dentists in the area, but if he did we haven't found them yet.'

That wasn't unusual. There was no national database for dental records, so it was a case of trawling around dentists' surgeries hoping to find the right one. I'd worked on investigations before now where the police had to resort to placing adverts in dentistry magazines.

Even so, this was a potentially important lead. Darren Crossly had already been positively identified as one of the interred victims, and it was looking likely that his sometimes-girlfriend, Maria da Costa, could be the woman found with him. And despite my reservations about his age and height, this missing Wayne Booth – not only a former porter at St Jude's but also a night-watchman after its closure – seemed likely to be the last victim.

It was tempting to tie all these strands up into a neat parcel, to assume that Lennox had been involved in stealing and selling hospital drugs with the other three, before turning on them and concealing their bodies in the old hospital. Even Christine Gorski could fit into that scenario: given money for one last fix by her brother, she could have gone to St Jude's intending to buy and blundered into a situation that led to her being killed as well.

Yet, tempting as it was, the theory was still pure supposition. And if the case against Gary Lennox fell apart, the rest of it would come crashing down as well.

I worked until lunchtime. Whelan had left long before, and so had Parekh. Strictly speaking, I could have finished sooner myself. I'd already had a good look at the burnt bones during the post-mortem. Unlike fleshed remains, these were too delicate to risk soaking, but beyond a gentle brushing down they didn't need cleaning anyway. Most of the joint surfaces were already visible and the few crisped scraps of tissue that remained either came away with the soot or were too small to worry about.

But I was still bothered by what Whelan had said about Wayne Booth. The former porter and security guard from St Jude's seemed a likely candidate for the bones that had been burned in the boiler, yet I was uneasy about the discrepancies between his age and height and my own estimates. I'd be the first to admit this wasn't an exact science. Genes and lifestyle could play a part, causing some people's joints to age sooner than others. And not everyone's limbs were in exact proportion to the rest of their body.

Still, I didn't like the idea of being so far out. So I spent a fruitless couple of hours poring over the bones again, checking and re-checking my calculations to see if there was anything I'd overlooked first time round.

There wasn't.

Finally, accepting I'd done all I could, I stopped for lunch. A late one, I amended, seeing the time. The bones still had to be cleaned before they were boxed away, and I hadn't got around to the partial palate we'd recovered.

A forensic dentist would be examining it at some point, but I wanted to take another look myself.

It could wait till after I'd had lunch, though. Since I hadn't brought anything with me and there were no facilities at the mortuary, I went out to find somewhere to eat. There were no shops nearby, but there was a pub I'd been to before. It was only a five-minute walk away, so I set off for that.

The day hadn't improved while I'd been inside. It was still gloomy, and the mist-like drizzle penetrated and chilled. The pub was two streets away, done over in a kitsch London theme. It was crowded, the smell of damp coats mingling with beer and hot food. There were law courts nearby and the clientele was mainly lawyers and barristers, their confident, plummy tones forming a noisy backdrop. I ordered a sandwich and coffee at the bar, then looked around for a table. Most were full, but there was an empty chair at one over in a corner. Careful not to spill my coffee, I made my way across. There was already someone sitting there, but it wasn't until I was closer that I saw who it was.

Mears.

The forensic taphonomist was the last person I wanted to eat lunch with. But there was nowhere else, and even as I hesitated he looked up and saw me. From his expression he was as enthusiastic about sharing a table as I was, but by then there wasn't much choice.

'Anyone sitting here?' I asked, indicating the empty seat.

He took a second to answer, as though considering lying, before giving a listless shrug. 'No.'

A half-eaten sandwich and a pint of beer were on the table in front of him. There was another empty glass next to it, and as I sat down he furtively moved it further away, as though to disclaim it.

'How's it going?' I asked, to break the silence.

'OK.' Another shrug. 'You know. Good.'

He seemed ill at ease, staring at his hands as he rotated his beer glass on the table. I had the feeling he'd like to have emptied it. I glanced around the press of bodies to make sure no one could overhear what we were saying. But the hubbub of conversation made it hard enough to hear ourselves.

'Has Ward got you working on the identification?' I asked, keeping my voice down anyway. I didn't say whose: he'd know I meant Maria da Costa.

'Who told you that?'

'No one. I just assumed you would be.' God, he really was jumpy. I hoped my sandwich wouldn't take long to arrive.

'Oh. Right. Yes, I'm, er, I'm working on it now.'

He took a drink of beer, almost gulping it down. Ward had touched on him having problems, and so had Parekh's thinly veiled hint earlier. Watching him now it was obvious there was something going on, but Mears's troubles were none of my business. It wasn't my job to nursemaid him. Telling myself that, I looked at the absurdly young face and tried not to sigh.

'Is everything all right?' I asked.

'Why shouldn't it be?'

'I just wanted to make sure. The last time I saw you—'

'Everything's fine! There's just a lot to do. Maybe if Ward gave me a chance to finish one job before springing another on me I might—'

He stopped himself, his cheeks flaming red. Here we go again, I thought, resigned.

293

'Is there something you'd like a second opinion on?' I asked quietly.

He bit his lip, blinking furiously as he stared at his glass. 'I can't seem to—'

'Cheese sandwich?'

A young woman stood by the table, holding a plate. I managed a quick smile. 'Thanks.'

Mears stared furiously at his lap as she set it down. I waited till she'd gone.

'Go on.'

But the moment had passed. 'Doesn't matter,' he mumbled.

Standing up, he gulped the rest of his beer and then pushed past the table, knocking it so that my coffee slopped into its saucer.

'Wait a second,' I said, but he was already forcing his way through the crush of bodies towards the door. One portly man in a pinstripe suit was jostled and almost spilled his drink as Mears pushed past.

'And that, gentlemen, is the sort of attitude we have to deal with today,' he announced, glaring after him.

I don't think Mears even noticed.

Chapter 24

I STAYED IN the pub only long enough to finish the sandwich. Outside, the drizzle hadn't eased up and the
people I passed all trudged along the slick pavements
with heads bowed, shoulders hunched miserably.
Although it was only mid-afternoon, the day already
seemed to be hurrying towards night. It was days like
this that made me wonder why I chose to live in the city.
I'd moved away once before, exchanged the clogged
streets and concrete of London for a tiny Norfolk village, where at least the autumn weather felt more like a
natural cycle, the steady turn of seasons. Here it just felt
dismal.

But I knew my outlook was probably tainted by the
incident with Mears. As I stood on the pavement edge
waiting to cross the road, I wondered again what was
going on with him. Few investigations ran smoothly,
and dealing with the unexpected was part of the job.
The young forensic taphonomist had all the necessary
skills, and even his lack of experience needn't be too
great a handicap. Provided he admitted it, to himself as
much as anyone.

I had a feeling Mears's ego might make that difficult, though. Combined with his brittleness under pressure, it made for a bad combination. The question was what I should do about it.

My phone rang as I crossed the road. I hurried under a shop awning to answer it, seeing as I took it out that the number wasn't one I knew. But the voice on the other end was immediately recognizable.

'Dr Hunter? It's Adam Oduya. Have I caught you at a bad time?'

I didn't bother asking how he'd got hold of my number: as he'd said before, he had his sources. 'Is this anything to do with the investigation?'

'No, I give you my word. It's another matter entirely.'

I looked at the drizzle, now fully fledged rain, dripping off the edge of the awning. 'OK.'

'When we spoke a couple of days ago I mentioned there was something I wanted to talk to you about. Nothing to do with St Jude's, I assure you. I wondered if you're free later this afternoon to discuss it?'

I kneaded my eyes. After the encounter with Mears in the pub I wasn't in a mood to contend with Oduya as well. Still, I didn't feel able to refuse out of hand. Even if I didn't agree with his methods, it was hard to fault the activist's motives.

'What is it?' I asked guardedly.

'How do you feel about pro bono work?'

I'd taken on pro bono cases in the past, but it depended on the case. Particularly when it came from Oduya. 'You'll need to tell me more about it.'

'I'm trying to launch an appeal for an individual convicted of murder ten years ago who I strongly believe is innocent. I think the evidence against him is flawed, especially the supposed cause of the victim's injuries. I'd like you to review it and give me your opinion.'

I hesitated, still wary.

'I understand your reluctance,' Oduya went on, and I could hear the wry smile in his voice. 'Obviously, you don't want to do anything that will compromise your work for the police. But I give you my word this won't. I was going to wait for things to settle down over St Jude's, but my client has already tried to kill himself twice and his family are worried he'll try again. They don't have much money, but if it helps I could see about a small fee to cover expenses?'

'The money's not an issue, but I'd want to know more before I commit myself.'

'Of course. That's why I'd like to meet to discuss it.'

The rain was dripping down my neck from the edge of the shop awning. I moved further underneath, thinking what I had left to do at the mortuary. Not an awful lot, but I still wanted to look at the burnt dental palate from the boiler.

'I can't make this afternoon,' I told him.

'This evening, then. Whatever time and place suits you.'

I was still reluctant, but I was curious now as well. 'I could meet you after work. I'm at the mortuary on Carlisle Street—'

'Near the law courts,' he finished for me. 'I know it. I used to spend a lot of time around there when I was in full-time practice. It's not far from the Tube station, and there's a pub close by called the Plume of Feathers. I could meet you there, say, seven o'clock?'

That was the same pub I'd just seen Mears in. But it was convenient, and that should give me more than enough time. I thought Oduya would be satisfied with that, but he hadn't finished.

'Do you know how Gary Lennox is?' he asked.

'I thought we weren't going to talk about St Jude's.'

'I'm not, but I'd still like to know how he is. As you've probably heard, I'm no longer representing Gary and his mother.'

'What happened?' Ward had told me Oduya had been fired, though not why.

'Lola had a change of heart and went with the duty solicitor instead. She decided she'd feel more comfortable with . . . Well, let's say someone more traditional.'

From what I knew of Lola, that didn't surprise me. And I couldn't see any harm in updating Oduya about her son's condition. 'He's not good, last I heard.'

'I'm sorry to hear that. Regardless of how it turns out, it's a sad situation.'

Yes, it was. 'Do Christine Gorski's parents know?'

'That I tried to help a vulnerable man and his elderly mother, you mean?' Oduya sounded weary rather than angry. 'It's no secret. I wasn't representing Sandra and Tomas in a legal capacity, so there was no conflict of interest.'

I moved aside to let a group of people into the shop. 'I was thinking more about frustrating the police's attempts to find their daughter's killer.'

'If you mean advising Gary Lennox's mother on their legal rights, again it's no secret. Whatever her son may or may not have done, he has the same rights as you or I. If the police have a case against him, let them bring it. But I won't stand by while someone's vulnerability is exploited. I've seen the justice system abused too many times for that.'

'What about justice for the victims and their families?'

'It's all part of the same coin. And please, don't insult either of us by assuming the moral high ground. I've sat with a mother who's just been told her pregnant daughter was lying dead in a derelict hospital for over a year. Believe me, I want whoever's guilty to be caught as much as you do. We just have different ways of going about it.' The amusement crept back into his voice. 'Anyway, Dr Hunter, for someone who didn't want to talk about St Jude's, you're not making a very good job of it.'

No, I wasn't. I hadn't meant to let myself get drawn into a discussion. Ending the call, I put my phone away, feeling annoyed with myself. As long as the police were unable to gather enough evidence to either charge Gary Lennox or exclude him from suspicion, the investigation would continue to be stuck in limbo. But however responsible I might feel for opening this particular Pandora's box, it was out of my hands now. Getting into a debate about it with Oduya wasn't likely to help.

It was only as I stepped from under the awning into the rain that I wondered if that was what he'd intended when he'd asked how Gary Lennox was. As I hurried back to the mortuary, I told myself I'd have to be careful when I met him that evening.

The partial denture was a mess. Heat from the fire and subsequent rough handling as the remains were removed from the boiler had melted the acrylic and deformed the metal. And although the flames hadn't been hot enough to shatter the porcelain teeth, something – presumably a blow or impact of some kind – had snapped them off close to the gum line. Since we hadn't found the broken-off false teeth among the ashes, it must have happened before the body was put in the boiler. It meant that, even if the police could track down Wayne Booth's dentist and establish that he wore a denture, matching it to the melted one might not be so straightforward. I wasn't sure it would even be possible.

A forensic dentist might have better luck with that. Even so, the prosthesis still told me a few things. The badly melted palate would have fitted to the roof of someone's mouth, making it an upper denture. And the shape of the broken stubs told me they would have been the front four incisors and the right canine. That would have left quite a gap. While one or two could have been due to decay or gum disease, a row of five missing teeth – including the front ones – suggested another cause.

They'd been knocked out.

That didn't necessarily mean from an assault. I'd once known someone who'd lost most of their front teeth when they came off a bike. He'd chosen to have implants rather than dentures but, since it involved extensive and expensive surgery, that option wasn't suitable for everyone.

Evidently not this individual, I thought. The denture was a very basic type, consisting of a rudimentary acrylic plate that covered the real palate and was held in place by metal clips. Although probably not immediately obvious, these might have been visible as tiny silver claws clamped around the adjacent teeth. It was a common enough design, with the emphasis on functionality rather than comfort or aesthetics. That suggested the owner either hadn't cared how it looked or couldn't afford anything more sophisticated.

My guess was the latter.

I'd planned to examine the foetal skeleton after that, having left it soaking in fresh water. But the palate's tangle of metal and plastic took longer than I'd expected, and I'd arranged to meet Oduya at seven. Another night's immersion wouldn't harm the tiny bones, though, and there was no real urgency. With a guilty sense of relief at being able to put off the unhappy task for a little longer, I decided to leave them till morning.

I stretched, wincing as my joints popped stiffly, then packed everything away. Switching off the examination-room lights, I went to change and then headed for the foyer. There was someone in front of me in the corridor, and I felt a by now familiar weariness when I saw Mears.

He was on his way out as well, wearing a waterproof jacket and carrying his shiny new flight case. He looked tired and slump-shouldered, his forehead furrowed as though he was deep in thought. When he saw me his eyes darted away, almost furtive. Then his chin came up and he straightened his shoulders, giving me a terse nod.

I'd been considering making one last effort but, seeing that, I decided there was no point. I returned his nod, waiting in silence while he signed out at reception. At the front door he stopped to pull up his hood. I hung back, taking my time signing out so we wouldn't have to leave together.

And with such small moments are lives changed.

A gust of damp wind blew into the foyer as Mears went out. It was dark outside, the rain bouncing down. Hunched against it, Mears started to cross the road as I went through the doors. I paused under the entrance canopy to fasten my own coat, and as I did someone called out.

'Dr Hunter!'

I looked up to see Oduya on the other side of the street. He had an umbrella and was heading from the direction of the Tube station. As he stepped off the pavement to come over, ahead of me I saw Mears glance towards him to see who was calling. In my mind the moment seems frozen: two figures crossing the rain-drenched road in opposite directions, the streetlight capturing them like a flash photograph.

I heard the car before I saw it. From off down the road there was a squeal of rubber. A car accelerated directly at Oduya, framing him in its lights. Even as his head snapped towards it, he was already starting to throw himself out of the way. But there was no time. With a sickening thump the car ploughed into him, slamming him against the bonnet and then back over its roof. As his umbrella was crumpled under its wheels, he spun through the air in a tangle of limbs, before smacking down on to the tarmac behind it.

The car weaved but didn't slow. Stranded in the middle of the road, Mears finally moved. Dropping his flight case, he tried to jump aside but the car's wing clipped him. It batted him to the ground, and I saw the rear wheel go over his lower body. For a second, the driver seemed to lose control, sideswiping a parked van in a cacophony of breaking glass and scraped metal before roaring away.

It was all over in a matter of seconds. Overcoming my shock, as the van's alarm wailed I ran into the street. Oduya was nearest. He lay motionless, limbs twisted at unnatural angles like those of a discarded doll. Blood had pooled around his head, glistening blackly under the streetlights as it mingled with rain. The slit of one eye stared unseeing at the rough tarmac, and as I knelt by him I could see that the shape of his skull was wrong. There was an utter stillness about him, an obscene contrast to the activist's energy and charisma. It was that as much as his injuries that told me there was nothing I could do.

Other people were appearing now, rushing into the road with exclamations of shock. Leaving Oduya, I hurried over to Mears. Covered with blood, he was sprawled near his flight case, the once shiny metal now battered and dented. He was alive but unconscious, breathing in wet, shallow gasps. One arm was obviously broken, but it was his lower body that had suffered the most. His right leg looked as though it had been caught up in a machine where the car wheel had gone over it, shards of white bone visible through the torn flesh and blood-soaked fabric.

I tried to throw off the numbing effects of shock and focus. Mears's injuries were far more severe than Conrad's had been, and I felt a sense of helplessness as I stared at the crushed leg. Blood was pumping from numerous wounds, too copious to simply staunch.

'Let me see. I'm a nurse.'

Slipping a sports bag from her shoulder, a young woman knelt down beside Mears. Her face was intent as she took in his injuries.

'Just hold on, love, ambulance is on its way,' she told him. He gave no sign of hearing or understanding. She glanced at me, peeling off her thin paisley scarf. 'Have you got a pen?'

My mind was beginning to function. Knowing what she had in mind, I took a pen from my pocket as she deftly wrapped her scarf around Mears's thigh. He groaned as she tightened it, but it was more a physical reflex than awareness. Sliding the pen under the scarf, she began to turn it, twisting to increase the pressure. It was called a Spanish windlass, basic but effective at restricting the flow of blood. I'd seen one used before, but in very different circumstances to this.

'Here, I'll do that. I'm a doctor,' I added, when she glanced at me uncertainly. 'See if you can stop the rest of the bleeding.'

I kept hold of the pen, maintaining the pressure while the young woman delved in her sports bag for a towel. 'It's clean,' she told me as she began binding it around a wound on Mears's other leg. 'I'd just finished a shift and was on my way to the gym. I didn't see it happen, I only heard it. Was it a hit-and-run?'

I nodded, turning to look at where Oduya was lying. People had gathered round him, the glow from phone screens casting a blue-white illumination. Someone had covered his head with a coat, and sirens were already sounding in the distance.

'Did you know him?' the young woman asked, seeing me looking over.

'Yes,' I said.

Chapter 25

'I DON'T KNOW.'
I tried to keep the frustration from my voice.
Across the scuffed Formica table, Ward and Whelan sat
in identical plastic chairs to mine, their faces blanked of
emotion. We were at a police station only a mile from
the mortuary, a tired red-brick building that seemed
designed to crush the spirits of anyone who passed
through its doors. I'd been in the dingy room for two
hours, first answering questions from a detective sergeant I didn't know, then waiting for Ward and Whelan
to arrive.

If I'd hoped things might improve after that, I'd soon
learned otherwise.

'Try to remember,' Whelan said. The DI looked
crumpled and tired, and the overhead lighting gave his
complexion a sickly tint. 'None of the other witnesses
were as close as you. You were right next to it.'

I didn't need reminding. But the entire incident was
starting to seem unreal, a before-and-after too raw to
think about. The young nurse and I hadn't been on our
own with Mears for long. Police rapid-response teams
were at the scene in minutes, cars and vans disgorging

dark-clad officers in body armour. For a while all had been confusion, the strobing blue lights lending a nightmarish quality to the scene until it was established there was no further risk. Gradually, some semblance of order had been restored. Paramedics rushed to tend to Mears, and as the nurse and I were led away I looked back to see screens being set up around Oduya's body.

That was the last I saw of him.

I'd been quizzed about what had happened, then given paper towels and antiseptic gel from the ambulance to clean up before being taken to a police car. The rain on the windows turned the coloured lights of the street into prismatic smears as I was driven to the station. Once there, I'd been taken to the interview room and brought a polystyrene cup of tea.

It sat in front of me now, untouched and with a scum of grease on its surface, as Whelan continued to quiz me.

'What sort of car was it?'

I tried to visualize it again. 'A hatchback. Not a Golf, but something the same sort of size.'

'Can you remember the registration? Even part of it?'

I shook my head. 'It was over too fast.'

'What about the colour?'

'Dark, but under the streetlights it was hard to tell.'

'Blue, black, red?'

'I don't *know*.'

'And you didn't get a look at the driver? Or how many people were in the car?'

'No, I've told you. It was dark and raining, and I couldn't see for the headlights. There must be street cameras around there, can't you pull something from them?'

'Thanks, that had never occurred to us,' Whelan said flatly. 'Could it have been accidental?'

'No.' I was certain of that much, at least. 'The driver must have seen him. Oduya called to me, and as soon as he started to cross the road the car pulled out and drove straight at him.'

'So it was waiting?'

I heard the squeal of rubber again as the engine was gunned, saw Oduya turn as the headlights picked him out. I tried to dispel the image. 'That's how it looked.'

'Some of the other witnesses say the car swerved to try and avoid Mears after it hit Oduya. Is that how you saw it?'

'The car seemed to weave around as Mears tried to get out of the way,' I said, trying to recall how it had happened. 'It could have been trying to avoid him, I don't know. But there was no chance of that, not at the speed it was going.'

Ward stirred. She'd been largely silent so far. 'What was Oduya doing there?'

I'd known that question was coming. 'I'd arranged to meet him.'

Whelan blew out a breath in disgust. 'Jesus Christ.'

Ward's expression didn't change. 'Why?'

'He called me this afternoon and said he'd got a pro bono case he wanted me to take. It was nothing to do with St Jude's, so I agreed to meet him after work to discuss it.'

'At the mortuary?'

'No, a pub nearby. The Plume of Feathers. I think he'd probably come by Tube and was on his way there, because he was coming from the direction of the station. It was just by chance that I left as he was passing.'

'By chance,' Whelan echoed. 'And was it by chance that the car happened to be waiting for him?'

'I've no idea. I didn't tell anyone I was meeting him, if that's what you mean.'

'You didn't tell us, that's for sure.'

'There was no reason to, it didn't have anything to do with the inquiry,' I fired back.

'All right.' Ward sounded too fatigued to be angry. 'Who suggested whereabouts to meet, you or Oduya?'

I thought back. 'He did. He said he knew the pub from his time at the law courts.'

Whelan gave a snort but said nothing. Ward nodded. 'Oduya didn't have a car, so anyone who knew where he was going could guess he'd get the Tube. All they had to do was park up and wait.'

I pressed my thumb and forefinger into my eyes, seeing him stepping out from the pavement: *Dr Hunter!* I shook my head, a physical attempt to dispel the images the words had provoked.

'Have you any idea why?' I asked.

'We can't entirely rule out terrorism yet, but this looks more like a targeted attack on Adam Oduya,' Ward said. 'It's possible someone had a grudge against Daniel Mears we don't know about, but so far everything suggests he's an innocent casualty. It was just bad luck he was crossing the road at the same time.'

'Good luck for you, though,' Whelan said. 'If you'd left the mortuary first it could have been you instead.'

He didn't need to remind me of that either. 'Have you any idea who the driver was?'

Whelan shrugged. 'Oduya made a career of upsetting people. If we're looking at anyone with a grievance against him, it'll be a long list.'

But I'd noticed the hesitation before he answered. I looked from one of them to the other. 'You do, don't you?'

Whelan glanced at Ward. She sighed. 'Keith Jessop's disappeared. We went to interview him yesterday about the asbestos and the assault at St Jude's. No one knows where he is. His wife last saw him three days ago, when he turned up drunk and abusive after the scene with Adam Oduya. She tried to throw him out, he started smashing things and then ran off when a neighbour called the police. It's logged, we checked.'

Jessop? I sat back in my chair, trying to fit the contractor into the equation. The man was a drunken bully who'd made no secret of his feelings for Oduya He'd blamed him for holding up the demolition work, even tried to assault him in front of police officers.

Still, there was a big difference between taking a swing at someone and deliberately running them down. 'You really think it could have been him?'

'I think I'd like the chance to ask him,' Ward said drily. 'We knew the delays at St Jude's had hurt Jessop financially, but it's worse than we thought. He's bankrupt. The banks have foreclosed on his debts, and because he'd put his house up as collateral he's going to lose that as well. And his wife's divorcing him, not that I blame her. He's lost everything.'

It was hard to think. I felt exhausted, emotionally and physically drained by what had happened outside the mortuary. Even so, something about this wasn't right. 'I saw Jessop's car at St Jude's. It was an old Mercedes. A saloon, not a hatchback.'

'He could have more than one car,' Whelan said irritably. 'It might be a work vehicle, or one he stole. We don't know yet.'

'What we *do* know is that Jessop's a drunk with a violent temper and a public grudge against Oduya,' Ward went on. 'That alone's enough to pull him in for questioning, so the fact he's disappeared doesn't look good. And it isn't only the asbestos he's been lying about.'

I rubbed my temples where a headache had begun to form. 'What do you mean?'

Ward paused, perhaps regretting what she'd said. The strain of recent days was etched on her face. Whelan folded his arms and stared at his lap as she continued.

'This doesn't go any further than this room, OK? We've learned Jessop had access to St Jude's sooner than he's been claiming. He was supposed to have surveyed the site a full year before demolition work actually started. We're still looking into the dates, but that potentially overlaps with when Christine Gorski and Darren Crossly went missing.'

'Wait a minute,' I said, struggling to take this in. 'Are you saying now he could be involved in their murders? Not just the hit-and-run?'

'I'm not saying anything yet. But earlier today we got a warrant to search Jessop's work premises. We found plastic tarpaulins in his yard like the one used to wrap Christine Gorski's body. And before you say it, yes, I know half the builders in the country probably use something similar. But Jessop had a guard dog in his yard, a black-and-tan Rottweiler. Same colour as the dog hairs we found on the tarpaulin from the loft.'

'Not much use as a guard dog,' Whelan commented. 'It was daft as a brush. It'd run out of food and water, so it was just pleased somebody had come to see it.'

I barely heard him. It was one thing being told that Jessop was suspected of the hit-and-run that had killed Oduya. But the sadistic murders that had taken place at St Jude's were something else entirely.

'Guard dog aside,' Ward continued, pointedly, 'most of the tarpaulins were coated in cement dust and powder, which, admittedly, is only what you'd expect, given his trade. But some of them had dried paint on them, the same blue as the paint on the tarpaulin from the loft. We're getting it analysed, but it looks identical. And Jessop's wife let us take some of his clothes, so we've got samples of his hair. If his DNA matches the human hair we found on the tarpaulin as well, then he's going to have some tough questions to answer.'

I sat back in my chair, numbed by this new information. 'So where does this leave Gary Lennox?'

Ward spread her hands. 'At this moment in time, he's still the main suspect for the St Jude's inquiry. But that was always going to hinge on whether his fingerprints match the ones from the false wall. We still haven't been able to check that, so in the meantime we need to find Jessop and—'

She broke off as her phone rang in her bag. Taking it out, her face cleared of all expression as she looked at the screen.

'I need to take this.'

Pushing herself to her feet, she left the room. Whelan and I sat in an uneasy silence after the door closed behind her. He took out his phone and began scrolling down the screen.

'This is going to be bad for her, isn't it?' I said.

For a second I thought he wasn't going to answer. Then he reluctantly lowered his phone.

'Yeah, it is.'

'Tonight wasn't her fault.'

'Doesn't make any difference. This whole investigation's been a PR train wreck. Might not matter so much if we'd anything to show for it, but we've got one suspect practically out of bounds in hospital and now another on the run. Doesn't look good, however you try to spin it.'

No, it didn't. 'Do you think she'll stay on as SIO?'

Again, there was a pause. 'It all depends. If we get a breakthrough with either Jessop or Lennox in the next twenty-four hours, she could still come out smelling of roses. If not . . .'

He shrugged.

If not, the finger of blame would be levelled firmly at Ward, I thought. An inexperienced SIO – and a pregnant one, at that – in charge of her first murder inquiry would make a convenient scapegoat, regardless of whether it was fair or not. This must have seemed a fantastic opportunity when Ward was appointed.

Now it could end her career.

The door opened and she came back in. Whelan and I both looked at her as she returned to her seat, but her face was unreadable.

'We've heard from the hospital,' she said, sitting back down. 'Daniel Mears is out of surgery. He lost the leg.'

Jesus, poor Mears. It was only a few hours before that I'd seen him in the pub, brooding and withdrawn.

Whatever had been bothering him would seem inconsequential now.

'At least he's alive,' Whelan offered.

'Is that supposed to count as a win?' she snapped. 'Only one dead and one maimed? Jesus.'

Whelan coloured, looking down at the tabletop. Ward gave a long sigh.

'Sorry, Jack.'

He nodded, though his jaw muscles didn't unclench.

Ward pushed a hand through her hair, making it even more unruly than before. 'OK, I think we're done here. I need to get back to headquarters. We'll have to prepare a press statement and Ainsley's going to want briefing.'

'Do you need me for anything else?' I asked. I was expecting her to say I could leave. Instead, she considered me for a moment.

'Actually, yes,' she said. 'We have another problem.'

Chapter 26

I DIDN'T SLEEP well that night. Thoughts of the hit-and-run kept me awake well into the early hours, and if I drifted off it was to jerk awake again, still hearing the screech of tyres and the thud of impact. I got up early and took a long shower, finishing with an icy-cold spray. It left me shivering and more alert but no less at odds. Images of Oduya and Mears in the street alternated with Ward's bombshell about Jessop. The enormity of what had happened was hard enough to grasp on its own, but realizing the cause was something so needless – so bloody *mundane* – made it worse. I'd felt some pity for the contractor before this, seeing that, for all his flaws, the man was suffering.

Not any more.

I badly missed Rachel. I wished I could call her, but that wasn't possible while she was at sea. Instead, I tried to act as if it were just another morning, hiding behind the comfort of routine. I resisted turning on the morning news until I was eating breakfast, making do this morning with two cups of instant coffee and a slice of toast. I was expecting the hit-and-run to be one of the lead stories, and it was. It felt strange to hear Oduya and

Mears spoken about in that context on the radio, difficult to reconcile that the activist's huge personality had
crossed over into the past tense. Mears's condition was
described as serious but stable, his injuries life-changing
rather than life-threatening. That was better than it
might have been, but still bad enough. Their role in the
St Jude's investigation was mentioned, along with the
inevitable speculation and criticism of how it was being
handled. Then came something I wasn't expecting.

'The Metropolitan Police are looking to question a
fifty-three-year-old man in relation to the incident,' the
newsreader intoned. 'The whereabouts of Keith Jessop,
a demolitions expert believed to have been working on
the hospital site, are currently unknown. Jessop is
thought to be potentially dangerous and, if sighted,
should not be approached.'

I put down the piece of cold toast, no longer hungry.
So that was it, then: Ward had chosen the nuclear option
of releasing his name. I guessed she'd be under pressure
from Ainsley to demonstrate that the police were taking
action, but I hadn't anticipated it so soon. There seemed
something irrevocable about it, like taking a blindfolded
step in the hope that the ground was where you thought
it would be.

Pouring my coffee down the sink, I got my coat and
left the apartment. There was a bin liner of rubbish to
take out, so I dropped it into the refuse chute on my way
to the lift. The vandalized bins had been replaced, and
the only sign of the fire was a cold odour of old smoke
when I opened the hatch. Whatever I might think about
Ballard Court, I couldn't deny the place was efficient.

Early as it was, the traffic was already heavy as I
drove in to the mortuary. Ward had asked me to go in

again this morning before I resumed searching with the cadaver dog team. She wanted me to examine the skeletonized remains of Darren Crossly and the woman they believed was Maria da Costa, whose identity had still to be formally confirmed. This was the 'other problem' she'd mentioned. For all his posturing, it seemed Mears hadn't bothered to let Ward – or anyone else – see his findings.

'Christ knows what he's been doing. He's been promising to submit his report for days, but there's always been some reason why it's not turned up,' she'd told me. 'We sent him the da Costa woman's dental records as well, so he could compare her chart with the teeth from the body, but he didn't get around to that either. Or if he did, he didn't tell anyone about it.'

'Can't BioGen access his files?' I'd asked.

'Not the ones that matter. For some reason he didn't upload them on to the company system, and his laptop and cloud storage are password protected. Until he regains consciousness there's no way of getting at them.'

Mears had grumbled in the pub that Ward wasn't giving him the chance to finish one job before springing another on him. I'd guessed he was struggling with something, but I thought there'd be more to it than this. He'd already identified Crossly's body, and comparing the female victim's teeth with Maria da Costa's dental chart should have been relatively straightforward.

Yet something had still derailed him again.

I'd been wanting to examine the two interred bodies ever since I'd first glimpsed them in the sealed room. There had been no time for more than a cursory look when I'd gone to help Mears, and ordinarily I'd have been keen for the opportunity to find out more. But not like this.

The road outside the mortuary was still cordoned off by police tape. I'd parked a few streets away, and as I walked towards it I felt a tightness in my gut. There was little sign of the previous evening's carnage. The overnight rain had washed the tarmac clean of blood, and even the van hit by the car had been towed away. Except for the shards of plastic from its broken wing mirror and the fluttering strips of tape, I might have imagined the whole thing. People walked past the street without giving it a second glance. Someone had died but the world went on turning.

As it always did.

With the road closed, I used the mortuary's side door. It wasn't until I was inside that it occurred to me Oduya's body might be there, lying in the dark of a storage locker. The sense of unreality grew stronger when I went to sign in and saw Mears's name scrawled on the line above mine from the night before. Seeing it brought it home again. Not only what had happened, but how easily it could have been very different if the order of those names on the page had been reversed.

I signed in and went to change.

The lights of the examination room stuttered into brightness. Going to one of the cold-storage lockers, I took out the box containing the cleaned bones of the female victim. Mears had packed away both victims' remains before he'd left, and he'd been as scrupulous about that as he'd been in laying them out.

Unpacking the woman's disarticulated skeleton from the box, I began to carefully reassemble it, placing each individual bone on the table in its correct anatomical

317

position. I had to concede it wasn't as neat as when Mears had done it, but it didn't need to be. This was about information, not aesthetics.

The yellow-brown burns on the bones looked like small smudges. Mears had already cut sections of them for examination under a microscope, and I was itching to take a closer look myself. But first things first.

Before anything else I needed to find out if this was Maria da Costa.

It was the same procedure I'd carried out for Christine Gorski. Once I'd reassembled the woman's skeleton, I carried out an inventory of her teeth, noting any cavities or defects as well as detailing the positions of fillings, crowns and other dental work. That done, I turned to Maria da Costa's dental records. Ward had told me they'd finally had some good luck, finding the missing woman's dentist on the second attempt. As I went through the records my sense of puzzlement increased. When I'd asked Mears about the identification when I'd seen him in the pub – it seemed impossible that had been only the day before – he'd bitten my head off. Yet I couldn't for the life of me see why. The comparison was even more straightforward than the one I'd carried out on Christine Gorski. The dead woman's teeth were in a better condition than the young drug addict's, suggesting that, whether she'd been dealing drugs or not, she hadn't been in the grip of such a severe addiction. More to the point, every filling and crown in the cleaned jawbones was consistent with those shown in the dental records of Maria da Costa.

It was as easy an identification as anyone in my profession could hope to make. Mears must have seen that too. So why had he been dragging his feet?

I looked at the dead woman's teeth again. The only new feature I'd found not shown in her records was that several of the molars were cracked. The damage was on both sides, upper and lower teeth, but there was no chipping or loosening to suggest it had been caused by any sort of blow to the face. The cracks looked more like the sort of damage caused by pressure, as though she'd clenched her teeth hard enough to crack them.

She was tortured and walled up inside a derelict hospital, strapped down and left to die in the dark. You'd grit your teeth as well.

But something was beginning to nudge at me. I thought about the lesions I'd seen on both victims, where they'd torn their flesh against the straps. Presumably struggling to escape, regardless of the damage and pain they were inflicting on themselves. As terrified as they must have been, it was probably a natural response, although . . .

I stopped. *A natural response* . . .

I picked up one of the woman's ribs which showed one of the burn marks. It was the same dirty yellow as nicotine on a smoker's fingers. Small, too, and unusually localized for a burn. My heart had started to beat more quickly as an idea began to form. *Jesus, could that be it? Is that what this is?*

Putting the rib down, I stripped off my gloves and pulled on a fresh pair from the dispenser. Going to another storage locker, I lifted out the box containing Darren Crossly's deconstructed skeleton. Mears had packed away the bones with his customary care, and what I was looking for was close to the top. Taking out the skull and mandible, I carried them over to a desktop magnifying lens and switched on its lamp.

Crossly's teeth were cracked as well.

The knock on the door startled me. I turned towards it, but before I had a chance to speak it had already opened.

It was Ainsley.

'Morning, Dr Hunter. Mind if I come in?'

Since he already had, there was no point answering. The commander looked fresh and fit, wearing a navy-blue suit with a crisp white shirt and pale tie rather than a uniform. The jacket was cut to flatter his trim physique. Stopping short of where I was working, he raised his hands.

'I know, I haven't changed but I won't touch anything. And I'm not staying.'

'Is everything all right?'

'There's been no more crises, if that's what you mean. I just wanted to stop by and see how you were getting on.'

Even from where he was standing, his aftershave was potent enough to mask the examination suite's other chemical smells.

'I'm just getting started.' I carefully packed the skull and mandible back in the box. I'd examine Darren Crossly's remains in detail later, but I'd seen all I had to for now. 'Any word on Daniel Mears?'

Ainsley considered the woman's skeleton. 'Not so far. You heard he lost the leg?'

'DCI Ward told me.'

'Terrible. You were there, I understand?'

I nodded, not wanting to go into it again. 'It said on the news you're looking for Keith Jessop.'

I wasn't going to mention what Ward had already told me, that the police wanted to interview the contractor

320

about the other St Jude's murders as well. Ainsley's mouth pursed, perhaps remembering how the contractor had hit him.

'It wasn't an easy decision to release his name at this stage, but we need him in custody. The man's a danger to himself and everyone else. It's a pity somebody didn't realize it sooner.'

By 'somebody' I guessed he meant Ward. The scapegoating had already started.

'So which one's this?' Ainsley asked, looking down at the reassembled skeleton. He might have been talking about car parts rather than human remains.

'It's the woman who was with Darren Crossly.'

'Ah, yes. The one we think is his Portuguese girlfriend. Are you working on confirming the ID?'

'That's right.'

Strictly speaking, it wasn't a lie. The dental exam had proved this was Maria da Costa, but I'd still to check for healed bone fractures or any other identifying features to support the identification. I could have said so to Ainsley, but I hadn't liked his implied criticism of Ward. Although he might outrank her, she was still SIO.

For now.

He nodded, not seeming interested in the answer. I knew then that he'd come here for more than a progress report.

'I approved of DCI Ward's decision to ask you to take over from Mears, by the way,' he said, turning from the remains to me. The blue eyes were as impenetrable as a china doll's. 'BioGen wanted to send over someone else, but I felt we needed continuity. You're already familiar with the case so you can jump straight in. And, without any disrespect to Dr Mears, I thought it would be better to have someone with experience.'

To hear him talk it might have been his idea all along. 'I'll do my best,' I said neutrally.

'I'm sure you will.' Ainsley brushed a fleck of something off his jacket, too small for me to see. 'I'm sure I don't have to tell you that the investigation's under a lot of scrutiny. Frankly, it's lurched from one disaster to another, and we can't allow that to continue. Obviously, no one was aware it would develop as it has, but while I've the utmost respect for DCI Ward, with hindsight it was probably unfair to expect her to deal with this level of responsibility.'

Here it comes. Whelan had foreseen that the blame would be focused on Ward, and Ainsley wasn't wasting any time. 'Because she's pregnant?'

He quickly backtracked. 'No, of course not. But this is her first case as SIO, so it's not surprising she's been . . . overwhelmed.'

'I thought she'd been coping pretty well.'

I wasn't just speaking up for Ward out of loyalty. She was under a lot of strain, but she'd been forced to deal with fast-moving events no one could have predicted. And Ainsley was conveniently forgetting it had been his decision to bring in a private forensic company, the results of which I was having to deal with now.

He nodded slowly, as though giving weight to my words. 'Unfortunately, I'm not sure events bear that out. Especially not after last night.'

I couldn't see how Ward could have predicted Jessop's attack, let alone prevented it. But I also knew there was no point arguing.

'Why are you telling me this?'

322

Civilian consultants weren't high enough in the pecking order to merit that sort of consideration. There was certainly no need for a Metropolitan Police commander to inform me personally if Ward was being replaced as SIO.

Ainsley regarded me thoughtfully. 'I know you and Sharon Ward have a strong working relationship, but we can't afford any more mistakes. Without apportioning any blame, I think it falls to the rest of us to ease the burden of pressure from her in any way we can. That's why I'd like you to report to me from now on.'

'You're asking me to bypass DCI Ward?'

'Not at all. She's SIO and you should continue to report to her as usual. But I'd like to be kept appraised of your findings as well.'

So Ward wasn't being removed. Yet. Just placed on probation, with Ainsley overseeing and no doubt micromanaging in the background.

'Does she know?' I asked.

'DCI Ward's a realist.'

I took that to mean she didn't. Ainsley slipped a card from his wallet and set it down on the worktop next to him. 'Do we understand each other, Dr Hunter?'

'I think so.'

'Excellent.' He shot his cuff and looked at his watch. 'I need to be going. The post-mortem briefing's starting soon.'

'For Adam Oduya?' It hadn't occurred to me that might be the reason for Ainsley's visit.

'Yes, it's scheduled for ten o'clock. Not here, at the Belmont Road mortuary,' he added, seeing me glance at the wall clock. 'It was felt that was more appropriate when he was killed right outside. I just took a detour en route.'

He started towards the door, then stopped and turned again.

'Oh, one more thing. I appreciate your bringing Gary Lennox to our attention, but please remember you're a civilian consultant. Any operational aspects – certainly involving potential suspects – are best left to the investigative officers. That said, I can understand why it happened, and it was a promising lead. It's just a shame it didn't work out.'

I was trying to decide if he was thanking me or reprimanding me, so I was slow to pick up on that last sentence.

'I'm not with you.' From what Ward had said the night before, they were still waiting to check Lennox's fingerprints.

'I thought DCI Ward might have let you know,' Ainsley said, a shade too smoothly to be convincing. 'We managed to obtain sets of both their fingerprints. Lennox's and his mother's. Neither of them matches the ones from the crime scene, so all that time and effort was for nothing. Well, not quite *nothing*. Lennox is getting proper care now, which I suppose is something. But a simple call to social services would have been a lot easier.'

The doll's eyes held mine.

'I won't keep you any longer, Dr Hunter. You know how to reach me.'

Chapter 27

I TOOK A break after Ainsley had gone. There was a water cooler in the corridor, so I went to get a drink while I thought through what I'd just heard.

The commander's visit had thrown me. The good news was that Ward was still SIO, and as long as that was the case then anything I had to report would go through her. I'd no intention of going behind Ward's back, as Ainsley wanted. But the fact he'd asked was troubling. Ward was more than capable of looking after herself, and I'd no doubt she'd be well aware of how precarious her situation was. Even so, for a senior officer to undermine her like that didn't bode well.

Ainsley's other news was even more disturbing. He was right about Jessop: the contractor was a threat to himself and others, and the sooner he was in custody the better. But unless the police could find hard evidence that he'd been involved in the St Jude's murders, the investigation was back where it had started, with no leads or suspects. I'd only just started to believe that Gary Lennox could be guilty and that his mother might be lying to protect him. Now it had emerged that the fingerprints from the crime scene didn't belong to either of them. We'd been wrong all along.

And I'd caused all that grief for Lola and her son needlessly.

I felt out of kilter, as though the ground under my feet was constantly shifting. Some of it was probably a reaction to the hit-and-run the night before. I'd seen a man I knew deliberately ploughed down and killed by a car, and another badly injured. If that had happened to anyone else, as a former doctor I'd be advising counselling or therapy. But I had my own way of dealing with things.

Finishing my drink, I dropped my cup into the bin and went back to work.

As the door of the examination suite slowly shut behind me, I felt my earlier focus begin to return. The cracked teeth on both Maria da Costa and Darren Crossly had provided the first intimation of what we might be dealing with here. Now I just had to prove it.

Mears had told me there were thirteen of the burn-like marks on the woman's skeleton, spread out on different bones, apparently at random. At first glance I saw only eight. There was one on the bony protuberance of the mastoid process, just behind and below the right ear. Another was on the right clavicle, and there were two more on the seventh and eighth left ribs. The pubic bone had what looked like a single large burn, several times bigger than any of the others, while the remaining three were all on the metatarsals of the feet, two on the right and one on the left.

With the exception of the one behind the woman's ear – which I was beginning to have an idea about – all of the yellow-brown marks were front-facing. Meaning they'd probably been inflicted when Maria da Costa was strapped to the bed. At first I was at a loss how Mears had counted thirteen rather than eight, before I looked more closely. The large patch of discolouration on the pubic bone wasn't one large mark but several, close enough together to overlap. I nodded when I saw that. A large burn wouldn't have fitted my theory, but several small ones did.

And I was in no doubt that's what they were: burns. Mears had been right about that. Although the small, tobacco-yellow patches looked insignificant, I knew they would have been agonizing. But I didn't agree that they were brands, or that they'd been caused by something similar to a soldering iron. True, that might have resulted in small, localized burning to the bones not dissimilar to these. It would also have resulted in far more tissue damage than we'd seen. The skin and flesh above the bone would have been almost completely burned away.

I picked up the skull, turning it to see the mark on the mastoid process. There was a chance it could have happened while she was lying down, her head turned away to expose behind her ear. I didn't think so, though. I thought this would have been done while Maria da Costa was standing. And it had been the first one.

Mears, what were you thinking? It was right in front of you.

I quickly carried out an inventory on the rest of her skeleton, finding nothing of note, then packed it back into its box. Wiping down the surface of the table, I changed my gloves again and then began to unpack and reassemble Darren Crossly's bones. They told a similar story to Maria da Costa's. Numerous small burns the colour of nicotine stains, all on bones that had only a thin covering of skin and subcutaneous fat. In his case, ribs, tibia, the metacarpals of both hands and feet. There was no sign of a burn to either mastoid process, which briefly puzzled me. But he had one on his sternum, low down towards the bottom of the blade-like breastbone. When I saw that I began to understand what had happened to him as well.

Packing away the former porter's skeleton, I turned to the sections of burnt bone Mears had prepared. Cutting a sliver thin enough to examine with a microscope – especially from fragile, burnt bone – isn't easy. He'd set the bones he'd selected in resin and then used a microtome – a specialized cutting tool – to pare off wafer-thin slices. That took a good eye and a steady hand, but whatever his other flaws the forensic taphonomist was meticulous when it came to fine details. The sections he'd made were perfect, saving me the trouble of preparing my own.

Putting one taken from Maria da Costa's rib under the microscope, I bent my head to the eyepiece.

The world became an illuminated display of brown-greys and white. I was looking specifically for the cylindrical structures called osteons, which the outer layer of lamellar bone is made up of. Osteons carry blood through a central canal, although there was obviously no blood in these any more. They'd been discoloured from the burn, and I could see where micro-fractures had formed between them. The periosteum – the fibrous membrane covering the bone's exterior – had suffered damage too.

In burnt bone that was only to be expected. What interested me was the scale. I'd been struck from the start by how small the burns were, the patches of discolouration tightly focused. Mears had concluded that meant whatever had made them was small as well, something like a soldering iron, where the heat would be concentrated at its tip. It was a reasonable assumption to make, and all his thinking had progressed from there.

That was his mistake.

I examined the rest of the bone sections, seeing the same thing each time. Packing them away, I considered calling Ward to let her know what I'd found. But there was one more thing I needed to check first.

Something I wasn't looking forward to.

The sun was struggling to emerge from behind the clouds during the drive to St Jude's. By the time I arrived at the gates it had won a temporary battle, gilding the stone pillars and rusting ironwork with a hard-edged light that was already dimming as dark clouds built up again.

The young policewoman and the older PC were on duty again. She gave me a cheery smile.

'Back again?'

'Hopefully not for much longer.'

'Tell me about it.'

She waved me through, and as though waiting for its cue the sun chose that moment to slide behind clouds once more. Driving past the humps of rubble, I felt the usual heaviness at the sight of St Jude's rising up ahead of me. Neither Ward nor Whelan had answered when I'd tried calling them. I'd left a voicemail confirming that the woman's remains belonged to Maria da Costa and that we needed to speak urgently but hadn't said why. It wasn't something to leave in a message, and I was due back at St Jude's anyway to continue with the cadaver dog search. I thought I'd probably find one or both of them there.

Parking with the trailers and police vehicles, I climbed out and saw them both on the steps outside the hospital's pillared entrance. They were talking to Jackson, the police search adviser. He was in a pair of dirty coveralls, and as I approached a few other white-clad officers were trooping out of the hospital's cavernous doorway. It looked like the search team had either finished or was taking a break. Not wanting to interrupt if Jackson was briefing Ward on their progress, I hung back until they'd finished.

I was shocked at Ward's appearance. She'd looked exhausted the night before. Now she was positively haggard, her face hollowed out and drawn. Even the unruly hair seemed lifeless as she nodded at whatever Jackson was saying before turning away. As the PolSA headed towards the trailers, she and Whelan came down the steps.

'If you've come for the cadaver dog search, you're too late,' she said, as I went over. 'The dog trod on a nail so his handler's taken him to the vet. Doesn't look too bad, so we should be OK to resume tomorrow.'

She sounded as tired as she looked, listless and flat.

'Did you get my message?' I asked.

'About Maria da Costa?' She nodded. 'Thanks. We're still trying to track down Wayne Booth's dentist to see if the palate from the boiler was his. You'd think someone would know if he wore a bloody denture, but no one seems sure.' She seemed to collect herself. 'You said you'd something else to tell us?'

330

'I've had a look at the burns on Crossly and da Costa,' I said. 'They're not thermal.'

'Come again?' Whelan said.

'They're electrical burns. The victims weren't branded. Someone repeatedly gave them electric shocks, strong enough to burn the bone.'

'Are you sure?' Ward's fatigue had suddenly gone.

'As sure as I can be. Visually, they're very similar, but thermal burns are bigger and less focused. That's why these were so small, and why there wasn't much external scorching. The current passes directly through the skin and muscle. Both types of burn can cause fractures, but with electrical ones there's damage on the microscale as well. You get microscopic cracks in the bone's structure, which is what I found here. It explains the other injuries too, like the larger fractures on their arms. And the abrasions from the straps weren't from them being beaten or trying to escape, they were from seizures. That's why both victims' teeth were cracked, because they'd been clenched so hard during muscle spasms.'

'Jesus.' Ward was fully alert now, assessing what this could mean. 'What was it, some sort of stun weapon like a taser?'

I shook my head. 'I don't think so. That wouldn't carry enough charge to cause injuries like these. But with no mains electricity in the hospital, it would have to be something portable.'

'We found car batteries inside,' Whelan said. 'We thought they'd just been dumped, but if someone ran jump leads from them would they have been powerful enough?'

'I don't know,' I admitted. 'Perhaps if there were enough of them.'

331

This was entering unknown territory. Not much research had been done on electrical burns to bone, and I'd come across them only a few times before. And they'd been the result of massive shocks from faulty wiring or workplace accidents, and in one case a lightning strike. Nothing remotely like this.

'Whatever it was, I don't think it was just used for torture,' I went on. 'From their placement, most of the burns look to have been made when the victims were lying down. But Maria da Costa had one behind her ear, and Darren Crossly had one in the middle of his breastbone. I think they were given shocks to stun them. Him when he was facing forward, and her by someone standing behind her.'

'Maybe she was trying to escape,' Whelan said. 'You'd stun the big one first because he's more dangerous, then the girlfriend as she tries to run away.'

Ward was nodding. 'Makes sense. But why the hell didn't Mears spot it?'

'I think he did. He just didn't want to admit it,' I said. 'He'd started off assuming the burns were thermal and then couldn't let go of the idea. Not once he'd committed himself and told you about it. I think that's why he was taking so long – he couldn't accept that the facts didn't fit his theory.'

It was known as cognitive bias. I'd known more than a few academics who'd fallen prey to it, stubbornly refusing to admit they'd made an error, despite mounting evidence. It happened with older individuals as well, but with Mears his arrogance had been compounded by inexperience. He'd been so desperate to prove himself on his first major case that he'd lost sight of what he was supposed to be doing.

332

It was the least of his problems now.

Ward obviously thought so too. 'Well, leaving Daniel Mears aside, at least we know how the victims were overpowered as well as tortured. That's a step forward. Was there anything else?'

It was said with the air of dismissal, but I hadn't finished. 'Actually, there is. I think the same thing happened to Christine Gorski.'

That got their attention. 'I thought she didn't have any burns?' Ward said, frowning.

'None that I could see, no. But she could have had one somewhere we wouldn't know about.'

I saw Ward's face change as she realized. 'You mean her stomach.'

'I think so, yes. We know there wasn't a big wound because there was no blood on her clothes. But she was wearing a cropped top that would have exposed her midriff, and a contact burn from an electric shock could have broken the skin without it bleeding. That'd be enough to attract flies when she died, especially if it became infected first.'

That met with a sombre silence.

'You don't know that for sure, though,' Whelan said after a moment. 'You said yourself there was nothing on her body to say that's what happened.'

'Not on hers, no.' I took a breath, loath to say it. 'But there was on the foetus.'

At first I'd thought the minuscule fractures on the delicate bones must have occurred when its mother's body was moved. But after I'd seen Darren Crossly's and Maria da Costa's injuries, I'd examined the foetal skeleton as well and seen how similar the injuries were.

'Muscle contractions from an electric shock can cause bone fractures,' I told them. 'That's what caused them on Crossly and da Costa, and I think that's what happened to the foetus as well. The womb and amniotic fluid might have offered some protection, but . . . not much.'

'Jesus,' Whelan muttered, shaking his head.

But Ward was unconvinced. 'If someone gave Christine Gorski an electric shock, why didn't she have any fractures herself?'

'They don't always happen. The foetus was much smaller and closer to the charge. And Christine Gorski did have a dislocated shoulder. The muscle spasms can cause that as well, so it's possible that happened at the same time.'

'Her waters broke.' Whelan's voice was a rasp. 'That's what those splashes were on the loft steps and loft insulation. Some bastard gave her an electric shock and her waters broke.'

I'd reached the same conclusion. And then, when she'd tried to get away, someone had followed her up to the loft and bolted it behind her.

Whelan seemed relieved when his phone rang. He moved further away on the steps to answer as Ward continued.

'So we're looking at the same person being responsible for all three victims.' She squeezed the bridge of her nose, rubbing her eyes. 'Christine Gorski, Crossly and da Costa, and probably Wayne Booth as well, although we can't prove that yet.'

'I spoke to Ainsley earlier,' I said. 'He told me they weren't Gary Lennox's fingerprints you found at St Jude's. Did Lola change her mind about letting you take them?'

Ward's earlier animation had died. 'No. She was still withholding consent, so we seized his feeder cup and a mug she'd used from their house. It wouldn't be admissible in court but it meant we could run their fingerprints against the ones from St Jude's. None of them matched.'

So that was that. After all the fuss and trouble, the case against Gary Lennox had been a waste of time, just as Ainsley had said. True, at least now he was receiving proper medical care, but I doubted that would count for much with Lola. *Good job, Hunter.*

'So where does that—' I began, but Ward raised her hand.

'Hang on.'

She was looking at Whelan. He was still on the phone, frowning as he listened to what was being said at the other end.

'Something's up,' he told her, before speaking into the phone again. 'Say that again, you're not . . .'

His frown deepened, and as it did I heard a car engine approaching. An unmarked red van was being driven slowly down the driveway towards the hospital. Walking in front, as though escorting it, were two uniformed police officers. I recognized the cheerful young PC and her older colleague who'd been on the gate, but even when I saw the van driver's hand extended from its open window, holding something aloft, I didn't realize what was happening.

Still on the phone, Whelan's face had turned ashen at whatever he was hearing. 'Oh, fuck,' he breathed.

'What's the hell's going on, Jack?' Ward demanded, as other police officers turned towards the strange procession.

There was no time to answer. Suddenly, the van accelerated, forcing the two PCs ahead of it to break into a run. The young woman I'd spoken to earlier stumbled and fell, and for an awful second I thought the van would run over her. Instead it braked and the driver's door was flung open.

Jessop climbed out.

The contractor carried a sports holdall slung over one shoulder, bulging and sagging from whatever was inside. He still had one arm raised in the air, and I could see there was something small and square gripped in his fist. At first I thought it was a mobile phone, but then I saw the wires curling from the open bag.

He was holding a detonator.

Chapter 28

WHELAN REACTED FIRST. 'Clear the area!' he yelled, signalling furiously as he pushed past me. 'Everybody get back! *Now!*'

Police officers and SOCOs seemed to be running everywhere, scrambling for cover behind cars and trailers. Still holding the detonator aloft, the contractor grabbed hold of the young policewoman by the arm. When the grey-haired PC made as if to intervene, Jessop thrust the detonator at him, thumb poised.

'Go on, then! You think I give a fuck?'

'Do as he says!' Whelan snapped.

The older PC reluctantly backed off. Next to me Ward was speaking hurriedly into her phone, her voice low as she requested support. At the bottom of the steps, Jessop shifted his grip on the PC, yanking her in front of him and pinning her to his chest with an arm crooked tight around her throat. The contractor's clothes were filthy. A grey stubble covered the loose skin of his jowls like a dirty frost and his eyes were yellowed and bloodshot.

Whelan spoke to me quietly. 'Move away, Dr Hunter.'

The hospital's mausoleum-like entrance behind me was the nearest cover and the only option that wouldn't involve going past Jessop. Looking into its dark maw, I hesitated, loath to leave the two of them.

'Now!' Whelan snapped.

Jessop's voice rang out. 'He's staying there! Nobody's going anywhere!'

Still holding the police officer around her neck, with his free hand he pulled open the top of the holdall. From where I stood I could see it was full of waxy slabs tangled with plastic-coated wires. A bottle of what looked like vodka lay among them, sloshing slightly with the movement.

'There's enough RDX in here to blow everybody to fuck!' He raised the detonator. 'Anybody comes near me, I'll fucking press it! I mean it!'

'All right, Keith, we believe you.' Ward stepped out from beside me, lowering her phone. 'Now you've got our attention, supposing you tell us what you want?'

She spoke conversationally, sounding almost bored. It seemed to unnerve him. As Jessop struggled for a response, the young PC he was holding spoke in a choked voice.

'I'm sorry, ma'am, he said if we didn't do as he said, he'd—'

Jessop tightened his arm around her neck. 'Shut the fuck up!'

'All right, Keith,' Ward said smoothly. 'Why don't you put the detonator down—'

'*Don't tell me what to do!*' Jessop glared at her, his mouth working. 'Nobody tells me what to do. Not any more.'

Ward raised her hands. 'Nobody's trying to. You're in charge, so why don't you tell me what it is you want?'

'What I *want*?' Jessop barked out a laugh. 'What I fucking *want* is my life back! Can you give me that?'

'I can help, but you've got to—'

'Do I look *stupid*?' The jaundiced eyes seemed to radiate heat as he glared at Ward. 'My picture's all over the fucking news! Everything's gone, and for what? Some stupid little bitch who'd no right to be here!'

'Her name was Christine Gorski.' There was an edge in Ward's voice. 'She had a life too. And a family. You saw them, remember?'

'So what? It's not my fault their daughter was a junkie!'

'She didn't deserve to die, Keith. Any more than Adam Oduya or—'

'I don't give a fuck about them!' Jessop yelled. 'What about me? Who cares about *me*? No one!'

'That isn't true, Keith. I'm sorry if—'

'You're *sorry*? You think I give a fuck about an *apology*?'

'Then talk to me. Tell me what you want.'

'I want to do what I should have done months ago!' He jerked his chin behind her, towards St Jude's. 'I'm going to blow that fucking place up!'

'That won't change anything, Keith.'

'Maybe not, but I'll die happy.'

'Will you?'

A breeze stirred the contractor's greasy hair as he stared at her, suddenly uncertain. Then he cocked his head, listening. A moment later I heard it myself.

The wail of sirens, growing louder.

'That your friends?' Jessop sneered. 'Thought you'd keep me talking until some fucker blows my brains out, is that it?'

'No, wait—'

But Jessop was already climbing the steps, forcing the female PC to walk ahead of him. When Whelan moved towards them, the contractor raised the detonator.

'Get the fuck out of the way.'

'I can't do that. Come on, man, think what you're doing.'

'I said, fucking *move*! You think I won't press this?'

Jessop brandished the detonator, his knuckles white. The sirens were much closer. I saw the older PC from the gate cordon start to edge nearer, but then the contractor's head whipped towards him.

'Fuck off! Now!'

'Do as he says,' Ward said quickly. She put a hand on Whelan's arm. 'Nobody do anything stupid.'

'I'll count to three,' Jessop spat. 'One!'

'No one's going to stop you from going inside. Just let her go,' Ward told him. 'Look at her, Keith. She's not much more than a girl. Do you really want to hurt her?'

'Two!'

The young PC had shut her eyes. She was half the size of Jessop. I could see her trembling but her mouth was clamped and determined. Ward seemed to have run out of words. As the wail of sirens drew closer, Jessop took a breath and raised the detonator.

'Take me,' I said.

The words tumbled out spontaneously. My voice sounded unnaturally loud. Whelan and Ward spoke at the same time.

'For Christ's sake . . . !'

'Stay out of this, David . . . !'

But I had Jessop's attention. I spread my hands, showing him they were empty. 'You want a hostage, take me instead.'

He looked at me, his arm still crooked around the PC's neck. Then his mouth turned down. 'Get out of the way.'

'Let her go. I'll come with you,' Ward said before I could respond.

Whelan turned to her, horrified. 'No way! That's—!'

'In another thirty seconds you're going to be in the crosshairs of about a dozen police marksmen,' Ward told Jessop, ignoring her DI. 'I can't let you take one of my officers in there, but I'll go with you instead. Or you can blow us all up now because, the way my day is going, I really don't care very much. Your call.'

'Ma'am, you don't have to do this,' Whelan implored.

She ignored him, staring at Jessop. 'Fifteen seconds.'

The sirens sounded inside the gates now. The contractor gave a nod. 'If you try anything . . .'

'Jesus, man, I'm six months pregnant, what am I going to do?' Beneath the show, I could hear the fear in Ward's voice.

'Sharon, don't . . .' I began, but she was already going towards where the contractor held the young policewoman.

'I can't let you do this,' Whelan said, moving to stop her.

'Stand aside, Jack. That's an order.'

Her voice cracked out, and Whelan faltered. Moving quickly, Jessop shoved away the PC and grabbed hold of Ward instead.

'Inside. Now,' he said, steering her up the steps.

'For God's sake, man, she's pregnant!' Whelan shouted, anguished.

So was Christine Gorski, I thought, numbly. Jessop backed through the shadowed doorway, pulling Ward in after him. Her bravado had gone now, and her face was pale and scared.

Then Jessop pushed the big doors shut behind them and they were swallowed up by St Jude's.

The next hour was one of the worst I can remember. The second Jessop and Ward had disappeared inside the hospital, Whelan began yelling instructions. As frenzied activity erupted all around, I stood on the steps, dazed and ignored. Dark vans screeched up with lights flashing, disgorging armed officers in body armour. The air was full of sirens, all of them growing louder, as though drawn towards the epicentre of St Jude's.

Whelan hauled me roughly down the steps. 'What the fuck were you *thinking*?'

He lifted a hand, as though wanting to hit me. Then, with a disgusted shake of his head, he turned and hurried away.

I was ushered away from the main building, forced into a run until I was behind the police trailers, where a police officer with a gun demanded to know who I was. Then I was instructed to stay there. More police vans and cars were arriving all the time, joined now by fire engines and ambulances. As the crackle of emergency radios sounded from all around, above the trailer I could make out the roof of the old hospital, a stark black silhouette against the grey sky.

Jessop hadn't blown it up yet.

Not knowing what else to do, I sat on the steps of the trailer. When I looked at my watch it didn't seem possible that less than half an hour had passed since I'd arrived at St Jude's.

'How you doing?'

342

It was the young PC from the gates, who Ward had replaced as hostage. She held out a bottle of water.

'Thought you could use this.'

I could have used something a lot stronger, but I accepted it gratefully. She hesitated.

'I wanted to thank you. You know, for back there.'

I just nodded. There was a sick, hollow feeling inside me that swallowed up anything I might have said. The PC looked past me, towards the hospital.

'She'd have done it anyway. If anyone's to blame, it's me. I should have stopped him.'

'How? You did what you could,' I told her.

'Doesn't stop you feeling shit, though, does it?'

No, it didn't. After she'd gone I took a drink of water. It was more to give myself something to do than from thirst, but I realized I was parched. As I recapped it, brisk footsteps alerted me to someone's approach. It was Ainsley. The commander stopped in front of me and gave me a cold stare as I got to my feet.

'We'll talk in the trailer.'

He trotted up the steps, leaving me to follow. Empty plastic chairs stood inside, arranged around an empty table.

'Any news?' I asked.

Ainsley seemed to consider whether or not to answer. 'No. We're still trying to make contact.'

'Is anyone else inside?' The cadaver dog search had ended for the day, and I'd seen one search team outside, but there could still be others in the basement.

He breathed out through his nose, nostrils flaring. 'Apart from my SIO and a suspect with a bagful of explosives, you mean? Thankfully not. The search was winding down so the hospital was empty.'

He turned a chair around and sat down. After a second I did the same. The china-blue eyes were hard to meet, but I didn't look away.

'So, Dr Hunter, would you mind telling me why you're here instead of at the mortuary?'

It wasn't the question I'd expected him to lead with. 'I'd finished there, so I came to help with the cadaver dog search.'

He stared at me without speaking. Hanging between us was our last conversation, his instruction to report my findings to him as well as to Ward. We both knew I'd flouted it, but I didn't care.

'Tell me what happened with Jessop,' he said at last.

I did, trying to dredge up every detail from my memory. Ainsley would have already spoken to Whelan before coming to see me, but he was all business now, wanting to hear anything I might add.

'Describe what you saw in the bag,' he said, interrupting.

'Rectangular blocks of what looked like dirty white putty, with wires stuck in them. Jessop called it RDX.'

Ainsley breathed out. 'It's an explosive used in demolitions. Can you say how many blocks you saw?'

'Not really, but the holdall was medium sized and looked heavy. About half full. And there was a bottle of vodka in there as well.'

It was worth mentioning in case no one else had seen it: alcohol and explosives were a bad mix. Ainsley nodded, as though I'd confirmed what he'd already heard.

'How would you describe Jessop's state of mind?'

I wasn't qualified to judge that, but Ainsley wasn't asking for a professional opinion. 'Angry, aggrieved.

Self-pitying. He didn't show remorse over Christine Gorski or Adam Oduya.'

'Would you say his threats were a bluff?'

My mouth was dry. 'No.'

The doll's eyes regarded me. 'Do you recall our conversation this morning about interfering in police operations?'

I took a breath and let it out. 'Yes.'

'Then would you mind telling me what you thought you were doing, offering yourself as a hostage to a hostile suspect armed with a bag of explosives?'

I'd been tormenting myself with the same question, asking if Ward would have volunteered if I hadn't done it first. But then Jessop would have taken the young policewoman instead, and I'd have been berating myself over not doing anything. There was no easy answer.

I stared back at the hard blue eyes. 'What would you have done?'

Ainsley's mouth pursed, but he didn't reply. He stood up, dusting something invisible from the front of his well-pressed trousers. I'd noticed him do that before: either his eyes were better than mine or it was an unconscious tic.

'I'll send someone to take a formal statement, then you can go. I'll arrange for you to be taken home.'

It hadn't occurred to me until then, but I'd parked in front of the main hospital building, on the wrong side of the new perimeter. My car wasn't going anywhere until this was over.

One way or the other.

'I'll make my own way,' I said.

'As you like.'

He left. I'd managed to stop myself from asking what was going to happen now. He wouldn't have told me, and I could guess some of it anyway. A police negotiator would try to make contact with Jessop, probably through Ward's phone, if the contractor's was switched off. They would try to talk him into giving himself up and releasing Ward. If that failed, the decision would have to be taken whether it was riskier to wait or send in armed officers. In a warren-like building the size of St Jude's, that would be a last resort.

Especially when Jessop might have rigged it with explosives.

It seemed an age before a plainclothes detective constable arrived to take my statement. I spent the time replaying the events on the hospital's steps and agonizing over what might be happening while I waited in the empty trailer. My neck and shoulders ached as I sat tensed, waiting for the roar of an explosion.

It didn't come. Once I'd signed my statement, I was told someone would be along to escort me through the outer police cordon, and then I could go. When no one had appeared after another fifteen minutes I grew tired of staring at the trailer's scuffed walls and went to wait outside. No one took any notice as I opened the door and went down the steps, but there was a palpable tension, a sense of expectancy in the air. It had been late afternoon when I'd arrived and the light had fallen while I'd been inside the trailer. Floodlights had been set up in front of St Jude's, bathing the austere face of the building as though it were a giant stage set.

Jessop's van still stood at the bottom of the steps, too close to the hospital for the police to approach. Its door hung open exactly as he'd left it, a physical reminder of what had happened.

'Dr Hunter.'

I turned to find Whelan approaching. I braced myself for more criticism.

But all his energy seemed to have left him. The DI looked to have aged five years in the last few hours, and I realized he probably felt almost as useless as I did. This was a tactical operation now. He'd have to take a back seat himself while other people took over.

'I wasn't sure you were still here,' he said. 'Look, about earlier. Maybe I was—'

The ground suddenly shook with a deep, solid *bump* that felt as though my heart had stuttered. An instant later it was followed by a huge, percussive *THUMP* that rocked the trailer next to us. I staggered into Whelan as the entire front of St Jude's seemed to shiver, and then the boards covering its windows were blown off. A sheet of timber caromed into Jessop's van, almost tipping it over before it was swallowed by a billowing cloud.

The din of car alarms filled the air as shattered brick and stone peppered down with the sound of hail on a tin roof. All around people were climbing to their feet, staring in shock at the hospital.

Whelan leaned weakly against the side of the trailer. 'Oh no . . .'

Beneath a billowing veil of dust, over half of St Jude's had ceased to exist.

Chapter 29

THEY BROUGHT OUT the first body just before
midnight.

The rescue operation had started even before the
dust swirling over the rubble had begun to settle. Grim-
faced rescue workers tried to clear a way inside,
ferrying equipment and machinery from fire tenders
and vans. More floodlights were set up, replacing those
shattered in the blast, and the strobing blue lights of
emergency vehicles added an icy hue to the scene. The
old hospital had been mortally wounded. Debris littered the ground in front of it, glass and shredded
timber scattered like fallen leaves. One wing had been
destroyed, the loft where we'd found Christine Gorski
and the hidden room beneath completely obliterated.
The other, including the main entrance, was still standing and retained most of its roof. But only the exterior
walls were intact. The explosion had brought down the
internal walls and floors, reducing most of the interior
to a vast heap of broken stone and plaster. What windows remained had been blown out, leaving blind,
blackened holes edged with jagged shards and broken
frames.

All had been confusion in the minutes after the explosion. As the last rumbles died down, Whelan had taken a few steps towards the hospital before stumbling to a halt as the smoke and dust had cleared to present a view of the wreckage.

'Oh, Jesus Christ . . .'

My ears were ringing, and the air had held an acrid stink I could taste at the back of my throat. 'What can I do?'

He'd looked at me as though he'd forgotten who I was. 'Stay here.'

Then he was running towards a group of officers, yelling orders. Ignoring his instructions, I'd headed for the ruined hospital until a police officer in body armour grabbed me by the arm.

'You! Where're you going?'

'To help,' I said dumbly.

'You think anyone's walking out of there? Stay behind the trailers!'

With that, he'd hurried away. He was right, I'd realized, as another group of uniformed officers rushed past. There was nothing I could do here. Dazed, I'd gone back to the trailers.

By contrast, everyone else had seemed galvanized with purpose. A semblance of order had already been established as the honk of fire engines blared in the distance, steadily growing closer. I'd slumped down on to the steps of a trailer, staring at the devastated hospital. In front of it, Jessop's van stood on flat tyres, paintwork dulled by dust and grit. Its door was hanging off and its windscreen had been stoved in by the broken plywood board that lay across its crumpled bonnet. I'd felt nauseous. I hadn't believed he'd do it. In spite of everything,

I'd thought the contractor would allow himself to be talked down, would have let Ward leave.

Not this.

The cloud of dust had began to thin when movement caught my eye above the hospital. Black wisps were trickling from the undamaged section of roof, fanning out against the darkening sky. Please don't let it catch fire, I'd thought, my stomach tightening. Then a breeze had cleared the dust and I'd realized it wasn't smoke.

The surviving bats were leaving St Jude's.

As night fell the rescue operation had taken on the relentless quality of a machine. I would have liked to help, but my offers had been tersely refused. No one had told me to leave, though, so I hadn't. At one point I'd seen police and fire officers huddled over building plans, and shortly afterwards rescue workers had began venturing through the main doorway. Ainsley had arrived not long after that, leading a tall man in casual clothes to a trailer. The man was in his forties and had walked with the shell-shocked look of someone who'd found himself in a nightmare. Although I'd never met Ward's husband, I hadn't needed to be told this was him.

One look at his face had made that clear.

It was an hour or so later when there was activity around the main entrance. Its doors had been blown off, leaving a raw opening like a toothless mouth. Now shouts came from inside. I scrambled to my feet as I saw paramedics jogging towards the entrance with an empty stretcher.

An odd silence fell just before they brought the body out. I was too far away to make out any details, and the figure on it was covered. But the funereal pace of the bearers as they carried it down the steps was message

350

enough. In the bright floodlights and flanked by the tall stone pillars, the procession looked almost theatrical. Desperate to know who it was, I looked round and saw Whelan watching solemnly from nearby. I hadn't seen the DI since just after the explosion. He looked exhausted, glancing at me without interest as I hurried over.

'Who is it?' I asked.

Whelan didn't take his eyes from the slow procession. 'Jessop.'

He said it without emotion. A little of the tension went from my shoulders as I watched the stretcher being loaded into a waiting ambulance.

'What about Ward?'

'Nothing yet. It was pure chance they found him. He was in the basement, on the edge of where half the floors above came down. It looks like he'd set the charges but wasn't anywhere near them when they went off. There wasn't . . . they haven't found anyone nearby, but it's going to take days to clear the rubble.'

His face reflected the bleakness in his voice. It confirmed what I'd known but not wanted to admit. This was a recovery operation now, rather than a rescue.

Whelan turned to me as the ambulance doors were slammed shut. 'I didn't know you were still here.'

'It's better than waiting at home.'

He nodded. 'You should go, though. There's nothing you can do here, and it'll be hours before . . . Well, before there's any news.'

'I'd rather stay.'

'Up to you. In that case you might as well . . .'

A shout came from the entrance to St Jude's. There was some sort of commotion going on among the rescuers gathered by the main doorway, a commotion spreading

351

outwards from them like ripples in a pond. Seeing it, Whelan tensed, and as though on cue his phone rang.

Snatching it from his pocket, he squared his shoulders as though preparing himself. I watched him, my stomach knotting.

'You're sure?' he said, his expression carefully guarded. 'There isn't any . . .?'

There was a long pause. I watched the broad shoulders sag. He put his phone away.

'They've found her.'

Rachel called me at seven o'clock that morning, nearly beside herself with worry. She'd heard about the explosion at St Jude's on the BBC's World Service. It had said only that there had been casualties following a hostage situation, but she hadn't been able to get through on the boat's satellite phone. She'd had to wait until they put in to the nearest marina before she'd been able to contact me.

'You're sure you're all right?' she kept asking.

'I'm fine,' I assured her.

Her call had woken me from an exhausted sleep, but I didn't mind. It was good to hear her voice. I didn't know what time it was when I'd got back to the apartment, except that it was late. I'd taken a taxi, since my car was still out of bounds at St Jude's for the time being. Even though I hadn't been close to the blast, I was still gritty with dust. But I'd been too tired to shower. After everything that had happened I just wanted to sleep.

It had taken several hours to bring Ward out. After instructing me to stay put, Whelan had hurried off, leaving me alone with my thoughts as I'd stared at the floodlit shell of St Jude's. Ward's husband had emerged from a trailer with Ainsley not long afterwards. He'd looked unsteady and almost overcome with emotion as they'd headed towards the ruined building.

For a long time after that nothing had happened. Then I'd seen a sudden flurry of activity outside the hospital. I'd moved to get a better view, hands clenched so tightly my fingernails dug half-moons in the skin of my palms. Emergency workers were trooping back from behind the shattered building, the reflective strips on their dirty protective clothing glinting under the floodlights. Paramedics came next, bearing a stretcher, and while I could only see a blanket-covered form strapped to it, I'd recognized Ward's husband walking alongside.

Then an arm had emerged from beneath the blanket as Ward reached up to grip her husband's hand.

Whelan came back over after the ambulance had left. He'd still looked drained, but now it was from relief instead of tension. He'd handed me a bottle of water.

'I wouldn't want another night like this,' he'd said, his voice hoarse.

Neither would I. The call Whelan had received earlier had been to tell him that rescuers had heard banging from beneath the rubble. When they'd hammered in return, the bangs had repeated the same rhythm. Somehow, Ward had survived the explosion and the building's collapse. After consulting blueprints supplied, ironically enough, by Jessop himself, they'd realized she was in the underground tunnel linking the basement to the now-demolished morgue at the back of St Jude's.

There was no way they could get to her through the hospital. The tunnel's entrance was buried under hundreds of tons of debris and any excavation would risk bringing the surviving structure down as well. Instead, the decision was taken to free Ward from the other end of the tunnel, clearing a route to her through the more manageable wreckage of the morgue.

The rescue had seemed interminable, and must have felt even longer for Ward and her husband. With her phone unusable so far underground, no one had any idea of her condition until the rescuers actually reached her.

'She's in pretty good shape, considering,' Whelan had told me, taking a drink of water. 'Shaken up, and she might have a perforated eardrum from the explosion, but other than a few cuts and scrapes she came out in one piece.'

'What about the baby?'

'They'll check her out at the hospital, but so far everything looks OK. She's a tough one, the boss. Tougher than a lot of people give her credit for.'

There'd been fondness as well as pride in his voice. I'd looked at the ruined shell of St Jude's, remembering the force of the explosion that had brought it down. Even now I still found it hard to believe anyone could have survived.

'How did she get away from Jessop?'

'She didn't. He let her go.' Whelan recapped his water. 'From what she's told us, he was hitting the vodka while he went round rigging the explosives. She managed to get him talking, and by the time they got down to the basement he was getting pretty maudlin. She tried to persuade him to give himself up, but he lost his temper and yelled at her to get out before he changed his mind. She'd made it as far as the tunnel when he triggered the charges, so she ran in there as the place came down.'

Remembering the tunnel's dark mouth, criss-crossed with police tape and asbestos warning signs, I didn't envy her. Trapped and alone underground, it must have been a hellish experience.

'Did she think he meant to do it?'

'God knows. By the sound of it he was drunk and not making much sense towards the end. But he did what he said he was going to, and if anyone deserved to have that place dropped on his head it was that murdering bastard.'

I wasn't about to disagree. But even through the fatigue and relief something didn't seem right.

'Why did he let her go?' I'd asked.

'She didn't say. Maybe because she was pregnant.'

'That didn't help Christine Gorski.' She'd been stunned by at least one electric shock before being left to die in the hospital's loft. And the degree of cruelty evident in the deaths of Darren Crossly and Maria da Costa, even the brutal snuffing of Adam Oduya's life and the callous disregard for Mears, were hard to reconcile with Ward being allowed to escape.

Whelan had shrugged, growing irritable. 'Then perhaps he had a fit of conscience, I don't know. He did, that's the main thing.'

It was, and that wasn't the moment to be questioning such an unexpected reprieve. Whelan left shortly afterwards, heading for the hospital for a more formal interview with Ward. With my car still off limits, I'd called for a taxi to meet me outside the main gates and then walked down the long, unlit driveway to the main road. Halfway along I'd stopped and looked back. The floodlights bathed the shattered hospital in a white glow, hard edged against the black sky. Like the church ruins in the woods, there seemed something natural about it, as though St Jude's had always been destined for this end.

Turning my back on it, I'd walked away for the last time.

The street beyond the police cordon had been packed with waiting media vans, cameras and spectators. I'd kept my head down as I hurried past, ignoring shouted questions as I saw my taxi waiting. One persistent journalist ran after me as I climbed in, but I'd slammed the door on her and told the driver to set off. Ignoring the woman's angry yell, I'd sat back in the seat, wanting nothing more than to fall into bed and sleep.

Which I had, until Rachel's call woke me. Finally reassured that I wasn't hurt, her attention swung to Ward.

'It's a miracle she got out alive. And the baby's OK as well?'

'So far as I know.'

I heard Rachel give a long sigh. 'God, when I heard it on the news . . . I thought you said it wasn't dangerous?'

'I didn't think it was. Things just . . . developed.'

'*Developed?* Jesus, David, you could have been killed!'

'I was a bystander, that's all. It was Ward who was inside the hospital, not me.'

'And what about the hit-and-run? The news report said that someone from the investigation was hurt then as well. It could have been you.'

I hadn't told her it nearly was, and decided that now wasn't the time. 'I'm fine. Really. If you were here, you'd see that for yourself.'

'What's that supposed to mean?'

'Nothing,' I said, taken aback. 'I just meant . . . there's nothing for you to worry about.'

'Seriously? I get to hear on the news that you might have been blown up, and then have to wait hours to find out you're OK? You call that nothing to worry about?'

I massaged the back of my neck, amazed at how quickly this had turned into a row. 'Look, I'm sorry you were worried. But it wasn't something I could do anything about.'

It sounded feeble even to me. I could hear Rachel breathing on the other end of the line. The silence grew awkward, but I couldn't think of anything to say that wouldn't make it worse.

'I didn't mean to bite your head off,' she said more quietly. 'This just isn't . . . I'll phone you later, OK?'

The line went dead.

Sleep was out of the question after that. The sky was lightening as I stared through the window at the apartments' tree-covered grounds below. From up here it was possible to see how well screened the place was, isolated from its neighbours by its high fence and electric gates. There and then, I made up my mind that I would move back into my own flat as soon as I could arrange it. It had been a mistake coming here, and there was no point in staying any longer.

I'd had enough of hiding from ghosts.

A hot shower and breakfast helped me feel more human, although the conversation with Rachel still preyed on my mind. My restless mood wasn't helped by lack of sleep, or the feeling of being in limbo. I'd been expecting to continue with the cadaver dog search at St Jude's for a day or two yet, but obviously that wasn't going to happen now. It left me with nothing planned, and nothing to do. I wasn't good at down-time and, while there was always work for me to do at the department, for once I didn't feel like going there either.

You really do need a change.

I'd made myself another coffee when my phone rang. This time it was Whelan, and my first thought was that something had happened to Ward or the baby.

I needn't have worried. 'They're fine,' the DI told me. 'They're talking about discharging her later today. Like I told you, she's a tough one.'

He sounded back to his no-nonsense self, the emotions he'd let slip the night before stowed safely out of sight again.

'Are you going to be around later?' he asked.

'I can be,' I said, trying not to sound too eager. 'Why?'

'There's something I wanted to ask you about. Might be nothing, just something the boss said that got me thinking.'

Now I was intrigued. 'About what?'

'Tell you later. There's a couple of things I want to do first. Let's say two o'clock at St Jude's. Don't bother checking in, I'll see you by the main gates.'

'You want to meet at the hospital?'

I couldn't keep the dismay from my voice. I thought I'd seen the last of that place, and I couldn't see any reason to go back now it was destroyed.

But Whelan was giving nothing away. 'I'll explain later. Do me a favour and keep it under your hat for now. Like I say, it might come to nothing.'

My restlessness was forgotten as I put my phone away. With Jessop dead and the crime scenes buried under tons of rubble, I'd assumed the investigation would start winding down. I couldn't imagine why Whelan would want to go to St Jude's again. Or why he needed to meet me there.

I looked at my watch, impatient at having to wait to find out. I still had a few hours to kill, but now I thought about it I could put the time to good use.

There was something I had to do as well.

Chapter 30

A BIN LORRY was blocking the street. I told the taxi driver to let me out at the corner, paid and got out to walk the rest of the way. The weather was as mercurial as ever, bright and sunny again after the morning's early rain. I unfastened my jacket, enjoying the thin sunlight on my face. The phone call with Rachel still cast a shadow, but I told myself it was what happened when people were tired, stressed and in different time zones.

Now, though, Ward's miraculous escape the night before made it hard not to feel a sense of optimism in the daylight and fresh air. *Well, not so fresh.* The sweet stink of the bin lorry accompanied me as it made its slow progress, hissing and clanking, down the street.

The handles of the brown-paper carrier bag dug into my palms as I approached Lola's house. There was no sign of life. The window shutters were still closed, grime and cobwebs adding a dirty film to the glass. Even the glossy finish on the front door seemed dulled. I still wasn't sure what good coming here would do, except perhaps appease my conscience. I was under no illusions about how Lola would feel after the disruption I'd brought into her life. Thanks to me, she'd been questioned by the police and seen her invalid son treated as a suspect in a murder inquiry. Even though the crime-scene fingerprints had cleared him, he'd still been taken from her care, and I didn't think she'd be the forgiving sort.

But now it was over I had to see how she was. I knocked on the door. There was no response. Halting a few houses away, the bin lorry's hydraulics groaned as it accepted another load. I knocked again, but I was already beginning to think I was wasting my time. Even if Lola was home, I was the last person she'd want to see. One of the refuse collectors shouted and banged on the side of the lorry. As it began rumbling along the road again, I caught a movement as the blinds shifted in Lola's window. *Well, she's in at least.* I raised the paper bag so she could see it.

'Lola, can you open the door?'

Nothing. I lowered the bag, feeling stupid for making such a cheap gesture. I'd known it would take more than another roast chicken to make up for my guilt, but I'd hoped it might persuade her to speak to me, at least. The bin lorry's brakes hissed as it pulled up to a halt at my back, blocking out the sun. I could hear more banging as bins were collected from the occupied houses across the road. I set the paper bag down on the front step and turned to leave.

The door was opened. Lola stared out at me, her face a cold mask. Her eyes flicked to the bin lorry looming behind me, then she moved back.

'You'd better come in.'

Well, that was easier than I thought. I picked up the carrier and stepped inside. The bin lorry blocked

361

even more of the light from the shuttered window. In the dimness I saw that the medical supplies that had cluttered the room before were gone. But the bed was still there and, while the stained mattress had been stripped of its sheets, a smell of faeces and urine still lingered.

The noise from the bin lorry was muted as Lola shut the door and turned to face me.

'What do you want?'

'I came to find out how you were.'

'Why?'

I couldn't blame her for being hostile. The shrine-like cabinet with its photographs of a young Gary Lennox faced the empty bed, even though there was no longer anyone in it to see them.

'I wanted to see if there was anything I could do—'

'Haven't you done enough? You've taken everything I had left – what more do you want?'

I was still holding the carrier bag with the roast chicken. It seemed a pathetic peace offering now.

'I'm sorry, I know you're—'

'Sorry? Oh, that's all right then! You waltz around, acting like your shit don't stink, and all the time you're planning this.' She flung a hand towards the empty bed. 'Happy now, are you?'

Lola glared at me, her chest rising and falling. Coming here was a mistake, I realized, wondering how I'd thought it could be anything else. There was a hiss from outside as the bin lorry pulled away from the window, letting daylight back into the room. I was about to leave when something seemed to shift in the deep-set eyes. She held out her hand.

'Here, give me that.'

362

Snatching the carrier bag from me, she dumped it down by the sink, pausing to sniff the aroma coming from it.

'I suppose you want a cup of tea now you're here.'

That was the last thing I'd expected, but she was already filling the kettle. She jerked her chin towards the scuffed dining table.

'You might as well sit down.'

Still surprised, I pulled out a chair and lowered myself on to it. I looked over at the cabinet with its old photographs of her son as a young boy.

'How is Gary?' I asked.

The kettle banged down. *'Don't you say his name!'*

I was startled by the sudden outburst, unprepared for the venom in her eyes. 'I'm sorry, I just wondered how he was.'

Lola controlled herself with a visible effort. She turned away again. 'Ask the doctors if you're so worried.'

The atmosphere in the small room was suddenly frigid. I wished I'd declined her offer of tea, but I couldn't leave now. Lola seemed unsettled as well. She picked a mug up and set it aimlessly back down, then opened the paper bag containing the chicken before bunching it shut again.

'How much do I owe you?'

'Nothing, it's—'

'I told you before, I don't want your charity!' The look she gave me was one of thinly veiled contempt. And something else I couldn't identify. 'I'll fetch my purse. Wait here.'

She went through the doorway in the corner of the room, and I heard her thumping tread going upstairs.

On the worktop the kettle clicked off, apparently forgotten. I blew out a long breath. I'd been prepared for Lola to refuse to speak to me or yell abuse, but not this barely restrained anger.

The trill of my phone made me jump. Taking it out, I saw the caller was Whelan. I debated ignoring it, but Lola was still upstairs and it could be news about Ward. With a last glance at the doorway, I answered.

'Everything OK?' I asked, keeping my voice down.

'If you mean the boss, she's fine. Already fretting about getting back to work,' Whelan said. 'Where are you?'

I looked at the doorway again. There was no sign of Lola coming back downstairs yet, but I didn't want to stay on the phone long. 'I can't really talk.'

'Then I won't keep you. There's been a change of plan. Can we make it four o'clock instead of two?'

I'd planned to go to St Jude's straight from Lola's. But the way things were going I'd have been early for the meeting anyway.

'Why, is there a problem?'

'No, just something that's come up.' His tone made it clear he wasn't going to tell me what it was. 'Oh, there is one thing. We found Wayne Booth's dentist. The remains from the boiler aren't his. Booth didn't have a denture, partial or otherwise. He still had all his own teeth.'

I shouldn't have been surprised. The only reason to think the missing ex-porter and security guard might have been the fourth victim was because of his connection to St Jude's and therefore Gary Lennox. But that theory had collapsed along with the case against Lola's son. Which left us with no idea of who the burnt remains might belong to.

I agreed to meet Whelan later and put my phone away. I could hear Lola still clumping about upstairs. Restlessly, I got up and went to the cluttered cabinet of photographs.

This was the first opportunity I'd had to look at them up close, without the distracting presence of Lola's son. The cabinet really *did* look like a shrine, I thought. As well as the framed pictures on its top there were mementos from Gary Lennox's childhood. Certificates for swimming and attendance of a college bricklaying and carpentry course, what looked like a home-made wooden jewellery box. There was even a faded Mother's Day card in which a message had been scrawled in childlike handwriting.

After what had happened to him, I supposed it was understandable for Lola to mourn what her son used to be. Even so, unintentional or not, it was cruel to confront him with it as well. Poor devil, I thought, looking at one of the school photographs. Its colours were bleached and faded, showing Gary Lennox when he was thirteen or fourteen. He seemed excruciatingly uncomfortable in a too-tight uniform, his discomfort evident despite a strained smile that revealed his crooked teeth. He'd been carrying too much weight even then, and had gained more in the later photographs. It was a shocking contrast to the shrunken man I'd seen lying in the bed.

I picked up the picture of Lennox in his porter's uniform. It was one of the largest there, and looked to have been taken when he was in his late teens. Probably not long after he'd started work at St Jude's. He'd become a hulking young man, although his awkward smile remained the same. I put it back down and started to turn away, then stopped. Something nagged at me. Picking it up again, I studied it more closely. His smile wasn't quite the same, I saw. His teeth were no longer crooked. It was noticeable in the other photographs taken when he was an older teenager as well. Although it didn't seem to have helped his confidence, at some point he'd had his teeth straightened.

The realization crept over me slowly, a prickling of tension I felt before I knew its cause. I looked again at the older photographs showing the younger Gary Lennox with crooked teeth. Then back at the one in my hand. The front teeth seemed too uniformly perfect to have been straightened by a dental brace, and none of the photographs showed him wearing one. Only the before-and-after results. More likely crowns or a bridge, then.

Or a partial denture.

I told myself it didn't mean anything, but every instinct said otherwise. Gary Lennox was in his thirties, within the age range for the burnt remains recovered from the boiler. Although the photographs stopped when he was in his late teens, the blueprint for the adult he'd become was still clear. A big individual. Large stature, heavily boned.

Unrecognizable as the wasted invalid Lola claimed was her son.

Right or wrong, Whelan needed to know about this. Putting down the photograph, I took out my phone to call him. But as I scrolled to the DI's number Lola's heavy tread began thumping back down the stairs. Opening a text panel, I tapped a hasty message: *Chk GL dentl recs* and pressed send. Hoping it would make sense, I quickly put my phone away and turned as the door opened.

Lola stopped when she saw me next to the cabinet. Her eyes flicked to the photographs I'd been examining, but I couldn't tell if there was any more suspicion in them than usual.

'He was a lovely boy, my Gary.'

I stepped away from the cabinet as casually as I could. 'When did he lose his front teeth?'

The question didn't seem to surprise her. She came into the room. She had a folded-over newspaper in her hand, but I couldn't see any purse. 'When he was sixteen.'

'That's a tough age for something like that. How did it happen?'

The small eyes were fixed on me. 'The bastard who called himself his father knocked them out. An accident, he said, but I knew better.'

The prickle of tension I'd felt was back, stronger than before. I'd guessed that the owner of the partial palate had lost his front teeth in some sort of violent event. Having them knocked out by an abusive father, accidental or not, was certainly that.

'Did he have a bridge or a denture?' I asked.

'What's it to you?'

There was no doubting her suspicion now. But I was saved from answering when my phone rang again, startling me for a second time.

Lola gave a scornful smile. 'Aren't you going to answer it?'

I took the phone from my jacket pocket. *Whelan.* He must have got my text, but I couldn't speak to him now. I cancelled the call, switching my phone on to silent before putting it away.

'Don't you want to talk to them?' she mocked.

'It can wait.'

Lola continued to stare at me with that knowing smile. I felt a sudden unease, some instinct urging *Get out, now.* But that was ridiculous. She was an old woman. And this had gone on long enough.

'Who was in the bed, Lola?'

'I don't know what you're talking about.'

'It wasn't Gary, was it?'

She glared at me, and again I felt that touch of disquiet. 'Think you know it all, don't you?'

No, I didn't. But I was beginning to guess at some of it.

'Gary's dead, isn't he?' I said quietly.

Her composure cracked. Her mouth quivered as her eyes went to the photographs of her son on the cabinet. A tear ran down a wrinkled cheek, joined by one on the other side.

'He was my boy,' she whispered, her voice broken and hoarse. 'My lovely boy.'

Despite myself, I felt sorry for her. 'I know you want to protect him, but you can't. Not any more,' I told her gently. 'It's over.'

'*Over?*' She spat the word. 'You think it's ever going to be over? My Gary's *gone*! All because of them . . . them three *scum*! They weren't fit to lick his boots!'

She dashed the tears from her eyes with the back of her hand. I'd heard enough. Sickened and weary, I reached for my phone.

'I'm going to call the police now, Lola. You need to tell them what Gary did.'

'What *he* did?' Her mouth curled in a sneer. She came towards me, still clutching the newspaper. 'I told you before, my Gary was a *good* boy. He wouldn't hurt a fly.'

She suddenly lunged, thrusting out the newspaper. I dodged back but the bed was behind me. As I stumbled against it the newspaper fell away to reveal a long, black tube. I tried to knock it away but the blunt end glanced off my chest. Agony seared through me.

And I stopped breathing.

Chapter 31

THE PAIN WAS worse than anything I'd known. The world seemed to white out in a bright flash as every nerve in my body screamed. I fell on to the bed, my muscles locked in spasm. There was a coppery taste of blood in my mouth. I could feel my heart stuttering, feel my lungs bursting with the need for oxygen. Then my chest heaved and I could breathe again.

Jesus Christ, I thought, trying to gasp in air, Jesus Christ, what just happened?

Someone was moving nearby. Heavy, shuffling footsteps. There was the scrape of a chair being drawn up, then Lola sat down with a grunt and picked up a mug from the table. *When did she make that?* Had I blacked out? I'd no idea. Lola took a noisy drink before lowering it with a sigh.

She looked down at me and smiled.

'Not so clever now, are you?'

My thoughts were muzzy, like thinking through a fog. I still couldn't move. There was still pain but it was somehow distant, as though I were anaesthetized at the same time.

The old woman took another drink of tea and smacked her lips appreciatively. She reached for something on the table. I wanted to shrink away when I saw it was the black tube, but I was unable to move. There were thick wires at the end she was holding, while protruding from the other were two stubby metal prongs.

She held it up to show me.

'About the only useful thing my husband left me, this. Brought it back with him from South America. Like a cattle prod, only stronger. The police there would charge them up and then . . .'

She made a jabbing motion towards me, stopping short with a grin. I would have yelled, but I couldn't even do that. I could only lie there, paralysed.

'Hurts, don't it? He tried it on me once when he was drunk. Just that once.'

Her grin had gone. She laid the thing across her lap, the end with the two stubby prongs pointed at me.

'I stuck him with it after he knocked Gary's teeth out. 'How do you like *that*?' I said. Pissed and shat himself like a baby, he did.' She looked down at me as though to check. Her mouth turned down with disappointment. 'Didn't expect it to kill him, but served him right.'

Sensations were beginning to return. I could feel the lumpy bed under me, smell its sour, unclean odour. I hurt all over but the sharpest pain was on my ribs, where the thing had touched me. A bright, hot burning. You've been shocked, I thought, dazedly. She gave you an electric shock. A bad one.

'My Gary was upset at first, but he was a good boy,' Lola was saying. 'Always did as he was told. "It'll be better now," I said, "you'll see. Just the two of us, it'll be better." And it was. He helped me clean up, get everything tidied away in case anyone came and asked about Patrick. Nobody did, though.'

She paused to take another drink of tea. My muscles were twitching uncontrollably, agonizing shivers running through them. I still couldn't move but my hands and feet had started tingling, a savage pins-and-needles. I told myself it was a good sign.

Above me, Lola's voice droned on.

'We were fine until that bastard Booth turned up.' Her mouth curled as she glanced down at me. 'It was him that got my Gary sacked from St Jude's. Did you know that, Mr Smartarse? Him and them other two, Crossly and that foreign slut. Made his life a misery, they did. Always picking on him, laughing at him for being big-boned. Crossly's girlfriend was shagging the head pharmacist, the nasty little bitch. Getting him to turn a blind eye so they could nick meds and sell them. Except they weren't as clever as they thought, so when Security started sniffing round they hid stuff in my Gary's locker. Made him look like a *thief.* The hospital must have known, but they didn't want a *scandal*, did they? So my Gary got sacked while Booth and them other two bastards stood back and laughed! "Who's been a naughty boy, then? Got caught, did you?" I'll never forget his face when he came home that night. Like a whipped dog.'

There was a thrumming in my chest. I thought it was a muscle spasm before I realized it was my phone. I'd switched it to silent before putting it back in the breast pocket of my jacket, and its rubber case must have insulated it against the shock. I could feel it vibrate and pause, vibrate and pause, against my ribs. *Whelan again?* I could have wept with frustration. But even if

Lola hadn't been sitting a few feet away, I could no more move my hand to reach my phone than fly.

She hadn't noticed. Her voice took on a crowing tone. 'Christ, didn't I laugh when they shut St Jude's down a few months later! Made the whole lot of them redundant! Boot was on the other foot then, wasn't it? My Gary had a job at the local supermarket while they were in the dole queue. See how they liked it!'

The vibrations from my phone cut off. *No, don't hang up!* Distracted, it was a few seconds before I noticed that Lola's flow of words had stopped. She was staring down at me, and I realized I'd been shifting my arm fractionally as the stunned muscles and nerves began to recover.

'Wearing off, is it?'

Her smile was cruel. She lifted the black tube from her lap. I tried to push myself away as she leaned towards me, but my muscles wouldn't cooperate. *No! No, no –*

There was a crackling *SNAP* as the two metal prongs jabbed into my stomach. The world whited out again as my nervous system screamed. This time I didn't lose consciousness. I was aware all the time as my back arched, lifting me juddering off the bed on just my heels and the crown of my head.

Then it had gone. I crashed back down again. Each ragged breath was a blessed relief and an agony, my shocked body quivering in protest. There was a smell of burning flesh and fabric.

Laying the tube on the table, Lola sat back and took another drink from the mug.

'Must have been about a year after that when Booth showed up at the supermarket where Gary worked. Crooked bastard had managed to get himself a job as a security guard at St Jude's. Him!' She shook her head. 'Thought it was a big joke finding Gary stacking shelves. Like being a night-watchman was anything special. A few days later he came back, and this time he'd got Crossly and his bitch with him. Started helping themselves to beer and wine, right in front of my Gary. Laughing in his face, telling him he'd already got the sack for thieving once, wouldn't want it to happen again, would he?'

Her mouth compressed in a bitter line.

'He was too upset to tell me. Oh, I knew *something* was wrong but he said he was just tired. He'd been under the weather for a bit, had to go for tests and things.' She glowered into the mug she was holding. 'Bloody doctors, what do they know?'

Without warning, she dashed the tea in my face. I choked, my paralysed diaphragm fighting for air. Lola put the mug down on the table and made herself more comfortable in the chair.

'Anyway, that went on for weeks. Then one night Gary didn't come home from work. I sat up half the night, worried to death. Three o'clock in the morning it was when he finally came back, clothes all torn and filthy, reeking of drink and . . . and . . . *her*!'

Lola's face twisted, her mouth working as though trying to rid itself of a bad taste.

'They'd waited for him after work. Made him get in the car with them, said they were having a party. Like they were his *friends*. Took him out to St Jude's, where they'd got this ward decked out with chairs and what-have-you. Booth wasn't working there any more, but Crossly and his bitch had got jobs at another hospital, so they were up to their old tricks. Nicking drugs and selling them, thinking they were clever, doing it from in there. Scum!'

She scowled, carried away by her memories.

'Thing was, business was slow. The pharmacy they'd been nicking from had tightened up, so they'd run out of stuff to sell. So now they were bored and wanted *entertaining*. My Gary wasn't a drinker, not like his old man, but they forced it down him. Egged him on to do things with that . . . that *whore*! He didn't want to – I know my own son better than *that* – but Crossly turned nasty. Started knocking him about, yelling at him. My Gary could have snapped him in half, but he never lifted a finger. And when he was on the floor, in tears, that fucker Booth . . .' She paused, her voice quavering with emotion. '. . . That fucker *pissed* on him. Like he was a dog! Who'd *do* that?'

She broke off, her mouth working as she drew in ragged breaths. Abruptly, she looked down at me, and I knew what was coming. My skin crawled as she picked up the black tube. I tried to push myself away as she extended it towards my face, still wet from the tea she'd flung in it. But none of my limbs would obey.

'You think it's hurt so far?' she hissed. 'If I stick this in your gob you'll know better. You'll scream loud enough when your teeth burst.'

The twin electrodes hovered inches away from my mouth. They were tarnished and stained, except for the very ends, which were burnished a dull brass. I could see in Lola's face how much she wanted to do it, but then her gaze went to the shuttered window. The thin slats of wood and single pane of glass were the only barrier between us and whoever might be outside. An expression of petulance crossed her face.

She stuck the tube against my chest.

When the spasm had passed, I could hear her moving about by the sink. Making more tea. I lay quivering, tears of pain wet on my cheeks. But as bad as it had been, I didn't think this shock had been as strong as the others. I could already feel my muscles twitching as the first inklings of use began to creep back. I didn't know how much charge the black tube held, but it wasn't connected to the mains electricity. Sooner or later, it had to run out.

I just didn't know if I'd survive that long.

Lola grunted as she lowered herself back on to the chair. Taking a dainty sip from the mug, she put it down on the table next to the tube. Sniffing, she wiped her nose with the back of her hand before resuming. As though telling a child a story.

'Crossly was easy,' she said, calmer again. 'We had to wait a couple of weeks till he showed up again at the supermarket, but I knew the rotten bastard wouldn't stay away for long. I'd told Gary to say he'd found a bagful of prescription painkillers I'd got stashed away. Codeine, opiates – all stuff they could sell. They knew I'd been a nurse. They used to torment him with stories they'd heard about me, and they'd never think Gary was lying. He didn't want to, but I knew he would. He was a good boy, my Gary.'

There was pride in her voice. I wriggled my toes, slowly tensing muscles to work some use back into them without being seen.

'Crossly wanted him to take them to St Jude's,' Lola went on, oblivious. 'Made him go in through the morgue, so he wouldn't get picked up by them cameras they'd put up at the front. Thought he was getting one over on Gary, making him go through that tunnel by himself. Except he wasn't. He'd got me with him. With this.'

She raised the black tube, her eyes shining. I tensed, thinking she was going to shock me again. But she lowered the tube without using it.

'I thought all three of them would be there, but it was just Crossly and his tart. Thought it was hysterical when they saw me. "Brought your mummy, have you? Need someone to hold your hand in the dark?"'

A slow smile split Lola's face. She patted the black tube.

'He was laughing on the other side of his face when I stuck this in his fat gut. Her too. She tried to run away, but she didn't get far, I saw to that. I'd only planned to ginger them up a bit, but when I saw the old beds standing there I had a better idea.'

Nodding to herself, she took another drink of tea.

'Gary wasn't happy,' she said, setting the mug back down. 'Shook like a leaf, bless him. It was only the second time I'd ever had to raise my voice, but I couldn't manage on my own. I needed help getting those fat lumps on the beds, and I couldn't build the wall myself, could I? I made sure they watched him doing it, though, I can tell you that. Still think he's useless, do you? I said. Who's laughing now?'

She'd picked up the black tube, grinning as she stabbed it in the air for emphasis. I flinched each time it came near me. Then her grin faded.

'The only pity was that Booth wasn't there with them, but I thought we'd get round to him later. Give him a room on his own. I didn't expect . . .'

Her voice faltered. She blinked away tears.

'He was strong as an ox, my Gary. Never an ill day in his life, never mind what those doctors said. And he never complained, not even when he had to bring all them blocks and stuff upstairs. Who wouldn't be out of breath, carrying all that lot? He'd made a lovely job of the wall, right down to the painting. It looked a treat. Another hour or so and no one would have known we'd ever been there. And then that . . . that stupid little *cow* walked in!'

My limbs felt wooden and heavy, as though my body had been shot full of novocaine. But some movement was slowly returning. While Lola was distracted, I tried flexing my leg, watching her to make sure she didn't notice.

She was too lost in her own story, though. 'I *told* him, I'd *said* to make sure he'd padlocked the ward door! Every time, I said about it! I didn't want no junkies coming in while we were busy, he *knew* that. But he'd been in a funny mood all day. Quiet, off his food. I thought he'd be all right once we'd finished in that place. If I'd known, I'd never have . . . I thought he'd just *fallen*, clumsy like he was. But he just lay there, his face all blue! I couldn't just *leave* him there, could I, my lovely lad? Not in that place, not with them!'

I wasn't even trying to follow what she was saying, intent on making my body work. Lola bowed forward, covering her face with her hands. Her shoulders shook, but then her head snapped up again.

'It was that pregnant little bitch's fault!' she spat. 'If she hadn't . . .'

Without warning she snatched up the tube and rammed it against my side. And then again. Fresh agony poured through me. I blacked out this time, greying back to consciousness as I felt myself being dragged from the bed. I landed on the floor with a jarring impact, winded on top of everything else. My limbs were dead as lumps of wood, and my heart seemed to be fluttering in my chest as I saw Lola stoop down, stiffly, and take hold of the rug I was lying on.

'Let's get you out of the way, shall we?'

The ceiling above me began to move as I slid across the floor in a series of slow, stop-start jerks. After a few seconds Lola stopped and straightened, panting and with her face flushed.

'Jesus bloody Christ . . .'

Grimacing, she massaged her lower back while she caught her breath. Then she bent to grip the rug again. Grunting with exertion, she took one staggering step backwards, then another.

The rug, with me on it, slithered a few more inches.

I could see an open doorway behind her. Inside it was a small, unlit hallway with a low ceiling that sloped downwards into the blackness of a cellar. The sight terrified me as I realized what Lola was intending. Even if I didn't break my neck when she tipped me down the cellar steps, once I was down there she could do as she liked. No one knew where I was, and my car was still parked at St Jude's. Lola could take her time, torturing me with the black tube without anyone to see or hear.

Just like Darren Crossly and Maria da Costa.

I tried desperately to will use back into my muscles. *Come on, MOVE!* As Lola wheezed and huffed, dragging me inch by inch across the floor, I was rewarded by the slightest twitch of my fingers. It was a start, but the cellar door was only a few feet away. Fresh panic surged in me as Lola heaved the rug nearer before stopping again. She mopped her forehead, gasping for air.

'Christ, my bloody back.' Her face was red and greasy with sweat as the small eyes rested on me. 'Woken up, have we?'

I saw her look over at the chair where she'd left the black tube, and could almost see what she was thinking. I lay completely still, knowing if she gave me another shock it was all over. *No! Don't do it!*

But no one was listening. My feet thumped down as Lola let go of the rug. She stepped over my legs to get to the chair, and as she did I felt a thrum against my chest as my phone began to vibrate. It was almost silent, but she was closer to it this time. Or perhaps something in my face gave it away: either way, she stopped. Her eyes narrowed as she looked at me.

'What's that, then? Someone trying to get hold of you?'

She reached down and wrenched my jacket open. With an annoyed click of her tongue, she pulled out the phone. She scowled as it vibrated again, more audibly now.

'Bloody things.'

Shuffling round me, she went to the sink and dropped the phone among the dirty dishes. It disappeared with a splash, giving one last *bzz* like a drowning insect before falling quiet. Lola turned back to me with a mean smile.

'Not be needing that any more.'

I closed my eyes as despair welled up. But the distraction had made her forget about fetching the black tube. Not that she needed it: my feet were already in the cellar doorway. Hands on hips, Lola regarded me as though contemplating her final effort.

'Right. Nearly there.'

Taking a deep breath, she began to step over my legs so she could drag me the last few inches. As she did, with an effort born of desperation, I raised my hand to grab her ankle. It was a futile attempt. My hand flopped, numbly, succeeding only in slapping at her foot.

'Oh, yes?' she snarled. 'Want some more, do you?'

Incensed, she turned to wrench free, and her other foot caught my outstretched legs. Her eyes widened as she stumbled, teetering in the open doorway. She clutched at the door, causing it to swing towards her. It struck my body and stopped, and Lola's hand slipped from it. Her cry was cut off as she tumbled backwards down the cellar steps, crashing down them in a series of slithering thuds.

Then silence.

I lay in the doorway, my heart racing. I half expected to hear movement from the cellar as she began to make her way back up the steps. But there was nothing. *OK, you can't stay here. Time to move.* Trying to force myself to sit upright, I succeeded in rolling on to my side. I lay there, gasping. My entire body felt wrong, numb and burning at the same time. There was a buzzing in my ears and my heart was still hammering too fast. *Stay calm. Breathe deep and stay calm.* Looking up, I could see Lola's landline on the sideboard. If I could reach that, pull it down to the floor by its cable, I could call for help. Throwing out an arm that was as unresponsive as a log, I attempted to drag myself across the floor. The buzzing in my ears grew louder, and my heart raced more than ever. I could feel it bucking in my chest, its rhythm ragged and stuttering as a grey mist seemed to fill the room. *Oh, Jesus, don't pass out. Not now, not yet.* I kept my eyes on the phone as I tried again to crawl towards it.

But it could have been a mile away. The buzzing was growing deafening. It filled my head as I lay back down. I couldn't feel my body any more. That worried me at first, but it was also a relief. An odd sense of peace came over me. So this is it, I thought, as my vision began to fade. I felt sadness for Rachel, then I pictured Kara and Alice. I heard my daughter's laugh, and before the greyness turned to black I smiled to think of them waiting for me at home.

Chapter 32

'HAS HIS GIRLFRIEND been informed?' Whelan asked. Ward shifted in the chair, trying to find a more comfortable position for her stomach. 'Not yet. We know she's out of the country but haven't been able to contact her.'

They sat in front of the window. Both looked tired, the strain of recent events evident. Of the two, Whelan looked the worse, the light from the window and the fluorescent fitting overhead combining to expose every hour of lost sleep. Ward looked marginally more rested, but the freshly scabbed grazes and a purpling bruise on one cheek told their own story.

'Better if she hears it from us rather than see it on the news.' Whelan blew out his cheeks. 'What the hell did he think he was doing, going back to the Lennox house?'

'I expect he felt sorry for her. And responsible, probably. Bear in mind he was the one who told us about Lola and her son in the first place. If not for that, we might still be—'

She broke off, looking towards the bed.

'Back with us, are you?'

I tried to speak. My mouth was dry and didn't work at first. 'What are you doing here?'

My voice came out a croak. Ward smiled. 'Good to see you, too.'

'I meant . . .' I swallowed, trying to moisten my mouth. '. . . Shouldn't you be in bed?'

'Tried it, got bored.' She said it lightly, but a shadow crossed her face. Then it was gone. She gave a tired grin. 'I'm fine. Besides, there's too much to do, trying to keep you out of trouble.'

I started to push myself up in the bed, then abandoned the attempt. 'What day is it?'

'Friday.'

That was right: I'd forgotten that I'd already asked the nurse when I'd first come round that morning. My thoughts were still a little fuzzy, but I knew I'd gone to Lola's on Wednesday. I'd lost a whole day.

'How do you feel?' Ward asked.

Strange was the first word that came to mind. The light hurt my eyes and colours seemed too vivid. Moving took conscious effort, as though my body no longer fitted properly. On top of that, I felt as weak as a kitten and ached all over. There were burn dressings on my upper biceps and torso where the pain was more focused, and ECG sensors were taped to my chest. Thin wires ran from them to a monitor by the bed.

'OK,' I said.

'How much do you remember?'

It was coming back to me now. *Lola. The black tube.* 'Enough.'

'Do you feel up to telling us what happened?' Ward asked, pouring me a glass of water.

I wasn't sure, but I did my best. I broke off to take a drink from time to time, and at one point a nurse came in to check my stats, but I managed to tell them as much as I could remember. Which ended when I'd lost consciousness on Lola's floor.

'It might not feel like it, but you were lucky,' Ward told me, refilling my water glass. 'That thing she used was called a picana. Like a beefed-up cattle prod but a lot nastier. This one had been customized so it could be recharged rather than run off a mains supply. It was running low by the time she used it on you.'

It hadn't felt like that to me. 'She told me her husband brought it back from South America.'

'We know. Apparently, various regimes used them to torture prisoners in the 1970s, but I'd not heard of one here before. She kept it under a floorboard in her bedroom. We missed it when we first searched the house, but in fairness we weren't looking for anything like that then.'

'How did you find me?' I asked, managing this time to push myself up in the bed. I was only wearing a hospital gown, but I was past caring.

'You can thank Jack for that. After he got your text and then couldn't get hold of you he called round to Lennox's house. One of her neighbours said she was definitely home, so when she didn't answer the door he forced an entry and found you on the floor.'

'Thought you were dead,' Whelan said, matter-of-factly.

So did I. 'What made you think I was there?'

But Ward was climbing to her feet. 'I think we've tired you enough. Get some rest. We can talk again tomorrow.'

There were still questions I wanted to ask, like why Whelan had wanted to meet at St Jude's in the first place, and what Ward had meant when she'd said *We know*. But even as I started to protest, a wave of fatigue washed over me. Suddenly, I couldn't keep my eyes open. I sank back down on the bed as the two of them left, talking in low voices to themselves.

'You didn't tell him about her,' I heard Whelan say, and Ward respond, 'Later,' but by then I was too far gone to worry about it.

I spent most of the next forty-eight hours drifting in and out of a sleep so deep it felt like unconsciousness. Often I'd wake to find someone by the bed, and then a moment later they were gone and I'd realize hours had passed. Rachel arrived on Friday evening after Ward's and Whelan's visit. She'd tried to call me back after our argument, but my phone wasn't working after Lola had dropped it into the sink. Growing increasingly worried, Rachel had called Jason and Anja to see if they knew where I was. They didn't.

Checking hospitals, Jason had been told I'd been admitted as an emergency, and then used his sway as a senior consultant to find out why. It had taken Rachel most of a day to get to an airport and make connecting flights back to London. She'd hugged me so hard she'd dislodged some of the sensors taped to my chest, before turning on me, furious.

'Jesus, David, *look* at you! I can't turn my back for five minutes, can I?'

Then she'd hugged me again.

Jason had been even more direct when he and Anja visited. 'You're a trouble magnet, that's your problem. It's uncanny.'

I'd undergone a variety of tests, X-rays and scans to determine if Lola's treatment had caused any lasting complications. The chief worry was my heart, which had been dangerously arrhythmic by the time I'd been found. There was some concern about damage to its muscles, and whether the electrical current had permanently disrupted their normal rhythm. I'd been seen by a cardiologist who explained that, while there was no immediate crisis, he wanted to see me again in a few weeks.

'All in all, you were very lucky,' he said.

People kept telling me that.

Piece by piece, I was able to form a clearer picture of what had happened. The first surprise was hearing that Lola was still alive. I'd assumed the fall down the cellar steps would have been fatal for someone her age, but she'd survived with contusions, a broken hip and minor fractures.

'She looked better than you did,' Whelan told me during his and Ward's second visit. 'What the hell were you thinking, going there?'

Not that an old woman would try to kill me, that was for sure. But even before I'd texted Whelan to check Gary Lennox's dental records, the DI was already forming his own suspicions about Lola and her son. After Ward's rescue from the tunnel, he began to think how the morgue would have made a convenient back door for anyone wanting to come and go from St Jude's without being seen.

'The CCTV cameras at the main entrance around the front were dummies, but most people wouldn't know that,' he said. 'There weren't any by the morgue, so until it was demolished anyone who knew about the tunnel could get into the hospital that way. I remembered you saying you'd seen Lennox's mother in the woods, so then I got to thinking how that was the quickest route from their house to the morgue.'

That was why he'd originally wanted to meet me, Whelan explained, so I could show him whereabouts in the woods I'd seen Lola. Then he'd received my text and realized we might have been approaching this from completely the wrong angle. And that the remains in the boiler might not be another victim's after all.

'There had to be a reason you wanted me to check Gary Lennox's dental records, and since I'd just told you the denture couldn't be Wayne Booth's it didn't take a genius to guess why,' Whelan said. 'When you didn't answer your phone I'd a nasty feeling you might have gone back to Lola's, playing the Good Samaritan again.'

'It's a good job he did,' Ward told me, pointedly. 'You wouldn't be here if he'd waited to check the dental records first.'

I was uncomfortably aware of that already. 'I'm glad he didn't.'

Whelan tried to shrug it off. 'I just didn't want you to balls things up before we'd had a chance to question her. I was already starting to think the man in the bed wasn't her son, and by then I had a pretty good idea who he might be.'

'Wayne Booth,' I said.

'Wayne Booth,' Ward agreed.

Lola had found out where Booth lived from Darren Crossly and Maria da Costa, Ward explained. She'd intended to torture and entomb him at St Jude's as well, but when Gary died she'd had to change her plans.

'She went to his flat, stunned him and then pushed him back to her house in an old wheelchair,' Ward said, sounding almost impressed. 'Five miles, with the picana tucked under a blanket so she could knock him out again when she needed to. Her neighbour even saw her taking him into the house, but she was new and just assumed it was Lola's son. Like the rest of us.'

There was a note of self-recrimination in her voice.

'So it was the electric shocks that did the damage to Booth?' The flesh around my own burns seemed to twitch as I asked the question.

Ward nodded. 'You remember I told you he was covered in old skin lesions? The doctors thought at first they were healed pressure sores or maybe same kind of fungal infection, until a dermatologist identified them as burns. By the time they got round to telling us ... Well, it would've saved us all a lot of grief if we'd known sooner. She must hope stopped using the picana on him when Booth had the stroke, but it's still a miracle he survived this long. I suppose Lola's nursing experience came in useful for something. She wanted him alive so she could keep on punishing him. Easier than blaming herself, I suppose.'

Don't take him as well! He's all I've got left! Not the plea of an overly protective mother, as we'd thought, but an embittered torturer deprived of her victim. The cabinet of photographs facing the bed hadn't just looked like a shrine. It had been one.

'Is Booth able to communicate at all?' I asked.

'He can respond to yes/no questions with nods and hand movements. The therapists are working on getting him to use a keypad, although that's going to take time. But Lola's told us most of it herself.'

'She's confessed?'

'I wouldn't call it a confession, exactly, I just don't think she cares any more. She knows there's no point denying anything now, and in between the verbal abuse I think she enjoys rubbing our faces in it.'

They'd told me that the fingerprints from the wall and the paint tins at St Jude's had matched ones on Gary Lennox's personal belongings. The *real* Gary Lennox, that was, not Wayne Booth. It was clear now why the fingerprints of the bedridden man hadn't matched those found at the crime scene. At the time that had been taken as proof that Lola's son was innocent. It never occurred to anyone that the man in the bed might be someone else.

'Has she said anything about how her son died?' I asked. From what Lola had told me, it had sounded like the shock of seeing Christine Gorski walking in on them had brought on a cardiac arrest.

Ward gave a grim smile. 'She was less talkative about that, but it came out in the end. She killed him.'

'She *what*?'

'Not intentionally. She lost her temper when he tried to protect Christine Gorski. She'd already stunned her once, and when Gary tried to stop her doing it again she used the picana on him. We know he had a weak heart, so maybe that's what happened to his father as well.'

A heart condition, inherited or otherwise, wouldn't have been helped by carrying building supplies all the way up to the top floor of St Jude's. And as a reluctant partner to his mother's crimes, her son would have been under enormous physical and emotional stress already.

'You were right about Christine's waters breaking,' Ward added, her tone studiedly neutral. 'She came round and tried to get away while Lola was trying to revive Gary, but only made it as far as the loft. Lola followed the splashes on the floor, and when she realized where the girl had gone she just bolted the door and left her in there.'

I didn't know which was worse, the fact that Lola had killed her own son or the callous way she'd delivered an electric shock to a pregnant young woman. And then left her to die in the loft of a derelict building.

'Some nurse,' Whelan said, in disgust. 'She couldn't carry his body, so she used an old wheelchair she'd found lying about to get him as far as the stairs. Then she tipped and dragged him the rest of the way to the basement.'

Ward took up the story again. 'We think that's why the ribs we found in the boiler were broken, and probably the denture as well. The plan was to take him out through the morgue, but she couldn't get the chair up the steps at the other end. So then she hit on the idea of cremating him in the boiler.'

Christ. I thought about Lola pushing her son's body through the darkened hospital, hearing bones and teeth snap as his dead weight thumped down every stair. *I couldn't just leave him there, could I, my lovely lad? Not in that place, not with them!*

'The only thing she won't tell us is what she did with the remains afterwards,' Ward continued. 'We know she made several trips back to the boiler room for them, although I'm not convinced that wasn't more to get rid of the evidence than sentiment. She admits she couldn't get everything out before the morgue was demolished, but she clams up when we ask what she's done with the bones she took away. Says we've taken enough from her already. We haven't found anything at the house, so I'm going to have the cadaver dog search it.'

'When?' I asked.

She shook her head. 'Forget it. You'll have to sit this one out. Don't worry, I'll let you know if we find anything.'

I was in no position to argue. But there was one subject that still hadn't been mentioned. Although I could understand Ward's reluctance, it had to be aired sooner or later.

'What about Jessop?' I asked.

Whelan pursed his lips and looked down at the floor. Ward folded her hands on her lap, as though to centre herself.

'We got that wrong,' she admitted. 'Jessop was hiding something, but it wasn't what we thought. One of his employees came forward after he blew up St Jude's. Neil Wesley. Only nineteen, but he claims he found Christine Gorski's body four months ago, when he went in the loft to do a routine check. Jessop didn't want any more delays, so he made Wesley help him move it. They wrapped her body up in the tarpaulin and then carried it further into the loft where it would be harder to find.'

'Didn't do him much good,' Whelan said harshly. 'If he'd reported it straight away none of this would've happened. We'd have thought she was the only victim, and chances are St Jude's would have been torn down months ago. We'd never have known about the others.'

I put my head back on the pillow, feeling drained. Jessop had paid a high cost for his mistake. So had a lot of other people. 'Why didn't this Wesley say something sooner?'

'He was too scared,' Ward said. 'He thought Jessop would report it when he told him, but he threw a fit instead. Said it was only some down-and-out who nobody'd miss, and that if Wesley told anyone he'd sack him and make sure he got the blame. It's been playing on the poor kid's conscience ever since. You saw him yourself, hanging round the main gates, trying to pluck up courage to come forward.'

It took me a moment to realize what she meant. The young man who'd stepped out in front of my car, distracted by what was going on at St Jude's, and who I'd later seen at the bus stop outside the entrance. 'That was Neil Wesley?'

Ward gave a token smile, although her heart wasn't in it. 'PC Hendricks told us about it. She's quite a fan of yours after you offered to swap yourself as a hostage.'

It was an attempt to move the conversation on to a lighter track. But there was still too much about this I didn't understand.

'Did Jessop say anything when you were with him in St Jude's?' I asked. 'Any sort of explanation?'

'He was a self-pitying drunk who'd made a mess of his life and only got himself to blame!' Whelan snapped with sudden heat. 'If he'd had any decency, he'd have topped himself quietly rather than making a big show of it!'

'All right, Jack,' Ward told him quietly. She sighed. 'He didn't say very much, no. But if he'd been the sadistic killer we thought, he wouldn't have just let me go. And I'm not even certain he meant to blow up St Jude's anyway. The state he was in at the end, I don't think he knew what he was doing. It could have been accidental.'

'I'd save your sympathy, ma'am. He still nearly killed you,' Whelan said stubbornly. 'He didn't give you enough time to get out. If not for that tunnel . . . Well.'

He stopped, reddening. But for once we were in agreement. 'Even if Jessop didn't kill the people at St Jude's, he deliberately drove the car at Adam Oduya,' I said, aware my speech was starting to slur with fatigue. 'And it won't be much consolation for Daniel Mears to know he was just an accident.'

The atmosphere in the room suddenly changed. I looked at them, my tiredness dropping away.

'What's wrong?'

Ward turned to Whelan. 'Can you give us a minute, Jack?'

'You sure, ma'am?'

She nodded. 'Wait for me outside.'

'Sure about what?' I asked her as Whelan left the hospital room. 'What is it?'

'I didn't want to tell you yet, but we've found the car used in the hit-and-run. At the bottom of a disused quarry off the M20. It looks like it was stolen, and the driver either lost control or else deliberately drove through the fencing and over the edge. Either way, she must have died immediately.'

My mouth was dry. 'She?'

Ward was looking at me with an odd expression.

'It was Grace Strachan.'

Chapter 33

I WAS DISCHARGED two days later. Rachel brought my clothes and drove me back to Ballard Court. Stepping outside the hospital, the world seemed a little unreal. Even though it was overcast, the daylight hurt my eyes. Everything seemed too bright and too loud, a sensory overload of sound and colour. Yet another after-effect of Lola's ministrations that I'd been assured would eventually fade.

Although some would take longer than others.

We didn't speak much in the car. 'Are you OK?' Rachel asked, as we waited at traffic lights.

'Yes,' I told her.

We watched the lights change in silence.

We let ourselves into the apartment. Rachel quickly put on some music and began busying herself in the kitchen. I went into the lounge but then lost track of what I'd been going to do. That kept happening, though not as much as it had. I'd find myself thinking about something, and then suddenly be unable to recall what it was.

Going to the window, I stared down at the street below. The trees had lost most of their leaves and the pavements were dark and glossy from rain. The cars parked outside looked too small to be real, like part of a model set.

'Why don't you sit down?' Rachel said, carrying a mug in from the kitchen. 'I've made you a coffee while I make lunch. I know how much you hate the coffee machine, so I bought a percolator. Saves you drinking instant.'

'I don't mind instant,' I said without thinking.

'Well, now you've got both.' She sighed. 'Sorry. It's just . . . you're very quiet. I don't know what to say.'

I made myself smile. 'I'm just tired.'

Her look said she didn't believe that any more than I did. 'Do you want to talk about it?'

'No,' I said, turning back to the window.

Just thinking about it was hard enough. I knew part of what I was going through was a reaction to what had happened at Lola's. It would take time for the psychological as well as the physiological effects of the electric shocks to wear off, and the memory of being paralysed and helpless still provoked a clammy sense of panic. But I was prepared for that. It was a natural response, something I could understand and deal with.

It was what Ward had told me in the hospital that I couldn't accept.

'We think Grace Strachan might have been stalking you for months,' she'd said after Whelan left the room. 'We're still trying to trace her movements, but it looks like she's been living abroad. She couldn't have kept off the radar all this time in the UK, so we believe she must have left the country after she stabbed you.'

'But that's . . .' I'd lost my words: it was too much to take in. I tried again. 'Someone must have been helping her.'

396

Grace had been too unstable to have remained free all this time on her own. When I'd known her before she'd had her brother, Michael Strachan, to protect her and contain the worst of her psychotic behaviour. Even then they'd had to keep on the move, until in desperation he'd tried to find refuge for them on a sparsely populated island in the Hebrides.

It hadn't worked.

'Someone could have,' Ward had agreed. 'But losing yourself is a lot easier if you're rich, and the Strachans were loaded. All the known assets belonging to her and her brother were frozen but there could be offshore investments we don't know about. And from what I understand, Grace was perfectly normal most of the time. She only turned violent when something triggered her.'

Like jealousy over her brother. Or blaming me for his death, I'd thought numbly. 'So what brought her back now?'

Ward had looked uncomfortable. 'We think you did. Your name was mentioned in news reports about the murder investigation in Essex earlier this year, and also after that mess in Dartmoor. They were both high-profile cases, so she could easily have read about them. It's possible she thought you were dead until then. The fingerprint we found on your front door was probably from a failed attempt to break into your flat rather than something that was missed after the first attack. You weren't home when she called, so we think she's been looking for you since then.'

The room had seemed to swim as her words sank in. All this time, I'd been blasé about the threat Grace posed. So confident that Ward and Rachel were worrying about nothing, that I wasn't in any danger.

All this time, I'd been wrong.

I'd swallowed the bitter taste that had risen in my throat. 'I can't have been so hard to find.'

'Not always intentionally, perhaps. But you were in the Essex marshes for the murder investigation there, and then you moved into the new apartment. Grace couldn't go around asking people where you were, so she had to wait until you resurfaced. We've checked CCTV, and we've seen a woman we believe was her outside the university building where you work on several different occasions. She was waiting there for hours at a time.'

'She went to the *university*?'

'I'm not going to say "I told you so," because, if I'm honest, I didn't believe there was any real threat either. But it's a good job you used the side doors rather than the main entrance.'

Jesus. I'd thought back to a few days ago, when I'd forgotten Ward's advice and left through the main doors. I'd convinced myself I'd imagined the trace of Grace's perfume outside, but it had been late and I'd been almost the last to leave the building. A chill ran through me to think about it.

Perhaps I'd just missed her.

'When we realized she'd been to where you work, we looked at CCTV footage from outside your apartment as well,' Ward had continued, almost gently. 'The security meant she wasn't able to get inside, and luckily you used the underground car park. But we think she was there on at least two occasions, possibly more. One of them was the same night the fire service was called out when someone torched the rubbish bins. They thought it was kids, but the fire officers reported having to remove a woman who was hanging round the grounds when the residents were evacuated. They thought she was just some gawker, but . . . Well, let's say I'm glad you weren't home.'

That was the night I'd gone to the mortuary to help Mears. I remembered speaking to the fire officer when I'd arrived back at Ballard Court. *We've already had to escort one of your neighbours away for being too nosy. Fires always bring out the weirdos.*

'How did she know where I lived?' I'd felt surprisingly calm, as though this were happening to someone else. 'I'm ex-directory and hardly anyone knows the address.'

Not even the university: I'd arranged for my post to be redirected, and I hadn't planned to stay long enough for it to be worth notifying many people. Ward sighed.

'We think she must have followed you from St Jude's. The murders were all over the news so she probably guessed you'd be working on the investigation. It wouldn't be hard to blend in with the reporters outside the gates. Or she could have staked out the mortuary, hoping you'd turn up there sooner or later.'

Which I did. *Oh, Christ.* I'd passed my hand over my face as the memory of that night came back.

'You said Adam Oduya called your name as you left the building,' Ward went on, relentless now. 'Mears was already crossing the road, so in the dark it probably looked as though he was shouting to him . . .'

I'd seen Oduya step off the pavement, umbrella tilted against the rain. *Dr Hunter!* Mears had looked towards him as he started across the road, backlit by streetlights and his face concealed by a hood. Even carrying a flight case like mine. Oduya hadn't been the target. He'd just

399

been in the way, and the car's swerve before it hit Mears wasn't a loss of control.

It was a steering correction.

'You're certain it was Grace?' I'd felt sick and winded, as though I'd been punched in the stomach.

'A street camera got a decent shot of her face as she drove off. She's aged a lot from the photographs we've got on file, but . . . yes, it was her. The car's registered to an address in Kent. We still think it was stolen but we haven't been able to contact the owner.'

'Oh, God . . .' I'd said, closing my eyes.

'Nothing like that, he's just out of the country,' Ward had said quickly. 'He's single and works abroad a lot, so he probably doesn't even know his car's gone.'

I'd tried to collect my thoughts. 'You said . . . you said Grace died in the crash?'

Ward had seemed relieved to move on to firmer ground. 'That's right. It could have been an accident or intentional, we're not sure yet. We still need to confirm the identity of the body, but—'

'Hang on, you're not even sure it's *her*?'

'As sure as we can be, but the car caught fire, so . . . What is it?'

I hadn't been able to breathe. For a moment I was in another time and place. I could hear a crashing like waves, smell burning flesh and bone.

'Are you OK?' Ward had asked, starting to rise from her chair.

I'd forced myself to slow my breathing. I'd nodded. 'Go on.'

'We can leave this till later . . .'

'No.' I'd unclenched my hands. They were clammy with sweat. 'No, I'd rather get it over with.'

There hadn't been much more to tell. The body had suffered severe facial trauma in the crash, so the police were hoping that viable DNA could be extracted from the badly burnt bones. But an expensive alloy suitcase had been recovered from the boot, its metal shell insulated enough for its contents to have survived the fire. That had yielded DNA from hair follicles off a brush, as well as fingerprints and various personal items all positively identified as belonging to Grace Strachan. There had also been a platinum bracelet on her wrist, badly charred but with a still-legible inscription: *To my beautiful Grace, with love. Michael.*

Her brother. It was only then I'd begun to accept it.

Grace was dead.

A superstitious man might have thought fate was involved in the manner in which she'd died. Fire had played a fundamental role in our relationship from the start. I'd gone to Runa, the remote Hebridean island where she and her brother lived, to examine burnt human remains. While Grace wasn't directly responsible for that victim's death, her actions had set in motion the events that caused it. As well as the deaths that followed, including that of her beloved brother, Michael.

And, almost, my own.

Irrationally or not, Grace had blamed me. She'd followed me back to London, turning up at my home to stab me when it was thought she'd died along with her brother. I'd barely survived the attack, and since then I'd been living under her threat for years. Not knowing where she was, or if she'd try again.

Now she had.

Under different circumstances I might have felt relieved that it was finally over. But an innocent man had lost his life and another been maimed because of me, accidental victims of Grace Strachan's crazed vendetta. Coming on top of the near-death experience at Lola's hands, the news left me shell-shocked. Over the next few days, physically I continued to recover. My coordination was still off and I was prone to light-headedness, but the burns from the electric prod were healing. And while I still tired easily, my strength and stamina were slowly returning.

But I couldn't settle. I felt as though I were a stranger in my own skin. When Ward phoned the day after I left hospital, I felt my stomach knotting in anticipation of more bad news. Instead, she was calling to let me know the cadaver dog had made a discovery at Lola's house.

'One end of the cellar had been bricked up with a false wall. This one was fully plastered, so if not for the dog we wouldn't have known it was there. When we took it down we found human remains.'

That made me sit up. 'Not Gary Lennox's, though?'

'No, almost certainly not. They're male but they aren't burnt, and it looks like they've been there for years. We think they might be his father's. Lola wouldn't say what she did with his body either, but it looks like the wall at St Jude's wasn't the first she'd made her son build.'

Of course it wasn't, I thought. Lola had all but admitted it to me. *He helped me clean up, get everything tidied away.*

Gary was a good boy.

The atmosphere in the apartment became increasingly strained. Although I tried, I couldn't seem to shake the lethargy that gripped me. I'd drift into a daze, suddenly coming back to myself with a shock to find Rachel looking at me with a furrowed, worried expression. Knowing this wasn't fair on her, I tried to make more of an effort, attempting something like normal conversation.

Then, without being aware of it, I'd gradually drift away again.

Rachel put up with it until the evening of my third day back. We were at the dining table, eating a casserole she'd had cooking all afternoon. Or picking at it, in my case. After a while it occurred to me that the music from the expensive speakers had stopped and we were sitting in silence. I looked up to find Rachel watching me.

'Sorry,' I said. 'Miles away.'

She played with the stem of her wine glass, her gaze troubled. 'How long are you going to go on like this?'

'Like what? I'm fine.'

'No, you're not.' Her green eyes bore into me. 'It isn't your fault, you know.'

She didn't have to say what she meant. 'Can we talk about it some other time?'

'When? I know you've been through a lot, but we both know this isn't just about what happened at the old hag's house. Grace Strachan—'

I stood up. 'Seriously, I don't want to talk about her.'

'Well, I do! If you don't want to talk to me, fine, but you need to talk to somebody! Get some professional help!'

'I don't need it.'

'Really? There's a name for what you're going through. It's called survivor guilt.'

'Oh, come on!'

'Well, what would *you* call it? Are you really going to stand there and claim you're not blaming yourself for what she did? That you don't feel responsible?'

I started to respond, but suddenly I was shaking. I sat back down, my legs unable to support me.

'I *am* responsible,' I said, my voice unsteady.

'No, you're not! Grace Strachan was driving the car, not you. You didn't even know she was still *alive*! I know it's horrible, but blaming yourself isn't going to change anything. If you want to blame anyone, blame her!'

'Grace was ill.'

'I don't care!' Rachel threw up her hands. 'Jesus, how can you be so hard on yourself and still forgive an . . . an evil *bitch* like that? So she had a shitty life, so what? People do! Look what *you've* been through! And my sister was murdered – you think that was a barrel of laughs? People die, and yes, it's awful, but guess what? We're still alive. And you need to decide if you want to carry on living or . . . or act like you're dead yourself!'

She got up and walked out, wiping at her eyes. I stayed at the table, knowing going after her now wouldn't help. I could hear her banging about, but gradually the noise subsided and the sound of the bedroom door shutting – not quite a slam but not quietly either – told me she'd gone to bed.

After a while I got up and loaded the dishwasher. I poured myself a glass of bourbon and took it into the living room. I sat in the dark rather than switching on a lamp. The dishwasher had long since stopped, and the apartment's quiet was broken only by the hum of the central heating when I went to a cupboard in the hall-way. I'd left most of my case notes and files at my old flat, but I'd brought one box with me. Taking it out, I set it on the dining-room table and opened it up. The familiar pang returned as I lifted out the photograph albums. They were the usual chronicle of family holidays, birthdays and Christmases, what few of them we'd had together. They charted Alice's growth from a tiny baby to a shyly smiling six-year-old the image of her mother. I went through them slowly, taking my time until I'd seen them all.

Then I carefully packed them back in the box and put it away.

The sky had started to lighten when I went into the bedroom. I sat on the edge of the bed next to Rachel. Sleep had smoothed away the stress of recent weeks and the earlier anger had left her face. A few dark curls had fallen across her cheeks, stirring slightly as she breathed. Resisting the impulse to brush them aside, I turned to look out of the window. The day was starting to come to life outside, shape and colour emerging from dark. A fresh start.

Something made me turn back to Rachel. She hadn't moved but now her eyes were open, green and thoughtful as they watched me. I looked into them as I moved the hair from her cheek.

'Will you marry me?'

Chapter 34

IT FELT LIKE I'd passed through a crisis. As though a dam had burst, the negativity and depression that had gripped me since I'd left hospital were washed away. The guilt over what had happened to Adam Oduya and Daniel Mears was still there, but I was able to view it in context now. I wasn't accountable for Grace's actions. Whatever demons had driven her were there long before I came along. I'd just been the latest target, not their instigator.

Ward told me that Mears was conscious and out of danger, though not yet ready for visitors. I doubted he'd want to see me anyway, but I knew there was an account there still to be settled. It might not have been my fault, but he'd lost his leg because Grace had mistaken him for me. Like it or not, that was a connection I couldn't ignore.

As often happens, my physical recovery seemed to keep pace with my emotional one. The electrical burns were healing well, my concentration levels had returned to normal, and I was able to do more each day without feeling tired. Rachel and I began going out again, and if the wet autumn weather hadn't improved, then it no longer seemed like a cloud on my spirits.

We had Jason and Anja round for dinner and told them the news. Anja hurried to hug Rachel while Jason solemnly shook my hand, before throwing a bear-like arm around my shoulders.

'You want my advice, do it before she changes her mind,' he'd told me.

Their delight was genuine, but although they hid it well I could feel their surprise. Rachel and I hadn't known each other very long and, except for one other ultimately failed relationship, I'd been alone since Kara and Alice died. They'd begun to see that as my natural state, and I suppose so had I.

But if there was one thing I'd learned from my work, it was that change is a part of life. My past was an integral part of me, but I'd long ago come to the painful acceptance that, while my wife and daughter were dead, I was still alive. Rachel's words had brought that home. And after almost dying on the dirty floor of Lola's house, I also knew how rare such second chances were.

They didn't last for ever.

Even so, at times it didn't seem real even to me. I'd find myself gripped by an almost out-of-body sense that this was happening to someone else, that I was an observer in my own body. Some mornings I'd wake with a vertiginous feeling of something like panic. Then I'd look at Rachel, sleeping next to me, and the feeling would evaporate like dew in sunlight.

We'd decided to stay on at Ballard Court for the time being. There was no point in moving back to my flat any more. Rachel didn't have any love for a place where I'd almost died and where I'd once lived with someone else. The apartment was bigger and more comfortable, and with several months still left on the lease it made sense to stay there while my old flat went on the market.

I found myself getting quite used to it.

We spent the next few days making plans and debating where to live, trawling through estate agents and property-guide websites. I was happy to leave most of that to Rachel, but there was one odd moment. It came when we were discussing the merits of staying in the city as opposed to moving elsewhere.

'I like London, but do we really want to live here?' she said, flicking through the print-outs of available apartments and houses. 'Neither of us are tied here by work, so maybe we should look somewhere else. Property's cheaper pretty much everywhere else, and we could get somewhere much bigger in a catchment area with good schools.'

She broke off as soon as she'd said it, reddening as she looked at me. 'Sorry, I'm jumping the gun a bit there, aren't I?'

We'd never discussed starting a family, and I saw I'd been stupid not to realize Rachel would want to. *Is that what you want as well?* I thought about Kara and Alice, my daughter forever frozen in my mind at six years old. There was the familiar ache as an image came to me of her laughing, squealing as Kara tickled her. *Bedtime. Say night-night to Daddy.* For a moment a sense of vertigo returned, a sudden feeling of enormity. Then it was gone.

'It's something we need to think about,' I said.

We'd settled on holding the wedding as soon as we could arrange it. Although there was no rush, there was no point in waiting either. We both preferred a small, civil ceremony with just a few friends. Jason agreed to be my best man, and Rachel's young niece, Faye, would be the sole bridesmaid.

'How about Vegas for the honeymoon?' Rachel suggested. She grinned when she saw my face. 'Kidding. Just so long as there's a beach where I can sunbathe and swim.'

I could live with that.

A week to the day after I'd left hospital, Ward phoned with an update. They still hadn't been able to locate Gary Lennox's missing remains, but there had been another, separate development. Kent police had found a yacht drifting in Oare Marshes, a wetland nature reserve on the south-east coast. There was no one aboard, but Grace Strachan's fingerprints were everywhere.

'It's been abandoned for quite a while. We're still trying to trace her movements, but we think that's how she got back into the UK and why she was able to avoid attention for so long. It looks like she'd spent the past few years in the Mediterranean, living on the boat and moving up and down the coast.'

That made sense. Grace was an experienced sailor. She and her brother had kept a beautiful yacht moored in a bay behind their house on Runa, and she'd used it to escape from the island during a storm. Although it had later been found wrecked, she'd evidently come by another. There were hundreds of miles of unpopulated bays, coves and islands along the Mediterranean coast, and provided the bigger ports and marinas were avoided, there'd be no need to worry too much about passports or paperwork. With enough money, it would be possible to live there virtually indefinitely.

'The yacht was registered to a company owned by an accountant based in Geneva. He was the Strachans' financial adviser, so you were right about Grace having help,' Ward continued. 'We're still trying to tie everything together, but the yacht was bought not long after she disappeared, so we think she persuaded the accountant to buy it for her. He was a lot older than her and recently divorced, so it isn't hard to guess how.'

No, it wasn't. My own memory of Grace had been skewed by her actions, but I could still remember the physical impact of first meeting her. She had the sort of beauty that dazzled, blinding you to what lay underneath until it was too late.

'Have the Swiss police questioned the accountant?' I asked.

'They can't. He went missing earlier this year. Everyone thought he'd absconded with clients' funds, but we found dried bloodstains in the yacht. Too old to say whose, although I think we can guess.'

The news that Grace had claimed yet another life was sobering, yet being able to fill in some of the blanks surrounding her after all this time was also a relief. It felt like a conclusion.

But there were too many distractions to dwell on it for long. As well as deciding where we should live, there was also the question of what Rachel and I would do for work. London was hardly the best place for a marine biologist, and there was no real need for me to be based there either. Although my position at the university seemed secure for the time being – Harris, the department head, was positively effusive after my involvement with such a high-profile inquiry as St Jude's – there were no shortages of other opportunities. Not so long ago I'd been *persona non grata*: now, to my surprise, it seemed like every day brought another offer.

One morning I received an envelope with an embossed BioGen logo on its front. I felt apprehensive as I opened it. According to Ward, Mears was continuing to make a good recovery but still wasn't ready for non-family visitors. I had the feeling she was being diplomatic, but I'd enough sense not to push. A letter from his employers seemed unlikely to be good news.

'What does it say?' Rachel asked. We were still at the granite island in the kitchen, taking time over coffee after a late breakfast.

'It's from the CEO,' I said, reading it. 'They're offering me a job.'

'You're joking.'

I handed her the letter, sitting back with my coffee while she read it.

'Senior Forensic Adviser in charge of Research and Operations,' she said, frowning. 'What the hell's that supposed to – oh, my God!'

She'd got to the part where it mentioned my salary. She read it again, open-mouthed, then set it down on the table.

'Are you going to meet him?'

'Would you mind if I didn't?'

'Of course not. Is it because of Daniel Mears?'

'Partly,' I admitted.

The letter had made no mention of the forensic taphonomist, and while the post they were offering was more senior than his, after what had happened to him I wouldn't have felt comfortable taking it. And a company that let someone inexperienced flounder on a major investigation wasn't one I wanted to work with anyway.

Folding the letter, I put it back in its envelope.

It wasn't only job offers that came my way. My involvement with events at St Jude's must have leaked out, because I began receiving interview requests from journalists. Including another from Francis Scott-Hayes.

'God, the man just doesn't know when to stop,' I grumbled to Rachel after reading it.

'Is that the same freelancer who's been pestering you?'

'For weeks. He doesn't understand what "no" means.'

'Maybe you should do it.'

I looked at her in surprise. 'Seriously?'

She shrugged. 'Why not? I know you don't like talking about work, but you don't have to discuss specific cases. Who does he write for?'

I read out his latest email. Rachel's eyebrows went up as she listened to the roll call of high-end newspapers and magazines Scott-Hayes had been published in, on both sides of the Atlantic.

'Wow, he sounds pretty serious,' she said, impressed. 'I think I even read that piece in *Rolling Stone*. Why don't you hear what he has to say?'

'I don't know . . .'

She picked up her coffee cup. 'Well, it's up to you. But if you're thinking about putting yourself in the job market, then an interview in a decent newspaper or magazine can't hurt your profile.'

'I'll think about it,' I said.

The registry office was booked for three weeks' time. That was the first available date, and we only managed that because an existing wedding had been cancelled. Our good luck was someone else's bad. I hoped it wasn't an omen.

But dark thoughts were few and far between. I no longer felt the sense of vertigo on waking, and any disbelief was tinged with anticipation. The days were like mayflies, here and gone in a rush. With so many things to do and decisions to be made, I forgot all about the journalist until Rachel reminded me. An online search for *Francis Scott-Hayes, journalist* produced page after page of his articles, along with photographs showing a lean-faced man in his thirties, stubbled and broodingly good-looking. There was even a short Wikipedia entry. He'd been embedded with armed forces in Afghanistan, reported on communities hit by the drug war in Mexico, even won a national press award for his investigation into human trafficking. By the look of it, most of his stories involved him travelling to war zones or some of the most dangerous trouble spots on the planet.

'Why would he want to write about me?' I asked Rachel after dinner that evening. 'I'm a forensic scientist, not some drug lord.'

'You're a forensic scientist who's worked on some of the biggest police investigations in the last ten years. People find that interesting.'

I was less sure of that than she was. Still, bolstered by Rachel's enthusiasm and a glass of wine, I reluctantly replied to his email.

An automated response came back immediately, saying he was out of the country without access to emails.

'Well, I tried,' I told Rachel, privately hoping that might be an end to it.

The next day he emailed back.

I would have been happy to leave the interview until after the wedding, but Rachel didn't think I should wait.

'He could have gone cold on the idea by then,' she said. 'At least say you'll hear him out.'

It was arranged that Scott-Hayes would come to the apartment for coffee the following afternoon. I was reluctant to invite him there, but the alternatives were either to meet at the university or else in a pub or coffee shop, which would be too public given what we'd be discussing. Besides, as Rachel said, it wasn't as if we'd be living at Ballard Court for much longer.

It was a Saturday, so I worked on my laptop in the study while Rachel made an early start on preparing dinner. Jason and Anja were coming round that evening and she'd insisted on cooking. Judging from the banging and language coming from the kitchen, she was beginning to regret it. The journalist was due at three o'clock, and as the appointment drew nearer I realized I was looking more at my watch than the laptop screen. Regretting ever having agreed to this, I watched the second hand tick up to the hour, then sweep past. After another ten minutes I went into the kitchen.

'He's late. I knew this was a bad idea.'

'No, what's a bad idea is me thinking I could make choux pastry.' Rachel pushed away the mixing bowl. 'He's probably just stuck on the Tube or in traffic. Why don't you put some coffee on?'

I filled the new stainless-steel percolator and set it on the hob before going back into the study. But with my mind on the meeting it was a waste of time trying to work. I'd just resolved to give Scott-Hayes another fifteen minutes when the intercom buzzed.

About time. I went into the hallway to answer it.

'Got a Francis Scott-Hayes to see you,' the concierge's voice came out of the speaker.

414

'OK, thanks.'

'Told you,' Rachel said from the kitchen.

I was saved from responding to that by the trill of my mobile in the study. 'Can you let him in while I get that?'

Leaving her to open the door for the journalist, I hurried back through the living room to the study. My phone, a replacement for the one Lola had dropped in the sink, was on the desk by the laptop. When I picked it up I was surprised to see Ward's name on the display. She didn't call so often now, and we'd spoken only the day before. Leaving the study, I walked back through the living room to the kitchen as I answered.

'Hello, I wasn't expecting—'

'Where are you?'

Startled by her urgency, I stopped in the kitchen door way. The percolator was bubbling on the hob, filling the air with the scent of fresh coffee.

'I'm at home. Why, what's—?'

'Is Rachel with you?'

The door leading to the hallway was at the far side of the kitchen. Through it I heard the murmur of voices. 'She's just answering the door—'

'No! Don't let her open it!'

But Rachel was already coming back to the kitchen. She had a bemused smile on her face as she walked through the doorway, raising a quizzical eyebrow at me.

'Frances Scott-Hayes is here,' she said, stressing the last syllable to emphasize the female spelling.

A woman was behind her, thin with greying hair cut in an unflattering bob. My first thought was that there had been a mix-up, that I'd researched the wrong journalist by mistake. My second was that there was something familiar about the woman who followed

Rachel into the kitchen. Then I caught a waft of her perfume, a heady scent of spice and musk I'd have known anywhere. It had burned itself into my memory as I'd bled out in the doorway of my old flat, a knife buried to the hilt in my stomach.

Ward's voice was still coming from the phone, but I barely heard it. Grace Strachan was almost unrecognizable. The breath-stopping beauty had been replaced by a cadaverous thinness. Her skin was stretched taut across the high cheekbones, revealing the contours of her skull. The dark eyes were sunken and shadowed, burning into me now with a manic intensity.

The smile fell from Rachel's face. 'David . . .?'

I was struck mute. With a nightmare sense of déjà vu, I saw Grace reaching into her shoulder bag as Rachel turned to her, and only then was I able to move.

'*No!*' I yelled, throwing myself forward.

Knowing I was too late.

Grace brought out the long-bladed knife and slashed in one fluid motion. Rachel gave a cry and reeled away, blood flicking from her on to the kitchen tiles. Then Grace was coming at me, teeth bared as she raised the knife. I grabbed for it as it swept down, not caring if it cut me or not.

Suddenly, Grace's head snapped back. She jerked to a halt as Rachel buried one hand in the grey hair and swung the heavy percolator with the other. The hot metal smashed into Grace's upturned forehead, steaming coffee gouting out as its handle snapped off. The percolator clattered to the floor as Grace collapsed, the knife falling from her hand. Kicking it away, I ignored the prostrate woman and rushed to Rachel. She was standing with one hand pressed against a long slice in

416

the flesh of her upper arm, eyes wide with pain and shock. The broken handle of the percolator was still clutched in her fist.

'Oh, Christ, are you OK?' I asked, frantically checking her.

She nodded shakily. Blood was running down her arm and dripping on the floor. The hand pressed against the wound had livid blotches where the boiling coffee had splashed it. Sparing a quick glance to make sure Grace wasn't moving, I steered Rachel to the sink and ran the cold water. Soaking a towel, I eased her scalded hand away.

'Hold your hand under the tap,' I told her, binding the wet towel around the deep cut in her arm.

She did as I said, gasping as the cold water hit the burns. 'You're shaking.'

I couldn't help it. I became aware of an animal keening. Looking down, I saw Grace had curled into a foetal position, arms covering her face.

'It hurts,' she whimpered. 'Please, Michael, make it *stop . . .*'

'Oh, God, look at her . . .' Rachel breathed.

'Keep your hand under the water.'

Leaving her by the tap, I went to the emaciated figure on the kitchen floor. Blood from a large gash on her hairline was intermingled with the coffee, turning Grace's face into a marbled mask. The skin was already starting to blister, and I flinched when I saw what the boiling coffee had done to her eyes.

Grabbing another towel, I soaked it under the cold tap and gently laid it on Grace's scalded face. She screamed at the contact, a bony hand clutching at my arm. It didn't let go as I looked around for my phone. I couldn't remember dropping it, but it hadn't disconnected. I could hear Ward's frantic voice as I picked it up.

'We need an ambulance,' I said, trying to keep my voice steady.

Epilogue

THE SKY WAS threatening snow. The low clouds were featureless, and dusk was already falling although it was barely three o'clock in the afternoon. In the room, though, it was stiflingly hot. A fluorescent light shone from the ceiling overhead, further muting the world beyond the glass.

'Won't be long now. Can I get you anything?' the overweight young man asked from by the door.

'No, thank you.'

He went out. I shifted position on the hard plastic chair and looked at my watch. I'd been waiting almost an hour and I'd a long drive ahead of me. I wanted to set off before the snow came down. But I knew that wasn't the reason for my impatience. I was nervous.

I should have done this long ago.

My phone chimed with the arrival of a text. I took it out and smiled. The image on the screen showed a red-faced infant, eyes screwed up and tiny fists balled. The caption with it said *Emma Louise Ward, born this morning 3.25am, 6lbs 3oz.* It was signed Sharon and Doug.

Still smiling, I texted congratulations and put my phone away. The news was a welcome patch of brightness, and there had been few enough of those recently. Not since the afternoon when Grace Strachan had walked back into my life.

I'd been at the hospital when Ward and Whelan had caught up with me. Staring into space in a busy A&E waiting room while Rachel had her wound stitched and dressed.

'How is she?' Ward had asked, taking the seat next to me while Whelan stood.

I looked at her. 'You told me Grace was dead.'

'I'm sorry, we thought she—'

'You said it was her body in the car.'

'Calm down,' Whelan cut in.

'Calm *down*? Are you serious?'

'We fucked up,' Ward said bluntly. She looked around the crowded waiting room. 'Let's go and get a cup of tea. I'll make sure they send for us if there's any news.'

We found an empty table in a corner of the hospital cafeteria. My insides still felt coiled with tension, an anger that was directed at myself as much as anyone else.

'I called you straight away, as soon as we got the DNA results back,' Ward told me, her face strained. 'We honestly thought the woman in the car was Grace Strachan.'

Until that moment I hadn't stopped to think what it had to mean for Grace to be alive. It felt like another punch to the heart. 'Who was she?'

'Her name's Belinda Levinson, a freelance web designer. Her boyfriend's a journalist who . . . What's wrong, are you OK?'

I'd bent over, suddenly feeling sick. A rushing like water filled my ears. 'Is his name Francis Scott-Hayes?'

The police had found the journalist's body at his isolated cottage in the Kent countryside. He'd died from
multiple stab wounds and the condition of the body suggested he'd been dead for several weeks. As far as they
could tell, Grace had been living on her boat since
returning to the UK earlier in the year, when she'd
hitched to London and made her abortive attempt to
break into my flat. The Oare Marshes, where her yacht
was found, were only a few miles from where Scott-
Hayes lived. He'd returned to the UK early from a
two-month stint covering the war in Yemen, and it was
thought he must have given her a lift at some point.

'We don't know why he took her back to his cottage
instead of her boat,' Ward had said. 'Can't rule out sex,
but he'd got a long-term girlfriend and by all accounts
wasn't the sort to go for casual pick-ups. And he was a
lot younger than Grace. If she still looked like she used
to it might be different, but . . . Well, you saw how she
is.'

I had. The Grace Strachan I remembered had exuded
a powerful sexual appeal, but there had been nothing of
that evident in the pathetic scarecrow on my kitchen
floor. 'Do you think she pulled a knife or forced him
somehow?'

Ward gave a shrug. 'It's possible, but he'd still have to
have stopped for her first. I think it's more likely he just
felt sorry for her and took her to his house to freshen up.
We've checked the weather reports, and there was heavy
rain around the time he came back to the UK. A middle-
aged woman, wet through and on her own at the side of
the road wouldn't have looked much of a threat.'

No, she wouldn't, I thought. Freshly back from a war
zone, the journalist must have felt safe in the familiar

421

landscape near his home. Bloodstains showed Scott-Hayes had died in the hallway of his house, probably not long after returning with his guest. His decomposed body was found in a small stone outbuilding behind his cottage, a former piggery now used for storage.

'How badly decomposed?' I'd asked automatically.

'Bad enough. And the answer's no, so don't even think about it.'

I hadn't been going to ask to take a look myself. Not right then, anyway. I'd not interrupted again as Ward explained how Grace had abandoned her boat and moved into the journalist's cottage. Isolated and quiet, it made a perfect hideaway, well away from social contact where her erratic behaviour might have been noticed. There was no immediate danger of Scott-Hayes being missed. He'd set up an automated email response before his trip – the same one I'd received myself – and the volatile nature of his job meant he was prone to changing his plans at short notice. Even his lack of social media posts didn't raise much concern at first, since he frequently worked in remote and inhospitable regions far from any wi-fi or internet connections. And, while she was unlikely to have planned it, at some point Grace must have realized that her dead host's occupation presented her with a rare opportunity.

Living in his house, it wouldn't have been difficult to gain access to his email account. While his phone and laptop required fingerprint verification, that would hardly have posed a problem with his body there. So Grace had stolen his identity as well as his life, emailing me in the hope of drawing me out. And when that had initially failed, another opportunity had offered itself.

'We found Belinda Levinson's car outside the cottage,' Ward had told me. 'Her friends say she was concerned when Scott-Hayes missed her birthday. She tried contacting his editors but no one seemed sure if he was back in the country or not, so she went to check on him. When she didn't come back her friends assumed the two of them must be enjoying their reunion.'

I rubbed my temples. 'Did Grace stab her as well?'

'The fire made it hard to tell if there were any stab wounds on the body, but we found a second blood type at the cottage. We can't say yet if it's Levinson's or not, but we're assuming it is. The likeliest scenario is that Grace killed her as soon as she turned up at the cottage, and then . . . Well, when St Jude's hit the news we think she probably put the body in the boot of Scott-Hayes's car and took it to London.'

I shut my eyes. *Jesus.* Grace had never planned far ahead when I'd known her before, but then she'd never had to. Her brother had always been there to look after her.

'You thought Scott-Hayes's car had been stolen,' I said, trying to keep the accusation from my voice. 'Didn't anyone go out to his house to check on him?'

'Of course they did. We asked Kent police to look into it. But at that time Jessop was still the chief suspect for the hit-and-run and there was no reason to think anything might have happened to the car owner. We knew Scott-Hayes worked abroad, so when there was no one at home . . .'

Ward gave an apologetic shrug. I didn't have the energy to argue, and I wasn't blameless myself. I'd agreed to be interviewed without bothering to speak to the journalist in person. Even emailed Grace

Strachan my address. When the concierge had called through on the intercom I'd heard only what I'd expected: *Francis*, not *Frances*, the female variant of the name she'd given him. And Rachel had simply assumed I'd made a mistake over the journalist's gender. She'd never met Grace, so had no way of knowing who was outside the door. If I'd been the one to answer it, I doubted I'd have recognized her straight away either.

Then it would have been a whole different story.

Rachel's injuries hadn't been serious. The scalding to her hand was superficial, and although the knife had sliced through the muscle of her upper arm almost to the bone, the doctors assured us that there would be no long-term nerve or tendon damage. Even so, because she'd lost enough blood to need a transfusion, she'd been kept in hospital overnight.

It gave me a chance to clean up the apartment. By the time I collected Rachel in a taxi next morning, there were no visible signs of what had happened. But the less tangible effects were harder to erase.

In the days following the attack, we'd tried to pretend everything was normal, but it was a strain for us both. Rachel found it hard to sleep, growing quiet and short-tempered. I'd never liked the luxurious apartment and now, even with its alarms and concierge, she no longer felt safe. We'd had a blazing row over moving back to my flat, and while we made up afterwards, things were never quite the same.

By mutual consent the registry office was quietly cancelled. We pretended to ourselves it was only postponed, but we both knew it was more than that. We just didn't want to admit it.

One evening two weeks after the attack, Rachel had been even more subdued than usual. It was during dinner. She'd been pushing her food around listlessly on her plate when she set down her fork.

'I'm going back to Greece.'

Although I'd been half expecting it, that didn't soften the blow. Objections and arguments flashed through my mind, until I looked at her face. Thinner than it had been, with shadows under her eyes. Rachel had always been strong, but there was a brittleness about her now I hadn't seen before.

I'd put down my own cutlery, what little appetite I'd had gone.

'When?'

'Sunday. They're letting me rejoin the boat for the rest of the research trip. And they've . . .' She'd paused, forcing the words out. 'There's a chance I can extend my contract. For another year.'

There was a dull ache in my chest. 'Is that what you want?'

'No,' she blurted. 'But we can't go on like this. *I* can't . . . I don't want to break up, but this is . . . I just need some time.'

I got up and went over. Her tears had wet my shirt as I held her, staring past her at the doorway through which Grace had entered our lives.

We'd sat up most of that night, talking it through. I didn't want her to go, but she'd made up her mind even before she'd told me. And part of me knew it was best for her. Violence had visited us twice in the short time we'd known each other, and that always came at a price. Rachel was still coming to terms with her sister's murder, so this attempt on our lives – in a place she'd felt safe

– had struck at her core. She'd responded with violence herself and, justified or not, the world seemed a different place after that. We couldn't pretend nothing had changed, and trying would have been slow torture. She deserved better.

Three days later, on a grey October afternoon, Rachel flew back to Greece. 'It isn't all that far. You could still come out for a holiday,' she'd said, as we'd stood in the hallway by her suitcases.

I'd smiled. 'I know.'

We'd see.

I'd moved back into my old flat. I'd wondered if it might feel strange, like going back in time. It didn't, but it didn't feel particularly good either.

Just familiar.

Professionally, I was more in demand than ever. There was a gruelling trip to Ireland that I wasn't physically ready for but took anyway, followed by a bizarre series of murders in the Welsh Borders. And I'd received another job offer, much more intriguing than the one from BioGen. A private company was looking to set up a new anthropological research facility, the first of its kind in the UK. There were legal and bureaucratic hurdles to overcome, but they felt it was something I'd be ideally suited to, given what they called my 'unique experience and expertise'. The letter didn't say what the facility was, but I could guess.

I'd trained at one like it in Tennessee.

I'd yet to make a decision, and meanwhile the fallout from St Jude's continued to rumble on. I'd watched on TV as a crane swung a wrecking ball into the surviving walls. After all the protests and demonstrations, all the needless blood and tears, the old hospital came down meekly in a billow of dust. One good thing that might yet come out of this was that, after such negative publicity, the developers were showing signs of backing down. A new proposal had been put forward to redevelop the entire site for social housing, and a petition had already been set up to name it Oduya Park.

Coincidentally, the day after that I'd heard from Ward that the activist's police 'source' had been found. He was a PC whose wife had given birth to their twin daughters in St Jude's and who was now approaching retirement. The officer's name meant nothing to me, until Ward mentioned it was the older partner of the young PC on the gates. He wasn't part of the main investigation team, but he had ears and people like to talk shop, regardless of their profession.

No one had the stomach for any more negative headlines, so the PC's retirement had quietly been brought forward. I was glad he wasn't punished more severely, though I wondered how things might have played out if details of Christine Gorski's pregnancy hadn't been leaked. Would Oduya still have spoken to me after the public meeting if he hadn't wanted to confirm what he'd been told? And if not, would events still have conspired to make him shout my name across the rainy street, just as a hooded Mears was crossing the road? Or would the course of all our lives have been changed, and I been the one picked out in Grace Strachan's headlights that night?

There was no way of knowing.

I'd met with Oduya's family, including his partner, a thoughtful man in his forties who I'd already met to collect paperwork for the pro bono case Oduya had wanted me to take on. The activist's parents had been restrained in their grief, not outwardly blaming me for their son's death. Still, it was a difficult meeting for all of us.

Though not as difficult as the one that followed. One afternoon, against Ward's advice, I'd gone to see Mears. The forensic taphonomist was out of bed when I went in, sitting in a wheelchair in dressing gown and shorts. One thin leg was bare, the other ended in a bandaged stump above the knee. He was staring into space, an open book face down on his lap. The red hair was lank and uncombed. At first he didn't see me, then a spectrum of expressions crossed his face. A flush flared on his cheeks.

There was an empty visitor's chair by the bed, but I didn't sit down. 'How are you?' I asked, the words sounding trite.

In answer he spread his hands, offering himself and the bandaged stump as evidence. 'How do you think?'

There'd been an intensity to his stare that made it hard to meet his eyes, but I wouldn't let myself look away. For days I'd been wondering what to say, and now I was there all the ideas I'd had deserted me.

'I'm sorry,' I'd told him.

I knew he'd been informed about who'd been driving the car that had hit him. And why. Mears tried to give a laugh, but it wouldn't come. The flush had spread across his entire face and neck, making the hollow eyes look feverish.

'You're *sorry*. Well, that's all right then. That makes everything hunky-fucking-dory, doesn't it?'

'Listen, if I could—'

'Could what? Could go back in time? Give me my leg back?' He'd turned his head away, his mouth trembling. 'Just leave me alone.'

428

Ward had been right: I shouldn't have gone. Wordlessly, I'd started to leave.

'Hunter!'

I'd stopped and turned. Patients in the other beds were staring. Mears looked close to tears, his hands clenched on the arms of the wheelchair. His voice shook.

'It should be you sitting here. Don't forget that.'

I'd let the doors swing shut behind me.

Ward continued to give me periodic updates about the St Jude's investigation. Professor Conrad was released from hospital and was expected to return to work before much longer. And Wayne Booth's condition continued to improve with treatment and therapy, although he would never regain anything like full mobility or speech. As for Lola, Ward had told me that she'd suddenly stopped cooperating, refusing to respond to or even acknowledge the charges against her. Her silence came after the police made another discovery.

'We dug back into the patient death the neighbour told you about. The fourteen-year-old boy who died from the insulin overdose,' Ward had told me. 'Lola wasn't prosecuted because there was no reason to think she'd done it deliberately. Everyone assumed it was an accident. But we've found out the boy went to the same school as Gary Lennox. He was two years older, so there wasn't an obvious connection, but guess who he'd been bullying before he went into hospital?'

'She killed a *child* because he'd bullied her son?' Even after everything else she'd done, I was still shocked by that.

'She's not admitting it, but that's what we think,' Ward said. 'If it wasn't tragic, it'd be funny. All those people died because an overprotective mother thought

429

they'd hurt her son. And then she ends up killing him herself.'

Ward had started her leave shortly after that, understandably deciding to concentrate on more positive maternal issues of her own. It was high time. The only loose end from the St Jude's investigation was that Gary Lennox's remains were still missing, and there seemed little prospect of his mother revealing where they were. Whelan had speculated that she might have simply dropped them into a wheelie bin, but I disagreed. The shrine she'd created on the cabinet hadn't been solely to torment Wayne Booth. It had been just that – a shrine. Lola wouldn't have disposed of her son's burnt bones simply to get rid of the evidence.

Not long after Ward had started her leave I'd had a call from Whelan.

'Fancy taking a dog for a walk?' he'd asked.

The church ruins had looked even bleaker at this time of year. Ivy still clung to the crumbling gable wall, and the moss looked thicker than ever on the fallen stones. But the trees surrounding it were bare now, the fallen leaves forming a rotting mat underfoot. A few rooks looked down from the black branches, feathers ruffled against the wind and rain. It was a foul day, but one member of the party didn't mind. Star trotted happily around the woodland clearing, the scents here far more to the Labrador's liking than the fustiness of the old hospital.

It had been Whelan's idea to walk the cadaver dog along the route Lola would have taken as she'd brought her son's bones back from the boiler. We'd started at the demolished morgue, its mound of broken bricks now dwarfed by the rubble of St Jude's, and let the dog sniff its way through the waste ground to the woods behind the hospital.

We found Gary Lennox's remains in the clearing. Or rather the Labrador did. They weren't even well hidden. After snuffling around the church ruins, the dog made a beeline for the lightning-struck oak. Split a few feet off the ground, the rooted part of the trunk was hollowed out by rot and surrounded by the bush of straggling shoots thrown up by the dying tree. At the base of the hollow, all but invisible inside the trunk, were charred human bones. The skull was at the very bottom. It was blackened and cracked, and its upper jaw was missing its front teeth.

As the last of Gary Lennox's bones were removed from inside the rotting tree, I'd thought about when I'd seen Lola there. How annoyed she'd been to find someone else in the church's crumbling remains. It had always seemed out of character for her to be collecting litter from around the clearing, but now I understood why.

She'd been tending her son's grave.

It had begun to snow outside. Small flakes clung to the barred window, slowly sliding down the glass as they melted. I shifted again on the uncomfortable chair, tempted to use the weather as an excuse to leave. Now I was here I wondered what I'd hoped to achieve. I still couldn't say for sure why I'd come, except that it wouldn't have felt right not to.

It was just something I'd felt I had to do.

I felt my stomach tense as I heard footsteps approach in the corridor, as though the scar beneath my ribs had a memory of its own. The door opened and an orderly entered. I half rose to my feet as the woman shuffled into the room behind him. She was painfully thin, dressed in a plain white gown through which the bones

431

of her shoulders clearly showed. The wispy grey hair was short and bristly above one temple where it had been shaved, showing the line of a healing scar.

Whatever threat had once existed in the frail figure had burned itself out. The orderly held on to her arm, guiding her into the chair opposite mine. The skin on her face was still livid and raw, although the scalds had now largely healed. But that wasn't the real damage. The eyes that darted fretfully around the room were milky, as though clouded by cataracts. The boiling coffee had been strong and viscous, badly burning the delicate corneas and causing permanent scarring. Surgery might have restored some sight but, even if the courts were to allow it, the psychiatrists felt the trauma would be too much for her fragile psyche. From now on, her world would be a grey mist.

She tilted her head, listening anxiously.

'Who's there?' Her voice was a whisper. 'Michael, is that you? I've been so *scared*.'

There was a desperate eagerness about her. For a moment, I saw a hint of her former beauty, the ghost of the woman she used to be. Then that too burned out and disappeared. I forced myself not to recoil as the blue-veined hands groped across the table towards mine. Her skin was icy to the touch.

I caught a faint smell of soap from her. Nothing else.

'Hello, Grace,' I said.

Acknowledgements

I was helped in the writing of this book by the generosity and expertise of people with far more knowledge than I have. Any inaccuracies in the text are entirely mine, not theirs. In no particular order, thanks to Tim Thompson, Professor of Applied Biological Anthropology at Teesside University, for patiently answering yet more odd questions; Tony Cook, the National Crime Agency's Head of Operations at CEOP, for procedural advice, and whose excellent *Senior Investigating Officers' Handbook* provided invaluable reference; Dr Martin Hall, forensic and veterinary entomologist at the National History Museum, London, for insights into blowflies and other insects; Patricia Wiltshire, Professor of Forensic Ecology at Southampton University, for providing wide-reaching background; Dr Becky Gowland, Senior Lecturer in Archaeology at Durham University, for the anecdote that inspired the foetal skeleton scene in Chapter 2; the Metropolitan Police press office for their prompt responses; and forensic anthropologist Dr Anna Williams of the University of Huddersfield, for information on cadaver dogs and the odours of decomposition. Details of her campaign for a UK body farm are available at http://htf4uk.blogspot.com.

Thanks also to my agents Gordon Wise, Melissa Pimentel and the team at Curtis Brown; my UK editor Simon Taylor, my German editors Ulrike Beck and Friederike Ney, and everyone working behind the scenes at Transworld and Rowohlt publishers; to my mom for her support, and to Ben Steiner and SCF for their fast read-through and comments.

Finally, a huge thank-you to my wife Hilary, first and best reader, for working tirelessly on this with me and sharing the good and bad. It really is a collaborative effort – I'm just the one at the keyboard.

Simon Beckett, January 2019

Simon Beckett's
Sunday Times bestselling
David Hunter thrillers

THE CHEMISTRY OF DEATH
When a woman is found murdered a close-knit
community plunges into a maelstrom of fear and
paranoia. And no one, not even Dr David Hunter, is
exempt from suspicion. . .

'Very distinctive . . . a cut above the average, with a
convincing central character, a gripping plot and a fine
store of morbid information'
Observer

WRITTEN IN BONE
On the remote Hebridean island of Runa a grisly
discovery awaits the arrival of forensic anthropologist
Dr David Hunter.

'Beckett cranks up the suspense . . . unexpected twists
and a gory climax'
Daily Telegraph

WHISPERS OF THE DEAD
In plain black letters were the words Anthropological
Research Facility, but it was better known by another,
less formal name. Most people just called it the
Body Farm. . .

'Intelligent, beautifully written and utterly gripping'
Sunday Express

THE CALLING OF THE GRAVE

Eight years ago they found the body buried on the moor. They were certain that it was one of Jerome Monk's teenage victims. Which left two more to find. . .

'As bone-chillingly bleak as its subject . . .
this doesn't disappoint'
Financial Times

THE RESTLESS DEAD

A badly decomposed body has been found in the mudflats and salt marshes of the Backwaters. Could it be linked to two unsolved missing person cases? But then more remains are discovered. And as these desolate wetlands begin to give up their grisly secrets, Hunter is reminded that it's not the dead we need to fear. . .

'A tense, gripping read'
Sunday Times

WHERE THERE'S SMOKE
Simon Beckett

'Inside the room it is even darker. It is like walking in ink. Blind, she feels her way through the half familiar landmarks of beds and bookshelves. Her heart thuds. Blood from the wound is sticky, and at her touch there is a white leap of pain that lightens the darkness. She hears the footsteps now, drawing closer. . .'

Meet Kate Powell. She is successful, single, and likes to be in control.

But lately her life has begun to feel a little shallow, a little meaningless.

Aware that her body clock is ticking, Kate believes she knows how to fix her problems. She wants a child.

Unable to imagine a world in which she's never met her baby's father, Kate advertises for a donor. Alex Turner appears to be the perfect match.

But appearances can be dangerously deceptive. . .

'Brilliant. One of the best novels I've read in years'
Martina Cole

STONE BRUISES
By Simon Beckett

'Somebody!' I half-sob and then, more quietly, 'Please.' The words seem absorbed by the afternoon heat, lost amongst the trees. In their aftermath, the silence descends again. I know then that I'm not going anywhere. . .

Sean is on the run. We don't know why and we don't know from whom. But under a relentless French sun, he's abandoned his bloodied car and taken to the parched fields and lanes. And now he's badly injured.

Almost unconscious from pain and loss of blood, he is found and taken in by two women from an isolated farm. Their father is violently protective of his privacy and makes his dislike of the young Englishman clear. Sean's uncertain whether he's a patient or a prisoner but there's something beguiling about this tranquil and remote place.

As he tries to lose himself in the heat and dust of a French summer, he begins to realize that the farm has secrets of its own. It is the perfect hiding place, but that means nobody knows he is there. . .

. . . which would make it the perfect place to die.

'Menacing, beautifully paced . . . marks Beckett's transition to established star'
Daily Mail